CW00641211

The Russian Tiara

Anne Melville

PIATKUS

By the same author

The Lorimer Line
The Lorimer Legacy
Lorimers at War
Lorimers in Love
The Last of the Lorimers
Lorimer Loyalties
The House of Hardie
Grace Hardie
The Hardie Inheritance
The Dangerfield Diaries
Snapshots
The Tantivy Trust
A Clean Break

Copyright © 1994 by Anne Melville

First published in Great Britain in 1994 by
Judy Piatkus (Publishers) Ltd of
5 Windmill Street, London W1

**The moral right of the author
has been asserted**

*A catalogue record for this book is available
from the British Library*

ISBN 0-7499-0246-9

Phototypeset in Compugraphic 11/12pt Times by
Action Typesetting Limited, Gloucester
Printed and bound in Great Britain by
Butler & Tanner Ltd, Frome

Contents

Prologue

St Petersburg
1908

Prince Kristov knew better than to dine at home when a baby was being born. His wife's rooms were swarming with midwives, nurses and maidservants, all behaving as though the arrival of a baby was not simply unexpected but unprecedented. Only the wet-nurse, who had been brought to St Petersburg from one of the Kristovs' country estates the previous day, sat stolidly in a corner, waiting until she was required.

In spite of all the fuss and flurry, the princess's labour was not yet far advanced. Between dramatic groans, she was able to smile as her husband bent over the bed to kiss her forehead.

'A boy this time,' she murmured. 'You should tell your mother.'

'I'll go there after the opera. Be strong!'

He kissed her again before making his way down the marble staircase. The coachman was already sitting outside on the sleigh, shaking the reins of the three bay trotters to keep them alert. As one footman helped the prince into his greatcoat, another stepped forward to open the door.

A boy in grey uniform stood in the doorway, one hand stretched out towards the heavy knocker. In the other hand he held an envelope, which he now handed to the footman with a bow.

Prince Kristov recognised the livery. He had seen it often enough in Paris, where he was a regular customer of the House of Cartier. He paused to tear the envelope open and extract the stiff card it enclosed.

M. Cartier, he read, presented his compliments to Prince Pavel Karlovich Kristov. He begged to introduce M. Louis Sarda, who had brought a selection of the House of Cartier's finest jewels to St Petersburg, and hoped to have the privilege of displaying the pieces to his most valued clients at 28, Quai de la Cour between December 6th, 1908, and the New Year.

Prince Kristov pushed the card into a pocket and forgot about it for the rest of the day. He dined with a group of his fellow officers before going on to the opera. But there was no one interesting to talk to there, so he left after the first act and paid the promised call on his mother.

He found her presiding over the samovar in her salon. After the death of his father she and her younger son, Alexis, had moved into one of the side wings of the Kristov palace, so that her elder son and his family could use the main part of the building as their winter home. Her new apartments were spacious enough, but she could not dine more than twenty guests at a time and so took more pleasure in her weekly soirées. Her reputation for wit and intelligence attracted ambassadors and philosophers as well as generals and grand duchesses to her Wednesdays, and the room was full.

The arthritis from which she had suffered for many years was causing her particular pain today, and she displayed little excitement at the news that she was about to become a grandmother for the second time. Instead, she changed the subject quickly to that of her own second child.

'Have a word with your brother soon if you please, Pavel Karlovich, and talk him out of this ridiculous idea.'

'What idea?'

'He's refusing to enrol in the Corps of Pages.'

This was indeed shocking news. Every Kristov boy for generations had been a member of the Corps before going on to serve the Emperor as an officer of either the court or the army. And it was not as though Alexis were unsuitable in any way. At the age of sixteen he was already a fine horseman and an expert fencer; last year he had won the golden épée at the Gourevitch Gymnasium.

'Why should that be?'

'It's all the fault of that governess. Miss Beatrice. Fortunately, you were never taught by her; she only came after you had left the schoolroom.' Like most of the nobility, the Kristovs had employed both French and English governesses for their children; but there was a fourteen-year difference in age between Pavel and his younger brother.

'What did Miss Beatrice do?'

'She taught him the language well, I grant you. But then she had books sent from her home. Dozens of them. Novels. Completely unsuitable. If I'd known ... Alexis said she made him read them to improve his English. But the effect — well, he says he wants to study in England. To make English friends. He'll be proud to serve the Emperor later, he says. If he gets to know more of the

2

world than just a regiment in his own country, he thinks he could be useful one day as an ambassador.'

'Send him there as soon as you can,' advised Prince Kristov. 'It's wet and foggy all the time, and the people don't like foreigners.' He had never visited England, but had become acquainted with a good many Englishmen when accompanying his mother on her annual visit to Carlsbad. 'A short stay should be enough. He'll soon realise the advantages of returning here, to his own circle. I'll speak to him on Sunday.'

He used the promise as an excuse to leave the soirée. The talk was above his head, and he wanted to spend the night in the apartment of his mistress.

At the age of twenty, Barisinova was the star of the Imperial Ballet and the toast of St Petersburg. Her temper had not been improved by the recent discovery that she, like her lover's wife, had become pregnant. In her case the birth was still a good many months away, but she and the prince both knew that it would not be long before she would have to suspend her career and retire to the country to avoid scandal. Their love-making was more subdued than usual, and before he left her bed the next morning the prince decided on a visit to the Fabergé premises on the Morskaya to fan the flames of love with a token of his affection.

A more urgent gesture, however, was an enquiry after his wife's condition, and at the palace he was pleased to learn that the baby had been successfully delivered. Here too, though, there was a disappointment. The baby was a second daughter, and not the son for which they had both hoped.

'Tanya,' said the princess, announcing the name she had chosen.

Nodding his acceptance, the prince repeated the name. 'Tanya. Yes, very well.'

She was a long baby, and what little hair she had was fair, like her father's. The Kristovs were a family whose ancestors had many centuries earlier migrated to Russia from Scandinavia. They were all tall, and most of them were pale-skinned and fair-haired. This latest addition to the family wore a serene and mature expression as she lay sleeping in the crib rocked by her nurse's foot.

'She'll be a beauty one day,' said the prince. 'Just like you, my dear.' He remembered the Cartier card which had arrived the previous day. 'I'm going straight off to buy something to celebrate the birth. An ornament for your hair for the New Year Ball at the Winter Palace. Your confinement should be over just in time.'

He bent over to kiss his wife, whom he loved dearly. It was only the purdah into which she retreated when she was pregnant that had driven him into Barisinova's arms. His mood was a generous one when, an hour later, he entered the room in which Cartier's treasures were on exhibition.

As a regular customer in Paris, known for his wealth, he received a warm welcome and particular attention. Tray after tray of unmounted gems and finished pieces was displayed before him by M. Sarda himself, M. Cartier's personal representative. It was hard to choose from amongst such beauty, but almost at once he ordered a diamond aigrette to be set aside. The stone was already mounted, lacking only the feathers which would give the piece height and individuality. A selection would be sent round to the Kristov palace that same day, M. Sarda promised, in order that the princess might make her own choice.

That was all that Prince Kristov had intended to buy for the moment, but the glittering array of jewels gave him pause. His wife was bound to find out about Barisinova sooner or later. Nothing in Petersburg stayed a secret for long. It might be best if he were to make a tearful confession and accompany it with a gift to reinforce his apology.

'I would also,' he said, 'like to order a tiara.'

'With pleasure, Excellency.' M. Sarda snapped his fingers behind his back and within seconds his chief designer, M. Lamartine, had taken up position beside him, 'In the French or the Russian style?'

'Oh, Russian, certainly.' Until now the two men had naturally been conversing in French, but Prince Kristov used the Russian word to make clear what he wanted. 'A kokoshnik.'

The Russian style of tiara was higher in the crown than the French. Instead of nestling in the hair it rose above it, allowing for a greater elaboration of design which could incorporate much larger stones.

'Have you anything special? Better than these?' With a casual gesture of the hand the prince waved aside an array of jewels worth thousands of roubles.

'Well, since you enquire ... For such a particularly valued client ... We're not making this generally known, but M. Cartier had the opportunity recently of buying part of the collection of the French crown jewels.' The Frenchman considered for a moment. 'M. Lamartine, the teardrop pearls, if you please.'

There was a short pause while a box was fetched and opened. Prince Kristov stared down at two of the largest pearls he had ever seen. Their shape − not round, but perfectly symmetrical and exactly matching − was as unusual as their size. M. Sarda had been exact in describing them as teardrop.

'These were a gift to Queen Marie Antoinette, to be made

into earrings,' the Frenchman explained, dropping his voice reverentially.

'But they're too heavy for that, surely.'

'Your Excellency is correct as always. That is the reason why they have never been mounted, and I wouldn't recommend them for that purpose. But in a kokoshnik ...'

He gestured again to the designer, who had been busily sketching as the two men conferred and who now moved his drawing pad to the counter so that it could be studied. He had drawn seven overlapping open circles, increasing in size towards the large central one.

'Each circle to be of diamonds,' he suggested now, pointing with his pencil. 'A small pearl to be fixed inside each of the outer six circles, suspended from the top on a trembler; and one of the teardrop pair in the centre.'

'Why not both?' demanded the prince.

'That would require two circles of equal size, Excellency, and in our experience ladies find it more becoming to have a single central point – especially with the kokoshnik, which rises so conspicuously. If I might suggest it ...' His pencil began to work again: 'the second pearl could be most suitably mounted in a necklace to complement and mirror the kokoshnik, curving downwards instead of up. The effect would be one of great richness and harmony.'

'And cost, I've no doubt.' But Prince Kristov had never yet enquired the price of jewellery before buying it, and he did not intend to begin now. 'Very well. Get them made up. To be ready for the New Year Ball. You'll mount the stones in gold, I take it?'

'With respect, Excellency, we prefer to use platinum. It enhances the colour of the diamonds, instead of imparting a yellow hue. It adds further animation to the life of the piece.'

'As you think best.' Prince Kristov, his business finished, was about to turn away when he had another thought. Why should he bother to go on to Fabergé when he could find a generous gift for his mistress here? He looked down at the drawing of the kokoshnik, into which the teardrop pearl had been inserted, shaded to give it a three-dimensional appearance.

'The design is good,' he said appraisingly. 'I might consider another piece. To have the same proportions but a quite different appearance. It would not be necessary for my wife to learn about this.'

The admonition was hardly necessary. No jeweller could hope to stay in business who did not know the importance of discretion. Without the mistresses of customers his trade would be more than halved. The designer quickly found a new page in his sketch pad.

'Could I suggest rock crystal for the circles in this case, Excellency,' he said. 'Engraved to catch the light. And instead of pearls, strings of the tiniest diamonds on silver wire, attached at the top only, so that they dance with every movement.'

Prince Kristov glanced at the two Frenchmen, but their expressions gave nothing away. Of course they had guessed who would wear this kokoshnik, but they knew better than to give the slightest sign of it.

'Very well,' he agreed. 'No hurry for this one.' He would mollify Barisinova by telling her that the piece was in preparation, but would present it in six months' time, when the child was born. As he was helped into his greatcoat he felt pleased with his afternoon's work.

When the door had closed behind him, the two jewellers noted the order numbers of the three pieces and separated to deal with their own paperwork. The rough drawings which had been sketched in front of the customer were not sufficiently accurate to guide a workman. After a few words of more detailed instruction from M. Sarda, the designer settled down with his rule to make a meticulous plan. With the two teardrop pearls in front of him to establish the necessary scale, he drew in each tiny diamond and specified beside it what weight and quality it should be, and how faced.

At the top of each page he wrote the order number, the name of the customer and a brief description of what was to be made up. It would have been sufficient to identify the pieces as kokoshniks — but for his own benefit, because he regarded each creation almost as though it were a child, he allocated individual names.

The headdress for the ballerina could suitably be called *La Danseuse*. Already his eyes sparkled in sympathy with the diamonds as he anticipated the lightness of its movement.

For the princess it was a different matter. Pearls were not his favourite adornment, although he was careful never to express this opinion aloud — especially in Russia, where they were popular with the nobility. He thought them heavy; not so much reflecting light as absorbing emotion. Diamonds expressed gaiety, but pearls were inclined to be dismal. In this case, the shape of the central gem imposed its own description. Above the drawing of the Kristov kokoshnik he wrote the only possible title.

'*La Lachrymosa*.' The tiara of tears.

6

Book One

Part One

Laura in Oxford
1910–1913

1

'The iced walnut cake today, I think,' said Dr Mainwaring. 'Yes, the iced walnut cake would be very suitable.'

'Yes, Papa.' Laura Mainwaring, standing straight-backed to face her father across the breakfast table, received his instructions as though she were the housekeeper. Later, she would pass them on to the maid in the voice that her mother, had she still been alive, might have used.

'At half-past four, as usual. And I hope, my dear, that you will be able to join us?'

'Yes, Papa.' Now she was the dutiful daughter, accepting her responsibilities as the lady of the house.

In the course of each day Laura played many roles, trying them on like new clothes in front of a looking glass, testing to see which best fitted her, which would be most comfortable when she moved into adult life. In an hour's time, seated at a desk in tidy school uniform with her long chestnut hair neatly plaited, she would be the clever, hard-working schoolgirl. In the luncheon break she would gossip with her friends, giggling as though she were a shop-girl. Walking home at four o'clock, she would be transformed into that pathetic figure, the motherless child returning to an unwelcoming house; for her father, when he was not in college, spent most of the day in his study. And at half-past four, like a middle-aged hostess, she would preside over the ceremony of pouring out tea.

These tea parties were regular features in the autumn term because Dr Mainwaring – an Oxford don – liked to invite all his new pupils, two or three at a time, to his home as soon as possible after their arrival at the university. They would receive a second invitation, for sherry, after they had taken their final examinations. Laura

9

wished very much that her father wouldn't do it. The undergraduates were too polite to refuse the invitations, but it was easy to discern how eager they were to escape to some more exciting activity.

The 1909 freshers had been a hearty set, far more interested in rugger and the river than in the subjects they were supposed to be reading. There was no reason to expect that the 1910 intake would be any more studious.

'Who will be coming today?' Laura asked. She needed to know the number, and liked to hear names in advance instead of having to struggle to remember them when the guests were introduced.

'There will be three on this occasion. Mr David Hughes, a scholar of the college. A very talented young man, although Welsh. Prince Kristov, from Russia. And the Honourable Charles Vereker, a younger son of Lord Knaresborough. A family with a great tradition of public service. His grandfather was Secretary of State for – '

'A prince, did you say?' Laura, who should have known better than to interrupt, was not interested in the family tree of the Honourable Charles Vereker. '*Prince* Kristov? Is he the son of the Tsar?'

'Of course not. The Tsarevich is only a child. The Russian nobility operates on a quite different system from our own. Mr Vereker will never become a peer, unless his elder brother dies without an heir. But in Russia every child of a prince takes the rank of prince or princess and passes it on in turn to all the children of the next generation. The result is that there's hardly a member of the upper classes who doesn't boast a title of some sort.'

'All the same . . .' Laura's brown eyes were bright with interest. Most of her father's pupils came from wealthy families – although from the tone of his voice it sounded as though Mr Hughes might be an exception. In the past four years, since her aunt had married and left her in nominal charge of the house in Norham Gardens, Laura had poured tea for a good many members of the British aristocracy. But never yet for a prince. Silently she considered how best to boast of the occasion to her schoolfriends. Should she announce it in advance or wait until the next day to describe it? Well, she could decide that as she walked to school. There was one more practical question to ask.

'How do I address him? Your Royal Highness?'

'Certainly not. I've just told you, he has no royal blood.' Dr Mainwaring was silent for a moment, considering the question, and Laura realised with amusement that her father, who was so well versed in British protocol, was for once at a loss.

10

'A servant might address him as "Your Highness",' he pronounced at last. 'But not you. In Russia, his friends would always call him by both his first names: Alexis Karlovich, Alexis, son of Karl. But in Oxford he'll have to get used to the other men calling him Kristov. In the same way, it would probably be correct for you to say "Excellency" if you were in Russia; but since you're not, I suggest that you call him simply "Prince Kristov". While he's in England he must accept English conventions.'

'Then shouldn't it be Prince Alexis? Like we'd say Prince George.'

'Call him what you like, my dear. He won't expect someone of your age to be *au fait* with the niceties appertaining to his rank.'

Laura's age was sixteen. It was unfair of her father to remind her of the fact when he was expecting her to behave as an adult hostess. But curiosity about this unusual guest overrode any annoyance she might have felt.

'Does he speak English?'

'Well, of course. You'd hardly expect a young man to attend a university whose language he didn't understand. All Russian children of the nobility are brought up by English nurses and French governesses, or vice versa. I understand that many of them hardly speak Russian at all, except to the servants. Should you not be leaving for school now, my dear?'

Yes, she should. Hurriedly she ran down to the kitchen, since that was quicker than ringing the bell, and gave instructions for the tea-party. Then, pulling on her hat, coat and gloves, she set off at the briskest pace which was allowed — for running in the street while in school uniform was against the rules.

The falling leaves, golden in the October sunlight, swirled around her face and feet and her imagination swirled with them. She saw herself in Russia, galloping through endless forests with Prince Alexis at her side. How different that would be from her occasional sedate trots round Port Meadow on a friend's pony! Or in winter they might skate together, with smooth, rhythmic movements keeping time to some unseen orchestra.

Port Meadow was Laura's ice rink in winter as well as her riding ground in summer, and she was in fact a fast and proficient skater. But the meadow rarely flooded deeply enough to cover all the tufts of reeds and grass, so that it was necessary to watch for obstacles all the time. In Russia, she felt sure, there would be great sheets of ice, frozen rivers, along which it would be possible to speed arm in arm, looking into the eyes of a companion instead of always down on the ground.

11

She sighed with pleasure at the thought, her feet unconsciously moving in a sliding movement through the fallen leaves. And when the orchestra ceased to play and the skating came to an end, they would be driven home, the prince and she, in a sledge covered with furs. They would arrive at a palace and in the evening there would be a ball. She would coil her hair high on her head and weave diamonds into its plaits to shimmer like a crown, and the prince ...

But at this moment she turned a corner and saw that the monitor on duty was about to close the school gates. She was just in time to slip inside. A few seconds later, and she would have had to explain herself to the headmistress. With the ringing of the assembly bell, her day-dreams shattered and disappeared like a spent firework. She was a schoolgirl again, pleased because the first lesson was French, her favourite subject, and she knew that she had prepared a good translation.

At the age of sixteen Laura Mainwaring was both ambitious and practical, a romantic and at the same time a realist. Her immediate ambition was to study at the university, and it was likely that she would achieve this, for she was clever enough to pass the necessary entrance examination. Although her father had little private income and only with difficulty maintained the household on his small stipend as a tutor, the death of her mother soon after Laura's birth meant that she was an only child: there were no brothers to be sent to expensive boarding schools. Because she had a home in Oxford and could enrol inexpensively as a Home Student, to be at the university would not cost much. Fortunately her father was not one of those who believed that education for women was unnecessary or even dangerous.

But the passing of examinations was unlikely to alter the course of her life. It might even make marriage more difficult, because not every man was prepared to take on a blue-stocking, and most girls started looking for their husbands when they were eighteen, not twenty-one. Nevertheless, Laura took it for granted that she would marry eventually and that the rest of her life would be spent in some country vicarage – or perhaps in a house identical to her present home – bringing up children and supervising servants and worrying over money.

Part of her mind not only welcomed this prospect but longed for the security it offered. But a far larger part was restless, demanding new experiences and a chance to see a wider world before immuring herself in one tiny corner of it.

These awkward tea-parties with her father's pupils did at least give her occasional glimpses of the way in which other classes of society lived. But she sensed that many of the young men who came to the university had little respect for scholarship and were constrained only by good manners to be polite to a tutor who was their social inferior. They took no notice of her now because she was only a schoolgirl, and probably they would pay no attention to her even when she was older. The only exceptions were likely to be the college scholars who were as ambitious and clever — and as poor — as Laura herself: men, perhaps, like Mr Hughes.

Her father, she recognised, would be able to do little to help her achieve the security of marriage when the time came — and even less to suggest any way of escape from the kind of life which her mother would have lived. Only in day-dreams could she invent adventures in which she was always the heroine, and create heroes to play a part in them.

Such dreams had full play while she hurried home at four o'clock. As a rule, for a social occasion which promised so little excitement, she was content to wear the high-necked white blouse and navy blue skirt which comprised her school uniform; but not today. Not for a prince! Instead she changed quickly into her blue Sunday dress. She had grown since it was made, and it was now too tight, straining across her chest embarrassingly to show the shape of her breasts. Still, it was the best she could do. Tugging it down, she adjusted the lace collar and stared critically at herself in the glass.

In front of her stood a tall girl — and one who was still growing. Everything about her was long: long arms, long legs, long body, long neck. She disliked the neck, which was not swan-like and graceful but straight and strong, giving an oddly perched look to the face above it. She held herself well — Aunt Barbara had always insisted on good posture — increasing the impression of height. Her long chestnut hair was naturally straight, but the thick single plait in which she normally wore it encouraged it to fall in waves to her waist when it was released. There were always a few short and unruly strands which fell forward over her forehead, but not enough to be called a fringe. Her complexion was pale, almost white, except for some unwanted freckles which she did her best to obscure with talcum powder.

Her eyes, dark and dramatic, were her best feature. It was with her eyes that she could indicate every change of mood or role. As she smoothed down her dress, the expression in her eyes changed from a schoolgirl's liveliness to a serious indication of interest in whatever her guests might wish to talk about. She was ready to entertain.

By half-past four the drawing room too was ready and the tea trolley laid. She tasted one of the cucumber sandwiches and gave a nod of approval to the maid. Running upstairs to her bedroom again, she looked eagerly out of the window, pressing herself against the wall so that she would not be noticed if her guests happened to look up.

And here, unmistakably, they came: the three men who – although Laura could not know it yet – would so greatly influence the course of her future life, approaching on foot from the University Parks. They were together and must be walking at the same pace, for the distance between them did not change; so it was odd that the small, dark-haired young man in the lead should appear to be striding out in a hurry not to be late, whilst his two companions, a few yards behind, sauntered in a casual manner. That the dark man was Mr Hughes, Laura did not doubt for a moment, and she gave him no more than a glance before turning her full attention on the other two.

Almost all Oxford men, as Laura had discovered long ago, cultivated an air of superiority, but these two had certainly been born with it. It was easy to decide which was which. The taller of the two wore no overcoat over his Norfolk jacket, although a long scarf was twisted several times around his neck; his arms swung with a military stiffness. It was the other who must be Prince Alexis. His foreignness was revealed in the way he gestured as he talked, and in the unusual length of his overcoat – so smartly cut that it must undoubtedly be fashionable somewhere, but not in England. He wore no hat, and his fair hair, like the overcoat, was longer than normal; not parted and trimmed but brushed back from his forehead. His face, like his hands, continually moved as he spoke, as though the lifting of his eyebrows and the shape of his mouth were intended to be as eloquent as his words. From her look-out on the first floor Laura could not see his eyes, which appeared from above to be almost closed, like those of a sleeping cat which without warning will become wild and ready to spring.

For a few moments they were out of sight. Then Mr Hughes appeared at the front gate. As though knowing his place, he held it open for the other two. Laura leaned forward in order to keep them in view. The movement must have attracted the attention of Prince Alexis, who looked up. His wide-set blue eyes opened wide and his lips parted in the smile of someone sharing a secret. Laura found herself suddenly unable to breathe, as though winded by a sudden punch in the diaphragm. This, she felt sure, was love at first sight.

'Bet you a tenner the stag moves first!' Alexis, sitting on a window seat at half-past three on the day of his tutor's tea party, was staring out at the college deer park as Charles Vereker came into the room.

Charles crossed to stand behind him. 'This has got to stop, Kristov,' he said. 'I'm not going to spend the whole term making footling wagers with you.'

Alexis, who was more interested in acquiring an idiomatic knowledge of English than in his academic studies, tucked the word 'footling' away in his mind before protesting. 'I thought English gentlemen would bet on anything.'

'We bet on races if we're just about to watch them,' Charles told him. 'And if you were to claim, for example, that you could run round Cloister Quad two hundred times without stopping, and I didn't believe you, we could put that in the wager book and either you'd do it or you wouldn't. But the movements of a stag are of no interest to anyone but a doe.'

'Oh, very well.' When Alexis first arrived at Oxford at the beginning of the Michaelmas term he had been told that his tutor would be Dr Mainwaring, but Dr Mainwaring was never likely to teach him anything more than the dry facts of history. It was Charles Vereker who could prove far more useful as a tutor, by introducing him to English life.

Prince Alexis Karlovich Kristov had not at first been pleased to discover that he was expected to share his set of rooms in Magdalen College with another man. But his nature was an easy-going one, and he was quick to make the best of the situation. The arrangement would only last for one year, since after that he would be allowed to rent a house outside college. And he did at least have a bedroom to himself; he had at once given this a feel of home by hanging his ikons and their night-light over the bed and replacing the bedspread, rug and curtains with his own. The shared sitting room which over-looked the deer park was fortunately a large one – big enough to take the piano which he had hired and still leave plenty of room for parties. And, most satisfactory of all, his roommate had proved to be a congenial companion.

Intelligent and friendly and rarely to be seen without a cigarette in his hand, Charles cultivated a calm, even languid, appearance. He too was reading Modern History but – unlike Alexis – proposed to take his studies seriously. This did not prevent him from spending most afternoons on the river or the rugger field, nor from drinking too much in the evenings. But he organised his days efficiently, setting aside sufficient time to work in the library, attend occasional lectures and produce the necessary essays for his tutors without a last-minute rush. His family had been sending its sons to Oxford for many generations, so that he was well able to make sure that Alexis observed all the proper customs and understood the university slang.

Charles's only failing was an insistence on tidiness and punctuality. Alexis, who rated both these virtues low, dealt with the first by giving generous tips to the scout who cleaned the rooms, but disregarded the other. The note of disapproval in his roommate's next question took him by surprise.

'Why are you dressed like that, Kristov?'

'I'm going up to see the horses.' Riding was Alexis's passion. Even his wish to absorb English life could not make him enjoy team games like rugger, but he had brought three of his polo ponies with him to England, and his groom had been instructed to find him a hunter. A message had arrived that morning to say that a fine chestnut was awaiting his inspection at the livery stables.

'Have you forgotten that we're going to tea with the Manner?'

'The Manner?' Although Alexis had had time to get used to the odd Oxford habit of changing words like breakfast to brekker. freshman to fresher and lecture to leccer, he was not always able to make the translation – especially in the case of his tutor, who spelt his name Mainwaring but pronounced it Mannering.

'Dr Mainwaring. We're due at his house at four-thirty.'

'Well, I can be there by five or so.'

'When you have a ten o'clock tutorial,' said Charles patiently, 'you are expected to arrive at ten o'clock. And when your tutor invites you to tea at four-thirty, you are expected to arrive at four-thirty. The occasion is a duty on both sides and will be abysmally dull, but we won't have to stay long and we need never go again. You'd better get into some respectable clothes at top speed.'

Alexis made a face, but moved towards his bedroom. With parents who attended the imperial court, he had been brought up to respect protocol. One of the delights of England was its comparative informality, but he had been quick to realise that Charles's pronouncements were usually correct.

'Shall we drive there in your motor car?' he asked hopefully. He had watched with open-eyed admiration his roommate's arrival on the first day of term ten days earlier in a Hispano-Suiza driven by a uniformed chauffeur.

'No. I told Richards to take it back home. All these pettifogging

16

rules about where an undergraduate can or cannot keep a car! It's not worth the trouble. I shall send a telegram for him to bring it up whenever I need it. We can walk to the Manner's house. But get a move on.'

'Walk!' Although he had paid little attention to the invitation, his impression was that Dr Mainwaring's house was somewhere out in the suburbs. But then a new thought struck him. 'Should I carry a gift for Mrs Mainwaring?'

'No. He's a widower. There's a kid daughter, I believe, who may do the honours, but she won't expect anything.'

The walk was pleasanter than Alexis had expected. From Magdalen's own extensive grounds they were able to cross into the water meadows and then stroll, still beside the river, through the University Parks. In spite of Charles's nagging — or perhaps because of it — they had plenty of time to enjoy the peaceful surroundings.

To a man who had grown up in Russia, where even the most modest of his family's estates included huge forests and extensive farmland, England was a country designed on a miniature scale; that was its greatest charm for him. Ducks and swans floated lazily on the water, and small boys, newly released from school, ran whooping over the grass: it was a delightful scene. He had made a mistake in wearing his overcoat, though, for the sun was shining warmly on the berried branches and golden leaves of the trees.

They had just reached Norham Gardens when they heard quick footsteps catching up with them, and turned their heads to see who it was. Dr Mainwaring took his pupils in pairs for tutorials — in order, he said, that they might sharpen their brains on each other; this was Alexis's tutorial partner.

Unlike Charles, who had obviously been chosen to share his rooms on grounds of social suitability, David Hughes came from a modest home and was already, only ten days into his first term, becoming anxious about money as he totted up the costs of such essentials as his gown and mortar board. But he was clever: the very first essay that he read aloud in Dr Mainwaring's room had been enough to show Alexis that.

It was clear now that he had been invited to the same tea party — and that he was anxious to get it over so that he could return to his work. He nodded in recognition as he overtook the other two; but then slowed his pace so that they would all arrive at the same moment. And they were nearly there now. Unlike the jumble of addresses in Russian streets, where houses were registered in order of their dates of construction, the numbers here moved in steady progression, so that Alexis could already identify their destination.

17

The house was large by the standards of Oxford family accommodation, although of course it could not compare in size with any of the Kristov palaces. It was built of yellow brick, pointed in dark mortar and decorated with lines of red brick which arched over each window. The proportions were wrong. Alexis paused for a moment to consider them. It was too tall for its width, with a steeply-pitched roof and high gables above the attics in which no doubt the servants slept. When there were so many beautiful buildings in Oxford, it seemed a pity that anyone should have to live in something so ugly.

A movement at one of the first-floor windows caught his attention, and he glanced up. The face he glimpsed must be that of the child whom Charles had mentioned: even at this distance he could recognise nervousness as well as curiosity. But she was tall: perhaps not a child after all. It was a matter of habit with Alexis to charm any woman he met. His eyes opened wide and his cheeks dimpled as he sent his smile up towards Dr Mainwaring's daughter.

At half-past five the three young men emerged from the house. As long as they remained in sight of anyone who might be watching from it they walked decorously, side by side. But as soon as they rounded the corner David quickened his step whilst Charles, lighting a cigarette after an hour of abstinence, yawned as though the air inside had been as stuffy as the conversation. Alexis, feeling the need to fill his lungs with fresh air, began to make fencing movements while he walked: bending a knee low as he lunged forward, or whirling gracefully in a circle. 'So, that's done,' he said.

'Why were you talking to Miss Mainwaring in French?' asked David curiously, slackening his pace again in order to hear the answer. 'And what did you say that made her blush?'

'I asked her what her favourite subject was at school, and she said French. So I spoke a little French, and her blush was of embarrassment because she found it hard to understand. She told me later that although she can read the language well she had never before had the chance to converse with a Frenchman.'

'You're not a Frenchman.'

'Oh, very well, but you know what I mean. French is my first language. The poor child has to study only from books, taught by an Englishwoman who obviously has an execrable accent.' 'Execrable' was one of Alexis's new words: he had to think before pronouncing it in the English way. 'What she needs – Miss Mainwaring, I mean, not her teacher: although yes, her teacher as well – what she needs is a weekly conversation with someone like myself.'

18

'Which no doubt you offered her?' said Charles, laughing.

'Well, I did say that if she cared to come to Magdalen ... She longs to accept.'

'Well, she won't be allowed to.' David spoke confidently. 'A sixteen-year-old girl exposed to a college full of dissolute under-graduates! And no mother to chaperone her! The Manner would probably have to sit in on your conversations himself, and I can't see him taking kindly to that.'

'You're right.' It was just as well. Alexis had not intended the invitation to be taken seriously. And yet there had been a certain look in her eyes when he made the offer. 'Although I think that Miss Mainwaring is a young lady of some determination. And also, she is a romantic and I am a most mysterious stranger. She would like to fall in love with me.'

'Oh, come off it, Kristov!' Even Charles protested at this. 'You shouldn't talk like that about a respectable girl.'

'Why should it be a criticism of a woman, that she is ready to fall in love? You may say that I am arrogant, if you like. But I'm not boasting, just telling what I see. If I were to say to Miss Mainwaring that she should come to our rooms next Monday for French conver-sation, she would come. And you, Vereker, could be the chaperon; I have no bad intentions.' He circled and struck with an imaginary foil even more vigorously than before; and so certain was he of his opinion that his claims became as extravagant as his movements. 'I bet you a tenner, Vereker − and you, Hughes − that in three years' time, when I go down, if I should choose to say to Miss Mainwaring, "Come with me to Russia," she would come.'

Charles came to a standstill, forcing the other two to stop if they were to hear what he said. 'In the first place, Kristov, it's bad form to talk about a young lady like that, and make her the subject of a bet. And in the second place, it's an invalid wager, because you could win it by simply saying when the time comes that you don't choose.'

'And in the third place − ' David was even more disapproving ' − it's about time you learned to balance risk and loss. If *you* lose a tenner, you won't even notice it. If *I* lose it, I shan't be able to pay my battels. That much money to me is the equivalent of − oh, one of your blessed polo ponies. If your stake was going to be something that you couldn't afford to lose, you might think more carefully before scattering your bets around.'

Had anyone spoken to Alexis like that in Russia it would have caused the kind of quarrel which can last a lifetime. But so secure was he in his social standing here that nothing an Englishman − or

19

Welshman — said could disturb him. As a boy he had accepted punishments from his English governess without protest, because he was still a prince in spite of them, and she was still only a governess. He shrugged his shoulders and walked on in a more sedate manner. By the time he was back in his rooms, he had forgotten all about the bet.

3

Oxford in June. A haze of heat shimmering off stone walls and hovering above untrodden green lawns. A calm, unruffled surface to the river. In punts moored beneath the willows undergraduates sprawled lazily in silence, relishing the last moments of their golden years, enjoying the bitter-sweetness of friendships which would never again be quite so intense or unreserved. Bottles of champagne, suspended on string, cooled in the water, ready to celebrate the end of final examinations. A cloudless sky, a cloudless mood.

Into the gardens of North Oxford, scented by roses, the sun penetrated even more brightly. Bees moved purposefully from blossom to blossom; butterflies spread their wings in brilliant display. But behind the closed curtains of her bedroom, Laura Mainwaring, aged nineteen and dressed in black, wept for her father and listened for the cab which would bring her aunt from the station.

A few moments before noon she heard the neat tapping of the approaching hooves and stood up, drying her eyes and taking a deep breath to steady herself before opening the curtains just enough to allow her to look down. Yes, it was indeed a cab which came to a halt outside the door — but the passenger who emerged was not Aunt Barbara but Prince Alexis.

She watched as he paid and — to judge by the smile on the cabbie's face — overtipped. What must it feel like, she wondered, to be so rich that money had no real value and could not be reckoned in terms of the effort required to acquire it? Well, she was never likely to know the answer to that question. She continued to stare down as the cab pulled away. Alexis consulted his watch and turned away from the house, strolling with a deliberate aimlessness which made it clear that he was killing time. No doubt he had arranged to meet a companion in order that the formality of offering condolences need not prove too awkward an occasion.

How lightly and gracefully he moved, and with what confidence, almost like a dancer. Laura allowed herself to remember how his first appearance at the house three years earlier had swept her off her feet. She had developed a schoolgirl passion for him which not even his total unawareness of her continued existence could subdue. His promise to spend time speaking French with her was never honoured, and in her sensible moments she had never expected that it would be. That realisation hadn't prevented her from writing letters to remind him of his offer and ask for a meeting, but she had better sense than to post them: they were all still in her handkerchief drawer.

Leaving school, growing up, had had no effect on the infatuation. How many hours had she wasted in this last year, since she became a Home Student, leaning dreamily on Magdalen Bridge in the hope that Alexis would pass in or out of college and notice her? But on every occasion when a Magdalen man did pause to converse with her, it was always Charles Vereker. Not until two terms had elapsed did she mention Alexis's name at home and learn that he no longer had rooms in college but had rented a house and installed his own chef and housekeeper there. She had even attended some of the lectures which related to Alexis's syllabus rather than her own — for she had chosen to read Modern Languages. But Alexis was not a man who went to lectures: that was something else which she should have guessed.

It was his smile which had charmed her at that first meeting. His appearance, certainly, was striking as well. The fairness of his hair, the blueness of his eyes, his wide, high cheekbones, foreign style of dressing and uninhibited gestures, all marked him out from the ordinary run of undergraduates.

Yet the other two guests on that occasion were handsome too: Charles in the clean-cut style of the young English aristocrat and David, whose dark good looks were sharpened by the flashing intelligence in his eyes. And both of them, naturally, had been perfectly polite to their tutor's daughter. Alexis, though, had been more than polite as he described other countries which she longed to explore. When he leaned towards her, speaking first in English and then in French, his smile was warm with understanding and sympathy, as though no one else in the world existed for him. How could a sixteen-year-old have been expected to resist someone so exotic?

But that was three years ago. Now, in 1913, she was no longer an impressionable schoolgirl. Two weeks earlier, as her father wrote invitations to his annual sherry party for undergraduates about to go down, Laura had realised that she would at last come face to face with Alexis again. That was the moment when she shook herself metaphorically by the shoulders and resolved that the meeting should be of no importance. If possible — as an act of self-discipline —

she would not even speak to him; but certainly she must be quite clear in her mind that their paths would never cross again. Today, in such changed circumstances, she could not avoid his visit; but that would make no difference to the closing of what could hardly even be called an acquaintanceship.

None of these good resolutions could prevent her from sighing as she glanced at herself in the glass. Her eyes were no longer as swollen as on the previous day, but there was no doubt that black did not suit her complexion. Angrily, as she went downstairs, she told herself that this was no time for vanity. She waited with folded hands in the drawing room until the bell rang and Annie announced the caller.

'Miss Mainwaring.' He bowed to kiss her hand. At that first meeting he had shaken hands in an ordinary English way, but that would have been because she was only a child then. As he straightened himself she saw those blue eyes flicker round the room with a suggestion of surprise or doubt. Perhaps he had abandoned his wait outside the house on the assumption that his friend must have arrived before him. Whatever the reason, he was quick to conceal it with a smile. 'I hope you are well.'

'Yes, thank you.'

'But in mourning, I see. I'm sorry. I hope it isn't depriving you of the pleasures of this beautiful English summer.'

Laura stared at him in amazement. What an extraordinary comment to make! Could it be that Russians for some reason were unwilling to talk about death? But in that case, why had he come? Puzzled, she invited him to sit down. Surely he would make some reference to her father's accident. But no; he continued to make the smallest of small talk — asking her whether she had achieved her ambition to study at the university, and congratulating her on her success.

'I promised to speak French with you,' he remembered apologetically. 'But there was so much talk of chaperones that I took fright. I'm sorry.'

'Your conversation was a help to me all the same,' Laura told him. 'It made me realise how much I needed practice. I was able to persuade my father that I should spend time in France, and he found a family in Paris willing to put me up and talk to me.' She felt the life returning to her eyes at the memory. 'Such a marvellous city! I'd like to spend the rest of my life there.' But her excitement was short-lived as she remembered how sombre now were the prospects for the rest of her life. She continued to talk quickly to banish the gloom from her mind.

22

'You've been taking your Finals this week, I suppose,' she said. 'How did you find the papers?'

Alexis lauged aloud. 'I have been playing hookey,' he told her, giving the word the careful enunciation of a new acquisition. 'Your father will have told you that I am his worst pupil. I've spent far too much time hunting or playing polo, and this year also I bought an apartment in London. There have been so many kind hostesses, so many parties, that it became tedious to return to Oxford every night. So last week I said to myself that there was no shame in not having an Oxford degree, because my friends in Russia have never even considered the possibility of such a thing. But to have a *bad* degree, or to take the examinations and fail, that would be a disgrace indeed. Instead of wasting my days in the Examination Schools, I've spent the past week in London, where the season has begun and young bachelors are greatly in demand for escorting young ladies to balls.'

He had been smiling as he spoke, but now the puzzled look returned to his eyes. 'Miss Mainwaring, you are very polite and welcoming, but I fear that I have made a mistake. In the time, perhaps, or even the date of your father's sherry party.'

'Oh, I see!' The shock of comprehending what had happened brought Laura to her feet. 'You've been in London. I suppose you've come straight from the station, without seeing the note I sent to you — and to everyone else.'

'The note?'

'To say that of course the sherry party had been cancelled because of my father's death.'

It was Alexis's turn to be startled. 'Dr Mainwaring dead!' He had risen politely to his feet when Laura herself stood up. Now he stared levelly into her eyes with a perplexed expression on his face. 'But he was not an old man. And seemed in good health a week ago.'

'It was an accident. A stupid, ridiculous accident.' Sensing that she was about to become upset again, Laura turned away and moved restlessly round the drawing room. 'The son of my hostess in Paris came to stay with us. It was his first visit, and we wanted to introduce him to Oxford life. So on Friday — ' unbelievably, it was only two days ago — 'we went on the river. My father is — was — a good punter. After an hour he gave Gerard a lesson, teaching him how to do it properly. Tossing the pole up with one, two, three movements of the hands before dropping it back into the water.' Laura, who could handle a punt herself, mimed the movement, finishing the demonstration with a sigh.

'He let Gerard take it back to the boathouse, practising what he'd learned,' she continued. 'We were nearly there, just about to go under Magdalen Bridge. Gerard threw the pole up too high, or too late and − and − ' Unable to continue, she pushed her clenched fists into her eyes as if they would hold back her tears. In her mind she re-lived what had at first seemed a moment of almost comic confusion as the pole struck the bridge and the punt swung wildly in a circle while Gerard attempted to control it.

'My dear Miss Mainwaring! Please don't upset yourself. I'm so sorry. So very sorry. And then I invade your home like an insensitive brute and − '

His hands turned her to face him, gripping her shoulders, drawing her close, and she allowed her head to press down on his arm as she abandoned the attempt not to weep. The gentleness with which he murmured sympathy and moved one hand to stroke her back soothingly had an almost feminine quality. He was encouraging her to cry her unhappiness out, and for a few moments she allowed herself that luxury. Then for the second time in an hour she used deep breaths to bring her emotions back under control, and managed to finish her story.

'The end of the pole hit the bottom of the bridge, at the edge,' she said. 'The stone is very old, I suppose, and not secure. A piece was dislodged. It was sharp as well as heavy. There was the whole river into which it could have fallen, but it landed straight on my father's head.'

He murmured his sympathy again, adding, 'It might have hit you.'

'I wish it had.'

'You mustn't say such a thing.' His hand was still gently moving up and down her back, comforting her with his touch. 'A young woman with your life in front of you.'

'What sort of a life?' she asked miserably. Until now it was a question she had not dared to put into words, because the loss of her father was sadness enough. But the effect of his death on her own ambitions had become clear to her almost at once.

'You'll continue your studies, surely.'

Laura shook her head. 'We could only afford them because I was able to live at home. But the house belongs to the college. I shall have to leave it. I can't afford lodgings. I can't even afford to pay the fees. My father left no money and I have none of my own. Not a penny.'

No sooner had she spoken than she was ashamed. To talk of money when she should be thinking only of her bereavement was discreditable. Indeed, she ought not to talk of money at all − and

24

especially to someone who had so much of it. It came as a relief when for a second time that morning she heard the sound of an approaching cab.

Aunt Barbara, bustling in to embrace her niece, looked shocked to find her in unchaperoned conversation with a young man. Alexis, sensitive to her reaction, waited only to be introduced before repeating his condolences and taking his leave. Once again he bowed his head and raised Laura's hand to his lips.

'If you will allow me, I will call again,' he said softly. 'Tomorrow afternoon?'

An hour earlier Laura had thought she would never be able to look happy again. But now, as she nodded her head, she realised that she was smiling.

4

There was no avoiding Aunt Barbara's presence in the drawing room the next day. Less expected, and less welcome to Laura as she waited to see whether Alexis would keep his promise, was the appearance of David Hughes, who had called to express formal condolences on the death of his tutor.

Unlike Alexis, David was a regular attender at lectures and had noticed Laura's unexpected appearances to educate herself in subjects which had nothing to do with her own course. Perhaps he had imagined that he himself was the attraction, for on each occasion he had waited behind to discuss the lecture with her, and even from time to time invited her to coffee at the Cadena.

Today, therefore, he had presented himself as an acquaintance of her own as well as a pupil of her father. He had come at teatime, and so he had been given tea. By now everything had been said that could be said, but he sat on as though he had set some kind of mental alarm clock with the correct duration of such a call and was unable to leave until it rang to release him from his duty. He looked relieved when Alexis arrived to take on some of the burden of conversation.

Alexis, for his part, did no more than greet David casually before leaving him to talk to Aunt Barbara whilst he himself carried on an earnest conversation with Laura.

'If it's not impertinent, Miss Mainwaring, may I ask what are your future plans?' He misinterpreted Laura's silence as disapproval, although its true cause was the lack of any plans to describe. 'I know it's too soon, that I ought to wait. But term ends on Thursday and

25

I'm expected in Carlsbad to join my mother, so I hoped you wouldn't be offended − '

'Oh, I'm not offended,' she told him. 'It's kind of you to take an interest. But I've nothing to tell you. I shall have to find some way of earning a living. But I'm not qualified ... Even schoolteachers nowadays are expected to have some kind of college diploma. I have no skills at all. I can't think of anything useful I could do, but something will have to be found very soon.'

'Your aunt − ?'

'Yes, my aunt has kindly invited me to live with her. But she has four young children and only a small house. I don't feel ...'

'I would like to make a suggestion to you, Miss Mainwaring. And please don't be too quick in deciding what you feel about it, until I've had time to explain, because at first it may seem a little, a little ...' His hands waved wildly in the air as he struggled and failed to find the word he wanted.

'What is it?'

'My sister-in-law has two daughters. Sofiya and Tanya. Nine years old and four and a half, I think. She needs an English governess for them.'

'Governess!' Astonished, Laura spoke too loudly, attracting the attention of the other two. It was not just that the idea of becoming anything as humble as a governess had never occurred to her: there would also be a special objection to this particular post. For, although it might mean that she would continue to meet Alexis from time to time, he would never regard her as anything but a servant.

'A governess in Russia is not at all the same as a governess in England,' he hastened to explain. 'I have been for weekend visits to houses in your English counties, and I have seen the governesses of the children there. Little grey mice who creep about the house with no companionship, despised by their employers, by the servants, even by their pupils. In Russia it is very different. In my own home, my English governess was my chief teacher and companion for many years.'

'She taught you very well,' murmured Laura, but Alexis continued to talk without acknowledging the compliment.

'She was the most important person in the household, under my parents,' he continued. 'The servants served her with respect. And to my mother she was a friend. She ate with the family. If there was a grand dinner, a great ball, she was always invited. She could dance with a grand duke if he asked her. My sister-in-law would treat a governess in the same way. And my brother owns many houses. If you were to join his family you would move between St Petersburg and Moscow and his country houses near there and in the Crimea. You would go to Paris again, and to Carlsbad. What work could you find in England to offer such opportunities?'

'But I'm not qualified!' Laura could not resist the interruption.

'Oh, Miss Mainwaring, your qualifications are perfect. Your duties would be only to teach English to my nieces, to speak it with them, to guide their reading and to act as their escort and companion. They have other teachers for French and mathematics and for music and dancing. You speak with the English of an educated lady, and you have lived surrounded by books. You will turn two little girls, whom you may find a little wild, into two young women who should be able to hold an intelligent conversation in any court of Europe.'

'Don't listen to him!' To Laura's astonishment, David Hughes sprang to his feet, apparently outraged. 'Kristov, you ought to be ashamed of yourself!'

He looked from one to the other, but it was on Laura that his gaze rested. 'I'm sorry, Miss Mainwaring,' he said more quietly. 'It's none of my business what you choose to do. But I hope you will consider very seriously before taking such an irretrievable step. You would be cutting yourself off from all your friends, and – and –' Flushed and stammering, and ignoring Alexis, he said goodbye to Laura and her aunt and left without finishing the sentence.

'What did he mean by that outburst?' Laura asked when the front door had closed behind him.

'He's angry with me because he's in love with you,' Alexis told her. 'And I am tempting you to move out of his reach.'

Aunt Barbara tutted disapprovingly at this new, frank turn to the conversation, but Laura took no notice of her signals to be silent.

'In love with me!' she exclaimed. 'Oh, don't be silly, Prince Alexis.'

'You must learn to read the language of eyes, Miss Mainwaring. He won't dare to confess it himself, but I can tell from watching him that what he feels for you is more than admiration. He would have wished for you to continue living quietly with your father whilst he set about making his fortune. But your life has been upset, and this upsets him as well. He has no money and knows that it will be many years before he can afford to marry. So he is angry with himself, because he is poor, and he expresses the anger against me, because I am rich.'

'Stuff and nonsense!' said Aunt Barbara. 'That's quite enough of that.' But again Laura paid no heed.

27

'You're very sensitive to people's feelings,' she told Alexis.

'I've already confessed to you that in these years in Oxford I haven't spent as much time as I should reading books. I came to England to make English friends, so I have learned to read people instead.'

Laura made no comment. Had he read her own childish feelings at that first meeting three years earlier? He could hardly be aware of what she thought now, since she didn't know herself. But he must have guessed at her indecision, because he made a smooth return to the discussion which David had interrupted.

'If you accept the post of governess, you will be generously paid. One hundred roubles a month, with no expenses to pay apart from your personal clothes. In as little as a year you could make good savings and return home if you wish.'

How could he be sure of all this? There had been no time for him to contact his sister-in-law since he heard of Dr Mainwaring's accident. Did the post really exist? It was possible, she supposed, that in some earlier letter he had been informed of the impending departure of a current governess and asked to look out for a replacement while he was in England. As for the money, Laura had no idea what a rouble was worth. Nor, for that matter, did she have the slightest notion what she could expect to earn if she stayed in England. She shivered with apprehension as she recognised yet again how totally unprepared she was for the independence which had so suddenly been thrust upon her.

Alexis smiled sympathetically as he stood up to leave.

'You'll need time to consider this suggestion, and to discuss it with your aunt.' He felt in his pocket for a card case and handed her an engraved card bearing an address in St John Street. 'A message will reach me more quickly here than if you send it to Magdalen. May I expect to hear from you before Thursday night?'

'So soon!' It was Monday already, and the next day would be taken up with the funeral. 'To change the whole course of my life — '

'A quick decision is often a good decision. Even if you wait longer to consider, nothing will alter. And if I know your answer soon, I can make the arrangements for your journey before I leave Oxford. Please believe, Miss Mainwaring, that I have nothing but your best interests at heart in what I propose.' He touched her hand with his lips before turning to make his adieux to her aunt.

'What an extraordinary young man!' exclaimed Aunt Barbara after Annie had shown him out. 'Foreign, of course. There can't be any question of your going, my dear.'

28

'I shall have to think about it.' Laura had been taken as much aback as her aunt. Had she been alone with Alexis, she might well have thanked him politely for the proposal and then declined it. But this automatic opposition brought its own reaction.

'To live abroad, so far from your family – '

'I very much enjoyed my visits to Paris,' Laura pointed out – realising as she spoke that there were unlikely to be any future invitations. Gerard, in a state of shock and guilt at the terrible consequence of a trivial miscalculation, had returned home hastily on the day after the accident and would almost certainly feel unable ever to face her again.

'Well, Paris, yes, but *Russia*! A barbarian country! Scarcely even in Europe.'

'I would hardly call Prince Alexis a barbarian.' But even as she spoke, it occurred to her that, sophisticated though he might be, he could be unreliable. Arrangements which were made might not always be honoured. She tucked the thought away on one side of the balance which would need to be struck. 'And it would certainly solve the immediate problem of what I'm to do and where I'm to go. I shall have to be out of this house before next term begins.'

'I thought we'd agreed, dear, that you would come and live with me. I've always thought of you as my own daughter. And you know how much the children love you.'

'You're very kind, Aunt Barbara, but you know very well that you haven't really got room.'

'Nanny's room will be available for you. It's time for her to move on in any case, with Mavis at school already and Bobbie just about to start. I'm sure you'd be willing to look after the little ones for me. And I could introduce you into a very nice class of society. You need to meet the right sort of young man. As a governess in Russia you'll never find an eligible husband. I know girls like you always think that there's plenty of time; but there isn't. Men want young wives, and you won't stay young for long. You must be sensible.'

'Please excuse me,' said Laura abruptly. 'I need a little fresh air. I'm going for a walk.' She had not been out of doors since her return from the hospital on the day of the river picnic which went so disastrously wrong, and suddenly the darkened atmosphere was stifling her. Without pausing even to pull on a hat she ran out of the house, along the road and towards the river.

The sun was bright, dazzling her eyes which had accustomed themselves to the dimness behind the drawn blinds. Her mourning dress had been bought for the winter death of her grandmother four years earlier and was far too warm and tight. She ran along the river bank, looking for a place where the willows and hawthorns would conceal her from curious eyes and shield her from the heat of the day. As she sat down, hugging her knees, a family of ducks swam hopefully towards her; but she had missed the opportunity of bringing a left-over scone with her, and after only a few moments they made off again in formation to look for a less forgetful visitor. Laura did not notice them go.

So still did she sit as she concentrated all her thoughts on her future that the wild life on the river, temporarily disturbed by her arrival, resumed its busy movement. Sedge warblers and reed buntings bustled in and out of their nests. A kingfisher posed on a twig, waiting to dive, whilst a water rat swam silently back to its hole. None of this did she see. Her eyes, fixed on the river, observed only the swirling pattern as the water parted to pass the fallen branch of a tree.

She had a methodical mind and moved efficiently through the pros and cons of a plan which could never be more than the best of a bad lot. There was certainly a great deal to be said against it. Alexis might let her down. His family might know nothing about his offer and be unwilling to receive her. She might even, if they moved between so many properties, be unable to find them. If she found them, she might not like them, or they her. The children − Alexis had suggested that they were 'a little wild' − might prove to be intolerable. She might discover that she had no gift for teaching.

That was the devil she didn't know. The devil she did was in many ways more daunting. Although Aunt Barbara, her mother's younger sister, had generously moved in to look after Laura when she was two years old, and had stayed for several years, the relationship between the two was not warm enough to replace that of mother and daughter. They behaved affectionately to each other, but love was missing. As for her uncle, who worked in a bank, he was the dullest man whom Laura had ever met, and if she was expected to pick a husband of the same sort out of Aunt Barbara's social circle, almost any alternative would be preferable.

Besides, it was all too clear that if she accepted the invitation to go to Bristol she would be a substitute nanny − even more of a domestic servant than in Russia, and unpaid. Laura was clear-minded enough to have realised by now how she was tilting the argument. It meant that she wanted to go.

'You have to be clear.' She started talking aloud to herself in an effort to discipline her thoughts. 'You may never see Alexis again, even in Russia. And if you do, he'll still be a prince and you'll be a governess, whatever he may say. So if you decide to go just because you hope . . .' Her voice trailed away. She didn't know what she hoped.

What she did know was that the thought of seeing more of the world was exciting, and every other possibility was by contrast drab. She had loved her time in Paris; and although mention of the Crimea suggested nothing but battlefields to her, she knew that St Petersburg was a beautiful city. She couldn't afford to continue her Modern Languages studies in Oxford, but wouldn't it be even more valuable to work in a country in which French was regularly spoken, and where she could learn Russian as well? There was nothing to be lost and a great deal to be gained by allowing herself a limited time − a year, say − for such an exciting experiment.

Before long the hard-headed side of Laura's character became submerged under a wave of romantic dreaming as she visualised the adventure of forests and palaces, furs and snow, balls and jewels, and trains which chugged for days across strange countries and continents. She deliberately moved through these day-dreams without a partner. All her life she had longed to travel, to explore different societies, and now the chance had been offered. What a fool she would be to turn it down!

To dispel any lingering doubts she reminded herself that she had nothing to lose, for she would be a pauper if she stayed. There was, though, one precaution she could sensibly take. A rail ticket from St Petersburg back to London could not possibly cost more than £20. Surely her father's estate, small though she knew it to be, would yield that much. With the price of a return ticket always in her pocket, she would have the means of escape from any disaster.

Yet why should she anticipate disaster? Alexis had made a kind and liberal offer. He was opening a door through which she could step to explore a wider world. The unhappiness of the past few days was forgotten for a moment as her eyes shone with excitement. This very evening, before she had time to change her mind, she would send a note to Alexis and, as soon as he could arrange it, she would leave for Russia.

5

As soon as he heard the news, Charles Vereker set out for Norham Gardens. He went on foot, to give himself time to think what he should say.

Charles was a natural diplomat. As a younger son he would need a career and it was taken for granted by himself, his family, and all

31

those connections who would ease his way, that he would quickly rise to the top of the Foreign Service. As well as a quick brain, he had a natural gravity of character which fitted well with his inbred courtesy.

During his three years at Oxford he had behaved much as any undergraduate of his kind was expected to behave. As often as any of his contemporaries, he became drunk after dinner, or climbed into college after the gate was locked, or joined the rowdy group which ragged the effete aesthetes. He was a hearty, in other words, taking time from the hunting which was his passion whenever he was needed to strengthen the rugger team.

Nevertheless, he had also found time to study. As though it were a secret vice, a matter of shame actually to be seen at his books, he applied himself during the vacations to his reading list and then, during term, worked into the small hours on the essays to be read aloud at weekly tutorials. He had not been marked out from the start for a First by his tutors in the way that, for example, David Hughes had; but secretly he hoped that his papers might be good enough.

With the beginning of Finals he had dropped any pretence of frivolity in order to do his best; and although the examinations were behind him now, his mood remained serious. In this last week of term there was nothing to do except play cricket and cement his Oxford friendships so securely that they would last throughout his life. In one sense his present mission was a part of that process, although from a different point of view it might seem a betrayal.

To think of Laura Mainwaring as a friend would be an exaggeration. College rules on his own side and the system of chaperonage on hers made it very difficult to develop a friendship with a girl at Oxford. But during the past year he had on several occasions, as he returned to Magdalen after a ride or a game, seen her leaning over the bridge, and had stopped to exchange a few words with her.

What interested him most was the change that came over her face and way of speaking as they conversed. Whilst staring down at the river, and in the first few seconds after he attracted her attention, her eyes were dreamy, as if she were yearning for something beyond her reach. But almost at once, as she gave him her full attention, everything about her sharpened into focus. She was intelligent, and years of living alone with her father had taught her to think before she spoke, enabling her to hold her own in a serious conversation. He would have said, until today, that she was a level-headed young woman; but now he was worried in case he might be wrong.

As he stepped from the sunlight into the darkened house and was

32

shown into the drawing room where she was sitting in her heavy black dress, any feeling of criticism was banished by sympathy. Her whole world had collapsed about her head. How could anyone expect so young a woman to be level-headed in such circumstances?

She stood up as the maid announced him. An orphan she might be, but there was nothing waif-like about her appearance. Unlike many tall girls she did not stoop. Instead, her head was held erect on an unusually strong neck. She had changed the style in which she dressed her chestnut hair, so that its plaits now crossed on top of her head, framing her face in a manner which gave it a businesslike appearance.

'How kind of you to come, Mr Vereker.' She held out her hand to shake his firmly. 'Thank you very much for your letter. I haven't had time yet – '

'No of course not.' Anxious to come to the point of his visit while they were still alone, he wasted no time on small talk. 'Miss Mainwaring, I was given some disturbing news this morning. I understand that there is some suggestion of your going alone to Russia.'

'Your informant, I suppose, was Mr Hughes. He seemed remarkably disturbed when the question arose. I didn't understand the cause of his concern. Won't you sit down?'

He was still holding her hand, he realised, and relinquished it as he took a seat.

'I do hope, Miss Mainwaring, that you're not seriously considering accepting such an invitation.'

'Why should I not consider it?'

'There are so many reasons.' He was reluctant to give the true one. 'To travel alone to a strange country, to live there without protection – '

'I *am* alone, Mr Vereker, whether in Russia or England. But I'm as capable as anyone else of making a journey unaccompanied. And if you have been given the details of the offer made to me, you'll know that I shall live under the protection of Princess Kristova and her family.'

'You mustn't go!'

'Then you must tell me why not.'

'Kristov is a friend of mine,' said Charles unhappily. 'I don't like to speak behind his back, but ... He's always in good spirits, bubbling with ideas, new enthusiasms. But none of them come to much. He makes appointments and doesn't keep them. He'll suggest a plan and then completely forget about it. And probably the plan had no firm foundation in the first place. In the year when we were sharing a set, I had time to get used to him, but you ... I can quite

33

understand how you might be swept off your feet by something which seems an exciting idea. I feel I must warn you that it could all crumble away and leave you nothing but disappointment.'

'I'm not such a bad judge of character as you seem to think,' said Laura. 'I understand what you're trying to tell me. And I've allowed myself one simple test. I've asked him to make the arrangements for my journey. I shall pay him back, of course, out of my first earnings; but if you're right in thinking that he will already have lost interest in an idea which only occurred to him on the spur of the moment, all he has to do is to do nothing.'

'You mean that you've agreed to go?'

'Yes,' said Laura. 'I sent a note to him yesterday.'

For a moment Charles was silent. He had hoped not to have to reveal the true reason why Hughes had been so appalled.

'There was a wager,' he said at last. 'Kristov bet ten pounds that he could persuade you to go to Russia with him.'

Now at last he had got through to her. He saw her face turn pale, even as she straightened her shoulders and drew herself even more erect than before.

'Naturally we didn't accept the bet, Hughes and I,' he said quickly. 'It's not the sort of thing that any gentleman would consider fit for a wager. Foreigners have different ideas, I suppose. We tried to tell him — '

'If you didn't accept the wager, there was no reason for him to try and win it.'

'Except that — money doesn't matter to someone like Kristov. But he might still want to prove that he was right.'

'When did this happen?'

'Three years ago, when we first came to tea and met you.'

'Oh, well, three years! And I shan't be going to Russia "with him" in any sense. Taking up an appointment as a governess, that's all. In any case, you make it sound as though he's, well — '

'For the past two years he's rented a house in St John Street,' said Charles, although probably she knew that already. 'He invites women there.'

He had gone too far. She was still pale, but her chin gave a jerk of determination as she stared into his eyes.

'That's none of my business, Mr Vereker, and I shouldn't have thought it was any of yours either. I need employment and Prince Alexis has offered me employment. That's all there is to it.'

Was he jealous of Alexis, Charles asked himself suddenly, already convinced in his own mind that there was a great deal more to it than that. What was it about his friend which enabled him to charm forgiveness from those who had the right to be angry and trust from those who would be wise to be cautious?

As he stared at the resolute young woman, admiring her courage even while he tried to undermine it, he felt strongly attracted to her. It was an emotion to be controlled, because he knew that he would do well to postpone marriage for eight or nine years, and anything other than marriage would be out of the question in her case. And even when the time came for him to set up his own establishment, common sense suggested that he should stay within his own class. Both those considerations were true of Alexis as well, of course: the difference was that the Russian didn't allow them to influence his present behaviour in any way, while Charles was constrained by his own good breeding.

He sighed, recognising that he had lost the argument, failing in his first attempt at diplomatic negotiation.

'I hope that at least I can ask one small promise of you, Miss Mainwaring. A cousin of mine is attached to the embassy in Russia.' He had written the name on the back of one of his own cards already, and proffered it now. 'Will you assure me that if you find yourself in any kind of difficulty you will apply to him for help?'

Laura smiled, dissolving the severity of her expression into sweetness.

'How very kind of you! Certainly I'll give you that assurance, and it will be a great relief to me to know that I can count on his support.' Her friendliness was as light-hearted as though they had not just been on the point of quarrelling.

Charles still had one card up his sleeve, and he kept it there as he made his farewell and wished her good fortune in her new life. Russia was one of the only two foreign countries for which a passport was needed. Almost certainly Laura would not know that – and it was unlikely that Alexis was sufficiently well-ordered to think of it. Whatever first plans he made for her journey might have to be postponed, and he was not the sort of man to start all over again with an arrangement. Better that she should be disappointed at once, in her own country, than find herself at risk in foreign parts.

Outside the house a motor car was drawing to a halt: a beautiful machine, with its brass gleaming and its engine purring with power.

'Good,' said Charles as the driver applied the brake and jumped down to the ground. But then he remembered. It could not have arrived to take him back to college, because it did not belong to him any longer.

Alexis had coveted the Hispano-Suiza from the moment he first set eyes on it, and the arrangement he proposed to his friend as the end of their Oxford life approached made a good deal of sense. Subject to a cash adjustment to cover differences in value, he suggested swapping his hunter for the vehicle. Charles, who knew the horse to be a superb jumper with first-class stamina, accepted the offer with pleasure for he could always buy another car. What he had not expected – and the discovery had annoyed him considerably – was that Alexis had enticed his chauffeur away with the promise of an outrageously inflated salary. It was difficult to blame Fred Richards, who depended on his wages and was probably as much attached to the car as to the family, but Charles's nod of recognition now was an off-hand one, and he passed on without speaking.

At the corner of the road he turned to look back. Richards was just being admitted to the Mainwaring house with a package in his hand. For once, perhaps, Alexis had not only made a plan but was preparing to carry it through.

6

Front door or back door? It didn't take Fred Richards more than a second to decide. At Knaresborough Hall, where one of the coach houses had been converted into a garage, the path from the stable yard led straight towards the servants' hall in which he took his meals. In the four years of his employment he had never stepped through the front entrance. Even when he carried luggage up the wide stone staircase it was always taken from him by a footman on the threshold.

This sort of house was different. The side door would be used only by the indoor servants and for tradesmen's deliveries. And although the message he carried was to someone who was going to be no more than a governess, she wasn't a governess yet. He rang the front door bell.

Waiting, he smoothed down the jacket of his new uniform, which was dark green and extremely smart. There would be a gold badge and a special braid to put on it when he got to Russia, His Nibs had promised. But even as it was, it turned his skinny body into a fine figure of a man. Only the peaked cap didn't suit him, for his springy thick hair was liable to push it too high off his face, giving him a cheeky look. For the moment, though, he had sleeked the hair down with water and was pleased with his appearance.

At the age of twenty-two, Fred was an ambitious young man. He hadn't had much schooling, because he was expected to bring home a wage at the earliest moment possible. But all the time he was doing his apprenticeship he had studied at night classes as well, learning to do book-keeping and to write a good letter. One of these days he intended to be his own boss and make his fortune.

A chauffeur's job in Russia might not seem the most obvious step in that direction, but he had been promised three times his previous wages. Since he would be getting full board and lodging and uniform as well, it should be possible to put most of the money aside for the future. One of the things he had learned from his classes was the importance of having a bit of capital saved, instead of needing to borrow it. The next three years of his life would be a kind of investment. At the end of them he hoped to find himself well set up and ready to go.

Although he was ambitious, that didn't mean that he had to be serious all the time. His eyes were bright as he stored every experience away for future use, and his attitude to life was light-hearted. He grinned cheerfully as the door was opened by a young maid in her afternoon uniform of black dress and white apron, with a frilly white headpiece like a tiara made of lace.

'Message for Miss Mainwaring. Personal.' If he were to produce the envelope he was carrying it would be taken inside and he wouldn't get a chance to look at her. It wasn't likely that he would be invited in but, as he had hoped, she came to the door herself. She was younger than he had expected and dressed unbecomingly in black.

'Miss Laura Mainwaring? Message from Prince Alexis Karlovich Kristov.' Taking off his cap politely, he held out the letter.

'Thank you. Are you to wait for an answer?'

'If you please. And the answer's to me, in a manner of speaking.'

She read the brief note without comment. 'You'd better come in,' she said.

An older woman, also in mourning, was knitting in the drawing room. Since no introductions were performed, he provided his own. 'Fred Richards at your service, ma'am.'

He was left to stand while Laura, returning to her seat, read the note for a second time.

'This doesn't do much more than introduce you,' she said.

'That's because His Nibs is leaving me to make all the arrangements.' As he had expected, she raised her eyebrows at this impertinent form of address, but did not interrupt. 'He's going off on the Channel ferry himself on Saturday. To visit people all over Europe before he gets back to Russia. But I'm to take the car direct from Tilbury to St Petersburg. And he reckons as how

37

the best thing'd be for you to travel on the same boat. So's I can give you a hand with your luggage, be around if you need me. But I have to ask you whether you have any objection to that.'

'No,' said Laura, but her voice was faint and she was unable to conceal disappointment. No doubt she had hoped for the company of the master, not the man, on the journey. He did his best to cheer her up.

'What an arrival we'll have, you and me, Miss Laura! Landing in St Petersburg, driving through the streets. Reckon the whole town'll be out to cheer us.'

It was one of the things which had persuaded him to accept the Russki's offer. The generous salary was certainly the main factor. But the expression almost of awe with which the prince had stroked his new acquisition, and his anxiety that the chauffeur should stay with his charge, had made it clear that such a vehicle was a rarity in Russia – and that a man who could not only drive but maintain it was worth his weight in gold. Fred's apprenticeship had been at the Morris Motor Works and he had worked for a year as a toolmaker before deciding that there were better things in life than production lines. He was confident of his ability to keep the Hispano-Suiza running, even if he had to make new parts for it himself.

It was this confidence and the sense of his own indispensability which made him reckon himself the superior of any mere governess. There was one at the Hall for Lord Knaresborough's granddaughter: a woman who seemed to have no proper place in the household at all. She ate neither with the family nor in the servants' hall. When she tried to give instructions to the servants they were obeyed only if it was thought likely that they represented her ladyship's wishes.

This governess, however, was presumably a young lady come down in the world and not yet settled in to her new position in life. She was staring at him doubtfully.

'Did Prince Alexis tell you to call me Miss Laura?'

'He said that's what your pupils would call you. And probably the rest of the family as well, because your surname isn't said the way it's spelt – and anyway, they don't know how to deal with people who don't have the proper kinds of name. He's been telling me, His Nibs has, how the Russkies do it, taking on their father's name all the time. But I'll use any name you like to give me. His Nibs calls me Richards, because that's what I'm used to, but you can call me Fred if you like.'

It was easy to tell that she disapproved of his cockiness. Since she had at least a maid, she would still think of herself as being on the employer's side of the social divide. And it was likely that she had never had any male servants. The fact that she didn't know how to deal with him ought to make it easy for him to get on top.

'I'm to book our passages,' Fred continued. 'So I've come to ask when you'll be ready to go. But I'm not sure how strong His Nibs is on practical arrangements. Do you have a passport?'

Laura shook her head.

'Me neither. So I thought, I could drive you to London and we could get them together. Unless you'd rather go by train and do it on your own.'

He knew what the answer would be. No one ever turned down the chance to ride in such a very special motor car. He paused only for a second before going on. 'I'll be needed all this week, finishing with the drive to Dover on Saturday. Any time next week that suits you. You'll need to get some photographs.'

They arranged a day, and when it came, he realised that she had never been driven in any car at all: her eyes shone like a child's with the excitement of the expedition. He was amused by her changes of mood. It seemed that the prospect of travel excited her, the uncertainties of her future employment alarmed her, and from time to time the memory of her recent bereavement overcame her again, wiping the smile from her face. But beneath it all he sensed a determination to be resolute: to do her best and to enjoy it. Even when, two weeks later, she stood on deck as the boat made its way slowly out of the Thames estuary and the coastline of England gradually receded from sight, she didn't cry.

It was Fred himself who was unhappy. Not about leaving England. His mother was dead and he had never got on well with his father: they were glad to see the back of each other. As for Florrie, she was a pretty little thing when she dressed herself up for her afternoon out, and they had had some good times together. But Fred had no intention of remaining at other people's beck and call for the whole of his life. He was going to make something of himself, and when he succeeded he didn't want to find himself tied to someone who would never be more than a kitchenmaid. It had been a mistake to go as far as he had with her; but since the damage had been done, he'd found it simplest to slip away without saying where he was going. She'd soon get over him.

So it wasn't the thought of Florrie which caused him to groan. The trouble was that he had never been to sea before and he didn't like it. He had expected it to be calm in July, but almost before they were out of the shelter of land he began to feel queasy. They had been travelling for less than eight hours when a storm blew up, whipping the North Sea into a grey landscape of mountains

39

and valleys through which the ship pitched and rolled. Miss Laura, grasping the rail with the foam flying against her face, stared expectantly towards the horizon; but Fred, sick and miserable, took to his berth.

7

The ship creaked and shuddered, sometimes heeling over so violently that Fred expected to be thrown to the floor, sometimes rising and rising and then hesitating, poised on one of the mountain peaks, before crashing down again. How could such an enormous hunk of heavy metal stay on the surface of the water? At any moment it must surely sink − but so great was his misery that he hardly cared.

There were supposed to be stewards, but they never came. Instead, it was Laura who knocked gently on the door and then, ignoring his lack of response, entered and stood beside him.

'I've brought some pills for you to take. Let me help you sit up.' She set down a glass of water which she was carrying and slid one arm under his back. Her fingers were cool on his skin and, as he struggled into a sitting position, he was conscious of the gentle curve of her breast touching his shoulder. To swallow − without immediately vomiting − was as great a struggle as to sit; but when he lay back again he did not at once close his eyes. Instead he stared up at the young governess's sympathetic face.

The wind had disarranged her hair and flushed her pale skin. She couldn't be called pretty in the sense that Florrie was pretty: there was too much of a clever look to her face for that. But she was young and attractive and she had character. 'Look for a girl with character,' his mother had always advised him, while she was still alive, but Fred had never known what she meant by that. Now he was looking at it: he still didn't know exactly what it was, but he could recognise what he saw.

'I'm supposed to be looking after you, not the other way round,' he croaked in a weak voice.

She gave a soft laugh. Smiling, her face was transformed. What could have possessed him to think that she wasn't pretty? It was because she had been putting on an act with him: that must be it. She was only nineteen or twenty and she had led a sheltered life. No doubt she felt the need to look prim and businesslike. It was a kind of defence − a defence against himself, amongst others. After all, he had set out to impress her with the fact that she was only a governess now, with nothing to be stuck up about. Why should he ever have thought that she would be stuck up? She was an angel. Whatever was in those pills she had given him, it was taking effect already.

'I'll go and get you a hot drink,' she said. 'After you've had that, the best thing will be to sleep.'

She came frequently again to bring him drinks and comfort, but perhaps it was time and geography as much as medicine which brought him relief, for as the ship approached the Kiel Canal the summer storm abated as suddenly as it had begun. Fred found that he could stand up without feeling his head swim or his legs stagger. He was hungry, and began to wonder when the next meal would be ready.

As soon as he was dressed he made his way on to the deck and searched for Laura. She was staring with interest at the banks of the canal.

'You're better!' she exclaimed, switching on that smile of hers.

'And very grateful to you. Thanks.' He hesitated, but there was no point in delaying his request. 'I shouldn't ask a second favour so soon, but ...'

'Yes?'

'I wondered,' he blurted out, 'I wondered whether you'd give me some lessons? In speaking French.'

She was surprised, and hesitated in turn. Before she had time to say no, he hurried to persuade her.

'You're going to be teaching, aren't you? You could get a bit of practice in on me. The thing is — ' He felt himself flushing. 'His Nibs said it would be easier for me if I could pick up a bit of French or Russian. Only the nobs speak English, he said. Well, I had a look at some Russian words and they don't even use civilised letters. But French ... I got myself a book. I can read it all right. But I don't know how the words are supposed to sound.'

Laura hesitated for a moment, but then nodded her head.

'It's difficult,' she agreed. 'All right, then. Where is the book?'

He had been holding it out of sight and now produced it. They went in together and sat down at a table in the saloon. When he recited the first words and phrases that he had memorised, she didn't laugh. He gave her full marks for that, because when she repeated the same words, they sounded completely different. A cat, for example, turned out not to be a chat, but a sha with a sort of grunt in front of it. She made him practise the new sounds over and over again, telling him whereabouts in his mouth or throat they should be made and demonstrating the shape that his lips should make.

'Not "wee"', she said patiently for the third time. 'Purse your

41

lips up as though you were going to whistle.' Her own lips, as she showed him, were small and rosy. Her expression was animated and friendly. 'Oui!' exclaimed Fred perfectly, and she clapped her hands in applause. Fred himself couldn't speak again for a moment. Nothing like this had ever happened to him before. Not the moment when Florrie had said, 'Well, just once, then': not even the moment when he first sat at the wheel of the Hispano-Suiza. Blimey! he thought. I've fallen head over heals in love with this Miss Laura.

So determined was he to spend every possible moment in her company that his pronunciation improved out of all recognition in the space of the all-too-short voyage. The thought of all the words which would have to be learned was daunting, but at least now he could hope not to be laughed at every time he opened his mouth. He was in a jaunty, confident mood as he awoke early on the last morning and packed his cabin bag before going on deck.

The ship was almost gliding up the Gulf of Finland and into the Neva towards St Petersburg. They were so far north that darkness fell for only an hour or two each night, so that in spite of the early hour it was already light. As he joined Laura on deck the sun was gleaming from the city's golden spires and warming the coloured façades of palaces and public buildings.

'It's beautiful!' exclaimed Laura. So incredulous was her voice that Fred couldn't help laughing.

'What were you expecting?'

'Oh, something rather chilly and grim, I suppose.' It was her turn to laugh at herself. 'It's ridiculous. I mean, I know it's summer, but my picture of Russia has always been of men with huge black beards, and snow, and wolves howling.'

'At least you were right about the beards.' They were slowing to a halt now and Fred's sharp eyes had already picked out a green livery similar to his own. A bearded coachman was holding the reins of a landau, and a luggage waggon was drawn up immediately behind. 'Listen, Miss Laura, there's something I want to say. Sounds a bit odd, perhaps, but, well, it's this. Wolves come in more than one skin. You're a long way from home. On your own. I don't know how much time His Nibs spends with his brother: how often I'll see you. But I just want you to know that any time you need help, anything I can do — well, I'll always be on your side. Remember that.'

'I'll remember. Thank you, Fred.' She held out her hand and he gripped it rather than shaking it. What he wanted to do was to take her in his arms and kiss her. But she was no longer the ministering angel, the helpful teacher, the carefree fellow-passenger. Neatly dressed, with her hair tidy again, she was disguising any nervousness she might be feeling under a cloak of straight-backed dignity.

He left her there while he went down to supervise the disembarkation of the motor car, but was forced to return and appeal for her services as interpreter. Although the coachman was accompanied by someone from the Kristov household who spoke French, Fred hadn't progressed far enough with his studies to understand.

'The children I shall be teaching are living in their summer palace at the moment,' Laura reported when the arrangements had been explained to her. 'But their parents are in St Petersburg this week for the celebration of the Romanov dynasty's tercentenary. There was an Imperial ball last night and they may not have returned home yet. I shall be travelling with them to the country tomorrow. Prince Kristov — that's Prince Alexis's brother — will speak to you about the car later in the day. It has to be cleared through customs, but one of his household will deal with that. Meanwhile, we are both to go to the Kristov palace in the trap, or whatever they call it.'

The journey was a short one and Fred was soon blinking at the width of the palace's frontage. As they approached a colonnaded portico the horse was jerked to a halt. Laura, assuming that they had arrived, began to move, but Fred put a hand on her arm to hold her back. There would be some less grand entrance for the likes of them. They had paused only because another, far more elaborate carriage was approaching from the opposite direction. Footmen came running to pull down the step and assist the two occupants to dismount.

The woman appeared first and Fred gasped at the sight of her. He was not someone who had ever been resentful of rank. He recognised that a man was born into a certain class of society and there was nothing that could be done about that. Some people were Fred's superiors and others were his inferiors. He liked to know exactly where he stood, but that was all. That didn't mean, though, that he intended to stand in the same place for ever. That was the reason why he was not envious of other people's wealth: one day he was going to be wealthy himself, although he hadn't yet worked out how to achieve it.

It seemed now, though, that he would have to revise his idea of wealth. He had once thought of Lord Knaresborough as being as rich as anyone could expect to be. Prince Alexis had changed that view for him within a few days of their first encounter, simply by showing that he placed no value at all on money: it was something to be scattered around as a child might scatter crumbs to birds, and there would always be more where it came from.

43

As he stared wide-eyed at the princess — for it could be no one else — returning from the ball, Fred was forced to revise his views once again. Even Prince Alexis had never vaunted his fortune in such a way.

Her long cloak hung open, revealing a cream satin dress panelled in patterns of tiny pearls. There must have been hundreds of them; even thousands. The décolleté neckline was so low as to be indecent in his opinion. But his eye was drawn from the swelling of her white breasts to the necklace of pearls and diamonds which encircled her neck. They descended in tier after tier until the largest pearl which he had ever seen fell as a pendant in the shape of a teardrop to rest just above the point of cleavage.

The necklace alone must represent a hundred times as much wealth as any ordinary person could earn in a working life — and that was not all. The princess's hair was swept up from her face to form a thick crown, and on this first crown was arranged a second. Mirroring the design of the necklace, it rose high on a silvery framework, sparkling with diamonds, softened by gently trembling pearls. From the highest point of the centre hung the twin of the pendant teardrop.

Like the fairy on the Christmas tree, thought Fred to himself in an attempt to belittle such ostentation; but despite himself he was overawed. Beside him, Laura too seemed frozen into silence. Together they had just been treated to their first glimpse of the Kristov kokoshnik.

Part Two

Laura in Russia
1913–1918

1

'It was kind of Alexis Karlovich to find me a new governess,' said Princess Kristova. 'Although it would have been kinder still if he had told me of his success. I received his message only when I returned from the country to Petersburg for the celebrations. My brother-in-law is a young man of generous impulses; but not always, shall we say, businesslike.'

'Do you mean that you don't want me, Your Highness?' Laura shivered with anxiety, in spite of the warmth of the day; but the princess's eyes were smiling as she raised a hand in reassurance.

'I am very happy to see you, Miss Laura. But before I take you to our summer residence, I must find another post for Miss Hetty. It would be unkind to turn her out of the door.'

'You have an English governess already?'

'Yes. But she may be better suited to a boy pupil. It is good to have discipline and order in the schoolroom, but not fear. Do you not agree, Miss Laura?'

'Certainly not fear. My belief is that most children are anxious to learn and that it is only necessary to present information to them in an interesting manner.' Alexis had made no attempt to interview her as a suitable teacher before offering her the post that was not in his gift, and now it seemed that his sister-in-law was about to accept her with an equal lack of investigation. Laura was left with the feeling that she ought to interview herself in order to inspire confidence in her employer.

'I will send some messages to my friends this evening and see what can be arranged before we travel tomorrow to Almyra, our house in the country. Tonight we shall dine early, *en famille*. We shall speak French, because my mother-in-law will be present.

You will join us, I hope, and give us all the news of Alexis Karlovich.'

'Thank you very much.' How many English aristocrats, Laura wondered, were in the habit of sharing their own dining table with their governesses? But this was just what Alexis had promised. He might be unbusinesslike, but he had not been deceitful.

The neglected interview took place over the meal. Prince Kristov's mother, severe in manner and stiff with arthritis, put the new governess through her paces during the first three courses. Laura's holidays in France now stood her in good stead, enabling her to converse fluently.

Throughout this part of the conversation Prince Kristov remained silent. He was considerably older than Alexis, unless it was merely his beard that aged him. His hair was as startlingly fair as his younger brother's, but more closely cut; and his eyes, instead of laughing with mischief, held a vague, uncertain expression. But perhaps that was because decisions about the schoolroom fell into the women's sphere and he was anxious not to intrude. Certainly his smile was pleasant and, as the meal progressed and the conversation became more general, he revealed himself as a cultured man who had read and travelled widely. If Laura found the evening a strain – and she did – it was only because everything was so strange and she was still worried lest something should go wrong. What if Miss Hetty caused trouble when asked to leave?

The Almyra estate, to which they travelled next morning, was fifty miles south of St Petersburg. Prince Kristov, after making it clear to Fred that Alexis's car was to be considered general family property until its owner returned to Russia, was a passenger in the Hispano-Suiza. Laura kept Princess Kristova company in a horse-drawn carriage.

She had gained the impression that the estate which enabled the family to escape from the swampy heat of the capital was an informal holiday home. So it came as a surprise to find herself arriving at what could only be described as another palace – modelled on a French chateau but situated in a park which was landscaped in the English style, so extensive that it took half an hour at trotting pace to reach the house after passing through the gates.

The two young princesses were having a lesson in the garden. Wearing white dresses and navy blue smocks tied at the waist they sat side by side at a table, their blonde heads bent over some task, while their teacher paced up and down behind them. The scene should have been idyllic: clear blue sky, warm bright sunshine, a background of graceful trees, and two pretty, privileged girls. Yet

46

even at a considerable distance Laura could sense that the atmosphere was not a happy one.

As though aware of her parents' return the younger girl looked up, gave a shout of happiness, slid down from the chair and began to run across the grass. A sharp command from the governess halted her and she turned slowly back to the table, gazing in silent appeal at her mother.

'Would you take a walk in the grounds for half an hour, Miss Laura?' said the princess. 'I must speak to Miss Hetty alone.'

Obediently Laura made herself scarce. Thirty minutes later she was summoned back to the house, where Princess Kristova awaited her in her boudoir.

'Miss Hetty will be leaving at once,' she said. 'Please supervise the rest of the lesson until it is time for luncheon, and then we will talk more about the timetable for the day. As I explained to you in the carriage, formal lessons are not necessary. I wish Sofiya and Tanya to speak English with you at all times. If you find subject lessons a useful way of improving their vocabulary, then good; but perhaps you will prefer a different approach. They are not clever, and they have no need to pass examinations. I wish them to be happy while they are children, and to become well-read and cultivated women.'

A nod of dismissal left Laura surprised by the casual nature of her instructions. She was startled still further by being ambushed — there was no other word for it — as she made her way down towards the garden.

'So! I suppose you're pleased with your success, Miss?' hissed her predecessor. 'Well, you may live to regret it. The girls are stupid and undisciplined, and if you try to establish order they'll be told by their parents that they need take no notice of you. Their father is a womaniser and their mother is vain and extravagant and idle. This is no place for a respectable woman and I'm glad to be out of it!'

She stomped away and Laura paused, giving her a start so that they need not descend the staircase together. From where she stood she could look down into the garden. The girls were happy again as they played a hiding and chasing game. They were both in hiding when Miss Hetty returned, striding furiously from the house to collect her handbag. It took her only a moment to catch sight of them and pull them towards the table.

'Mama!' called the little girl, Tanya, struggling to free herself. 'Mama!' She broke away, but was immediately caught. In a single spiteful movement Miss Hetty lifted her back on to her seat and slapped her fingers hard with a ruler. Tanya began to wail.

By the time Laura had run downstairs and found her way out into

47

the grounds, there was no sign of the dismissed governess. Tanya was still howling, while her sister tried to comfort her.

'Hush, hush!' said Laura. 'Let me see.' She took hold of the chubby fingers and frowned at the dark red line across them. 'Shall I kiss it better?' She touched her lips lightly along the line. 'All better now?' she asked, while Tanya stared at her wide-eyed. It was a moment which was to prove important later; and even at the time both child and woman recognised its significance in the beginning of a new relationship.

'I'm your new governess,' Laura told them. 'Miss Laura. Do you understand what I'm saying?'

It was Sofiya, the ten year old, who answered – in English.

'Oh, yes. But not "kiss it better".'

'Well, it seems to have worked.' The howls had stopped. 'Now then.' Laura had always been good at casting herself in a new role and playing it well. This was no time to reveal doubts about her capabilities. Her voice must be kind but businesslike. 'Miss Hetty is leaving. And in future this ruler will be used only for measuring, or for drawing straight lines. Nothing else. What lesson were you doing?'

'Geography.'

'And what had Miss Hetty asked you to learn?'

'The rivers and prin-ci-pal towns of England. But Tanya is too young. She has only just left the nursery. She can't read. And she doesn't understand maps.'

'Of course not. Let's forget about England for today.' Laura was not at all sure that she could remember all the rivers herself. 'We'll talk about maps. In fact, why don't we draw a map ourselves? Of your grounds here. There seems to be a lot of land, and if I go for walks I might get lost. That's what maps are for, to stop people getting lost.'

Tanya removed her fingers from her mouth. 'I like draw,' she said.

'Good. First of all, we'll put the house in the middle.' But as she drew a square in the centre of a piece of paper, Tanya shook her head vigorously.

'I draw house.'

She pulled the paper towards her and reached for a pencil. Laura left her to it and, under Sofiya's instructions, began to arrange various articles on the ground to illustrate the making of a plan as seen from above. Books represented the main house and the private theatre and porcelain gallery which flanked it. A handkerchief served as the lake, handfuls of leaves as woods, and pencils

48

and the dreaded ruler as avenues. When they were ready they called Tanya to join them. She brought her drawing with her.

'My house!'

Laura stared at it, impressed. How old was she? Not yet five, her mother had said. Like any small child she had drawn the house as a two-dimensional façade; but not many children of her age would have made as good an attempt at the double stone staircase which led to the entrance on the first floor, or the towers at each corner, with their pointed roofs. Whether from memory or by instinct she had got the proportions right and fitted the windows neatly into the right places. Most impressive of all, she had sketched in some of the trees at the side of the house. Although they were only scribbles, the fir tree scribble was recognisably different from those which represented aspens or birches, and the poplar scribble was different again.

'That's very good, Tanya,' said Laura sincerely.

Tanya beamed with pride, and at the sight of the little girl's smile Laura's heart gave a lurch. She was overcome by the weight of her new duties. How selfish she had been until now, thinking only of herself, seeing this post merely as an arrangement to solve the problem of her immediate future! How frivolous it had been to accept with so little thought the offer which Alexis had made with even less – and how shameful that part of her reason for accepting was the hope of seeing him again!

This was the first moment at which she realised what power she had been given over two young minds. Did she possess the skills needed to exercise it wisely? It was her responsibility now to discover what talents the two little princesses might have, and to develop them. She must teach Tanya to read, and later she must introduce her to books which were worth reading. They must both be helped not simply to converse fluently in English, but also to have opinions worth expressing. It was a task to which she would need to devote years, not months.

As a maid approached over the grass to tell them that luncheon was ready, Laura made a promise to herself that she would do her duty by her charges. Whatever part of her life ought to be devoted to them, they should have.

2

Roses. Roses everywhere. Their fragrance filled the air, reminding Laura of her last summer in England eighteen months earlier: on the day of her father's death the roses of North Oxford had been at their

49

best. But that was in June. Here, in the Crimea, the flowers were still in full bloom in November. Winter would already be tightening its grip on other parts of Russia, but a wall of mountains protected the Crimean peninsula from the north winds, lengthening the season of grapes and melons and allowing the governess and her two charges to spend much of the day out of doors.

The mild climate offered many pleasures. They could walk down through the pine forests to the sea, and there bathe or sail or picnic. Or they could ride. Although Laura's schoolgirl daydreams of galloping over the steppes with Alexis by her side had not come true, she had learned to ride well enough on the quiet horses which were chosen for the girls and their governess.

These, though, were afternoon activities. Mornings were reserved for lessons. At this moment they were sitting in an open-sided gazebo of Chinese design, whose elegant roof was supported by five narrow pillars. It was still warm enough for summer clothes: Laura was wearing a wide-brimmed straw hat and a neat blue cotton dress with a low square neck, while her pupils each sported a white and navy blue sailor top above a white skirt.

It was hard, in such peaceful surroundings, to remember that much of Europe had been at war for more than three months. Although the Russian army had suffered a serious defeat at Tannenberg almost as soon as hostilities began, none of the aristocratic families who owned villas on the Crimean coastline had made any change in the pattern of its days: picnics and parties continued without interruption.

Prince Kristov was an officer of the Imperial army, but there seemed to be no suggestion that he should actually fight. When Laura first joined the household, his duties had appeared to be mainly ceremonial, attending on the Tsar. Now he was spending more of the year than usual in the capital, acting as an aide-de-camp to the grand duke on the General Staff who was in charge of military supplies. To someone like Laura, who had seen at first hand the prince's inability to manage the Kristov estates properly, it was appalling to think that he should be one of the men responsible for equipping an army.

His occasional absence was the only change in the household routine. Certainly Laura's life with Sofiya and Tanya continued as though the war did not exist. They were at work this morning, having a nature study lesson. The table between them was covered with petals and leaves and flowers. Each of the girls had earlier pulled a rose to pieces, petal by petal, in order to study its structure. Now they were drawing a complete flower. When they were ready, Sofiya would be helped to label its parts — in English, of course — whilst little Tanya practised writing some appropriate descriptive words. By now Laura had taught her to read, but spelling was proving more of a struggle.

Sofiya hummed to herself quietly as she worked. Her drawing was slapdash, and two or three times she scribbled impatiently through what she had done and pulled a different flower towards her to act as a model. Tanya, although younger than her sister, was making a better attempt, continually looking from the rose to the drawing and biting her lower lip with concentration as she pressed her pencil down.

Laura herself, whilst keeping an eye on their work, studied the book which enabled her to keep one lesson ahead of Sofiya. She had realised soon after her arrival how many subjects she was not competent to teach. Alexis, who still kept an account at Blackwell's in Oxford, had authorised her to order anything she needed for his nieces, and an unknown but helpful assistant in the bookshop had chosen and despatched a set of textbooks for her use.

Neither of the girls was bookish. Had they been allowed to choose, Sofiya would have spent her whole day dancing and Tanya drawing and painting. But they were both affectionate and anxious to please. As Miss Hetty had warned, they were not accustomed to discipline and routine: but once Laura had succeeded in enlisting the support of the princess, her daughters were quick to learn that an appeal to their mother would be answered by: 'You must do as Miss Laura tells you.'

They had come to regard their governess as a companion — almost an elder sister; just as she was treated almost as a younger sister by their mother. She had become a member of the family — and the timetable which she imposed, wherever they might find themselves, gave the girls a sense of security in a life which was so often on the move.

By now Laura was familiar with the annual pattern of her employers' movements. The mines and agricultural land on which the family's fortune was based were never visited: nor did the children go to any of the country estates whose purpose was to provide good shooting in the autumn for Prince Kristov and his guests. The summer palace to which she had been taken on her first arrival in the country was reserved for the hottest months. The villa in the Crimea was visited twice in each year — once in the spring, when the blossom of cherry and lilac trees proved a greater attraction than the puddled chill of St Petersburg as the snow began to melt: and again, as now, in late autumn, when the cold was establishing its grip on the north. The family would return to the capital just before Christmas.

Winter was the season of balls and banquets, and was spent in one of the two winter palaces. The grand Kristov palace in the capital was the favourite, and so Laura had visited Moscow only briefly. She found the building there gloomy — more a fortress than a palace — and formed the impression that the family's short stay was mainly in order that the Moscow servants should have something to do.

It surprised the young governess that so many servants should be maintained in idleness in the various Kristov properties. Naturally there had to be a steward in control of each farm or forest, and managers to run the mines; but most of the domestic staff seemed to be employed merely to look after each other, called upon to clean the house and serve their employers for only a few weeks of each year. Prince Kristov grumbled about the costs of their wages — and often also about the shortfalls in the revenues he had expected. But he took no steps to control them.

Even as a schoolgirl Laura had been accustomed to keep an account of all the expenses of the household and to check the books submitted by every tradesman. She could hardly bear it when she saw her employer blatantly cheated. On one occasion, because it fell into her own sphere, she pointed out that the girls' dancing master had submitted an account for twice the number of lessons which they had actually attended. The information was greeted with a shrug of the shoulders. Clearly the nobility regarded it as an inevitable consequence of their position in society that they should be overcharged. It would be undignified to check a bill before paying it — just as it would be unheard of to pay it too quickly.

The drawings were finished. Laura gave each in turn the expected praise. But before she had time to test the young princesses on the new words they had learned, the lesson was interrupted. 'Uncle Alexis!' shouted Sofiya; and Tanya too abandoned her drawing and ran to greet him. 'Uncle Alexis! Uncle Alexis!'

How long had he been standing there, watching them? Laura felt the blood rising to flush her face, and turned away to tidy the table in order that he should not see. But within a few minutes he had crossed the lawn to join her, with his two nieces jumping up and down in excitement beside him.

'Sofiya, Tanya, go and tell your mother that I am here,' he ordered them. 'Otherwise there will be nothing for me to eat.'

There could hardly have been a less likely excuse. At every meal the chef prepared food for a dozen visitors — because often enough a dozen unexpected guests did indeed arrive.

'Well, Miss Laura,' he said when they had gone. 'How is it with you?' He lifted her hand to his lips. His eyes were laughing, as though he knew that the gesture which came so naturally to him was to her an exotic one.

For a moment Laura still could not speak. She had seen Alexis on several occasions since leaving England, for there were rooms specially kept for him in all the Kristov houses. He had made a point of looking her up at the end of his travels in Europe the previous year, to satisfy himself that she was happy. Later he had spent six weeks in St Petersburg, enjoying the winter season − a bitter-sweet time for Laura, because there had been much teasing about his doomed love for some married woman.

Very often during that period she had seen him wearing the uniform of the nobility − a black frock coat trimmed with gold braid, worn above tight white broadcloth trousers. Today, though, he was in a different uniform: that of an officer in the Horse Guards. She caught her breath as she realised its significance.

'Oh, Alexis Karlovich! So soon?' Most of the nobility were commissioned into the Imperial army as a matter of course but, in choosing to go to Oxford, Alexis had taken a different path. For the past three months he had been undergoing military training: but three months were surely not long enough.

'The need is urgent, and others will be in command. All that the Guards require is that I should be able to charge at full gallop, waving my sword above my head, and what better preparation is there for that than the polo field? All that His Imperial Majesty asks is that I should imbue my men with love of their homeland and be the first to lead them into the cannon's mouth; and for that I'm qualified by birth. Don't look so pale, Miss Laura. A little sea air; that will bring the roses back to your cheeks. Come: a walk.'

'I have to look after Sofiya and Tanya.'

'I saw Mademoiselle on my way out and asked her to take charge of them for an hour.' Although Laura was in charge of the girls' education, Mademoiselle Lamaire was also a member of the household, to teach them French and fine sewing. 'So come.' He offered his arm and Laura allowed her fingers to rest lightly upon it.

They strolled beneath a pergola entwined with climbing roses as far as the cypress grove which marked the end of the villa's cultivated grounds; and then, still without speaking, walked on through the pine forests which sloped down towards the sea. Was it the rich scent of the pines or the closeness of Alexis which made Laura's senses swim? Near the end of the headland, at the very edge of the forest, they came to a halt.

'How long − ?' asked Laura.

'I have three days' leave before I go to the front.' He turned her to face him and kissed her on the lips: the first time he had ever done this. 'Three days and three nights.'

There could be no possible doubt about what he meant. For a few seconds he paused, as though allowing her time to react. But although the sun was shining brightly and the breeze which stroked her bare arms was warm, Laura felt as though she had frozen where she stood. She ought to move away, but could not. Too often in the past four years she had embroidered a day-dream in which Alexis took her into his arms, kissing her passionately, murmuring words of love. And now it was happening. His lips pressed on her mouth, her cheeks, her neck; his arms pressed her closer and closer to his body. She felt dizzy, as though she were about to faint. Had he not held her so tightly, she would have fallen to the ground.

There had never been any ending to the day-dream. Whenever she ran through it in her mind it had faded in a hazy mist, ready to be replayed from the beginning. The novels she read ended with kisses and promises, and her imagination had never been able to take her any further. But now Alexis was moving beyond the dream. His hand was unbuttoning her dress, sliding over her skin. 'No!' she exclaimed. 'You mustn't − '

He sealed her lips with another kiss and she had to struggle to free herself. 'I can't − We ought not − ' Her incoherence brought her near to tears.

'You're a beautiful woman, my little Larisha. Do you know how beautiful you are? Well, I can show you. And you can give me a happy memory to take to war with me.'

Trembling, she shook her head, stepping backwards away from him and fumbling with the buttons of her dress. 'I'm sorry. But − '

A moment or two passed before he was ready to believe her. 'There's an English word I learned for girls who let themselves be kissed but will give no love in return.'

'I do love you. You know that. You've known that all the time.'

'What sort of love is it that says no? An English love, I suppose, that spells itself out with wedding rings. But you're in Russia now, where love is the breaking of a wave, the rushing of the wind through a forest, the meeting of two bodies in one moment of ecstasy.'

'I can't escape so easily from my upbringing.'

'You mean that while Dr Mainwaring was teaching me to understand history, he was teaching you how to become − ' For once

Alexis had to hesitate before hitting on the right words: 'how to become an old maid.'

It was not her father who had taught her anything about life at all. She had learned from books – and from the real-life example of what happened to girls who gave way to passion and found themselves within a year alone with a baby. Love, true love, ought to last a lifetime. Alexis was not offering her that, and she could never expect him to. Beneath the rosy dreams of a romantic lived the good sense of a realist. Laura needed to dig deep before she could draw on that good sense, but little by little her breathing steadied and her eyes made it clear that she meant what she said.

'So.' Alexis sighed. 'You are frightened of love. I am expected to be a hero, but I am not allowed to carry your favour into battle with me. When they tell you that I have died for my country, you won't weep.'

'Alexis!'

'In a moment you will tell me that we may be friends, yes?'

Unable to speak, she shook her head helplessly. She knew that what he wanted was wrong, but had never imagined that it would be so difficult to do what was right. No one had ever kissed her like that before; and Alexis might be correct in warning her that no one ever would again.

Waiting for his anger to break, she was surprised when he merely gave a rueful shrug and turned away as though he had never been interested in her as a person, but only as a female who was young, unattached and conveniently to hand in the short period before he left for the war. Could that be true? The pain of the thought increased her unhappiness. She watched as he disappeared into the forest, his footsteps silenced by the cushion of fallen pine needles, and then flung herself to the ground, weeping.

She wept not so much for the loss of Alexis as for the ending of her fantasies. No longer could she allow herself to imagine a situation in which she and Alexis expressed their love for each other: because that moment had come and passed, teaching her only that neither of them loved the other enough. And yet at this moment she felt that no passion could be deeper. Now, when it was too late, she was prepared to sacrifice anything, everything – but that was an impulse which did not last. Once again the realist in her beat back the yearnings of the romantic. She had made one sacrifice that day, and it must be a final one. It was her dream which had died.

3

Arrival in Petrograd was always an excitement to Laura. The city's name, St Petersburg, had been changed after the outbreak of war because it was too German-sounding, but it was still a European city rather than a Russian one. There was, as a rule, a lightness about the atmosphere which lifted her spirits, just as its colour delighted her eyes — the painted walls of imperial and noble palaces, the deep purple of the clouds which patterned the winter sky, the subtle shades of the frozen Neva throughout the winter season, or, in summer, the golden reflection of globe-shaped lamps in canals and rivers.

Most of the largest buildings were sited so that they could be seen across an open space, whether it was a paved square or crescent or an expanse of water. The Kristov palace looked out across a public square towards the Neva and backed on to a smaller watercourse, the Moyka. Its walls were painted in a pale pinkish-red, the wide expanse of the façade broken by white pillars and friezes.

The interior of the palace was ostentatiously opulent and vast. Along the whole of the front ran a suite of first-floor entertaining rooms — ballroom, music room, salon, the grandest of the three dining rooms and a variety of ante-rooms, all having their high and elaborately plastered ceilings and cornices decorated with gold leaf; their walls were panelled in pale pink and green marble slabs or hung with rich red silk. Venetian chandeliers illuminated the oil paintings on the walls and were reflected in full-length mirrors in intricately carved and gilded frames. Antique French furniture stood on parquet or marquetry floors patterned in three colours of highly polished wood, and were themselves scattered with *objets d'art*.

Each of the two side wings contained suites of reception rooms on a scale only slightly more modest. Prince Kristov's mother used one of these, and it was in her wing that Alexis lived when he was in the capital. On Prince Kristov's side there was another salon, another dining room, a large library and a room of more intimate size in which close friends could be received.

Although there were so few family members to fill the space, the number of servants meant that the Kristovs were normally greeted back in Petrograd with a cheerful, noisy bustle. In the February of 1917, however, everything was different. Sofiya and Tanya and their mother and household had stayed in the Crimea longer than was customary, because the prince had written to warn them of food and fuel shortages in the capital: no amount of money could buy goods which had been stranded hundreds of miles away by the collapse of the railway service.

They were returning now only because the prince's mother had had another fall, and it was thought that she would not live long. The coachmen who sat stolidly waiting at the station in their padded coats wore gloomy faces, recognising that this was no time for smiles. The people in the streets were sombre as well − but for different reasons. They were shabby and hungry, and amongst them were many soldiers with amputated legs or bandaged heads or arms in slings.

Like its citizens, the city itself displayed the wounds of war. The yellow trams which rattled along the streets were dirty and battered, and the wide, dignified avenues had become filthy with litter. Even the cold seemed somehow to be worse than usual. Laura turned up the sealskin collar of her shuba, the extra-heavy winter coat which had been a gift from the princess at the onset of her first winter. She was glad of the bearskin rugs which the footmen hurried to pull over her legs before the sleigh began to move over the frozen snow.

The two children, together with Laura and Mademoiselle, had a suite of rooms which occupied the whole second floor of one of the palace's side wings. Laura paused only to see that the luggage had been brought up before sending a maid to collect any letters which had arrived during her absence.

Reading letters from home was one of her chief pleasures − although all too often in the past two years they had brought sad news of deaths and woundings on the western front. Aunt Barbara wrote once a month, detailing the activities of her growing family. Two of her schoolfriends, and another friend who had been a Home Student with her, sent less regular news, mostly of engagements and marriages within their circle − and even, in one sad case, of widowhood.

These were events which gave Laura pause for thought. She was twenty-four years old now: almost on the shelf already. As a schoolgirl she had felt stifled by the prospect of moving from the household of her father straight to that of a husband, with no likelihood of any further milestones in her life except the birth and bringing up of children. But since leaving Oxford her life had been anything but dull: she had enjoyed more experience of travel than most young women of her age.

Besides, her definition of a dull future had changed: there was a warning close at hand. Attached to the English church in Petrograd was a club attended by most of the British governesses working in the city. When she looked at those of them who were no longer young and who seemed doomed to spend the rest of their lives as dependants in a foreign country, the thought of marriage became attractive − even essential − after all.

57

But where should she look for a husband? Or rather — for Laura had been brought up to believe that a woman must expect to be chosen rather than presume to choose — where should she place herself in order that a possible husband might find her?

She had not been altogether without suitors during the past three years. Although members of the Russian nobility scrutinised the pedigree and fortune of any possible bride in their own society with meticulous attention, a few of them seemed to regard a foreigner as being outside these conventions. There had been several flirtations — and one of these had shown signs of becoming serious.

The princess, watching Count Beretsky's courtship with amusement, had given a friendly caution, but it was not necessary. Educated Russian men, when they were sober, could be charming, almost irresistible. But they were also subject to great swings of mood; too often careless and lazy and untidy and unpunctual and, in a word, unreliable. If there was one thing which Laura would demand of a husband it was reliability. She didn't intend to spend her life wondering whether someone who had made an arrangement was merely going to be a few hours late or had forgotten it altogether. She might have been able to forgive all this in Alexis, because she loved him; but Alexis had shown no inclination towards marriage. As for the count, she had tactfully persuaded him that she was not good enough for him and that he should look for a wife in his own social circle — which by now he had done. She no longer had a Russian suitor.

For this reason there were some letters to which she particularly looked forward. The son of her Parisian hostess wrote from time to time, his guilt at causing her father's death replaced by a sense of responsibility for her well-being; and David Hughes was a regular correspondent. David's contemporary at Oxford, Charles Vereker — who to the last moment had tried to dissuade her from travelling to Russia — had been in touch only once in her first year there, asking to be reassured that she was happy in her situation and that she had remembered the name of his cousin in the embassy. But he was one of the first to volunteer when the war began and had suffered lung damage in a German gas attack at Ypres.

She had heard about his injury indirectly, through Fred, and had sent a note of sympathy to which he replied from hospital. By now he had been invalided out of the army and had resumed his career in the Foreign Service. Since his discharge he too wrote several times a year, each time hoping to persuade her that she ought to return to England as soon as possible. There were letters from all three men waiting today.

When she had read her correspondence for a first time, Laura put it away and made her way down towards the great hall. Before reaching it, however, she encountered Prince Kristov and asked politely what the news was of his mother.

'Bad, Miss Laura. Very bad. Not more than two days, the doctors think.'

'I'm so sorry.' She was about to pass on when the prince called her back.

'Miss Laura. I wonder if I could ask you . . . A message.'

'But of course, Pavel Karlovich.'

'To Barisinova. To tell her only that I shan't be able to visit her while my mother . . .'

'Yes, certainly. I'll explain.'

The girls were happy having tea with their old Russian nurse. Laura dressed for the cold weather again in her shuba, fur turban and knee-high felt boots. She found it difficult not to smile as she set out on her errand. She knew − probably everyone in the household knew − that Barisinova was Prince Kristov's mistress, but the prince himself appeared to think that to send one of the footmen on such an errand would be to reveal a secret which no one had guessed. Or perhaps such an open acknowledgement of the affair would not be thought proper.

By now, of course, the centre of Petrograd was as familiar to Laura as the streets of Oxford. During her first year she had used free afternoons, or the hours when her pupils were having their music or dancing lessons, to explore widely. But the contrasts within the city had shocked and even alarmed her.

There was a central district which included the proud array of palaces along the bank of the Neva, the fashionable shopping streets of Nevski and Morskaya, and the two great squares with their hotels, theatres and restaurants. But only a short distance behind all this splendour were decrepit blocks of overcrowded apartments rising from dirty streets, and wooden shacks hugging the sides of canals which here seemed foul and sinister rather than picturesque. In winter the snow was piled in high banks over which a walker must climb to cross the streets, and in summer an unhealthy miasma hung above the water. At any time of the year there were human shadows which seemed to melt away as she disappeared, leaving her uncertain whether she had seen or only imagined them. Laura was not a timid woman, but there was no pleasure to be found in such explorations, and by now she had abandoned them.

Barisinova, naturally, lived at a fashionable address not far from the theatre. Laura found the famous dancer in a domestic mood, playing cards with her seven-year-old son. Leon, who had inherited his father's blond hair — in his case, so pale as to be almost white — had the face of an angel: but he was used to having his own way. His governess had to be summoned to deal with the tantrum he threw when asked to leave the room so that his mother could receive a message from her lover in private.

To Laura's dismay, this governess proved to be Miss Hetty, whom she herself had so abruptly displaced in the Kristov household. The ballerina misinterpreted her expression and sighed.

'Yes, she doesn't like me and I don't like her,' she said, speaking in French after the door had closed on the struggling boy. 'But what can I do? It's so difficult.'

It was easy to guess what she meant. Many of the English community in Russia had returned home when the war began, and there were few replacements prepared to risk a voyage past U-boats. Those who had remained were for the most part churchgoers with strict moral standards, unwilling to care for an illegitimate child in an irregular household.

Out of politeness Laura accepted a cup of tea, but once she had delivered her message she was anxious to return to the palace before darkness fell. At this time of year, in February, the hours of daylight were few.

'Did you come with a footman?' asked Barisnova. 'No? Then one of mine will escort you home. If you've only just returned to Petrograd you may not have heard. There were riots yesterday, because of the bread shortage. People broke into the bakeries and looted them. There are rumours of more demonstrations to come, so you should hurry back.'

It was only polite to accept the offer of an escort since — feeling the need of exercise after the days and nights on the train — she had come on foot. She did not, however, take the shortest route back. Instead she called at the English shop on the corner of the Morskaya and the Nevski Prospekt, because from time to time a pang of homesickness made her long for a taste of Golden Syrup or a slice of rich Dundee cake.

She was out of luck. The shop was almost empty of supplies. Emerging on to the Nevski Prospekt, she frowned slightly at something unfamiliar in the scene. Then she realised what it was. The trams had stopped running. In fact the wide avenue — usually busy with every kind of vehicle and crowds of pedestrians — was almost deserted. But even as she watched, a squadron of Cossacks appeared on horseback, taking up positions along the road. Laura felt a moment's alarm, knowing their reputation for charging into a crowd without pausing to distinguish between demonstrators and innocent passers-by; but Stefan, the footman, gave a reassuring murmur.

'No whips.'

He was right. None of the horsemen carried the lethal metal-tipped whips which they used to break up trouble. They were young recruits, because all the trained men were fighting on the Galician front, and their faces expressed uncertainty about what they were supposed to be doing. Keeping well out of the way of the horses, she was about to turn along the Morskaya when a second unusual sight stopped her in her tracks. The bridge across the river from the industrial Vyborg section of the city was black with marching men: and, as they reached the Nevski Prospekt, women appeared from every side street to join the procession with shouts of 'Give us bread!'

What was happening?

4

The young Cossacks made no move to disperse the procession of demonstrators, but the atmosphere was an uneasy one. Behaving sensibly at last, Laura scurried back to the palace. As she approached the entrance, she heard behind her a familiar sound. It was that of the Hispano-Suiza, being driven cautiously over the icy surface before coming to a halt in front of her. Fred jumped out of the driver's seat and hurried to open the door for his passenger. Catching sight of her, he gave a cheerful wink before standing correctly to attention.

It was Alexis who dismounted: but an unfamiliar Alexis — not the dashing young cavalry officer concerned chiefly that his boots should be well polished. This was a tired and worried man, dressed in the khaki of the battlefront and no doubt upset by the news of his mother's illness. He had not noticed Laura as the motor car passed her, and now hastened inside, taking the stone steps two at a time.

It was natural that, after visiting his mother, he should join his brother's family for dinner that night; but when Laura came down, dressed for the meal, she could hear long before she saw them that the two brothers were having an argument. It was part of Alexis's charm that as a rule he seemed to take nothing seriously, but there was no laughter in his eyes now.

'Pitchforks!' he exclaimed. 'Clubs and axes! As though we were a medieval rabble. Against machine guns and cannon. Can you wonder that more men are deserting every day? Is it surprising that a soldier who does get hold of a rifle will probably use it to shoot off his toe

61

in the hope of getting a discharge − without realising, of course, that when he gets to hospital there will be no bandages, no disinfectant, and he may lose his whole leg. For God's sake, Pavel Karlovich, what is happening to all the supplies?'

'How should I know?'

'It's your job to know. It's your responsibility to get them to the front. Are they sitting in warehouses, in trains? Someone must know. Is it nobody's business to read the indents we send and find out what has happened to supplies which should have been despatched. I tell you, Pavel Karlovich, if my men decide that they'd rather shoot me and go home instead of waiting to be shot by Germans, I'd have no right to complain. I'm supposed to care for them, but I've nothing to offer. And it's all your fault − you and the rest of the General Staff. Ah, Miss Laura.' He had noticed her quiet arrival at last. 'How charming you look!'

He raised her hand to his lips in the gesture which had so much delighted her at their first meeting in Oxford. But his expression remained grim. Laura had long ceased to be a schoolgirl. Now Alexis had ceased to be a carefree dilettante. It was the war which had changed him, but no doubt the mere politeness of his attitude towards herself reflected his memory that nothing was to be gained by flirting. She was Miss Laura again, no longer Larisha; and the evening was painful.

For the next twenty-four hours she had little to do. As though straw had been laid on all the floors to silence their footsteps, the servants − usually so noisy − crept about the palace. The two young princesses were taken by their parents to join the vigil at their grandmother's bedside. Laura had letters to write, but found herself restlessly wandering towards the window of her sitting room.

From here she could see the frozen river as it curved towards the gulf and it was one of her winter pleasures to watch the changing colours of the ice: sometimes a ghostly blue or green, sometimes a sunset pink, often a shadowy purple. Today − in spite of the clear blue of the sky − the ice was grey: a cold, heavy colour. But what was most curious was its emptiness. As a rule the whole area was criss-crossed with sleighs doing business between one side of the city and the other, but now nothing moved. The streets, too, were empty, and late in the afternoon she thought she heard the sound of rifle fire.

Prince Kristov's mother died that night and during the elaborate routines of mourning which followed none of the family left the palace. The servants began to whisper together in corners, passing on rumours to each other − but not to the foreign governess. Only when Alexis sought her out to say goodbye, did she learn a little of what was happening.

'I have to return to my regiment,' he told her. 'Although there's nothing I can do there. Except hope that the Germans never realise that they only have to push and we shall all fall down. But for an officer the streets of Petrograd are as dangerous as a trench in the front line.'

'What do you mean, Alexis Karlovich?'

'I mean that there is widespread mutiny here. The Volinsky regiment, the Semonovsky – even the Preobrajensky Guard. The soldiers are refusing to fire on the workers and are killing any officer who tries to make them obey their commands. I believe that they would even kill the Tsar, the Father of the People, if he were to show himself now. My brother, like all the General Staff, is greatly at risk. I've tried to persuade him that he ought to leave Petrograd at once. And although he won't thank me for saying this, Miss Laura, when my nieces love you so much, I think you ought to consider whether it's wise for you to remain in Russia.'

'Alexis!' Laura was hardly able to listen to what he was suggesting for herself, so upset was she by the danger of his own situation. He was saying goodbye now with a solemnity which suggested that he never expected to see her again, holding her hand longer and more firmly than usual.

'Goodbye, dear Miss Laura. Go back to safe, sleepy Oxford. And when the good times come again, I will walk beside the Cherwell, beneath the willows, and look for you there.'

She would have kissed him then and thrown conscience or prudishness, whichever it was, to the winds. But already he was gone, leaving her trembling to face a situation which she still could not comprehend.

Prince Kristov would explain. But before she had an opportunity to speak with him, a message was brought from Fred Richards, asking if she could spare a moment to come to the wing in which the old princess had lived and died.

What was a chauffeur doing outside the servants' quarters, Laura wondered as she was shown to what was clearly his own suite of rooms.

'When His Nibs first went off to the war, he told me to look after Mum while he was away,' Fred explained. 'These last few months she started using me as a walking stick whenever she got dizzy. And after her fall, I was the one she wanted to carry her around. Seemed to trust me more than any of her Russki servants. So I had to be handy, like, to get up in the middle of the night. Well, that's all over now.'

'Yes.' Laura was still feeling subdued after parting from Alexis. Fred had become almost a stranger, for their meetings during the four years since their ship had docked had been infrequent. They had both changed. Laura's responsibilities had made her serious; Fred's had increased his confidence. There was a hint of authority in his voice.

'I'll be laying up the car today,' he told her. 'His Highness — ' this was Fred's way of differentiating between Alexis and his elder brother — 'thinks he's going to take it over as usual while His Nibs is away, but he doesn't realise what's going on. Much as his life is worth to be seen on the streets in that at the moment. So I'm finished here. Back to the old country with two nice little parting presents in my pockets — even though I suppose it means that the army will get its hands on me at last. Question is, hadn't you better consider going as well?'

'Prince Alexis has just made the same suggestion.'

'Well, we've got a couple of months' thinking time. No way we can get out of here by train across Europe in wartime. And no ships leaving this place till the ice melts. But I thought I'd just put it in your mind. Out of here together on the first ship in April.'

'I expect you're right, yes. What will you do till then?'

'Depends on His Highness. I've been a bit more than just a walking stick here. More like a kind of house steward. Keeping an eye on what goes missing and getting some of it back again. Hasn't made me the most popular chap around. But when His Highness disappears — and to my way of thinking that's what he'll have to do for a bit — he might be glad to know that I'm around. Up to him. Anyway, you be thinking about that ship, Miss Laura.'

'Yes, I will. Thank you, Fred.'

The anxiety which Alexis had fuelled and Fred had fanned to a blaze was hardly quenched by the appearance of Prince Kristov in the schoolroom an hour later.

'You must leave Petrograd as soon as possible with my wife and the girls, Miss Laura,' he said.

'Has something new happened?'

'Something new is happening every moment. The Duma has defied an Imperial order suspending it and has taken responsibility for the government. And there is an organisation which calls itself a Soviet of Soldiers' and Workers' Deputies which also believes that it can govern. The result is nothing but anarchy.'

Laura hesitated briefly. Was this the moment to tell her employer that she planned to return to England and so needed to remain near the port? No. As Fred had pointed out, there could be no possibility of sailing for at least two months.

'Are we to go back to the Crimea?' she asked.

'Yes, that will be best. At least there will be food there, and the servants will be loyal to the family. Unlike those here, who can no longer be trusted. You may have to pack for yourself. I shall send Richards with you as an escort.'

'Are you not coming yourself, Pavel Karlovich?'

'I cannot afford to be seen. They are shooting − ' He gave a groan of uncertainty or despair. 'That I should have to hide in my own country! Hurry now, Miss Laura. You must all leave at once.'

5

If one of the outdoor staff of an English stately home had barged in through the front door and walked bold as brass up the main staircase to the nursery floor he would have been sacked on the spot. But this was Russia at the beginning of 1918. As Fred Richards made his way upstairs to find the Kristovs' governess in their Moscow palace, the hazards he faced were of a very different kind.

His hopes of leaving Russia as soon as the ice of the Neva melted and opened the port of Petrograd in the summer of 1917 had been dashed by Laura's refusal to abandon her two pupils in the Crimea: and he for his part was determined not to abandon Laura. Even after the abdication of the Tsar, it had seemed safe enough in the south at first. Russia was a huge country and the hot-heads of Petrograd and Moscow were far away. But a second revolution eight months after the first had in effect given a licence to loot. Without warning, a newly-formed Soviet in Sebastopol opened the prison doors and allowed a mob to burn down all the villas of the nobility, forcing the Kristovs to flee.

Once upon a time they could have chosen between half a dozen retreats; but all their farms and mines had been taken over by the peasants or the workers and they dared not show their faces in any of them. The army had mutinied, shooting many of its own officers. Fred didn't know whether His Nibs was still alive − and if he were, he would be on the run, because from the moment of the second revolution in the autumn, when the Bolsheviks seized power, every officer who was a member of the nobility was under sentence of summary execution.

That applied to Prince Kristov too, of course. His earlier escape to the Crimea had been hazardous enough. The danger to him now made it impossible for him to return to Petrograd, where he was too well known. For want of an alternative the household had moved to Moscow. In their palace there, one of the prince's ancestors had built a concealed stairway and passage for the purpose of discreetly visiting his mistress. Through this dark approach Prince Kristov was smuggled, so that no one knew the head of the family to be living on the premises.

Fred had long ago discarded his uniform. Anyone might have thought that to be identifiable as the down-trodden wage-slave of a princely family would attract sympathy from a revolutionary crowd, but it didn't seem to work like that. Anyone who appeared to be claiming a connection with the nobility was stopped and questioned on every street corner and would be lucky not to be beaten or thrown into jail. The only safe course these days was to be indistinguishable from everyone else, and that meant looking shabby. Fred was a man who took pride in his appearance, so it wasn't an easy decision to throw away his smart uniform and put on second-hand clothes. But it was better to be ragged and alive than neat and dead.

A good many of the people who were camping out on the lower floors of the palace had once been the Kristovs' servants. It had not taken them long, after Kerensky was overthrown by Lenin and Trotsky, to form a soviet of their own and make demands for food and clothes and money which the family could not now meet. No service could any longer be expected of them; nor could they be evicted from the rooms they had occupied. There was an uneasy atmosphere in the house, of emotions coming to the boil, and the city was full of agitators who stirred up trouble wherever they went. Fred had decided that staying put had become more dangerous than attempting to escape. It was time to get out.

He found Laura sitting in an unheated room, supervising the two Kristov girls as they bent their heads over their sewing. Mademoiselle, who would normally have undertaken this task, had taken a boat to France from the Crimea, and quite right too.

For a few moments, before he was noticed, Fred stared at Laura. How pale she was! Well, her complexion was naturally fair: it went with the chestnut hair. But now there were increasing signs of stress.

She had been worried and unhappy the first time he ever set eyes on her, he remembered; and black hadn't suited her. That memory, though, had quickly been banished in the moment when he opened his eyes in the middle of a North Sea storm and saw her smiling, compassionate face looking down at him. From then on he had regarded her not exactly as beautiful but certainly as desirable. He had fallen

66

not only for the brightness of her eyes but for the tall, stretched look of her body; that long, strong neck; those slender arms. She didn't flaunt herself like these Russian princesses when they dressed up for an evening out in what Fred considered an indecent manner, but he took pleasure in imagining what was concealed under her high-necked blouse.

Had any man been given the chance to make that exploration, he wondered. Almost certainly not. She was the sort of girl who would have been brought up to say no until she was married. And by now she must be wondering whether she ever would find a husband. That was what was wrong, Fred realised suddenly. Yes, she must be anxious, and yes, she must be tired and perhaps even hungry. But the change in the shape of her face could be explained more simply than that. At the age of twenty-five, she needed a man.

As though sensing that she was being stared at, she looked up. Her smile transformed that strained face. 'Fred!'

'Can I have a word, Miss Laura?'

'Of course.'

She waited for a moment for a moment before realising that he did not intend to speak in front of the girls. Pausing to inspect their work and make a suggestion to Tanya, she came outside and followed him along a corridor until they were out of earshot.

'It's time to be up and off, Miss Laura. All this that's going on is nothing to do with you and me, and the sooner we're out of it, the better. In my opinion it's going to get very nasty any day now.' The nastiness had begun already, but he didn't want to tell her what he had heard unless he really had to.

'I can't leave the girls.'

'There's nothing you can do to protect them. The way I see it, the only hope for them — the whole family — is to go to ground, lie low, pretend to be the same as other people. Whether they can do it, I doubt. But certainly they'll have to do it without servants. A governess is a giveaway, and what would an Englishwoman be except a governess?'

'If they tell me they don't want me, then of course — '

Fred shook his head vigorously.

'You can't just hang around, waiting for things to explode. This is a private quarrel, but it's a bloody one. It's not like England. People are dying. Being killed. It's time to get frightened.'

He could tell by her expression that he had not yet convinced her, and so moved to his reserve position.

'Just think about it this way, Miss Laura. The last ship has left from the Black Sea. The last ship has left from Petrograd, with anyone who had any sense aboard it. There's only one way out of Russia now. It's only open to foreigners and Lord knows how long it'll be allowed to go on running.'

'The train through Siberia, you mean?'

'That's right. To Vladivostock. Now you may think today that you don't want to catch it, but if you were to change your mind when you hear that the last train is about to leave, you wouldn't be able to just run and jump aboard. You need papers. Permits to travel. Permits to leave the country. Papers to say that you are who your passport says you are. You know all this as well as I do. It can't do any harm to get all the paperwork done. It may take weeks, so the sooner you get started, the better. Then when you come to make your choice, it really will be a choice. I've got mine. All but the date of the train I'll be travelling on.'

'You're really going to leave?'

'You know why I came to Russia, Miss Laura? Not exactly to make my fortune, but to build a platform on which a fortune could be built. Saving my wages. All the little presents I was given. His Nibs was always generous, and so was the old princess, that time when she was so ill. The first year, I sent my savings home. Thought I could trust my father at least to hold it safe for me. Tossing money on to the fire, that was — or into a beer mug, more like. So the rest I've kept in a bank here. Watched it grow. Ready for me to go back home and start my own business, make something of myself. What's that money worth now? Not a farthing. You're in the same boat, I'll be bound.'

Upset, she nodded her head.

'Well then, there's no reason to stay and every reason to go.'

'When are you going?' she asked, her voice faint.

'I'm waiting for you.'

'But you said you'd got your permits to travel and leave already.'

'Yes. That's why I want you to get a move on with your paperwork.' He understood the meaning of the uncertainty in her eyes. Why should he take such risks for her? To explain the real reason for the protectiveness he felt might alarm her; but there was another way of putting it. 'First mention I ever heard of you, Miss Laura, was when His Nibs ordered me to look after you. I told you that time on the boat that you could rely on me any time you needed help. It takes twenty days to get to Vladivostock. I'm not going to let you make that journey alone. Twenty days in a country where you can't trust anyone any longer not to slit your throat. Well, you can trust me.'

'Yes, I know.'

'Well then. It's for my sake you need to get cracking.' Putting it like that would make it easier for her to decide that it was time to abandon a family she could do nothing to help.

'Yes. Although – ' There was a painful pause. 'Might Prince Alexis not need you?'

That was the question he had hoped she wouldn't ask.

'No.' But an answer of such brevity would invite more questions. 'Him and me's the same as your girls and you. He can't afford to be seen with servants.'

'But he can't pretend – I mean to say, his men all know who he is.' Her eyes flashed with a sudden fear as she waited for reassurance and wasn't given it. 'Is he all right, Fred? Have you heard?'

'Haven't heard nothing, no, and that's the best news there could be.' He hesitated, and then decided to be brutal. 'You must know what's happening on the front, Miss Laura. Mutiny and desertion. If an officer tries to stop the men going, he gets shot. And if an officer is a prince, he gets shot anyway. None of them are safe – not His Highness here: not His Nibs out there.' He watched as the remaining colour drained from her cheeks. 'He'll have known that, see. He'll have made a dash for it.'

'But you don't know.'

'Can't hardly expect him to bob up and tell me. I reckon, though, that if he was dead we'd have heard, one way or another. No news is good news.'

'But where could he go? What will he do?'

'Join the White Army. And that's another reason why we need to get out, you and me. Revolution's bad enough, but civil war on top of it ... There's nothing for us to stay for. You're going to get on with it, the permits, aren't you, Miss Laura? For my sake as well as your own. And for the Kristovs.'

'Yes. I'll have to tell the girls.' There were tears in her eyes. She was fond of them, he supposed. But her nod of agreement was a firm one, and Fred sighed with relief. Three weeks if they were lucky, and five at the worst. Then they would be on their way back to England together.

6

'Yes, of course you must go,' said the princess. 'But oh, my dear Miss Laura, how we shall miss you! How we shall weep when you leave!'

Tanya, always the most emotional of the family, was weeping already. Laura held out her arms and hugged her like a baby, rocking her backwards and forwards. Fearing this reaction, she had not revealed her plans immediately. But all the applications for the various permits she would need had been submitted. Judging by the experience of others with British passports, she expected the formalities to be completed in due course.

'We'll meet again, dearest Tanya,' she promised now. 'You must come to England. I shall give you the address of my aunt, so that you can find me.' Even as she spoke, Laura was chilled by the thought of her own future in a country to which she had so few links. How would she live? What work could she do? But this was no time for such trivial fears.

'Not England,' said the princess. 'It's too hard for us to obtain visas. We will meet in Paris.'

'Paris?'

'Yes. We have money there. Pavel Karlovich transferred it just in time. Not enough, but something. We must appoint a rendezvous now, my dear Miss Laura. You will want to travel first to your own country and to take a holiday with your family. But when you are rested, come please to Paris so that we can assure ourselves of your safety. We will register with the Russian Embassy there as soon as we arrive so that you can find our address — unless, of course ...'

Her voice faded as it no doubt occurred to her that the Imperial embassy would be closed down. 'Well, in case there is difficulty, we will make our rendezvous in a restaurant. The Café de la Victoire. Anyone will tell you. One of the most famous in Paris — at least, in 1913 ...' Once again she was overcome by doubt. The world she knew had collapsed. It was impossible to rely on anything any longer.

'Is poor Miss Laura to sit and eat for weeks and weeks until we come?' asked Sofiya. It was a long time since anything had made her smile.

'Of course not,' her mother reproved her. 'You must make yourself known to *le patron*, Miss Laura. We are well known to him. He will give you a message if he has one, or else hold a message from you. Remember: the Café de la Victoire.' But Sofiya's interruption had troubled her; perhaps because this was a conversation which the girls ought not to overhear. 'We will talk more later.'

Before such a conversation could take place, Fred arrived breathlessly and once again indicated that he must speak to Laura alone.

'I've got to go to Petrograd,' he told her.

'Why?'

70

'Dunno. Prince Kristov says he's got a job for me to do. Can't trust any of the other servants, he says. Doesn't seem to realise yet that when we get there, there won't *be* any servants.'

'How long will you be gone?'

'Two days, he thinks it'll take. Plus travel time, of course. He won't tell me what the job is, and I don't suppose he's got the foggiest idea how long it takes anyone to do anything, so let's say four days there to be sure. I'll be back within a week.'

Trying without much success to conceal her alarm, Laura swallowed the lump in her throat. Now that she had taken the decision to leave with Fred, anything which threatened their arrangements was frightening.

'You're not to worry. Now listen. I'll have to keep my identity papers with me. But if I let you have all the rest, all the permits, you should be able to buy a ticket for me when you get your own. If they won't let you, well, a week's delay won't matter too much; but I don't see why there should be any problem. Here's the money for the two tickets.'

It was Bolshevik money. How had he managed to get his hands on so much? Laura's own savings, like Fred's, had disappeared when the banks closed and Imperial bank notes ceased to be worth the paper they were printed on.

'I sold some furniture.' Fred was answering the question she hadn't liked to ask. 'And don't try to say it's stealing. In the first place, the Kristovs don't know the half of what they own. In the second place, they're lucky to have a whole floor to themselves here still. They'll be packed into one room any minute now, and what good will their possessions in the other rooms do them then? And in the third place, that lot outside would have taken all the furniture for firewood if I hadn't got my hands on it first.'

That last point was true enough. Laura didn't bother to argue the ethics of the transaction — but she was still worried about the timetable.

'Hadn't we better wait until — '

'No. The sooner the better. If you see that you'll be ready to leave two weeks from now, book us both on the train for then. Like I say, I expect to be back in one week, but in two for certain. Even if I have to give up in the middle of the job.'

'Do you — ' Her voice faltered, for she was conscious of disloyalty. 'Do you really have to go?'

Fred's face, which recently had been looking grim and forceful, softened into a smile.

'Well, the poor old bugger, he doesn't know the time of day,' he said. 'Can't blame him, I suppose. Bottom's dropped out of his world. Forty years of saying "Do this. Do that," and suddenly the only answer he gets is "Do it yourself". If I let him go alone he'll be picked up on the first street corner. And they'll shoot him, you know. Even out of uniform, if they find out who he is. I've got to get him a pass in a false name so that he can get a travel permit in a false name and a food card to go with it. He still believes that he's a decent old codger who treats his servants well and deserves to be loved by them all. He hasn't realised yet that he's an enemy of the people. He's not safe to be allowed out alone. I'll have to go, Miss Laura. But two weeks from now, you can count on it, I'll be with you on that train.'

'But just suppose – ' They must, surely, have some contingency plan. What should she do if he didn't get back in time? In Russia even at the best of times it was rash to assume that everything would go according to plan; and this was the worst of times.

'There's nothing to suppose. If I don't catch that train with you, then I'm dead. I told you right at the start of this that I was going to look after you, and I am. Do you understand me?' He gripped her shoulders so tightly that it hurt. She opened her mouth to protest, but the look in his eyes silenced her. He wanted to kiss her. Without a shadow of doubt he was longing to take her into his arms. She could feel in the tension of his muscles how fiercely he needed to restrain himself. It was his turn now to swallow the lump in a dry throat. As he relaxed his grip, she gave an imperceptible nod of understanding. Yes, indeed, she need not doubt that when the train pulled out of the station, he would be there.

That evening, after Sofiya and Tanya were asleep, the princess summoned Laura to her room.

'Sit down, please, Miss Laura,' she said. 'I ought not to have spoken of Paris in front of the girls this afternoon. Children chatter, and no one can be trusted any longer: no one except you.'

'You're planning to leave Russia?'

'Yes. As soon as it can be arranged. I'd hoped we could go into the country. But none of our estates is safe for us now. And Moscow is full of spies.'

'But how will you escape? All the frontiers are closed.' Vladivostock was the only port of exit still open, and only foreign nationals were allowed to use it.

'We shall go through Finland. During the summer, the roads were guarded. But now the snow is settled and we can go by sledge. Across the countryside. The frontier is so long. Even the Red Guard can't be everywhere at once.'

'Then I could come with you. There's no need for me − '

'No, Miss Laura. It's too dangerous. The risk is worth taking for us, but you have a safer route out, and you must use it.' She put up a hand to silence any further objection. Then her voice, usually so vague and pleasant, became businesslike. 'You'll need money.' She put a purse on the table.

'I have enough for the ticket, thank you.'

'To Vladivostock, perhaps. But you will still be only halfway round the world. You will have to cross America, the Atlantic Ocean.' She tipped out a pile of gold roubles. 'Here. As roubles they have no value, but gold is a currency anywhere in the world.'

Laura hesitated. She had recognised that her situation would be difficult, but had to hope that there would be a British consul in Vladivostock authorised to assist refugees − for many others beside herself must have seen all their savings disappear. But if the consul were to offer only a loan, she could give no security and would have no means of repaying it.

'Thank you, Anna Ivanovna,' she said. 'You're very generous.'

'I have something to ask.' Now it was the princess's turn to hesitate briefly. 'Pavel Karlovich believes that all this is a nonsense which will soon be over, and that we shall be able to return. Myself, I'm not so sure. If we are to spend the rest of our lives in France, we shall need money; far more than the little we have there. We shall take what treasures we can with us to Finland, but the load must not be too heavy for the horses. I have some jewels here in Moscow. Would you carry some of them out with you? You must think before you answer. It's not a small thing.'

Laura knew that well enough. If any of the Kristovs themselves were found trying to smuggle their possessions out of the country, they would be shot without even the pretence of a trial. It was possible that a foreigner might be allowed to board the Trans-Siberian train without being searched: possible, but not certain. And at any point of the journey the Cheka might stop and board the train. They would undoubtedly scrutinise all identity papers with care; and who could tell what other inspections might be imposed? There were so many new laws. It was an offence to carry a firearm. It was even an offence to travel with more than one change of clothing. The penalty in each case was death.

Nevertheless, on this occasion Laura needed no time to consider. In five years she had become closer to the Kristovs than to her own aunt and cousins. They were her family now. 'If they can be hidden, I will take them,' she said.

'My dear Miss Laura!' The princess embraced her before unlocking

73

the travelling jewel case which always moved with her from one palace to another.

'This necklace.' She drew out one of her most valuable pieces. Three tiers of graded and perfectly faceted Cape diamonds descended from a choker formed from a hundred tiny stones. 'I will take it to pieces. Some of the stones may be covered with cloth. Then they can be sewn on to your coat as buttons for extra decoration. and this − ' she indicated the choker − we can again wrap with cloth and sew into the hem. Or the lining of your hat. If you agree, I will help with the work.'

Princess Kristova had no domestic skills of any kind. Never in her life had she cooked a meal or cleaned a house or mended her children's clothes. Even now, with her staff gone, she was relying on the loyal Ukrainian woman who had cared for Sofiya and Tanya as babies. But, like her daughters, the princess had been taught fine sewing. She could embroider and smock and do drawn-thread work, and no doubt in this time of crisis she could disguise a diamond as a button. Laura, though, looked doubtful as she picked up the choker and examined it.

'A lot of the weight of this is the setting, which has no value,' she pointed out. 'Larger stones, which can be mounted, might be easier to sell.'

There was no lack of those. Laura had often enough gasped at the extravagant display of jewellery in which her employer set off for some grand court function, but this was the first time that she had seen so much of the collection at one time. She went to fetch the clothes in which she proposed to travel, and the two women settled down at once to the sewing.

The plan to make buttons from diamonds was abandoned as requiring too much time and being liable to draw attention to the coat. Instead, Laura produced one of her skirts which was decorated at the bottom with three rows of raised zig-zag braid, sufficient to disguise any lumpiness: forty stones were stitched into the hem.

It could not all be done in one evening. Several days passed before the work of concealment was finished. Or, at least, Laura thought it was finished. But there was one more request to come. The princess opened a separate jewel case and Laura found herself looking at *La Lachrymosa*: the Kristov kokoshnik.

7

At the sight of the kokoshnik, Laura gasped. 'Anna Ivanovna, I can't take that!' It was too high, too rigid, and the teardrop pearl which had given it its name was too large.

Without speaking at once, the princess took the tiara out of the case, still on its velvet tray. Beneath it, on a separate tray, lay the companion necklace, with a matching pearl.

'These are the most valuable of all my jewels,' she said. 'And I treasure them in particular because they were a gift for Tanya's birth. The necklace, when I have enclosed it in felt, will fit round Tanya's waist. No one will search the undergarments of such a young child. But the kokoshnik . . .' She looked appealingly at Laura. 'The gallery will divide into sections,' she explained, her fingers struggling to find the joins even as she spoke. 'It was designed, you see, so that for variety it could be worn as a stomacher instead of always in the hair.'

She had found the first of the tiny bolts now, and carefully drew it out. Within minutes the rigid curved top of the tiara was separated and put on one side. Turning the remaining part over, she held it against her slim waist. The pearls which were usually suspended within the diamond-studded hoops swung down to hang over her stomach. 'We could sew it inside your corset. No one could possibly know.'

This time Laura was not so quick to answer.

The princess stroked the jewels sadly with one finger.

'I wore this for the first time at a New Year's Eve Ball in the Winter Palace,' she said. 'We have a belief – a superstition, I suppose – that if you are wearing something new as the new year begins, you may make a wish on it, and the wish will come true. My wish was that one day my baby Tanya would wear the kokoshnik on just such a glittering occasion and would be the most beautiful woman present – and the happiest. But now . . . Unless you will help us, Miss Laura . . .'

Laura still hesitated. Although the large pearl must certainly be of great value by itself, she had learned something about jewellery during her years among the nobility in Russia. The diamonds which were now scattered about her clothing could be either sold separately or re-assembled into necklaces without any loss of value. But the kokoshnik would be far more valuable as a single piece than as the sum of its parts. There was no point in suggesting that it should be dismantled, more than had been made possible by the jeweller's bolts.

As a single piece, however, it would pose a great danger to its carrier. It would, in addition, be extremely uncomfortable. Fred had warned her that the journey to Vladivostock would take twenty days – and that was assuming that there were no unexpected hold-ups. For twenty days or more she would have to sleep in her clothes. If she were to carry the kokoshnik, that would mean sleeping in her corset as well; and to the everyday rigidity of the whalebone would be added the hard lumps of the jewels.

But what did a little discomfort matter in a situation which might well prove one of life or death for the family which had welcomed her into its midst? Prince Kristov and his wife had already lost all the land from which their income had derived, and there was no way in which they could ever hope to earn a living. Even if they were able to cast off every memory of their background and demean themselves by looking for work, their practical skills were almost non-existent. If Sofiya and Tanya were not to go hungry in their new life, they must start with as much capital as possible. Doing her best to disguise her reluctance, Laura nodded her head in agreement.

Crying with relief and thanks, the princess kissed and embraced her. But there were still, it seemed, two more items to be taken from the jewel box.

'You will need money yourself, dear Miss Laura. These emerald cuff links, and the studs – '

'You've already given me the gold roubles, Anna Ivanovna,' Laura reminded her.

'Those are for the journey. After your return to England, too, you must live. You are to regard yourself as still in our employment, but of course there will be no monthly salary. So these emeralds are for you to sell for your own benefit, to keep you while you are waiting to rejoin us in Paris. There must be no argument. Now, if you will take off your corset . . .'

'I have another.' Laura had already set aside the clothes in which she would travel, to ensure that they would be clean when she was ready to go. She fetched the corset now and together they unpicked some of its tiny stitches. It was only lightly boned, for Laura's body was firm and slender and her narrow waist needed no tight lacing. The kokoshnik's gallery could be divided into sections, and these were sewn back into the channels from which pieces of whalebone were taken. Disguising the shape of the large teardrop pearl was a more difficult matter and by the time the whole piece had been made smooth by layers of cloth, Laura suggested laughingly that she would be able to claim special treatment by appearing to be pregnant.

'You'll be protected by your passport,' the princess assured her when the work was finished. 'I wouldn't let you do this for us if I thought − '

'You mustn't worry for me. I shall be anxious for you, but I'm in no danger myself.'

She spoke with a confidence which she was unable to feel, for the journey which lay ahead presented a daunting prospect.

So much could go wrong while she was still in Russia, a country which had become unpredictable in its lawlessness. Suppose after all there were no ships to take her away from Vladivostock? And if there were, where would they deposit her? She might discover that the only passage available was to Japan. Even if she were successful in reaching the United States, there would still be the whole of that continent to cross, and then the Atlantic Ocean, in which no doubt German submarines were still operating. That night, before going to sleep, she fetched the atlas which Sofiya and Tanya used in their geography lessons and memorised the American railway routes, so that she would know that she was moving in the right direction.

All this time she was worried by Fred's absence. There was no real cause for anxiety: he had promised to be back within two weeks, and that time had not yet passed. But the next day, after queueing for six hours and learning that no further passenger trains were running on the Trans-Siberian railway, she at last obtained two tickets for a goods train. From that moment onwards every second seemed to tick away dangerously fast. Come on, Fred. Please come soon.

There were still three days to go until the limit he had set for his promised return − and two more before the train's departure − when Laura was awakened before dawn by Tanya, who crept into her bed, hugging her and crying.

'What's the matter, dearest?'

'We have to leave. Papa has sent for us. A message came in the night. Perhaps I shall never see you again.'

The messenger must surely be Fred. Laura comforted the little girl as much as she could before dressing quickly. She found the princess staring helplessly around, unable to decide what she should take with her and in the end scooping up scraps of food and pieces of her children's clothing in an apparently haphazard manner.

'Ah, Miss Laura, a message has arrived from Pavel Karlovich, to say − '

'Yes. Tanya told me. Did Fred Richards bring the message?'

'Tanya told you? Tanya, that was naughty. I said you were to keep it a secret.'

'But not from Miss Laura.'

'Of course Miss Laura is allowed to know, but I am the one to tell her. You must learn now, Tanya, that when you promise to keep a secret that means you must tell no one at all. One day your life may depend on it. Do you understand?'

Biting her lip, Tanya nodded.

'It won't be long before we meet again in Paris,' Laura promised her. 'But that must be a secret as well. Anna Ivanovna, was the messenger — ?'

'Not Richards, no.' It was clear that the princess did not intend to give any details. 'Miss Laura, when does your train leave?'

'In five days.'

'It dismays me that we must leave you alone. I'd hoped to go with you to the station, to assure myself that you were safely on your way.'

'I shall be all right here. And Fred Richards has promised to act as my escort. He'll be back soon. If you have a chance to make your escape, you mustn't delay.'

'Yes, it must be at once. You won't forget the Café de la Victoire, my dear Miss Laura. We shall meet again.' They were all crying now as they embraced each other. Only at the very last moment did Laura remember something which had occurred to her in the middle of the night.

'Anna Ivanovna, could you spare just a second to write me an authority to sell the jewels you were kind enough to give me for my expenses? So that I shall not be suspected of stealing them.' She hurried to find paper and a pen and ink and watched as a quick note was scribbled and signed.

'I've addressed this to M. Louis Cartier,' explained the princess, thrusting it into her governess's hand. 'The pieces were made in his workshops and so he will give you the best price: I have asked him to do so. But if you can't wait until you reach Paris, he has a brother in London — and this authority can be presented to anyone, wherever you need it.'

There was more kissing. The two girls had become silent now, frightened because they did not know exactly where they were going, or what would happen to them when they arrived. Within a few moments Laura was alone.

There were many other people living in the palace, but so thick were the walls that nothing could be heard. Outside, snow was falling heavily, deadening any sounds of horses or walkers in the street. Once before, after her father's death, she had known what it was to feel lonely, but at least then there had been someone nearby to feel concerned about her future. Now she felt completely abandoned.

No, that wasn't fair. There was Fred. Fred had promised that he

78

would always be on her side. He had promised that she could rely on him to help her return to England. He had promised that he would return to Moscow no later than Thursday. All those promises she must believe.

He would be hungry when he arrived, and there was no food on the premises, for the princess had taken the remains of the black bread for her journey. Nothing more was due on Laura's ration card for another two days, but she was already accustomed to deal in the black market, for no one could live on official rations alone. She filled a bag with Tanya's best dresses. Their owner would never wear them again, and the wife of some Bolshevik commissar would smile to see her own children looking like princesses.

It was a good thing to have something practical to do, to take her mind off the waiting. Laura dressed herself warmly, concealing her fur turban under the hood of the shuba − for to wear fur in the streets these days was to brand oneself as at least a bourgeois, and therefore an enemy of the republic. Then she tied a scarf across it to cover most of her face.

It was a dry snow which was falling today, crisp underfoot and beating against her eyes with a gentle touch which did something to rouse her from her depression. Walking steadily, she made her way to what was still called the rag market, although nowadays all the goods on sale were of the highest quality.

In another market peasant women were sitting in the snow, each with a few goods to sell. The only fresh meat was horsemeat, and Laura lacked the fuel to cook it for long enough to make it tender. She contented herself with buying bread and cabbage and smoked sausage − by the standards of the past few weeks, enough for a feast. Now there was nothing to do but wait.

8

The last day of the two weeks passed. This was the date for which Fred had told her to buy their tickets. As it happened, there was no train running for another two days, but he could not have known that. Where was he? If I don't come, I'm dead, he had said. But Fred couldn't be dead. Not Fred. He was a survivor.

Perhaps, believing that he had left his return to the last minute, he had gone straight to look for her at the entrance to the platform. Why hadn't she thought of that before? Hastily Laura scribbled a note for him to find if he came to the palace and then hurried towards the station. Even from a distance she could see chalked notices announcing cancellations due to shortages of fuel and the closed barriers which would show Fred, if he came, that no trains would be running that day. Red Guards were patrolling the area, stopping even the most casual passers-by in order to check their passes. She was careful not to approach too close and was glad of the concealment afforded by the falling snow.

Turning away, she suddenly remembered the promise which Charles Vereker had elicited from her five years earlier. In her correspondence with the young diplomat since then there had been only one further reference to his cousin – and at that time she had felt sure that the kindness with which she was surrounded would make it unnecessary for her ever to call upon the protection of the British Embassy in Petrograd. She had allowed the name to slip from her mind. What a fool she was! Petrograd was too far away now, but there was a mission in Moscow. She made her way to it at once.

Its offices were as cold as those of any other building in Moscow; but what a relief it was to be able to speak English in the confidence that this would be her passport to admittance rather than a cause of suspicion.

'My name is Laura Mainwaring and I would like to speak to the head of the mission,' she said. 'I have been given an introduction from the Honourable Charles Vereker.' To refer to him as 'the Honourable' in speech was, she knew, incorrect; but after so many months in which to use any kind of title was to risk execution, it gave her pleasure to emphasise his aristocratic connections. 'The introduction is to his cousin, Mr Henry Marriott,' she added. It was unlikely that Mr Marriott would still be accredited to Russia; but the mention of his name and Charles's should be enough to earn her a hearing.

The young man in the outer office gave her a curious look before inviting her to wait in an empty office. The wait was a long one, until Laura began to feel alarmed. But no harm, surely, could come to her on what was almost English soil. She wandered about the room, studying the maps which hung on the wall, until at last the door opened.

'Miss Mainwaring!'

It was Charles Vereker himself. The relief of seeing a familiar and friendly face overwhelmed her. Laughing and almost crying at the same time, she ran towards him, clasping both of his outstretched hands with her own.

'Mr Vereker. I had no idea – '

'I've been here only a few days,' he told her. 'There's a room at my disposal upstairs, with a fire. Let me take your coat.' He continued to

80

talk as he showed her into the cosy study of the Head of Mission. 'I've been anxious for your safety. Your aunt told me, when I wrote to her, that you were still in Russia and that she had had no recent news. So as soon as I arrived I tried to make enquiries. But I could ask only where the Kristovs might be, and of course in their own interest they had made that question a difficult one to answer. I'm so pleased to see you safe. And well, I hope? Come closer to the fire.'

'Thank you.' Laura found herself so weak with the pleasure of the encounter that she could hardly speak.

'You've left it very late to make use of the introduction I gave you. You must leave Russia at once.'

'Yes, I plan to do so. I have tickets for the Trans-Siberian train on Thursday, and hope that there are still ships leaving from Vladivostock.'

'We have an office there. I'll cable and tell them to reserve you a berth. There's great pressure on accommodation, as you can imagine.'

'I should be most grateful. Two berths, if you please. Not in the same cabin, though. I'm due to be escorted on the train by another British citizen, Mr Fred Richards.'

'Richards? The same Richards who was my chauffeur once?'

'Oh, I'd forgotten about that. Yes, of course, he left your service for Prince Alexis, didn't he?'

'He was stolen. There's only one thing more ungentlemanly than stealing a fellow's chauffeur, and that's stealing his chef.' But Charles was smiling.

'There's a difficulty, though.' Laura explained how worried she was that Fred had not kept his promise to return. 'If he doesn't arrive tomorrow, I must go to the railway office and try to change the tickets for a later train.'

'You must do no such thing.' Charles sat down on the other side of the fire and spoke earnestly. 'In the first place, if you miss the *Estella* there will be no other suitable ship for at least six weeks. There is an American cruiser in the harbour, but it may not be prepared to wait or to take civilians on board.'

'Six weeks is not — '

'Six weeks could be the difference between life and death. I'm here in Russia on a special errand from the Secretary of State. I'm not in a position to tell you its purpose: but I can say, in the strictest confidence, that before very long any British citizens who remain in Russia may find themselves regarded as more than merely class enemies. You must catch that train without fail. I can ensure that you are provided with companions. Half of the mission staff are being sent

81

home, together with the families of those who are to remain; and a party from the American Embassy in Petrograd has also arrived in Moscow this week in order to catch the same train. If I thought there was any danger that you might stay on for an insufficient reason I should have you arrested immediately so that you could be delivered to the station in handcuffs.'

Again he was smiling, and it was a smile which carried Laura straight back to her life in Oxford: a life in which handsome, carefree young men came to tea and she had nothing more to worry her than the thinness of the cucumber sandwiches or the next morning's test of French irregular verbs. To her shame, she found that she could not prevent herself from crying. Charles moved quickly from his chair and, leaning forward on one knee, offered his handkerchief.

'How stupid of me!' She sniffed herself under control at last. 'It's just that it's so long since I talked to anyone like you, or without having to think, am I saying the right things? But, Mr Vereker — '

'Won't you call me Charles?' he said, still smiling. 'Look, I'm down on my knees as I ask you. And then perhaps I may be allowed to call you Laura? Because that's how I've always thought of you to myself. When I first saw you at your father's house, you were just a child; and so young that I could guess what pleasure it gave you to be addressed as Miss Mainwaring. Now, though — '

'Oh yes, of course. But what I wanted to say was that I can't simply abandon Fred. I've got all his travel permits, and his ticket. I don't know what's delaying him, but if he turns up a day or two too late — '

'You can leave me to deal with that. I shall come down to the station to see you off. Bring all his papers with you, and hand them to me at the last minute if he doesn't turn up. Leave a message somewhere he's likely to look, so that he knows what's happening. I'm travelling on a diplomatic passport, and if he reports to me I can employ him again.' He moved back into his chair. 'Richards will be all right. What happened to the motor-car?'

'It was commandeered by a commissar. Fred had kept it so beautifully. It looked as good as new. But he doesn't believe that anyone except him will know how to look after it. They won't do the right things before laying it up for the winter, and then they won't be able to start it in spring.' An hour ago she would have been unable to speak and smile about such trivialities, but Charles, just by sitting there, seemed to have taken all her worries on to himself.

Those worries returned, however, when the time came for her to board the train. From the first moment of dressing in her jewel-laden clothes she felt stiff and uncomfortable. At every step the diamonds hidden in the hem of her skirt slapped against her ankles, and if she allowed the straightness of her back to relax even for a moment she could feel the pressure of one part or another of the kokoshnik. It was necessary to hold her head high and pretend that nothing was amiss.

There was still no sign of Fred: not even a message. The Red Guards at the station's control point were surly; but the young man to whom she had first spoken at the British mission was standing beside them, ticking off agreed names and refusing to allow any interference. Charles was on the platform, looking out for her. He hurried her to a wagon which had small flags pasted to the side to show that the passengers were British or American. Five men, too smartly dressed to be Russian, stood in front of the two doors to make sure that no one boarded without authority.

There were quick introductions, but anything more than a mere exchange of names would have to wait until they were on their way. Laura already knew that she would have to travel by a goods train, but was dismayed to find that her home for the next three weeks would be a convict wagon, used normally to transport prisoners to Siberia.

The wagon was divided by wooden walls into six windowless compartments which opened into a corridor. Each compartment held nine bunks made of wooden planks, and two buckets. One of these, she was told at once, would be used for clean water and the other must serve as the communal lavatory. At each end of the corridor was a stove which could be used for heating food and keeping the wagon warm. Charles had already secured for Laura a top berth in one of the compartments nearest to a stove.

'I can't save one for Richards,' he told her. 'If the train pulls out with an empty space, God knows who'll be put in to fill it. No word from him?'

Laura shook her head.

'He'll bob up again, don't worry. If you ask me, he's probably made a dash for it across the Finnish frontier. That's the route which the nobility are using now. All Richards needs is to get his hands on some kind of sledge and he could fill a trunk with Fabergé titbits and set himself up for life.'

'He wouldn't — '

'Yes, he would,' said Charles easily. 'He's a practical chap. He'll look around and see stuff that doesn't belong to the Kristovs any longer because they've made a run for it, and then he'll ask himself whether the Bolsheviks have any better right to it than Fred Richards. That's why he hasn't come back to Moscow, I'll be bound. He couldn't carry his loot on a train − but smuggling it over the snow is a different matter. I don't think you need worry about our Fred. I'm sorry you've got to put up with this, though.' His hand gestured at the hard planks, the bleak buckets.

'It's not important. Charles, thank you so very much for all your help. I can't tell you how grateful I am.'

'What are friends for?' He waved her gratitude away. 'When you get back to England, Laura, please don't disappear again. You can write to me at the Foreign Office. So that I have at least an address. I think I need to get off now.' Both the fifteen-minute and the five-minute bells had been rung. 'Have you got Richards's papers for me?'

She handed them over. After the two doors of the wagon had been closed she pulled open the small window in one of them and leaned out. For the last time her eyes searched the platform, hoping to see some disturbance, a running figure, a last-minute leap.

'If I don't catch that train with you, then I'm dead,' Fred had told her. In any other country at any other time such a statement would be fanciful, a piece of rhetoric; but she was well aware that in Russia today it could all too easily be true. Should she now be mourning him? Or was Charles's guess a correct one? Fred had helped himself to the Kristovs' possessions once before, to pay for the train tickets. It would be naive to think him incapable of lining his pockets.

The questions spiralled in her mind, offering no answers. As the train began to move, Charles walked beside the door for as long as he could, his hand raised to touch hers. When at last he had to fall back Laura continued for a little while to lean out of the open window. There was no last-minute leap. She felt her eyes misting over − not entirely because of the cold. Fred had promised to look after her and she had believed that he meant it. Either he had let her down; or else . . . The slowly clanking wheels began to hammer an unwelcome refrain.

'If I don't catch that train with you, then I'm dead, then I'm dead, then I'm dead.'

9

Fred had spoken the truth when he told Laura how reluctant he was to accompany Prince Kristov to Petrograd. His unwillingness was caused primarily by his wish to stay near her, ready to get out as soon as she had all the necessary permissions; but there was a second reason for anxiety. Every train journey was risky. The Red Guards had erected barriers at each station so that intending passengers could be scrutinised and their papers demanded for inspection.

Petrograd was a particularly hazardous place. Prince Kristov had emerged from hiding with his blond beard shaved, but too many people there might recognize him. Not only was he a prince, not only had he been an officer, he had been attached to the Imperial court for many years and, since the opening of hostilities, had worked in the department of state which was blamed for most of the disasters of the war.

Strictly speaking, of course, Fred's employer was still Prince Alexis. However, ever since His Nibs left for the war it had been taken for granted that his chauffeur was now at the disposal of the whole family. There had been no reason to object to that, since tips were generous and, during the period when the old princess was ill and needed to be carried about, Fred had found himself effectively acting as her steward as well. Managing her affairs a good deal more efficiently than Prince Kristov's steward had done, in his own opinion — and although he had not turned away the bribes with which tradesmen competed for the household's custom, at least he made sure that goods weren't paid for unless they had been delivered.

He had been a fool, no doubt, to remain for so long in a country which had become so dangerously chaotic. The collapse of the old social structure had left even foreigners vulnerable to death by slow starvation or summary shooting. Part of the reason for his delay was an appraisal of the welcome he was likely to receive in England. The army would grab him for sure, and Fred had heard enough about the horrors of trench warfare to know that he didn't want to be a hero. Florrie, too, would be on the warpath if ever she learned that he was back in the country. There was no doubt that England was a dangerous place for Fred Richards. But he had to get Laura out of Russia; and if she was to make the journey safely, he must stay at her side.

There was a risk, he knew, that the Kristovs might consider him too useful to be released from service, and that was why he had not yet given any notice of his intention to leave the country. Until he was prepared to announce his departure, he had no excuse for refusing to go to Petrograd, and loyalty to the family had persuaded him to agree. But he left Moscow on the day after his conversation with Laura without knowing what he was expected to do.

He wasn't likely to find out in the train, which was crowded with deserters returning home from the front. To speak English to Prince

Kristov would brand him as a spy, to speak French would link him to the nobility and, although in the course of five years he had picked up enough Russian to get by, no one would take him for a native speaker. A pretence of sleep was the safest course.

On arrival, with hats pulled over their foreheads and scarves wound round their chins, they walked side by side from the Nicholas station. It was not an easy journey, for it was apparently no one's duty now to keep the streets and pavements clear, so that to cross any road meant climbing over slippery banks of frozen snow. This was probably the first time that the prince had ever made the journey on foot, and as they approached the Kristov palace he slowed in dismay. The grand porticoed entrance was boarded up. A notice roughly painted across the boards proclaimed that the building was the property of the people and that looters would be shot on sight.

'How do we get in?' The prince, bewildered, halted in his tracks.

'Keep walking, sir.' Fred had long ago ceased to use the dangerous word 'Excellency'. This was no place to draw attention to themselves by stopping and staring. 'We come back at night,' he said. 'There's a way in from the Moyka cut. Let's hope they haven't noticed it.'

The rear of the palace stretched along the narrow river which in its passage across the city had been tamed into a canal. A private cutting at one end allowed the Kristovs to sail directly in from the Neva if they wished, and moor their smaller yachts under their own windows. Fred had often used the cut to return in the small hours from visits to one or other of his lady friends without having to arouse the night watchman. In summer it meant stepping sideways along a narrow wall above the water, but at this time of year all the waterways were frozen. It was possible to walk along the ice and use the iron hoops, which protruded from the walls for the mooring of boats, to act as a ladder up to the door above the watergate.

Darkness fell early. At this time of year, indeed, there were very few hours of daylight. Making this unlit and slippery approach to his home for the first time, the prince was hesitant and slow. When at last they reached the entrance, Fred pulled himself up to examine it. The door was bolted on the inside, but the window of the room which the boatman had once occupied proved to be broken. Throwing his coat over the sharp teeth of glass Fred climbed through and unfastened the door from inside, bolting it again behind them.

'What have we come to do?' he asked, shivering in the unheated building.

The prince did not answer immediately. He was listening; worried lest the palace might be occupied by squatters. But the silence was heavy and dead. The local soviet had unintentionally done the family a good turn by safeguarding the palace from the kind of mass invasion which had occurred in Moscow. There was no one inside.

'To the salon,' he commanded. There was a crash as he knocked into a piece of furniture. Fred produced a torch from the pack which he carried slung across one shoulder. He had long ago ceased to expect that any Russian prince would be practical enough to consider in advance what might be needed. He shone the light on the stairs as they made their way up to the great entertaining rooms.

'If they've really managed to prevent looting!' murmured the prince. 'Give me the torch.' He swept its light round the walls for a moment before Fred sprang at him to grab it back.

'Do you want to get us shot?' Many of the shutters were closed, but not all. 'If I'm to help you, I need to know what's to be done.'

'We have to leave Russia,' said the prince. 'The whole family. There's no future for us here. No chance of survival, even. But this anarchy can't continue for ever. We shall return. Build up our lives again. And not, if we can help it, entirely from nothing. Small things, jewels, we can take with us when we go. But there are greater treasures.'

'You want to hide them?'

'Yes. The Rembrandts. The Perugino. Some of the family portraits. They can be taken from their frames. If necessary, they may be rolled, though it would be best if possible to leave them on the stretchers.'

'Is there a strong room?'

'Yes. And my wife has a jewellery safe built into her dressing room. But of course those are the places where anyone would look first. And they are protection only against casual thieves – not against official orders of sequestration and the use of dynamite.'

'You be choosing the things you want to keep, while I see if I can sniff out a hiding place,' said Fred.

If the prince resented the manner in which the chauffeur was giving him orders, he did not like to show it. Over the past nine months he had been confronted with every kind of insubordination. In Petrograd the servants had walked out. The Moscow staff had stayed on only in order to keep a roof over their heads, and they had formed themselves into a soviet, with new demands made daily. If anyone was still working in his farms and mines and forests, it would not be for him. It was small wonder that he might feel this English mechanic to be the only employee he could trust.

Fred gave him a second, smaller torch and left him to his choices. His own first action was to visit the suite of rooms in the old princess's wing which had been reserved for her younger son, and help himself to an elkskin coat which had fur both inside and outside. The palace was icy cold – and the train journey across Siberia in a couple of weeks' time would be even colder. Then he sat down in the darkness to think.

So vast was the building that it was difficult to imagine every corner of it being thoroughly searched. Yet any hiding place might be stumbled on by chance. It would be dangerous to use any space, such as a chimney, in which a fire might be lit. To move a section of wooden panelling and refix it to conceal a doorway seemed for a moment to be a good idea, but the big cities were already suffering from a shortage of fuel, and it was all too easy to imagine a mob breaking into the palace and making off with any wood they could find. Even the parquet floors were liable to be pulled up to be burned, so the spaces beneath those could not be considered safe either.

In his mind Fred explored the palace. There were dozens of rooms which he had never entered: but anywhere that could be lived in was bound to provide a home for someone before too long. He allowed his imagination to carry him down and down, and when at last he stood up it was to the cellars that he made his way.

They stretched under the whole extent of the building: a little estate of their own. Those which bordered the Moyka were dank and musty, unsuitable for storing pictures. Next to them was a range of windowless rooms in which were racked painted dinner services and etched glass, sufficient to serve an eleven-course meal to several hundred guests at a time. But these rooms, whatever the board outside might claim, would sooner or later be looted and stripped. He moved on.

He found the solution at last in a very large space devoted to wine. The looters had been here already – or perhaps it was only the servants who had thrown themselves a party before leaving. To judge by the mess, the orgy had ended with the throwing of bottles to smash against the walls. Most of the cellars were lined with bins and racks: but leading off one of them, up three narrow steps, was a small room containing nothing but a table and chair. Perhaps it had been provided for the cellarman to make a note of what he handed to the butler – although Fred's experience of the household made him doubt whether such a system had ever been operated.

The good thing about it was that no outsider would expect the room to be there. Its stone walls felt dry, and the steps would be helpful in building a false wall. Pleased with his success, Fred went back upstairs to report.

He had been right to expect that Prince Kristov would underestimate the time needed for the task he had in mind – and wise, too, to anticipate that it would not occur to a prince to provide himself with food. Luckily — for Fred's pack held only enough for two days — there were still some pickings to be found in the kitchens and storerooms, and a constant supply of wine made the work go merrily. Not without difficulty half a dozen heavy pictures were lowered, taken from their frames, carried down and stacked. Into the secret room also went valuable icons, two malachite urns which had been a gift from a Tsar, a gold dinner service moved from the strong room, two old rugs which the prince said were Persian and priceless, and some of the bulkiest pieces of silver table furniture: vases, salts, wine carriages and candelabra.

By the time he was ready to seal the room, Fred had discovered a basement workshop with a selection of materials needed for the repair and decoration of the palace. As someone who had done his apprenticeship in a motor car factory, he knew how to use his hands. There was no problem about making ready, but he could not unaided carry down slabs from the courtyard to build up the steps and construct a new wall.

When he went for help, the prince was nowhere to be seen. In such a labyrinth, there was little point in trying to look for him, so Fred made himself comfortable in the salon. Some people certainly had all the luck! Fancy being born into an inheritance like this. Just this one room was larger than the entire home of any ordinary family. Against the marble-covered walls stood pieces of furniture decorated with tortoiseshell and brass in a style which Fred recognised from Knaresborough Hall, although he had forgotten its name. From the painted ceiling hung enormous chandeliers, and even though the six most valuable pictures had been removed, there were plenty left. And the second piece of Prince Kristov's luck was that the notice outside seemed to have had some effect. Unlike the Moscow palace, whose treasures had disappeared, would-be squatters had been deterred from invading this one.

Time passed. Fred risked a look from the window and was appalled to see tell-tale footprints in the overnight snow which had settled on the ice. Had the man no sense? Or had their presence been discovered by someone else? Uneasily he waited.

10

When Prince Kristov at last returned he gave no explanation for his absence and a different kind of uneasiness invaded Fred's mind. Might his employer consider it unwise to have someone alive who knew where the Kristov treasures were concealed? Fred couldn't help remembering the story of that Tsar who had commissioned the building of St Basil's Cathedral in Moscow. He had been so delighted by the beauty and originality of the design that he had the architect blinded to prevent him ever repeating his masterpiece.

No, it was ridiculous to credit Prince Kristov with such deviousness: he wasn't clever enough. Shaking off his suspicion, Fred explained what help he needed and together the two men carried down large slabs of stone. The prince proved a clumsy labourer's mate and on one occasion allowed himself to be sworn at without showing any resentment. Perhaps he had still more favours in mind to ask.

The two hours which they spent straining and heaving together made an odd impression on Fred. He had no instinctive sympathy with the Bolsheviks. Although in England the contrast between prince and peasant, unimaginable wealth and desperate poverty, was not nearly as marked as in Russia, he had been born into a society divided into classes, and he saw nothing wrong with that. If there were no aristocrats, there would be no chauffeurs. Although he considered himself a skilled man, it was a fact that he had been in service for eight years: and for that situation to be tolerable it was necessary to believe that his employers were in some sense his superiors. Lord Knaresborough and Mr Vereker, Prince Alexis and Prince Kristov had all by the accident of birth earned the right to give him orders.

At least, that was what he had thought yesterday. But now, as he glanced at the filthy, breathless dunderhead obeying his instructions, his attitude changed. Fred was the competent master builder and the prince his unskilled apprentice.

He might have gone on from there to consider the unfairness of such wealth belonging to one of them and not the other; but instead his thoughts moved in a different direction. He had never quite been able to establish his position in relation to Laura. She, like himself, was a servant: their skills were different but equal. Yet he had never been able to shake off the knowledge that she was his social superior. Even when he was practically ordering her to leave Russia, he had felt deferential.

No longer! She was a woman and he was a man and he loved her and would make her love him. Who had he been trying to fool when he pretended that all he wanted was to protect her?

For a moment he was unable to work any longer, but pressed his body against the wall, overcome by desire.

'I can manage by myself now,' he said gruffly, and was as glad

90

to be alone again as the prince was to escape. For perhaps an hour he sat with his hands, numbed by cold, pressed into his groin as he rocked himself to and fro. But if ever he were to see Laura again, he must get this job finished. With renewed briskness he returned to work.

All the water in the palace was frozen. He hacked ice out of the fountain, melted it to mix a plaster, and then slapped the mixture over the closed doorway. Smoothing it to a professional standard was beyond him in such conditions – but no one would expect perfection in a cellar.

The plaster whitened as it dried: too clean, too new. He should have mixed some dirt with it. But that could be rubbed in afterwards – and for good measure, he would splash the area with wine until it was as badly stained as the rest of the wall. To finish the job he would move a rack in front of it. Exhausted and dishevelled, he returned to the salon.

Prince Kristov was filling an empty flour sack with treasure. The princess carried only a small selection of her most valuable jewels with her: he had retrieved the rest from her safe. To these, wrapping them quickly to prevent scratching and rattling, he was adding Fabergé ornaments, gold watches, silver photograph frames studded with diamonds – anything he could find which was both small and valuable. He looked up as Fred arrived.

'It's all done.' The 'sir' had gone the way of 'Excellency' now. 'Except for about an hour tomorrow morning, dirtying it up. Then we can get out of here.'

'Good. Thank you, Richards. My wife and daughters will be arriving on the train tomorrow. The horses and sledges will be waiting at the end of Ekateringofski Prospekt, ready to take us away as soon as it's dark. Let me show you where we're going.'

He led the way into a library, where a map was spread out on a desk. A line had been drawn from Petrograd to the Finnish frontier, some way north of the gulf.

'It's not the shortest route, but the Red Guards are likely to be watching near the coast. Now that the lakes are frozen, there'll be no problem taking the sledges across.'

Fred gave a casual nod. The Kristovs' escape route had nothing to do with him.

'We shall try to stay together, of course, but in case of emergency here is a compass for you; and here – ' he ringed a small town on the Finnish side of the border ' – would be our rendezvous.'

'What do I need a compass for?' asked Fred. 'I'm not coming with you.'

'Oh, but yes, naturally. Do you think we would leave you behind in this barbaric place?'

'Thanks for thinking of me, but I can get out legally, on a British passport. I've got a place booked on the Trans-Siberian.'

'But we need you with us, Richards.' The prince took only a second to abandon all pretence that the invitation was primarily for the chauffeur's own benefit. 'We shall have to take two sledges, and there's no one else I can trust to act as coachman.'

'You don't need two sledges for four people, not when two of them are children.' Fred too was abandoning pretence − in his case the pretence of respect.

'We must carry some of our possessions, if we are to keep alive afterwards. And there will be six, not four, besides yourself. Barsinova and her son will join us.'

'If I may say so − '

'He is my son also. I can't leave him behind.'

'His mother's genius is greatly respected. Under any regime she will be protected by her art.' The flowery phrases were a way of camouflaging Fred's genuine feeling of distaste. He was no saint: he needed women. There had been other girls beside Florrie in England, and a succession of maids and shop-girls in Russia. But a prince ought to have higher standards! It was dishonourable of him to ask his wife even to recognise the existence of her husband's mistress.

'In any case,' Fred added, 'I don't know anything about horses.'

'The horses will find their own path. All that's necessary is to set them in the right direction. But going over unknown territory, rough ground, there may be accidents. A sleigh which overturns will need two strong men to right it.'

'Sorry, but I can't help you. You didn't say anything about this in Moscow. I've done what I thought I came to do, and now I've got to get back.'

He had never expected the mysterious job to be completed in as short a time as he had been promised, but it had overrun even his own estimate. Although he still had a few days in hand, Laura would be getting worried. There was no reason why he should not tell the truth to explain his refusal.

'I've promised to act as Miss Laura's escort on the train,' he said. 'I can't let her down.'

Every thought of Laura now excited him; every mention of her name. He couldn't wait to get back, to see her again, to set off for safety and the beginning of a new life which surely she would

92

share with him. There was nothing the prince could possibly say which would shake his resolve.

'You may fetch yourself another sack.' The bribe was clearly stated. 'As much as you can carry is yours. You will be a rich man. You need never work again.'

It was a temptation. To be rich was Fred's ambition, and the loss of all his savings when the imperial currency became valueless had hit him hard. But he loved Laura more even than wealth, and if he abandoned her for the sake of a few Fabergé trinkets she would rightly despise him for the rest of her life.

'No,' he repeated. 'I'll finish off in the cellar tomorrow. And then I must get back to Moscow.'

The task of ageing the plaster next morning took longer then he had expected. By the time he had dirtied it and splashed wine over it and dragged an empty rack in front of it, the concealment was so successful that he took the precaution of scratching his initials down near the floor to help in some future identification. How long would it be, he wondered, before the hidden room was re-entered?

He was hungry now, as well as cold and dirty; but this seemed no time to hang around. He didn't really suppose that Prince Kristov would force him to make the journey to Finland by holding a pistol to his head, but all the same . . . Fred scribbled a quick note to say that the job was done and to wish the family well. Then he made his way towards the watergate.

The sound of voices startled him. Princess Kristova and her two daughters were approaching along the ice: in broad daylight and not even in silence. His heart pounded in alarm on their behalf as he opened the door, gestured to them to hurry, and hauled them up and inside one at a time.

'Where's your father?' he demanded of Sofiya, the last to climb in.

'He'll be here in a moment. There was someone on the street selling cabbages.' His alarm had infected her and her eyes were wide open and full of fear.

'We'll wait for him, then.' The door ought not to be left unbolted for a moment longer than was necessary.

Prince Kristov, like his family, seemed not to have realised the danger of being seen near the palace: and his luck had run out. As he raised his foot on to the lowest of the iron mooring hoops a shout rang out from the further side of the narrow canal. 'Looters!' There was the crack of a rifle shot, and another, followed by a thud.

Princess Kristova caught her breath and flung herself towards the broken window of the boatman's room. But Fred reached there first and, as she opened her mouth to scream, he put his hands across it, silencing her and pulling her down to the floor at the same time.

'Quiet!' he commanded – and, to the girls, 'Get down on the floor and keep still. If they realise that there's anyone here, they'll come and shoot us all.' Releasing the princess, who lay shuddering on the floor, he crawled back to the door and slid the bolts across. 'Follow me.' Still keeping below the level of the window, he prepared to lead the way out.

'We can't leave him there!'

'We must, until they've gone.'

'But he may still be alive.'

She was becoming hysterical. At any moment she would start to scream again. Already the two girls were crying, without understanding exactly what had happened. It was a struggle to get them all upstairs. In one of the inside rooms they could not be seen and probably could not be heard. He guarded the door, fighting against the princess as she struggled to get out, forcing her head to press into his shoulder to muffle her shrieks and moans, until suddenly he realised from her stillness and weight that she had fainted.

'Look after your mother while I see ...' He made his way quickly to one of the rooms overlooking the canal and moved a shutter to conceal his face as he peered down. The two soldiers who had shot a presumed looter were not averse to a little looting themselves. Standing over the prince's body, they were helping themselves to the frost-blackened cabbage which he had just bought, while blood stained the snow and his open eyes stared upwards. There could be no doubt that he was dead.

'I'm very sorry,' he said to the princess, after he had confirmed the sad news.

'We must bring his body in. The rites must be observed.'

'It's too dangerous.' Fred knew how much store the Russians set by their funeral services and the lying-in-state, but his sympathy didn't extend to getting himself shot. He prayed to God that there was nothing on the prince's body which would identify him as the owner of the palace. Princess Kristova, meanwhile, was saying other prayers of her own. Not liking to interrupt, Fred turned towards Sofiya.

'I have to return to Moscow, to leave with Miss Laura,' he said. 'Have you brought food with you?'

'Yes. But we can't stay here. And we don't know where to go.'

'I'll show you on the map.'

He turned to lead the way towards the library, but the fourteen-year-old did not follow.

'Mama isn't strong enough. None of us is. Papa said we'd all be killed if we stayed in Russia, that we'd got to get to Finland, but we can't manage on our own. Papa said you'd be coming with us.'

'No, that's not right. I told him I couldn't.'

'But you must! Please, please. We can't do it without you. We need you. We shall all die if you don't. Please.'

Her voice choked on the word, and Tanya was already weeping. Princess Kristov, white as the flour which dusted the sack of treasure, had risen to her feet. Unable to speak, she stared beseechingly in his direction.

Fred couldn't speak either. He was thinking of Laura. Laura waiting anxiously, wondering why he was so long delayed. Laura making her way to the railway station, upset and disappointed. Laura, alone as the train pulled out, bitter at betrayal. Love and desire flooded his veins, warming his body in the frozen city. If only there were some way in which he could explain. But she would never know. Probably he would die in some frontier forest and she would never understand why he had deserted her.

A small hand — it was Tanya's — slipped into his. It was a theatrical, sentimental gesture — except that of course it was sincere and unstudied, a child recognising her only hope of survival. He had no choice.

'Bloody hell!' he exclaimed. 'Bloody, bloody hell!'

11

Grunting with effort, and so slowly that a runner might still have caught up with it, the train had pulled away from the station. When Charles could no longer be seen, it was time for Laura to become acquainted with the strangers who would be her close — very close — companions for the next three weeks.

From the British mission in Moscow there were three wives. One of them was accompanied by her husband, Joseph Strang, a clerk in poor health. The American party from Petrograd also included two wives who were being sent home for their own safety, as well as the son and daughter of the Minister. Billy Lee Wright was only sixteen, but determined to play his part as one of the few men in the party. His eighteen-year-old sister, Helen — a pretty girl whose hair fell in long ringlets as neatly as though she had dressed for a ball — was by contrast ill at ease in a situation she did not like or understand.

Like guests at a party when the host has forgotten to provide refreshments, the nine travellers stood awkwardly in the small open space, putting up a steadying hand to the edge of a berth whenever the train jolted over points on its way out of Moscow. They introduced themselves in turn, and Mrs Strang immediately suggested that all food should be pooled in order that it could be cooked and distributed in a controlled manner. It was tacitly agreed that she had earned the right to take charge by her forethought — alone amongst the party — in providing a kettle and a stewpan.

After the flurry of handshakes, there was a silence as they all came to terms with the uncomfortable conditions in which they were travelling. There was not enough headroom between the berths to allow them to sit up, so that they had to choose between standing and lying on the hard wood. In Laura's case, the kokoshnik sewn into her corset meant that only when she was lying on her back could she find any comfort on the berth. However, Charles had sent a man to help her to the station with her luggage, so she had taken the risk of rolling two bearskin rugs inside ordinary blankets. If the Cheka boarded the train, the rugs might be confiscated; but she hoped that the heavily stamped diplomatic papers carried by most of the party would earn immunity from search. Once again Mrs Strang took charge, giving three of the nine at a time enough space to make up their berths by suggesting that the other six should stand in turn in the corridor.

Laura and Helen had berths on the same level, and were able to chat quietly. Anxious to establish an intimacy, Helen described how their father, when first posted to Russia, had left them behind because their mother was in poor health. They had travelled out to join him only after her death, arriving just before Kerensky took power. After describing the experiences in Petrograd which convinced him that they must return to their aunt in New York, she declared that it was her turn to ask questions.

'Who was the handsome young man who saw you off? Is he your beau?'

'Heavens, no.' Laura laughed. 'Just a friend. I knew him in England. When I met him again here, he was very helpful with my arrangements.'

'He seemed most attentive for just a friend.'

Laura considered the comment with interest. It was true that Charles's manner had been warm, even affectionate; and she herself had felt an unusual pleasure at encountering him again. But although they had corresponded, this was their first meeting for more than four years. And although he was working for his living, Charles's aristocratic background was so different from

96

Laura's that he was never likely to think of her as anything closer than a friend.

'No,' she repeated. 'Nothing more.'

'Then there must be someone else. Do tell me. We're going to become the greatest friends, you and I, and I shall tell you about all my beaux at home in Mississippi; but you must start.'

Helen's ingenuous prompting struck just the right note. For five years, as a governess, Laura had been treated with deference, by her employers as much as by her pupils, and the need to be responsible and businesslike had made her feel older than her age. A half-frivolous conversation, one young woman to another, was just what she needed to cheer her through the journey.

What was the true answer, though? Helen might have been more specific. Whom do you love? Who makes your heart break with happiness when he's with you and with sadness when he's away? Whose touch is it that robs you of breath? Who is it who makes your body ache with longing? Whose name, even spoken casually by a stranger, brings the blood flushing to your cheeks? The answer to any of those questions must be Alexis -- and, indeed, the very passage of his name through her thoughts made Laura blush.

'I knew it − there is someone!'

Laura shook her head. She meant nothing to Alexis, and so − even assuming that he was still alive − he must mean nothing to her. It was foolish to allow a schoolgirl's dream to linger for so long, misting her eyes and perhaps making it difficult to recognise a real suitor, to consider a future which was not impossible.

'Well,' she said slowly, 'I have another friend called David.'

'In England?'

'At the moment he's fighting in France. But yes, usually he lives in Oxford.'

David Hughes had been awarded the first-class degree which Dr Mainwaring had confidently predicted for him and had then been elected to a fellowship at All Souls College. He had interrupted his career by volunteering for the army, but as soon as the war was over he intended to return to Oxford to take up an appointment as a tutor. Probably he would become a professor one day. He was one of Laura's most regular correspondents, writing about Oxford, about books, about his life in college, about the events leading up to the war and the horrors after it had started. His letters contained no endearments − nothing personal at all, in fact. Nevertheless, Laura had felt for a long time that his reason for keeping in touch with her was so that they might be ready to develop a closer friendship when

97

she returned. She had answered his letters regularly and at an equal length.

'Will you marry him, Laura?' asked Helen. In the unusual circumstances of their meeting, they had moved to the use of Christian names straightaway.

'He's never suggested it.' But as though the young American were making a proposal on his behalf, Laura suddenly felt quite sure that he would one day. And if he did, what would she say?

'I remember, when I was your age,' she told Helen now, 'I was full of romantic dreams. I wanted to travel, have adventures. The idea of getting married and settling down in the place where I'd been living all my life seemed too dull for words. As though I'd simply be living my mother's life all over again. But now . . .'

'I guess you must feel that you've had your share of adventures.'

'Or that it would be nice to have someone to look after me.' There had been a thread of loneliness running through all those years in Russia. She had never been alone. There had always been company and friendship — and in the case of her two pupils, even love — but never anyone to whom she was of special value.

'And who else is there?' asked Helen. 'If you're not prepared to count Mr Vereker.'

'Why should there be anyone else?'

'You must always have two. So that the one you choose knows that he's been chosen.'

'How very experienced you are! Well, I suppose there might be Gerard. A French friend of mine.' Gerard had returned hurriedly to France after the accident which caused her father's death. But his mother had insisted that he must not cut himself off from the orphaned girl, and his first letter of deep regret and abject apology had been followed by others which were lighter in tone.

'Was he the one you were looking out for at the station?'

It startled Laura to realise that her anxiety on Fred's behalf had been noticed, and she was unsure how best to answer. That anxiety had been based on trust. It was because she had been so sure that Fred would keep his promise that the only possible reason for his non-appearance had seemed to be his death. But when she thought about it more soberly she realised that Charles's explanation might be right. Money was the most important thing in Fred's life, and the prospect of wealth would undoubtedly override a pledge given to a mere governess. There was no point in troubling herself further about Fred.

'No,' she said; and the abruptness of the monosyllable brought the conversation to a close. Only after an hour or two did Helen speak again.

'Laura, I can't wait any longer. I simply must – ' She gestured in the direction of the toilet bucket. 'Would you screen me?'

Laura could understand her embarrassment, but suspected that this was something they would all have to learn to ignore, for there were berths on three sides.

'I'll do what I can,' she agreed. 'You could put your skirt over the bucket.'

'Billy, you're not to look,' commanded Helen. This had the unintended effect of drawing everyone's attention, and her cheeks reddened as she swung her legs down to the floor. How often, Laura wondered, would they be able to empty and clean the bucket. This was not going to be the most pleasant journey in the world.

It was certainly one of the longest, and new discomforts revealed themselves daily. A grimy dust from the engine smoke penetrated even the closed doors of the wagon and settled on skin and clothes and every possible surface. There was so little clean water that it was reserved for drinking. Only when the train stopped at a station was it possible to dash out for the boiling water which was usually available and make a hasty attempt to clean faces and hands. In happier days, food too had always been offered from station platforms, but now this was not always the case, and on some days rations were meagre. The two stoves in the corridor heated the air just sufficiently by day, but at night the temperature became colder and colder as the train crossed the Urals and began the long haul across Siberia.

For days on end there were no forests to break the monotony; only the seemingly endless snow-covered steppes. Laura's eyes throbbed from the glare, her body ached with stiffness and her stomach was turned by the stench which filled the compartment. Not even Mrs Strang's efforts at organisation could overcome the insanitary conditions in which they were forced to live. And throughout the journey Mr Strang coughed and coughed until it seemed that his lungs must be in shreds. The others wound scarves tightly across their mouths in the hope of escaping the sick man's germs.

They found themselves with unwanted fellow-passengers, left aboard after earlier journeys – although it might have been expected that the cold would have killed all insect life. Helen and Laura, finding their long hair infested, took it in turns to give each other a trim. Their inexperience and the small size of Helen's nail scissors produced jagged effects, and their attempts to remedy this led to much shorter cuts than they intended. But it would grow again, they assured themselves, and for the time being they combed

99

their cropped heads clear of intruders and wrapped scarves round their newly-exposed necks.

There were many unexplained stops. So long were the distances between stations that fuel must be taken on from railside stores. At those times all the passengers needed to be on alert, for ex-convicts who had been released from imprisonment with no legal means of returning to their homes were known to make for the railway line. On at least two occasions the Siberian Red Guards boarded the train and interrogated every male aboard, looking for ex-officers and carrying out a thorough search for weapons. Laura, conscious of the weight of the diamonds in the swinging hem of her skirt, and the bulge of the jewels concealed in her corset, was alarmed lest even the persons of foreign women might be searched. But young Billy Lee Wright stood manfully in the entrance to the compartment, whilst Laura herself, the only one of the nine who spoke Russian, made an equally forceful claim on behalf of all of them to diplomatic privilege.

On they travelled, through Omsk and Irkutsk, round Lake Bakail, to Chita and Khabarovsk. All the fifty-four passengers in the long wagon took it in turns to spend half an hour standing in front of one of the two windows. By day the snow glittered more brightly than the diamonds which had once sparkled round Princess Kristova's neck; but Laura's favourite time was sunset, when the sky blazed like a bonfire with flames of scarlet and yellow before the black clouds of night extinguished them.

By now the train was moving at no more than fifteen versts an hour and the station stops were so lengthy that it was possible for the passengers to take exercise on the ground and breathe the pure, transparent air, as long as some of their number remained on board to guard their accommodation. There was more variety in the faces of the would-be passengers or pedlars who thronged the platforms — Mongolians and Chinese as well as Cossacks, Siberians and Russians. More variety too in the food on offer: roast snipe, hard biscuits, local cheeses and sometimes eggs.

After the monotony of the steppes, forests of fir and silver birch once again provided a more interesting landscape. Laura, returning with a chilled nose from a short spell near the window, laughed aloud as she settled back into her place in the compartment.

'What is it?' asked Helen, who during the past week had been made so miserable by the dirt and foul smell that she could hardly be persuaded to move from her berth.

'I was just remembering how I was teased once, before I ever arrived in the country, because my picture of Russia was of snow

100

and forests and wolves and bears. And I was quite right, for here it all is.'

Helen sighed. 'How much longer?' She had been marking off the days with her scissors. There were twenty-three scratches already on the edge of her berth. Laura did not reply; she was growing apprehensive, and reluctant to reveal it. The train was running late. Would the boat wait? At least now they were steaming southwards again, which meant that they must have rounded the intruding finger of Manchuria.

On the twenty-fifth day after their departure from Moscow the train began to travel even more slowly than before. Laura rushed to the window where Billy politely ceded his place so that she could look out. They had arrived at Vladivostock. In full view ahead was the great harbour in which five naval ships flying British, American and Japanese flags lay at anchor. But it was a sixth vessel which caught her eye and made her cry out with delight. That, surely, must be a passenger ship, the *Estella*, for it was flying the blue ensign.

In the relief of recognising her own country's flag, Laura made herself a promise. There were to be no more romantic dreams. She had been lucky enough to be born in one of the most beautiful cities in the world, in a law-abiding country, powerful enough to protect its citizens wherever they might be. She was proud and happy to be British. When at last she reached home, she would have to plan one more journey, to keep her rendezvous with the Kristovs and hand over their jewels. It was likely that she would need to postpone her visit until the war had ended. But once that duty was performed, she would be glad to spend the rest of her life peacefully in Oxford: in England.

12

Oh, the relief of it! To be on a British ship, to hear English voices all around, to breathe pure air – and, above all, to feel in safe hands for the first time in many months.

Cabins must be shared, they were told, but to have a single companion was no hardship after the communal life of the past weeks. Laura's cabin-mate proved to be Helen, who had already become a friend. The two young women hugged each other in delight at the discovery that they would still be travelling together.

'There are showers!' Helen announced. 'Lordy, what will it feel like to be clean again! We are *disgusting*! I've been wearing a layer

101

of dirt like an extra set of underclothes. Guess I'll catch my death of cold when it's all scraped off.'

Even as she spoke she was unbuttoning her outer clothes which fell in a crumpled pile round her feet. Unlike Laura, who had taken seriously the official prohibition on travelling in Russia with more than a single change of clothing, each of the American diplomatic party had brought a cabin trunk from Petrograd and had it loaded on to a goods wagon of the train. Helen now pulled a light summer cape from her trunk and tossed it towards Laura.

'You can use this as a robe. After you're clean.'

'Thank you.' It seemed a long time since she was last able to worry about decency. Laura took the cape and a large bath towel and made her way to the shower room which consisted of a row of double cubicles with metal walls. The outer section of each was furnished with a bench and a row of hooks; the inner one with a shower head, soap tray and piece of duckboard over a drain in the floor.

Bleak as it looked, it was all Laura needed. While the *Estella* lay in harbour the tanks were filled with fresh water and it was warm. Working the soap to a lather, she scrubbed herself down, rinsed off and washed from head to foot a second time. What bliss it was to be clean again! She was tempted to indulge in yet a third soaping, but it was part of the luxury to realise that she would be able to wash whenever she chose now. After rubbing her hair and body dry, she twisted the bath towel into a sarong, fastened the cape above it and, holding her dirty clothes at arms length, returned to the cabin.

Helen had not yet returned from the showers. Her discarded clothes still lay in a pile on the floor, filling the cabin with the ammoniac smell of the train. Laura pushed them into a corner with her foot, and took advantage of the full space of the cabin. Quickly she dressed in her clean − although crumpled − clothes. She would have preferred to throw away her filthy undergarments, but that would leave her unable to change her clothes again until she reached America and could go shopping. So instead she bundled everything washable into one of the ship's laundry bags − except for the corset which held the pieces of the kokoshnik. This for the moment she pushed into a drawer which could be locked, and hung the key around her neck.

Her heavy winter skirt was beyond any hope of cleaning. Bloodstains spoke of the difficulty she had had in coping with her monthly period with no privacy or washing materials, and in one place the material was charred almost to a hole where she had brushed against a brazier. For nearly a month she had had to stand or walk on a floor awash with urine, and there had been additional accidents when the train stopped suddenly, swirling the contents of the toilet bucket out and over the nearest bystander. The stench was appalling. She had almost ceased to notice it while she was aboard the train; but now that she was clean the idea of ever wearing the garment again was insupportable.

The first thing to do was to remove the diamonds from their hiding place in the hem, and for that she would need to borrow the scissors with which Helen had cut her hair. For the moment, until her friend returned, she hung the skirt up on the back of the cabin door, rather than allow it to pollute the small amount of wardrobe space which they were allowed. While she still had the cabin to herself she took the opportunity to stare at her reflection in a small mirror which was mounted to the wall.

It was the first time for twelve years that she had seen herself with short hair, and for a moment she felt as though she were fourteen years old again. Vigorous towelling had flushed her pale cheeks with bright pink patches, like those of a doll. Without the coiled plaits to frame it, her face looked ridiculously small and childlike. Her chestnut hair, still damp, hung straight down at each side, although the ends were beginning to turn under as they dried. It was too short, barely reaching the bottom of her ears. She began to laugh at herself, as though she were looking at a picture.

A shudder vibrated through the cabin. The engines had started. It must mean that they were about to sail. Pulling on her shuba, Laura hurried out of the cabin and on to the deck.

It was not suprising that she felt emotional at leaving the country in which she had spent five years of her life, most of them happy. It was a beautiful country. She had loved its immense spaciousness – the snowfields and above all the great birch forests which stretched for miles and miles and miles. She had loved its contrasts – between the grim, grey townscape of Moscow and the sunny, sweetly scented gardens and woods of the Crimean peninsula: between the opulent formality of the social season in the elegant capital and the casual chaos of the country houses.

Most of all she had loved St Petersburg in the days when it was still St Petersburg. The rich colours of town houses reflected in summer in the water of the rivers and canals, and the more subtle colours of the winter ice and snow at different times and by different lights: moonlight, sunlight, lamplight. The golden spires and the domes so perfectly shaped that they seemed to have been stroked into their curves. The harsh, sad sounds of singing which echoed through churches hazy with incense and glittering with icons.

All that was slipping away from her now as the *Estella* moved slowly along the channel cut by the ice-breakers, gliding out of the harbour, between the islands and into the bay. The wind grew colder as the ship left shelter and began to pick up speed. Laura shivered and crossed her arms over her chest to keep warm, but was not ready yet to move away. She could still see on the horizon a range of distant mountains which at first looked purple and then faded to grey and at last sank behind a hazy blue mist.

So it was gone. It was unlikely that she would ever return to Russia. All she could do was to treasure her memories and hope that at some time in the future she would meet some of her Russian friends again.

Alexis. Was Alexis still alive? So many officers had been shot by their men in mutiny or executed for being of the nobility. How could she dare to hope that he had escaped? Yet just because so many of these deaths had been reported, there could be hope as long as his name appeared on no list. She must hope. The thought of Alexis — carefree, laughing Alexis — lying in the mud of a battlefield with a bullet through his brain was unendurable.

As for the others — Sofiya and Tanya and their parents — how confidently could she expect that they would succeed in making their escape? Almost every week the Red Guards had claimed to have killed a new batch of enemies of the state attempting to flee the country, and perhaps the claims were true. But from messages which filtered through it was known that a number of the refugees had reached Finland safely. Why should the Kristovs be any less fortunate than their friends? They would all meet again in a happier time and place.

The wind by now was bitingly cold and there was nothing to be seen except water. Laura hastened back to the warmth of the cabin and found that once again it was empty. Helen must have been and gone, for her discarded clothes no longer lay on the floor. The steward, too, had been in attendance. The sheets of the two berths were turned down and the laundry bag had been removed.

Helen had left her toilet bag on one of the narrow shelves and would surely not mind if her scissors were borrowed. But when Laura closed the cabin door in order to attack the skirt she had hung on its hook, her heart bumped with panic. The garment was not there.

It must have been stolen. The cabin door had not been locked. Anyone could have come inside and made off with it. Fumbling with anxiety, Laura unlocked the drawer to make sure that the kokoshnik at least was safe. And the ship was already moving when she had left the cabin, so the thief and the skirt must still be on board. She was doing her best to soothe away her panic, but it was hard to keep calm.

Why should anyone decide to steal a disgustingly filthy garment? No one could have known that a fortune was concealed in it: she had never mentioned the diamonds. Of course! she realised. It must be the steward who had taken it away. Collecting the laundry bag and noticing the stench of the skirt he could reasonably have assumed that it had been left out of the wardrobe for cleaning. Yes, that must be it. She went at once in search of him.

Fifteen minutes later, numbed by more than cold, she returned to the cabin. The steward had agreed that he could have hardly have been unaware of the presence of the skirt on the door and the pile of clothes on the floor, but he had taken only the bag and left everything else as he found it.

Helen had returned and was brushing her wind-swept hair into tidiness. Clearly she too had been up on deck. She turned, smiling, as Laura came in.

'My, but you're pale. Have you seen a ghost out there?'

'My skirt has been stolen.'

'Stolen? *That*? Oh, come on! Don't look so shocked. I've got another outfit ready for you here. You're a trace taller than I am, of course, but skirts are being worn shorter nowadays.' There was a navy blue skirt lying on the lower berth: she picked it up and held it to Laura's waist.

'I want my own. Helen, are you saying ...? Do you know something about it?'

'I know all about it. I threw it out, with all my own stuff. Grand gesture, to mark our freedom from confinement. Lordy, Laura, we couldn't ever have worn them again. The smell when I came back into the cabin!'

'Yes, I know, but I must have it. Where did you take it?' Her mind raced ahead of the answer. If it had been sent down for incineration, would diamonds survive a furnace, and how could they ever be recovered?

'I threw it overboard.'

'You did what?' Laura's legs would no longer support her. She collapsed backwards on to the berth, hardly able to believe what she had heard.

'I threw it over. Only because I knew I'd got something else to give you instead. I wouldn't have left you ... Oh my goodness, Laura, have I done something wrong?'

'How could you?' Laura's fists were pressed against her teeth, so that her words could hardly be heard. 'You had no right – mine – how dared you?' By now tears were streaming down her face.

'Laura, honey, don't cry. Tell me what I've done. I felt in the pocket. Was there something else, something hidden?'

'Didn't you stop to think?' demanded Laura, her misery fuelled by fury. 'Living as anyone with any money at all has been living in Russia, needing to make provision for the future, travelling when at any moment we might all have been robbed — probably everyone on that train was carrying some kind of reserve, and not talking about it. Didn't any of that even occur to you?'

'No,' said the girl, crestfallen. 'Billy looked after all that. Laura, I'm so sorry. We'll be responsible. For all your travel costs home, everything you need. How much was it?'

Laura shook her head hopelessly. What was the point of burdening the young American with a truthful answer, when she could never hope to replace a fortune in diamonds.

'Too much,' was all she said. 'Not mine, you see. I was carrying it for someone else.'

'Oh, Laura! What can I do?'

'Just leave me alone.' She waited until the cabin door closed and then threw herself along the berth, burying her face in the pillow. She was more angry than she had ever been in her life before, but by now the anger was directed at herself. She should never have let the diamonds out of her sight. She had been trusted to guard them, and had broken her trust. The Kristovs would escape and make their way to Paris, confident that she would meet them there with the treasure they had entrusted to her. Would they have enough to live on without this part of their fortune? Would they believe the story of what had happened, or suspect her of making off with the diamonds herself? Could she bear to face them and see the suspicion and dismay in their eyes?

Yes, she must do that, because otherwise she would seem to confirm their suspicions. And some kind of restitution must be offered. Not in money: that would be impossible. But she could work for them. As a housekeeper, perhaps, asking no wages — or earning a wage herself and bringing it back to help support the household.

This was not how she had envisaged spending the rest of her life, but it was impossible for her simply to walk away from the disaster. Only by coming to a conclusion of this kind could she avoid a lifetime of guilt. By the time she stood up again, smoothing down her crumpled clothes, her eyes were dry and her mind resolved.

Helen's offer to help with her travel costs could be accepted, and that would enable the jewels and the gold roubles which she had been given for her own support to be kept for the future. She would need a little time to rest in England; to look up Aunt Barbara and the friends with whom she had been corresponding; and to have new clothes made. Then, as soon as the war ended and ordinary travel became possible again, she would be ready to keep the rendezvous in Paris, to make apologies and offer her services.

After all, she would not arrive there entirely empty-handed. There was another reason why she must go to Paris: to hand over the kokoshnik.

Part Three

A Proposal of Marriage
1918

Oxford, like St Petersburg, was a city built on a marsh. As the first rays of the summer sunshine broke through the clouds, a white mist rose from the placid surface of the river, stroking the muddy banks and rippling over the towpath like an incoming tide. Leaning over Folly Bridge, Laura sighed to herself with enjoyment of the peace and stillness of the scene. She did not look up even when she heard footsteps approaching and slowing to a halt behind her.

'Laura! Oh Laura, will you marry me?' exclaimed David Hughes.

She spun round so quickly that she almost overbalanced, but David's hands gripped her elbows to steady her. He was in uniform — the uniform of an army officer. Would she have recognised him, she wondered, had they passed on the street without warning? It was five years since they had last met. David, still an undergraduate at that time, had been confident of his intellectual ability but socially unsure of himself in a university where few of his contemporaries had to worry about money and the need to earn a living. It had been a world in which most men were tall and confident, but he was small and unassertive. She had not, if she were to be honest with herself, paid much attention to him.

What a difference she saw in him now! The uniform made his body appear sturdier than before, and he even looked taller, perhaps because he held himself better. There was no longer any sign of the uncertainty she had once recognised in his eyes; the doubts about whether he should push himself forward. There was another change as well. His black hair was cut short and he was of course wearing a cap, but she could see a streak of white hair at the end of the scar which cut across his left temple. A great deal had happened to each of them in the past five years, but David must still be in his twenties. A young man. A young man in love.

This meeting was not, of course, accidental. Laura had written to tell him that after her journey round the world she was back in England and staying with her aunt. A second letter, in June, had mentioned a forthcoming visit to one of her school friends in Oxford. David had arranged this rendezvous as soon as he knew that he was coming home on leave. So she had no reason to be surprised at seeing him. But that he should open the conversation with a proposal of marriage could certainly not have been expected.

'Yes, I know.' David was reading her thoughts. 'Last time we actually spoke to each other we were Miss Mainwaring and Mr Hughes. But your letters ... I can't tell you how much your letters have meant to me, Laura. I feel I know you better than if we'd spent the past five years in each other's company. I realise that I should have worked up to this gradually, but I've only got a few days in England. There wouldn't be time. If you'll only say yes at once, I can get a special licence and go back to France a married man. A happy man. I love you, Laura. Please – oh, let's go down.'

Taking her by the hand, he led her across the bridge to the steps which led down to the towpath. There, out of sight of passers-by, he could kiss her. But even as he began to draw her into his arms, Laura put out a hand to keep him at his distance.

'David, wait a moment. I need to think.'

'But I need to show you that I love you.'

Her wish to hold him off was not strong enough, although he was not – like Alexis once – trying to sweep her off her feet by the force of his passion. Why should she think of Alexis now? Even were he still alive, he had no place in her life. David's was a loving kiss: the kiss of a man who would care for her, look after her. Only a few weeks earlier she had dreamed of exactly this kind of secure future with a husband she could care for and respect. That, though, was before she had lost the diamonds.

'David, I'm sorry, terribly sorry, but I can't rush things like that,' she said, breaking away from him. 'I have responsibilities – left over from Russia. Things I must do in Paris as soon as the war is over.'

'Couldn't you do them as a married woman?'

She shook her head. 'No, and I don't know how long it will take.'

The Kristovs were by nature generous. They might be grateful for what she had rescued and forgive her for what she had lost and send her back to England to pick up her own life again. But that must be their choice: it could not be hers.

'I could wait for weeks – months if necessary – as long as I knew you were coming back to me.'

'But it could be years.' She had promised herself that she would support them if necessary. Had the promise been to anybody else she could have asked for a release, but her own conscience was a strict taskmaster.

To hold to that decision was no easy matter. When Alexis had kissed her, her romantic yearnings for a first experience of love had been over-ruled by the common sense which was a stronger element in her character. But the love which David had to offer – married love, the love of a dependable man with, in peacetime, a congenial way of life – was exactly what the sensible side of herself had been waiting for.

'What is this mysterious responsibility?' David asked gently.

It was tempting to tell him – to hear him assure her that no one could possibly blame her for what had happened, that the family had almost certainly smuggled out other valuables themselves, even that the rule of the Bolsheviks would prove to be only temporary and the old regime would soon be restored. There was no real need to keep what had happened a secret. What made her reluctant to answer was the suspicion that in revealing the truth she would make him feel that she was balancing his love against a debt of money and deciding that it did not weigh heavily enough. She shook her head helplessly.

'Another man?'

'Oh, no. No one else.' This time she was successful in keeping Alexis out of her thoughts.

'Well, in that case . . .' He took her hand and they began to walk side by side along the towpath. 'I'm sorry I rushed you. I hoped . . . But I do see that I'm a stranger in a way. These five days of mine. May we spend them together? Here, where we were both happy once. And at the end of them, before I leave, I'll ask you again. When you've had more time to think about it. If you would agree just to be engaged, that would be something.'

'It wouldn't be fair. To tie you up in that sort of way when I might never be able . . .'

'Don't let's talk about it any more now. Except that I'd like to say one thing. It's not much fun over there at the front. Easy to get depressed and start wondering whether anything's worth while. Men take the wrong sort of risks because they've given up caring whether they get home safely or not. What each of us needs – and we all know it – is a reason to survive. Someone to come home to. All you girls on the home front, you have a responsibility to keep

110

someone happy. I'd like *your* responsibility to be me, that's all.'

He was smiling now: a friendly, light-hearted smile. 'Come on. No more dawdling.' He squeezed her hand tightly and they continued their walk at a brisker pace.

'You've cut off all your beautiful hair,' he commented when they paused later to rest.

Laura explained the circumstances, describing the dirt of her long journey across Siberia. 'I started to grow it again when I reached America. But it felt so odd after having it short.'

While resting for a few days with Helen's aunt in New York she had visited a proper hairdresser, who tut-tutted at the untidy line left by the nail scissors and then trimmed it so that the ends turned under, level with the bottom of her ears. Although, as she soon learned after her return to England, many factory girls had started to wear their hair short so that it should not catch in machines, hers still attracted looks in the street.

'It saves me an hour a day,' she laughed now. 'Brushing and plaiting. And don't tell me that I look like a Dutch doll, because I've heard that from all my nieces.'

'You look very young,' David told her. 'And very pretty.' Then he seemed to remind himself that he must not spend the whole of his leave courting her. 'Tell me about the revolution,' he said instead. 'When I come back to Oxford I shall be teaching history. Writing books about it, perhaps. One tends to think of it as something that's over and done with, just waiting there to be studied by people who never experienced it. It's an odd feeling to realise that of course what we're living through today is what will be in the history books tomorrow. I'm an eye-witness of the war, though I might prefer not to be. And you're an eye-witness of the Russian revolution.'

'There's something else that's odd,' Laura said. 'Everyone in England talks of "the revolution"; but there were two. One of them was a revolution against the other.' She described what she knew about Kerensky's movement and Lenin's.

'That must partly explain what's happening in the civil war,' David suggested.

'Civil war?' In the past few weeks, as she travelled on visits to all her friends, she had ceased to keep track of events in Russia. In her aunt's house hung a large map of Europe over which her uncle moved different coloured pins. She had arrived there to find the German pins sweeping forward in a manner which left the household alarmed and depressed, although the need to acquire a new colour to represent American troops had provided a moment of cheer. But the Russian front had collapsed soon after she left the country. The Crimea, in

111

which she had spent so many happy months, was now in German occupation, and her understanding was that fighting had stopped: Russia was no longer at war.

'It all sounds chaotic,' David told her. 'Lenin and Trotsky have a Red Army. Kerensky has raised an anti-Bolshevik army in Siberia. I believe most of his men are Czechs who were prisoners of war and due to be released from Vladivostock, but presumably he's hoping to pick up local support as well. Then there's a Tsarist Army somewhere in the Ukraine, which is against both of them. Now we — the British — are sending a force to Murmansk to stop it falling into German hands.'

Laura pondered on this latest piece of news and on the anarchy she had come to know so well. How could the Bolsheviks survive with three different forces ranged against them? It must surely mean that the Tsar would be able to reassert his authority and make it safe for the nobility to return to their old homes. Perhaps, after all, it would not be necessary for her to devote any more of her life to the service of the Kristovs.

This was not a hope to be put into words, and she did her best to dampen her optimism. But she could not prevent it from affecting her attitude to David and her answer to the question which she knew he would ask on their last day together.

'I love you,' he said when that time came. 'I want you to be my wife. And I'm not going to leave any loophole for you to express doubts. If you'll agree to an engagement, starting from today, then we could agree that in twelve months from now, if we're not yet married, either of us would have the right to withdraw. I mean to say, obviously an engagement can be broken at any time; but this would be an appointment, almost, at which we could talk the situation out. There might be disappointment on one side, but there wouldn't be any reproaches or hard feelings. Will you do that? Tell me now that you'd like to marry me as soon as you feel free, and that you'll let me know, without waiting to be asked again, if that moment arrives. I'd never hold you against your will: you know that. But it would mean such a lot to me to go back with your promise. Say yes, Laura. Please.'

She had had five days to think about it, and still had not managed to come to a reasoned answer. Most girls were married long before they reached the age of twenty-six. They knew about marriage, about love, in a way that she didn't.

Alexis, who would be an impossible husband, had aroused in her a passionate yearning for his touch, his kiss; making her body ache with the desire to surrender to his and be swept away — as he

112

had laughingly promised — like the surge of a wave or the wind in the trees.

David, who would be an ideal husband, did not excite her in the same way. But she liked him. No, more than that: she thought she loved him. In a calmer, more friendly manner; that was the only difference. The question she couldn't resolve was whether those two kinds of love ever came together. Was it possible to be at the same time — and with the same man — a contented wife and a passionate lover? She simply didn't know the answer.

It was settled, in the end, by the appeal in David's dark eyes. She couldn't let him go back to the front not knowing that she was so fond of him, even though it was a love too calm to sweep her into the marriage he desired.

'Yes, David,' she said. 'You have my promise.'

Part Four

Laura in Paris
1919—1930

1

Did the Parisians, like the Londoners, dance in the streets on Armistice Day? Did church bells ring and bonfires blaze as the war which had taken so many lives came at last to an end? If there had been celebrations in November, no trace of the rejoicing was to be observed when Laura arrived in the city in the first week of January, 1919, after a Christmas spent with her young cousins. The streets were dirty and the people who walked them were shabby: the atmosphere was one of mourning rather than triumph.

But that applied only to the public areas. When she stepped through the doors of the Café de la Victoire on the evening of her arrival in Paris it was as though the years of hardship had never been. Behind its curtained windows and almost anonymous entrance, polished silver and clusters of wine glasses sparkled on immaculate tablecloths. She had come early, before any diners had arrived; but not too early to be confronted with baskets piled high with dessert fruit, glass-domed trolleys laden with a variety of cheeses, trays on which half a dozen types of bread were arranged in geometric patterns and an ice sculpture surrounded by a still life of lobsters and shellfish. For more than two years, in both Russia and England, she had endured rationed and poor quality food, but it seemed that in Paris the rich at least could enjoy whatever they chose.

Although neatly dressed, she knew her clothes to be unsuitable for such a restaurant – and in any case, no lady would arrive unaccompanied to dine. She needed to put her enquiry swiftly to the *maître d'hôtel* before he informed her that if she was looking for work she must use some other entrance. He raised his eyebrows at the question, but answered politely enough.

114

'Prince Kristov? No, mademoiselle, he has not been here for many years.'

Although Laura had tried to prepare herself for this answer, the certainty with which it was pronounced chilled her heart. Yet what else could she have expected? Although she might assume, or at least hope, that the family had managed to reach Finland in safety a year earlier, where could they have gone after that, with the Germans on the offensive across Europe and Finland itself soon to close its frontiers to contain its civil war? Laura herself had been forced to wait until several weeks after the Armistice before embarking on the rough Channel crossing and the cold train journey.

'I was hoping that there might be a message for me here,' Laura told him. 'It was an arrangement made a year ago in Moscow, in a time of great trouble.'

The *maître d'hôtel* had already inspected the tables and studied his list of reservations and so now − perhaps moved by her pale face and obvious distress − was willing to spare her a few moments.

'Indeed I understand, mademoiselle. You should speak to *le patron*. He's here always after the opera. He may have received a letter from your friends. I suggest you return later in the evening.' He did not need to tell her in so many words that she could not afford to eat in his establishment.

'Yes. Thank you. Perhaps you could tell me, though − have many of your Russian customers from before the war returned here?'

'To Paris, yes. To dine here − well, now it is on special occasions, not regularly. Tonight, for example, Count Beretsky entertains eleven of his friends to celebrate the birth of his son.'

'Count Beretsky? Why, he's a close friend of Prince Kristov!' That he had once proposed marriage to Laura was not something to be mentioned. 'Perhaps he will have some news.'

'He also should be here if you return in three hours. The Russians dine late. And the English, early,' he added − for at that moment a group of half a dozen men appeared in the doorway. Laura, recognising that she must not keep him from his duties, turned towards the door herself; but then paused as she heard her name called.

'Laura! What are you doing in Paris?' It was Charles Vereker, whom she had last seen on the station platform in Moscow.

'I might ask the same of you.' She took his outstretched hands, smiling with pleasure at the encounter.

'We're all here for the peace conference. Feeding Mr Lloyd George with facts and figures − ammunition to stand up against M. Clemenceau. And writing innumerable papers. Come and join us for dinner.'

115

'I can't do that. I'm not dressed.'

'Then I shall abandon the others. Hold on a moment.'

'But Charles ...' She did not press her protest, for he had already gone, and she had been wondering earlier how best to pass the next three hours on her own.

He was back within a few seconds, offering his arm and hesitating only briefly before deciding where they could find a less pretentious place to eat.

He chose a small restaurant in the same street, and began to question her as soon as they had given their orders.

'I'm hoping to meet the Kristovs here,' Laura explained. 'We had a kind of rendezvous. Not for any particular time, just for a place – the Café de la Victoire. Is something wrong, Charles?' His expression, until then full of the pleasure of seeing her, had become grave.

'Bad news, I'm afraid.'

'Alexis?' She was hardly able to speak his name.

'No, no. I've heard nothing about Alexis. But his brother was killed a year ago in Petrograd. Shot as a looter. Ironic, really. He was trying to get into the Kristov palace. If anyone had recognised him as its owner, he'd have been shot for that instead.'

'A year ago! You mean that they never left Russia at all?'

'I don't know about the rest of the family. That's not to say ... I mean, I've had no reason to enquire. They could well have escaped and be living quietly somewhere.'

'And Fred Richards? Did he ever turn up?'

'Not while I was in Moscow. I hope for his sake that he got out somehow. I don't imagine the British are very popular these days, since the Intervention and the blockade. My own guess is that he's sitting on a small fortune somewhere. Probably under another name, in case the true owners ever arrive to claim it. There's a second tragedy building up here in Paris, you know, Laura.'

'For the Russians, you mean?'

'Yes. If Princess Kristova did manage to escape in time, she'll find herself just one of a whole community of exiles. All believing that they're going to get back one day. But nearly all, in the meantime, beginning to wonder where their next meal will come from. A few of them managed to think ahead. But there are quite a lot who were out of the country when the war began – just taking their usual holiday in Biarritz or Cannes or Carlsbad – and haven't been able to get their hands on any of their fortunes since then. If you meet any of them here, you'll find a brave show on the surface, but real hunger

116

and real despair beneath. Still, enough of that. Are you planning to stay? Where are you living?'

Even to Charles Laura did not mention the kokoshnik which she had brought to Paris with her and had immediately deposited in the strong room of a bank; but she did explain her hope of making contact with the Kristovs.

'I've no job in England,' she confessed. 'So I might as well look for something here while I'm waiting to find out what's happened to them. I haven't got an address yet, though.' She had no intention of spending long in her present hotel. 'There's a family, friends of my father's, who had me to stay when I was a girl, and I'd hoped that I might be able to lodge with them. I wrote to say I was coming, but didn't get a reply — and when I went to their apartment this afternoon I found it wasn't there any more and nor were they. The professor has died and his son hasn't been demobilised yet and Mme Duval herself went to live in Normandy after the apartment was hit by a shell from Big Bertha. But it won't take long to find somewhere.'

'If I can't contact you, you must keep in touch with me, let me know where you are,' said Charles. 'The whole of the British delegation is staying at the Majestic, and we have offices in the Astoria. I might be able to get you some work. There are all sorts of papers which have to be translated. I imagine you're pretty well bi-lingual French-English, aren't you?'

'Yes. And a little German and Russian as well.' How the day was looking up! Earlier she had been depressed by the dowdiness of Paris, by her inability to contact the Duvals and by the news that the Kristovs had not yet kept their rendezvous. None of that had changed but Charles had the knack of making everything seem simple. Suddenly light-hearted, she felt the cares which had weighed so heavily on her mind slip away. Shabby or not, Paris was still a city which filled her with excitement; and until the princess arrived there would be no need to confess to the loss of the diamonds. Her eyes sparkled with gaiety as she allowed herself to enjoy the evening, leaving the future to take care of itself.

Almost as though she were a Russian.

2

'Where are you living?' Count Beresky asked Laura the next day.

On returning with Charles to the Café de la Victoire on the previous evening to ask whether any messages had been left for her, she had found the count's dinner party in full swing; but he was sober enough to recognise the young woman with whom he had once been madly in love. The handsome young calvary officer whose dark eyes had once sparkled with gaiety was now an exile – and a husband. He insisted that she should call on his wife the next day at their villa in Passy.

When she arrived in the afternoon he was there as well to welcome her, and for the past hour the three of them had been describing their adventures as they left Russia. More fortunate than many of his fellow-countrymen, who in happier days had chosen to rent apartments or stay in hotels on their annual expedition abroad, the count had bought this property on his twenty-first birthday in 1912. From his remarks, Laura realised that it was now filled with exiles.

'I've been looking for lodgings this morning,' she told him. 'I haven't found anything suitable yet, but I have some more addresses to try tomorrow.'

'Well, then.' The count glanced across at his young wife, who smiled in answer to the unspoken question. 'We have a room here. It was for my mother, but she has died. In hospital, not in the house. She had the influenza. You've heard, I expect, how many are dying? It's like a plague. And she was old, and very sad after leaving Russia, with no wish to go on living. Come, let me show you.'

It was a large room on the first floor of the villa – untidy and rather dirty, and at first sight gloomy. But when the count opened the shutters, the bright January sunshine flooded in, reflecting off the golden icon which still hung in one corner. The window looked out on to the villa's own wooded grounds, through which two small waterfalls trickled with a soft splashing. To lodge here would bring the benefits of living in the town and the country at the same time. There was a Metro station not far away – Laura had used it for her journey that afternoon – and yet the wooded acres of the Bois de Boulogne were practically on the doorstep.

'The Racing Club is just over there, out of sight,' said Count Beretsky, pointing from the window. 'And the steeplechase course of Auteuil there. You can guess why I chose a villa here.' In Russia he had been famous for his horsemanship.

Laura smiled her understanding, but her mind was on the subject of rent. She had no work and no idea how long she would need to spend in Paris: nor did she know how much she would get for the emeralds which must support her through this period. But when she raised the subject, it was brushed away.

'Rent? There's no question of rent. I'm glad that I can offer a

118

roof and a bed to some of my friends whose affairs have fallen out less fortunately than my own.'

'But I couldn't possibly ...' Laura paused to think. She knew what pleasure it gave her Russian friends to be hospitable, and was anxious not to offend the count. But in the course of her visit she had become aware that at least six couples, and possibly more, were already sharing the villa with him. Was he not asking any of them for money? Although he was indeed lucky to own the property, he must have lost his previous sources of income to the Bolsheviks.

'You'd have to let me contribute to your costs, Excellency,' she said firmly. 'I know how much pleasure it gives you to be generous, but we in England take a different sort of pleasure, in paying our way.'

'Costs. What costs?'

'Well, there must be electricity bills. And servants to do the cleaning, perhaps.'

'There are none. My wife has a maid for a little while, because of the baby; but for the rest, everyone in the house does what needs to be done. Or at least ...' He threw up his hands expressively.

'You mean that everyone is supposed to, but doesn't.'

'Well, they're not accustomed. How can I ask ...?'

'*I* could ask,' said Laura. 'If you would like me to, I mean. I'm a foreigner. If I offended your friends, they would be angry only with me, not with you. And with a little organisation ... In exchange for the room, I could be a housekeeper for you, if you liked.'

For a moment he allowed his astonishment to reveal itself on his face, and then began to laugh: a great roar of a laugh, which must surely have made everyone in the house fall silent for a second and wonder what was going on. Then he kissed her: not like a suitor, as he had kissed her five years earlier, but first on one cheek and then on the other and then back to the first, in a gesture of welcome and affection.

'We'll have a party tonight,' he told her. 'There's enough champagne left in the cellars for one last celebration. So that everyone can meet you and learn that from now on Miss Laura from England is to rule the household with a rod of iron.'

'If you say that, they won't let me through the door.' But Laura was smiling as happily as her host. The disappointment of her failure to find the Duvals had disappeared. She was no longer alone in a big city. Already, in Charles, she had re-encountered a friend. Now, in addition, she had a home; and that home would bring her not just companionship and a kind of occupation, but an address.

With an address she could leave a message for the Kristovs – in

119

the hope that the princess and her daughters had managed to escape after Prince Kristov's death — without needing to make frequent calls at the Café de la Victoire. With an address she could more easily keep in touch with Charles, who had half-promised her work. And with an address she could hope to receive letters directly from David, instead of having to use their *poste restante* arrangement. She felt as happy now as though she had already drunk her ration of the evening's champagne.

Only one small problem remained to be solved, and Count Beretsky was just the man to advise her.

'Oh, certainly, my dear Miss Laura, I can tell you how to dispose of the jewels you've been given. In fact, I'll come with you. I need some more cash myself. There's no need for us to speak to M. Cartier in person. He's set a room aside especially so that people in our situation can do our business in private. If you show me now what you wish to sell, it will help me to have an idea of its value, to be sure that you're not treated ungenerously.'

Laura had kept the emeralds on her person since leaving England, and set them out before him now — the cufflinks, the studs and the cravat pin with its ostentatiously huge head.

'Ah, poor Pavel Karlovich. I remember him wearing those studs to the New Year Ball at the Winter Palace.' The count sighed at the memory after the news which Laura had brought him of his friend's death. 'And Anna Ivanovna was appearing for the first time in her new kokoshnik, *La Lachrymosa*. Such a handsome couple they made. And now, you say ... Ah, well.'

They travelled by cab, although Laura would have been happy to return to the city centre on the Metro, by which she had come. Was Count Beretsky living solely on the sale of whatever jewels he had managed to bring out from Russia, she wondered. And, if so, how long would they last him? To someone like herself, who had been brought up to look ahead and budget and economise, the philosophy that tomorrow would look after itself was a hard one to accept.

She was glad of his support, however, during the negotiations with the jeweller. If she wished to sell outright, she was told, she would be given only the value of the stones, judged by their weight and quality, because they would be remounted in a more modern setting before being put on to the market again. But since the pieces were Cartier originals she could, if she wished, ask for them to be put on display in the showroom in their present state, and would then receive half the proceeds if they found a buyer. She chose to take the money at once.

Leaving Count Berstsky to his own negotiations, she emerged to

120

find that snow was falling. Not the dry snow of Russia, which could stroke the skin like a fine powder or, when the wind was fierce, attack it like an abrasive blast of sand. This was a wet snow, falling in large individual flakes and melting as it touched her cheeks. It was unlikely to lie for long, so she allowed herself time to enjoy it as it swirled around her.

Instead of returning immediately to the hotel to pack, she walked to the river and crossed to the centre of the Pont des Arts. For perhaps half an hour she stood there without moving, watching the snow settle briefly on the trees at the tip of the Ile de la Cité and pick out the spires of the Sainte-Chapelle and Notre-Dame with a white edging.

In happier days she had stood like this above the frozen Neva in St Petersburg, looking down at the sledges which criss-crossed the ice in a bustling activity very different from this silent thrusting flow of the swollen Seine. She had admired the delicate golden spires of palaces and churches in that most beautiful of cities. Beautiful it might have been; but it was necessary to remember that the most elegant spire of all had belonged to one of the grimmest prisons. And she would never again be able to think of St Petersburg without sadness, because it had brought death to a whole way of life, as well as to the people she had loved.

Firmly now she put it out of her mind and instead, turning slowly, began to identify some of the imposing buildings which had become familiar to her as a schoolgirl on holiday: the Louvre, the Grand-Palais, the Mint. Her eyes, as she looked from one familiar landmark to the next, brightened with the thrill of once more living in Paris.

Ever since her first visit at the age of sixteen she had felt this to be the centre of the world and it had been one of her many day-dreams that one day she might find herself there as a resident rather than a visitor. Although she loved Oxford, that was a sleepy city — and a man's city: a city in which husbands dined on High Table in college while their wives stayed at home with the children in North Oxford; in which female students, segregated from the men by strict rules, were now as a grudging favour allowed to take the same courses and examinations, but not to be granted degrees. Oxford was not a place in which a woman who had tasted independence would find it easy to settle down — and at a moment like this Laura was finding it hard not to regret that she had given a promise to David Hughes which would one day draw her back there.

The true excitement was that she was independent. She was responsible for herself — and for no one else — and the smoothness with which everything was falling into place heightened her self-confidence.

It was almost certainly that exhilaration which that evening caused her to become a little drunk for the first time in her life. Even before the first champagne cork shot up to the ceiling her spirits were bubbling.

Another cause of inebriation was the lack of food at the party. For over four hours the inhabitants of the Villa des Cascades drank and sang and danced to the strains of a balalaika. But it was not until after one o'clock in the morning that two of their number, who had apparently found employment as waiters, returned from their evening's work laden with food from the restaurant — anything which could not remain fresh enough to serve on a subsequent day.

Only as she ravenously seized a bread roll did Laura realise how light-headed she had become. She should be mourning the death of the unfortunate Prince Kristov. She should be wondering where her two pupils, Sofiya and Tanya, were now and whether she would ever see them again. She should be asking herself what had happened to Alexis, and to Fred. She should be missing David, who loved her, but whom she might not see again for months.

None of these sombre thoughts was able to cast a shadow over the evening. As she loaded a plate with tired salad ingredients and scraps of meat, she began to giggle quietly like a schoolgirl preparing for a midnight feast. Tomorrow she would be a sober and efficient Englishwoman, imposing order and cleanliness on the chaotic and grubby household. But for the moment, she was thinking and feeling like a Russian amongst Russians. This was a happy day — and tomorrow could look after itself.

3

Spring came early to Paris in 1919. Standing at her window in the Villa des Cascades on a bright March morning, Laura could not distinguish any individual buds or leaves on the trees, and yet the woods were flushed with colour in clouds of red or yellow or the brightest, lightest of greens — as though they were posing for a Monet painting; whilst willow trees, shot through with gold, leaned gracefully in the Japanese style.

With every dawn the song of the birds in the Bois de Boulogne awakened her to happiness. Living in Paris brought her a feeling of *joie de vivre*, filling her with energy. For the first time since childhood she was young and carefree. It was necessary to remind herself that Russia was starving: the victim of terror and civil war and the allied blockade. Another sobering thought was that with every day that passed it seemed less likely that the surviving members of the Kristov family had managed to escape from the country. If they were free, even though they might not yet have reached France, they would surely have sent a message.

When should she give up hope? It was not strictly necessary for her to stay in Paris. She could leave contact addresses both at the restaurant and amongst the Russian emigré community. Then she need return only when she was summoned, to hand over the kokoshnik and see whether she was required to perform the penance which she had laid down for herself after the loss of the diamonds. But if she went back to England, David would expect her to stay; and she was not quite ready to settle down as his wife.

She enjoyed reading his letters, though. As a rule they arrived at regular weekly intervals, but the most recent had come twelve days ago. It contained the long-awaited news that he was about to be demobilised. No doubt he was on the move at the moment — going through all the formalities and visiting his family before returning to Oxford to take up his fellowship again. Might he even fit in a quick surprise visit to see her in Paris; or was he not a man for surprises? She didn't know, and not knowing allowed her to hope.

The moments when she thought about Russia were sad, but at every other time she was filled with satisfaction at her new life. Charles had duly found her some translating work, although this proved to be badly paid. Better still, he had introduced her to the wife of a French diplomat who required an intensive course of English lessons before accompanying her husband to a new post in Washington. So successful were the daily sessions that her pupil had offered wide recommendations throughout her circle of friends. By now Laura was giving a dozen or more private lessons every week, as well as taking classes in English conversation at a girls' school in Auteuil. She had not needed to spend the money given for the emeralds — and indeed, proud of her ability to support herself, was steadily adding to her savings.

Her running of the villa was equally successful. Determined to be as tactful as possible, she had spent several days analysing what needed to be done and how much must be spent each week to keep the house in reasonable order. The idea that pampered members of the nobility could be expected to keep kitchens and shared bathrooms in a tolerable state of cleanliness had to be quickly dismissed. In the old days they had not washed so much as their own hair themselves. Even Laura, despite her much more modest circumstances, had never used a scrubbing brush until the last difficult weeks in Moscow. But there was no reason why she and they should not each learn to take responsibility for some less demanding part of the house or garden.

So, like the head girl of a school compiling her rota of prefects' duties, Laura made a list of housekeeping needs and invited each of the villa's guests to make a choice. Including herself, but not the Beretskys, there were thirteen people who could be asked to sign. She had listed eight domestic duties and five financial contributions – intended to cover some of the costs of running the villa as well as the wage of a maid-of-all-work.

The effects of her initiative were interesting. Three of the women received it coldly and only agreed to put their signatures to a choice under pressure from their husbands, two of whom had already faced reality and taken work as waiters. But a grand duke whose garden in Tsarskoe Selo had been famous for its elaboration of parterres and pergolas, lakes and groves, rose gardens and topiary – all, of course, maintained by a large staff of gardeners – had expressed an unexpected delight at the thought of dirtying his own hands and straining his own muscles to keep tidy the grounds of the Villa des Cascades.

His wife and one of her friends had asked Laura if she knew of any paid work for which they might be suitable. Their only skills were embroidery, painting and playing the piano; but with the help of one of her language pupils Laura had managed to find them employment in Coco Chanel's millinery boutique near the Hotel Ritz: one to sew and the other to act as a *vendeuse*.

She was pleased with her efforts, and by now had made friends with several members of the household. In this way she had become part of emigré society in Paris, which sometimes appeared to be enjoying one continuous party. The idea of saving for an uncertain future was completely foreign to these Russians. Any exile with anything to celebrate – whether it was a new job or an advantageous sale of possessions – let it be known that he was holding open house, with food and drink available to all-comers until it ran out. Laura thought this attitude to money unwise to a degree, but found the atmosphere of gaiety and good fellowship irresistible.

She had also, in great contrast, found a niche in the circle of peace conference advisers to whom Charles introduced her. They were for the most part earnest and hard-working, discussing the work of rebuilding Europe even in their free time. At least once a week, on Saturday or Sunday, Charles took her out to lunch. Smoking almost non-stop, in spite of his damaged lung, he talked to her as seriously as though she were one of his colleagues, enthusing about the proposal to set up a League of Nations. 'There must never be another war like this one,' he said; and she nodded her agreement.

It was after one of these lunches that he dropped a bombshell. They had not driven out into the country as they usually did, but spent the morning walking round the collection of Impressionist paintings in the Palais du Luxembourg before making their way to a restaurant in the Boulevard St-Michel.

'I've been called back to London,' he told her. 'The usual Foreign Office system is that as soon as you know anything about a country, you're moved to a different department. But someone has decided that it might be useful to have a chap who has actually visited Russia on the Russia desk. I even learned a bit of the language before I went out last year. There's a lot going on all over Europe in respect of that part of the world. Plotting to overthrow the Bolsheviks.'

'The emigrés will be glad to hear it.' But Laura's voice did not express her usual liveliness, and she was not surprised that Charles noticed it.

'Shall you miss me, Laura?'

'Yes. Very much. You've done such a lot to help me, and I've so much enjoyed these Sunday excursions.'

'Would the thought of missing me be enough to make you consider coming back to England with me?'

'To do what?' She was slow to realise what he was suggesting.

'To be my wife.'

She could only stare at him. So great was the pleasure that his friendship had given her during the past months that the thought of its developing into something closer had never occurred to her. As a schoolgirl in Oxford she had been aware that her father's aristocratic pupils tended to regard their tutors as not far removed from servants. Perhaps since that time there had remained at the back of her mind the feeling that Charles's world was different from hers — that the social class into which he had been born might not inhibit his choice of friends, but would certainly influence his decisions about marriage.

They had finished their meal by now, and the table was cleared. For once Charles was not smoking. He reached across to take her hand and hold it tightly.

'In the summer of 1913,' he said, with what seemed at first to be little relevance, 'my younger sister, Deborah, came out. For the Season, I mean. I was roped in to be an escort and to make sure that my friends were on hand to partner her. Two months of dances and dinners with eighteen-year-old girls. The cream of

125

society, I suppose. Pretty girls, a lot of them. All looking for husbands — though not much interested in me, a younger son, unless it should turn out that there weren't enough dukes to go round that year. I suppose there must have been intelligent girls amongst them, but I never came across any. Wardrobes full of clothes, to be changed four times a day; but heads empty of any interesting thoughts. I can't tell you, Laura, how much I enjoy being with someone like you, talking to you.'

'But you don't choose a wife just for her conversation!' Laura laughed affectionately at the idea.

'Why not? It seems to me that there's a great deal to be said for choosing to marry a friend, instead of acquiring a wife and hoping that a friendship may develop. I mean, all the years a husband and wife are likely to spend together, it's important that they should like each other, as well as love. I enjoy your company so much that I want to have it for ever. But I do love you as well, my darling Laura. I've got every sort of reason for wanting to marry you. Please say — '

Did all men propose marriage with so little warning, Laura wondered, almost tempted to laugh. Suitors traditionally gave hints of their feelings with flowers and compliments and love letters. But Charles . . . and David before him . . . At that thought Laura gasped, and her face flushed with shame.

'What's the matter? Laura, dearest, what is it?'

'I didn't realise,' she stammered. 'You never gave me any hint. If I'd known how you felt, I would have told you before this.'

'Told me what?' He waited, but she was unable to answer at once. 'Is there somebody else? You're not married, surely? Are you telling me that you're engaged?'

'Well, it's more a kind of understanding.' But no, that wasn't true. David had insisted that it should be called an engagement, even though it was one which might be broken. She shook her head in denial of her own statement. 'I'm engaged, yes. I ought to have made it clear to you as soon as we met again. It's because we haven't any immediate plans for marriage that I — well, I simply didn't think about it.'

The true reason, of course, was that she had become engaged to David in order that he should return to the battlefield with something to live for. She had not allowed herself to think too much about the real prospect of marriage until she knew what her obligations to the Kristovs might prove to be. But if she couldn't marry David, then she wouldn't be able to marry Charles either. 'I'm sorry, Charles,' she said. 'Very sorry.'

126

He gave her hand one last squeeze and tried without much success to conceal his hurt feelings with a smile. 'Who's the lucky man? Anyone I know?'

'I met him in Oxford, on the same day that I first met you. I don't suppose you've kept in touch, though. David Hughes.'

'Hughes!' His astonishment at the name was as great as hers had been when he proposed: as though he were unable to take his fellow-undergraduate seriously as a rival.

'But it may never happen. The marriage, I mean. I've explained to him, if Princess Kristova and the girls manage to escape from Russia, I have an obligation to help them.' She told him – as she had not told David – the story of the lost diamonds. Was it because she hoped that he would try to persuade her that she had done her best in dangerous circumstances and could not be expected to offer more? But then, why should Charles reason in such a way when David, not himself, would reap the benefit if his argument were to be successful?

He did not in fact make any attempt to change her decision. Nor did he even suggest that she might tell him if her understanding with David were ever to be abandoned. Instead, she could see him retreating into his disappointment, regretting that he had spoken. For her own part, she felt guilty. She ought to have been wearing a ring, or in some other way making it clear that she was reserved. Far from doing that, she had flaunted her pleasure in organising her life as an independent woman. No wonder he had been misled.

So now she had lost him, in a manner which seemed cruel. When he left Paris, he would maintain contact with the men who had become his friends here, but not with her: she felt sure of that already. Her choice of a man for whom probably he felt little respect would have diminished her in his regard. As they walked through the Luxembourg gardens, down the double avenue of chestnut trees which at any other time would have delighted her with their bright thrust of new life, they were each silent and sad: Charles from the humiliation of rejection and Laura because she was already mourning the loss of a friend.

4

The influenza epidemic to which Count Beretsky's mother had fallen victim spread relentlessly throughout Europe, soon rivalling the tally of those killed in four years of warfare. The Russian exiles, under-nourished and living in homes which they could not afford to heat

127

adequately, were particularly at risk, and Laura found herself having to nurse the woman who had become her particular friend in the Villa des Cascades.

Countess Irina Alexandrovna Gribova, a young widow, had been the third of the villa's female occupants to recognise the necessity of earning a living. Her slight figure unfitted her for any work requiring physical exertion and she possessed no marketable skills, but she had swallowed her pride and taken a position in the boutique of a fashionable couturier, selling gloves. At the first sign of illness she was sent home, lest customers should be frightened away by the fear of infection – and the news that her post had quickly been filled by someone else did nothing to cheer her spirits or speed her recovery. For several days she had been near to death, too weak and unhappy to fight for her life. Laura had needed to do the fighting for her, alternately bullying and coaxing her back to health.

David also, demobilised and back in damp, misty Oxford, had succumbed to the epidemic. His most recent letter was brief and badly written, as though his eyes had difficulty in focusing. But its tone was cheerful as he described the care with which his college scout kept the fire in his room blazing and made his bed comfortable. Without putting it into words, he was telling Laura that she need not worry on his account: but behind this one unspoken message was a second – that the most certain cure for his illness would be her company.

'I ought to go back to England for a little while,' Laura said to Irina. 'But before I leave I want to see you sitting up and eating properly.' By now the countess's illness had almost run its course: she was going to be one of the survivors.

'Must you go?' Pale and thin and still very weak, Irina looked pleadingly at her friend and put out a hand as if to hold her back.

Yes, she must. Charles's proposal some weeks earlier had disturbed Laura, forcing her to realise how lightly she had been taking her engagement to David. She mentioned it now to her friend for the first time, and was amused to see that it had a therapeutic effect. Irina struggled to sit up and demonstrate that she no longer needed to be nursed.

'Yes, of course you must leave at once. You ought not to be here at all. How can you bear to live in a different country from your lover?'

'We agreed to wait for a year. He was in the army, you see.'

'But the war is over!' Irina shook her head uncomprehendingly, and Laura realised how odd the arrangement must seem to an outsider. Now the separation was about to end. Almost the whole of

128

the year for which she had agreed to sustain the engagement had passed. It would now be impossible for her to withdraw.

Why should she wish to do so? David was everything she could once have wished for in a husband: intelligent and loving, considerate and reliable. She could tell herself that she loved him, and it would probably be true. Not quite so successful would be any attempt to persuade herself that she was in love with him.

She knew what it should feel like to be in love. She had been in love with Alexis, even though common sense had prevailed in the end. More worryingly, she had realised even as she rejected his proposal how attractive she found Charles Vereker. His behaviour towards her was always that of a gentleman: polite and restrained. He had never kissed her or done more than hold her hand or take her arm. But he had wanted to — and she had wanted it as well. There had been a moment in which she wished passionately that they were not both so well-behaved. If only Charles had made his offer before David! Then she could have loved and been in love at the same time; she felt sure of it.

But that was water under the bridge, never to be thought about again. It was David to whom she was engaged — and perhaps the lack of passion in her feeling for him was the necessary price to be paid for that considerate reliability which she valued. Did it matter that he wasn't a man who ever seemed likely to sweep her off her feet?

Any of her Russian friends would have long ago confided such hopes and doubts to all her circle and discussed their advice at length. Laura, inhibited by her English upbringing, could only force herself to speak of a second reason for hesitation.

'I've been looking after myself and other people for a good many years now,' she told Irina. 'Earning my own living. Taking responsibilities. Sometimes it's been a struggle, but mainly I enjoy it. When I go back to to England ...'

'When you go back to England, you will find yourself one of the fortunate ones. There are so many women today who will never marry, because the men who should have been their husbands are dead in the war. So many women, too, who are widows and will never know the blessing of becoming a mother.' Irina's eyes filled with tears and she sank back again on the pillows, her brief energy exhausted. 'So many women who may never experience the joy of being held in a lover's arms. Have you had that experience yet, Laura?'

Laura felt herself flushing. In England, the correct answer for an unmarried woman to give to such a direct question would be 'Of

129

course not'; but she could tell from her friend's tone of voice that such truthfulness would provoke pity, so she said nothing.

'You must leave at once, dearest Laura. I am quite better now, and it will make me sad if you stay on my account. A woman without a man is incomplete — and soon you'll be too old to have children.'

'Nonsense.' But the urgency of Irina's prompting was having its effect. Already she had recognised that her place was at David's bedside. No one else had an equal claim on her. Prince Kristov was certainly dead, and every month that passed without news made it seem less likely that the rest of the family had managed to escape on their own. If they did, they would find any message which she might leave at the Café de la Victoire. So there was no good reason why she should remain in Paris.

By returning to England, even for a brief visit to nurse her fiancé, she would be committing herself to the engagement. Marriage and motherhood would follow inevitably: it was all destined to happen. She would become, as Irina had pointed out, one of the fortunate women of her sad generation.

Because of course her friend was right. Laura allowed the truth to force its way through her inhibitions. She wanted to be held and kissed and loved. Acknowledging this to herself, she could almost feel her body unfolding, waiting to welcome her lover. David in the flesh had not succeeded in inspiring her desire; but at a distance the thought of him as her husband was enough to excite her. She was ready for love.

'I'll take the night train,' she told Irina, trying to keep her voice steady. 'By tomorrow morning you'll be strong enough to get out of bed for a little at a time, and I shall ask Olga Mikhailovna to bring you broth and make sure that you are warm.'

She went back to her own room and wrote notes apologetically cancelling until further notice all the English lessons she was due to give. Then she began to pack everything needed for a fortnight's absence. Although this decision would effectively bring her life in Paris to an end, she would need to return in order to settle her affairs. The kokoshnik, for example, could not be casually taken out of the bank's strong room and added to her luggage for a Channel crossing. Some formal arrangement must be made which would allow the princess to claim it if she ever arrived in the city, and there was no time to think about that now. Laura closed her suitcase and was in the process of tidying her room when the doorbell of the villa rang.

It was answered by General Sablin, who had a room on the ground floor in which a small group of conspirators regularly met to plot the overthrow of the hated Bolshevik regime. The general possessed neither money nor domestic skills, so his contribution to the running of the villa was to act as concierge, scrutinising all comings and goings. He appeared at the door of Laura's room holding a cable.

'From England,' he said. 'The boy is waiting to learn if there is an answer.' He too waited as Laura tore open the envelope and read the brief message.

'Regret inform you dear David passed away Wednesday Oxford stop letter follows stop Eirwen Hughes.'

David dead! Numb with shock, Laura stumbled towards her bed and sat down. It wasn't possible. He had survived so many years of war, had survived the bullet which left its scar on his head. How could it happen that a young, healthy man could be swept away by a mere infection? She stared down at the faintly typed words as though the letters might somehow rearrange themselves and tell her that she had misread the news they brought. But of course there was no change, and no possibility of mistake. Eirwen Hughes was David's mother. They had never met, but Laura had received friendly letters from her ever since her son had confided the secret of his engagement.

'My dear Miss Laura, you are not well. Is there bad news?'

Unable to speak at first, Laura nodded her head.

'No answer,' she whispered.

The general went downstairs again, leaving behind him a deathly silence. In every room of the villa her friends would now be chatting, changing their clothes, making preparations for dinner. Quietness was a rare luxury in such an overcrowded home, but at this moment she was unaware of any sounds at all. When General Sablin reappeared in the room with an anxious expression on his face, it was as though he had floated up the stairs like thistledown. She saw his lips move, but her ears refused to register the words. He turned towards the door, and she could tell that he was shouting, but only when Countess Beretsky appeared in a fluster could she guess what he had said.

She wanted to cry, but the tears would not come. She shivered with cold, although her body felt hot and feverish. Passively, as though she were a doll, she allowed the countess to take off her shoes and travelling clothes and put her to bed, where she at once turned her face to the wall: refusing to believe what she had been told; refusing to explore her reaction to the news.

Three days later − although she did not immediately realise how much time had passed − she awoke to find Irina sitting beside her bed.

'Good.' Irina put down her sewing. 'You have returned.'

131

'I haven't been anywhere.' Laura's voice was husky with disuse.

'Oh yes, a long way away, I think. I have to tell you, Laura, that I read the cable. Only I; and I said nothing to the others. We were all frightened for you, and I was the most frightened in case you had caught the influenza from me. It was necessary to know the cause of your illness before it could be treated.'

'There's no treatment. And nothing wrong with me. I'm sorry to have alarmed you.' Heavy with loneliness and depression, Laura sat up and prepared to get out of bed.

'We are the ones who are sorry − and I especially, knowing how you must mourn your David. I had only fifteen months with Boris before he was killed, but you have had no time at all. You must remember that you have friends, Laura. Many friends, who care for you.'

'Yes, I know.' Laura accepted the young widow's kisses and embrace. It was true that the emigrés amongst whom she had lived for the past few months were emotional and demonstrative, showing their affection in a manner quite different from the restrained relationships which passed for friendships in her Aunt Barbara's circle. But that assurance did little to assuage her feeling of desolation as she wrote to Mrs Hughes, apologising because her collapse had caused her to miss David's funeral, and set about the task of resuming her life.

She had delayed too long before opening her heart to love, and was unlikely ever to have another chance. How bitterly now she regretted that she had been too selfish and short-sighted to make David happy by agreeing to an immediate wedding in 1918! In the back of her mind was a more shameful sadness, which she did her best to smother. Already she had had to stifle the regret that Charles Vereker had not proposed to her earlier, while she was still free: to it now was added a second regret − that he had not waited until later. Instead, less than three months after leaving Paris, he had announced his engagement to one of the debutantes he had affected to despise.

There was no point in dwelling on might-have-beens. For a second time she wrote to her pupils, hoping that her previous notes had not caused them to find another English teacher too quickly. She was going to need the money she earned from them, little though it might be. In an attempt to make realistic plans, she sat down one evening to consider her future as a spinster. All her arrangements for the past few months had been matters of chance, accepted with pleasure because they were only temporary. It was time to recognize that she would have to depend on herself for the rest of her life.

132

She must find regular work; a living wage. But what work was she fitted for, except to be a governess — a form of employment which had promised and delivered adventure for a short period, but presented itself as a form of slavery when considered as a career.

It was at this moment, when her spirits were at their lowest ebb, that a letter arrived from Mrs Gillespie.

5

Mrs Mary Lee Gillespie was the aunt of Helen Lee Wright, Laura's companion on the long train journey from Moscow and the voyage from Vladivostock to San Francisco. It was she who had arranged for the two young women to be met off the boat and transferred to a comfortable sleeping compartment for the further journey to New York.

After their arrival at her home there, she had insisted that Laura must stay with her for a few weeks to rest after the hardships of the years in Russia and the anxieties and discomforts of escape. More than that, she had generously made and paid for the arrangements for her guest's onward journey to England. It was Helen, still overwhelmed by guilt, who had begged her to do this; but since Mrs Gillespie knew nothing about the disaster of the lost diamonds, her actions stemmed from a generous nature and not from any sense of obligation.

She wrote now from London, where she was enjoying the opening weeks of the Season at the beginning of a visit to Europe. After a brief trip to the Highlands of Scotland to see the birthplace of her late husband's grandfather, she planned to spend a month in Paris before travelling to Nice or Monte Carlo for the winter. She looked forward to meeting Laura again and, since she spoke no French, would be grateful if a suite could be booked on her behalf at whichever hotel was reckoned to be the best in the city.

Even in her depressed state Laura could not resist a smile at the request. It was unlikely that either the Ritz or the Hotel Bristol would find difficulty in meeting the requests of a wealthy American, whatever language she spoke. But she did as she was asked and wrote to offer her services as a guide to the city when the time came. She was still looking for more pupils for her English classes, and there were all too many free hours in her day.

In her own community Mrs Gillespie was a respected figure: a patron of the opera, the organiser of a ladies' literary club, a society hostess and a member of numerous charity committees.

She was generous in supporting not only an art gallery but some of the city's young artists who were struggling to keep alive until their talent should be recognised. So she thought of herself as being in the artistic swim.

In France, however, she felt out of her depth. Art had taken a new direction here, and as she puzzled over the works of Braque or Picasso she began to lose confidence in her own taste. Even her clothes, the most fashionable that money could buy in Manhattan, were clearly behind the times in Paris, where skirts were shorter by day, and evening styles less structured. One of her first requests after her arrival was for an introduction to one of the haute couture houses, so that her wardrobe might be brought up to date. In addition to this, her inability to make herself understood left her nervous: worried lest she should be doing the wrong thing or missing something she ought to see or experience. For this reason she not only wanted Laura to suggest and arrange what she should do, but begged for her company whenever possible.

This sense of insecurity on the American's part brought Laura some unexpected treats. It took her one evening to the ballet, sitting in a box which she could certainly never have afforded on her own. Diaghileff's company was performing; and although Diaghileff himself was an exile not from the revolution but from the Tsarist regime, he had gladly given employment to some of the talented dancers who had fled the country in the past two years. One of these, she noticed from the programme, was Barisinova.

Her heart missed a beat as she caught sight of the name. Prince Kristov's mistress would surely have news of the family. Would it be good or bad? She turned to her hostess.

'I find that I'm acquainted with one of the ballerinas,' she said. 'I believe she would be willing to receive us after the performance if that would interest you?'

As she had expected, Mrs Gillespie glowed with pleasure: it was for experiences like this that she had come to Paris. They found the dancer's dressing room crowded — but not, as would have been the case ten years earlier, with rich and handsome young men jostling for her favour. Now she was no longer a rising star, the toast of a city, but a tired woman in her thirties, with the end of her career approaching more rapidly than she liked. Her admirers were older and poorer. Mrs Gillespie, a stranger amongst them and barely able to understand their conversation, revelled in the buzz of congratulation and asked Laura to act as interpreter for her own compliments.

To these, Laura added a question of her own.

'What news have you of the Kristovs?'

134

Barisinova sighed. 'My dearest Pavel Karlovich is dead.'

'I'd heard that, alas. But what of the princess and the girls?'

Barisnova shrugged her shoulders – not uncaringly, but in despair. 'I know nothing. My son and I were due to leave Leningrad with the family. It was all arranged. We sat at home all night, waiting for the message to tell us that the horses were ready, but no one came. It was three days before I learned the reason: that Pavel Karlovich had been shot. You can imagine, it would have brought danger to Anna Ivanovna if I had made enquiries. And to myself. In Russia today one must choose commissars rather than princes as protectors. Or else foreign generals. Leon and I would still be there if we hadn't managed to reach the Ukraine while the Germans were in occupation. They brought us out when they evacuated the area.'

'May we talk again? Do come and visit me.' Quickly Laura wrote down her address.

'You won't mind if I bring Leon?' The dancer gestured into a corner of the dressing room, where a fair-haired boy was playing with a model car on the floor, oblivious of the chatter around him.

'Of course not.' It was time to return her attention to Mrs Gillespie, who left the theatre thrilled by this glimpse of bohemian life.

It occurred to Laura that the American had something in common with the Russian exiles. Rich though her marriage had made her, she had been born in the South, in Mississippi, to parents who had experienced the same collapse of a society, the same sense of ruin as their properties were burned or confiscated, leaving them to scratch a living by digging their gardens and selling their treasures.

Like the emigrés, too, Mrs Gillespie was warm-hearted and impulsive, generous and demonstrative. On an impulse of her own Laura asked whether she would like to visit the Villa des Cascades.

'I'd just love to meet all your friends, but it would be better for *me* to entertain *them*, I guess. From what you say, they don't exactly have the money to throw away on strangers. Why don't I give a party in your honour, to thank you for the way you're looking after me here, and leave you to invite the guests? Is there some place where you know they'd like to eat?'

'Well, there's a restaurant called La Coupole ...'

'You fix it up for me, then. Take a private room and order whatever you think is right.'

How delightful it was to be hospitable at someone else's expense! Laura made out her list and set out to deliver the invitations in

135

person. Her first call was on Countess Beretsky, whom she found playing with her baby.

'I'm so glad, dear Miss Laura, to see a brightness in your eyes again,' she said after greeting the prospect of the party with delight. Many of Laura's Russian friends continued to call her 'Miss Laura' — perhaps because they were always accustomed amongst themselves to use two names and were put out by her lack of a patronymic. 'We've all been so worried for you. I'm going to say something that I know will shock an English miss, but you must listen to me all the same. You should take a lover. No, really, listen ...' For Laura had drawn in her breath to protest. 'Every woman needs someone to protect her and pay her compliments and send her presents.'

'There's rather more to having a lover than that,' suggested Laura, laughing.

'Well, of course. And you should have that more. You're still a young woman, and beautiful, but you behave as though you think yourself plain and forty-five.'

The smile faded from Laura's face. 'It's too soon after — '

'No.' The countess interrupted firmly. 'This is the right time. Before you turn your back on love and forget how to please.'

'Well, it's an interesting idea, but there isn't anyone.'

'Of course there isn't, because they're all, the young men, afraid of you, Not truly afraid, I mean. But they see a fence round you, with a notice to say "Don't touch". All you need is to give the smallest signal: a smile would be enough. You'll discover how many friends you have who would like to be more than friends.'

'I'm grateful for your interest, Olga Mikhailovna, but I really don't think — '

The countess sighed, jigging her baby up and down on her lap.

'I was afraid you would say this. So I must move on to my second plan.'

'And what might that be?' But the only answer was a mysterious shake of the head.

It was on the night of Mrs Gillespie's party that Laura discovered the nature of the reserve plan. The count and countess had decided to make her drunk — and they had more than half succeeded before she realised what was happening. From the first moment the party was a riotous success. Exhilarated by the prospect of eating and drinking well, the emigrés had dressed in Mrs Gillespie's honour as though for an Imperial ball. Only Laura knew that the glittering jewels they wore were mostly paste imitations of the heirlooms they had been forced to sell.

136

Almost all of them could speak some English, and they used that language to discuss with their hostess the culture of their city of refuge. They described to her the new fashions in art as well as in apparel, they discussed all the new plays, they mentioned the names of poets and novelists – some of them American – who, as yet unknown, would certainly be famous one day. Long after the lavish meal had been consumed, the room was still noisy with laughter and conversation as the waiters continued to make the rounds, keeping every glass filled.

Mrs Gillespie was in heaven – flattered by the attentiveness of her guests, genuinely interested and pleased by the feeling of being in the swim and, above all, overwhelmed by the exalted rank of each person who was introduced to her.

'So many princes and princesses, generals and admirals!' she gasped to Laura. 'They'll never believe me at home when I tell them. And such cultivated people. I can't tell you, Laura dear, how much I appreciate this chance to get to know them.'

Laura was tempted to tell her that the prince to whom she had most recently been introduced was one of the doormen at the Ritz, who even before tonight's party had experienced her generosity in the form of tips. But it would be unkind to cause embarrassment and spoil the atmosphere. Smiling, she accepted yet another refill of her glass.

During her years as a governess, she had become accustomed to drink a glass of wine with her meals, but her upbringing had left her abstemious. Tonight, she realised with increasing muzziness, she must have drunk far more champagne than ever before; without noticing how much, because her glass was unobtrusively refilled before becoming empty. Well, did it matter? The count and countess would make sure that she reached home safely, and although she had already come to suspect that they were deliberately encouraging her to drink too much, no harm was likely to come of it. Tossing her head with a Russian disregard for tomorrow's hangover, she continued to drink.

By two o'clock in the morning the laughter and chatter had died away, and they were all singing. Singing the songs of their homeland with a sadness which might have seemed maudlin had it not come so deeply from the heart. Laura found herself weeping in sympathy. She felt for a handkerchief; but before she could find it was startled into sobriety for a moment by the opening of a door which sent a cold shaft of air into the stuffy, smoke-filled private room. Standing in the doorway was someone she thought was dead. Fred Richards.

No, it couldn't be? Could it? She must be imagining it – seeing

137

figures from her past as other people saw pink elephants. And yet ... She started to rise to her feet, but the movement sent the room spinning round and round. Losing her balance, she fell back into her chair and would have overturned it had her neighbour not put out an arm. Her eyes, misty with tears from the singing which still continued, were not focusing properly. Finding the handkerchief at last, she gave them a vigorous rub. When she looked towards the doorway again, there was no one there.

6

No hangover! Laura sat up in bed and moved her head, cautiously at first, from side to side. She had expected to feel dizzy or sick, or at the very least to have a headache, but it seemed that there was no price to pay for overindulgence in champagne.

Except one. She had no memory at all of the end of the party. Her friends must have brought her home and taken off her outer clothing. Oh, and there was something else as well, for when she drew the curtains she found the sun high in the sky. She had slept, disgracefully, right through the morning, and would have to move quickly because she had promised to help Mrs Gillespie buy some shoes to match her new outfits.

Hurriedly washing and dressing, she was just in time to keep the appointment. Mrs Gillespie acknowledged her punctuality with a smile of approval, but seemed in no haste to leave on their expedition. Instead, she spent some time enthusing over the previous night's party and the new friends she had made. Then, almost shyly, she had a request to make.

'I told you, when I wrote, that I'd be going on to Nice for the winter season. I've been wondering, Laura dear, whether I could persuade you to come with me?'

'To do what?' Laura was taken aback.

'Just to keep me company. I can't tell you what a pleasure it has been to me, seeing Paris with you instead of meeting with other Americans all the time. You've made me feel really at home here, introducing me to people, showing me things I might never have found for myself, and acting as interpreter. I do appreciate that. If you could do the same for me on the Riviera as well, it would make such a difference.'

'But I can't just abandon my pupils here, I'm afraid.' It was not that they couldn't survive without her, but that they provided her only income now that Charles and some of his fellow-delegates had left Paris and the flow of translations had dried up.

'Perhaps I didn't make it clear. I'd want this to be a business arrangement. Obviously, you'd live in my suite at the hotel and we'd have all our meals together. But I would also pay a salary for your help. You've been so generous with your time and trouble here, I couldn't possibly ask you to come without making it worth your while. Let me leave you to think about it while I go and put my hat on.'

She was gone for a long time, obviously realising that she had given Laura a lot to consider. A paid companion! Was that how she was to see her future? From her childhood Laura remembered that her grandmother had a companion, a downtrodden woman who was sent scurrying to pick up balls of knitting wool or scold the servants. She was allowed no time for herself and was expected to be grateful for her board and lodging, without any salary in addition.

In Russia, on the other hand, it was taken for granted that any member of the nobility who was widowed or fell on hard times would come to live with a more prosperous branch of the family with no duty except to be sociable. The position of a companion was only demeaning if her employer proved to be a tyrant, and Mrs Gillespie was not likely to change her nature just because she held the purse strings. It was possible, indeed, that she felt no real need of a companion and was making the offer because she had realised what a struggle it was for her niece's friend to make ends meet. Laura remembered that she had felt exactly the same doubts when Alexis first suggested that she should become a governess, but in the Kristov household she had never been made to feel that she was a servant.

More serious was the drawback that the winter season would last only a few months, and then Mrs Gillespie would return to New York. But Laura shrugged that off. Although she would lose her present pupils in Paris, she would surely be able to find new ones and, living with all her expenses paid, she should have been able to save. By the time Mrs Gillespie returned, she was ready to accept the invitation with a smile of gratitude and pleasure.

Later that afternoon, when the shoe-buying expedition was over, she returned to the Villa des Cascades to be greeted excitedly by her friend Irina, fully recovered from the influenza although depressed at the loss of her job.

'You have had a visitor,' she told Laura. 'An English gentleman driving a Rolls-Royce!'

An Englishman with an expensive car. Could that mean that

139

Charles had returned to Paris? How she had missed him! But she pulled herself up. If he were here, it would probably be on his honeymoon. She chided herself for her moment of expectation, and Irina misunderstood the reason for her change of expression.

'Don't worry, he's coming back again. At seven o'clock this evening, to take you out to dinner.'

She must establish who it was before then. 'Did he leave his card?'

'No. He said, "Tell her it's Fred".'

Fred! Only then did Laura remember what she had seen, or thought she had seen, on the previous evening. So it was not a hallucination. And it had not been death which prevented him keeping his promise to escort her out of Russia. Joy at the news of his survival mingled with a feeling that Fred had a good deal of explaining to do.

Arriving on the stroke of seven, he was shown up to her room by General Sablin. Before the revolution Laura would have considered it most improper to receive a man in the room in which she slept, but such inhibitions had disappeared during the crowded months in Moscow. Here in the villa she had become accustomed to use her spacious bedroom as a sitting room as well. She rose to her feet to welcome him.

'You've cut your hair,' said Fred. 'All your beautiful hair!'

It was an unexpected greeting after such a lapse of time. Laura stared at him as curiously as he was staring at her. He too had changed, although in a manner less easily identifiable. Except during his bout of sea-sickness, he had always been self-confident; but now he was well-dressed and there was an air of prosperity about him: an easiness in his smile. Even in the old days he had done his best to make it clear that a chauffeur was as good as a governess any day, but a certain deference had insisted on showing itself. There was nothing deferential about his bearing now: only admiration – admiration so unconcealed that Laura was embarrassed by it.

'I thought you must be dead,' she said, in as inappropriate a greeting as his own.

'Because I missed the train? I've come to tell you about that. Can we get it out of the way before we eat? What happened in Petrograd to keep me away.'

She nodded, casting her mind back to that sick moment of realisation that he was not going to arrive in time. She hadn't known then whether to mourn him as dead or be angry because – as Charles had suggested – he had probably seized an opportunity to make his escape with a stolen fortune.

'May I sit down, then?'

140

'Oh yes, of course; I'm sorry.' She moved to sit on a sofa beside the window and noticed, when he moved towards the chair which faced it, that he was limping slightly.

'We're going back eighteen months now. I don't know how much you've heard. They were all set to make a run for it – the prince and princess and the two girls.'

'Barisinova told me that she and Leon were due to be in the party as well.'

'Yes, well, that was his highness's idea. I didn't think much of it personally. It's not right for a wife to see a mistress given the same attention as herself. And anyway, after he died – you knew that, did you, that he was shot?'

'Yes, I heard.'

'That was why I had to go, you see. God knows I didn't want to. But two kiddies blubbering and the princess fainting and none of them having the least idea what they were supposed to do next, and no one else to help them ... Well! I wanted to keep my promise and come back to you, Laura. I can't tell you how much.' He leaned towards her and gripped both her hands with his own. 'The thing was, I knew you'd feel let down but it wouldn't stop you getting away. If I'd turned my back on the others, though, they wouldn't have had a hope. Not that they had much anyway, poor devils, but I wasn't to know that.'

'And Barisinova?'

'I couldn't manage more than one sledge on my own, and there were two sacks of goodies as well as the three of them. That was why there was no room for little miss twinkletoes. But she was all right. A pretty dancer and no blue blood to be ashamed of. It was a right old mess anyway. I did what seemed best at the time, Laura. I want you to understand that.'

In the old life he had never called her simply Laura; but so much had changed that it seemed right now. She nodded her head, and felt him squeeze her hands even more tightly.

'So what happened to them all?' she asked quietly.

'Nothing good.' Fred was silent for a moment. 'Part of it was my fault. I never pretended to be much good with horses, and I'm used to roads, even if they're full of holes. I didn't always see patches of soft snow coming. Prince Kristov would have gone faster, I expect, and not had so many spills. But mostly it was bad luck. With a frontier that length it was a matter of chance whether we ran into a Red Guard patrol or not; and we did. We can't have been more than half an hour from the frontier – but in the middle of a snowfield, there's nowhere to hide.'

141

'Did they capture you, then?'

'Nothing so civilised. Just loosed off with all their guns as soon as they got close enough. Pretty wild firing, it was, but it's hard to miss a horse. One horse pulled the others down and the sledge went over again and we were sitting ducks. I tried to draw the soldiers off. That was when I took a bullet in the leg myself.'

'So it didn't work?'

'Well, the thing was, they found the sacks. Dividing up the spoils must have seemed a better bet than running after a refugee. They let me get away.'

'And the others?'

'Not good news, I'm afraid, Laura. I went back afterwards, after the patrol had gone. They were all lying there dead.'

'Oh!' Laura pulled her hands away from his grip and covered her eyes in shock. The sofa rocked as Fred moved to sit beside her and put an arm round her shoulders. As if recognising that nothing he could say would comfort her, he remained silent until she had pulled herself under control again.

'They were all of them shot?' she asked. It was hard to believe.

'The princess was shot. The two girls had their legs trapped when the sledge overturned. Sofiya's head . . . I reckon it must have been kicked by one of the horses.'

'And Tanya?'

'Tanya was lying underneath her sister. I don't know whether she'd suffocated or died of the cold. It was some time before I could get back to them. Don't cry so much, please. You must have suspected already . . .'

'Yes, I did. But I didn't cry for my suspicion. I can't just say goodbye to them without grieving. They were my family, my children, for five years.' Her voice broke again. She stood up and walked over to the washbasin, pressing a cold sponge against her eyes.

And yet, although it had come as a shock to hear the words, Fred's comment was a pertinent one. In her heart she must have realised that her two young pupils were unlikely to have survived. Whatever she might say now, Laura's grief had in a way already spent itself. The real effect of Fred's news was to close the door finally on her life in Russia.

7

'You've taken a long time to tell me all this, Fred,' said Laura when at last she could keep her voice steady.

'I searched high and low, but I couldn't find you. I could guess what you thought of me for letting you down. I wrote to that house you used to live in, in Oxford. I even went there. But nobody there had heard of you. I remembered you had an aunt somewhere, but you never told me what her name was. There weren't any clues. If you knew how hard I tried . . .'

Laura managed a smile as she turned back to face him again. 'How did you find me in the end?'

'Just luck. I arrived in Paris a couple of days ago and was having dinner in the Coupole last night. Setting up a little business deal. We heard the singing from upstairs. Russian singing. I made some comment to the waiter and he told me the name of the person who'd booked the room, because it was English.'

'So it really was you I saw? I wasn't sure whether I'd dreamt it. Why didn't you come in?'

'Because you were tiddly, that's why.' Now that the bad news was over, Fred was grinning in his old way. 'A gentleman never takes advantage of a lady when she's tiddly.'

It would have been offensive to query the description "gentleman", so Laura repeated another word instead. 'Advantage?'

'You know what I've come for, don't you, Laura?'

'To take me out to dinner, I was told.'

'I'm not hungry. Not for food, anyway. Only hungry for you.'

'What can you mean?'

Fred sprang to his feet when Laura stood up. He followed her across the room and took hold of her hands for a second time.

'Two things I've been wanting to tell you all these months,' he said. 'First one was that I didn't have any choice about letting you down, that time. Nearly broke my heart, not even being able to let you know. Do you understand now?'

'Yes.' Laura's voice was only a whisper. She had no difficulty in guessing what was coming next.

'Second thing is that I love you. Always have, right from when we were on the boat. No point in saying so then. I could tell it was His Nibs you were interested in, not me. I should have told you before I went off to Petrograd, though. But it was all such a scramble. No time for fancy words. Too important a thing, I thought, just to throw out casual-like and then disappear. On the train, that's when I was going to say it: when we'd have all the time in the world. Well, I've learned my lesson the hard way, and that's why I'm not wasting time now. Say what you feel as soon as you feel it, is my motto. So what I'm saying quickly, before we get separated again, is that I'm in love with you. And I want . . . I want . . .'

143

His lips pressed against hers, so that neither of them could speak, and he held her so tightly that she was unable to fill her lungs with air. She could fell his fingers fumbling with the tiny buttons at the back of her dress and instinctively began to struggle free. That was, after all, how a well-brought-up young woman was expected to behave in such circumstances.

How, then, was Fred in turn expected to behave? Was she expressing a genuine wish that he would stop and go away? Or was she secretly hoping that he would subdue her struggles with his strength? The first of those questions answered itself quickly as, still keeping his hands on her waist, he allowed her to take one step backwards.

'I'm not a bully,' he told her. 'If you don't want ... But I love you so much. You and me together, we could ... I could make you happy, if you'll let me, Laura. Will you?'

The silence which followed was long and intense. Laura seemed to have forgotten how to breathe, and certainly she was unable to speak. 'You should take a lover,' Countess Beretsky had told her, and now a lover had presented himself. He had chosen the right moment: a moment of loneliness, when it seemed that all the people to whom she had been closest had disappeared for ever.

Was it fair to Fred to use him as a comforter? She wasn't in love with him as she had been in love with Alexis. She didn't even love him as she had loved David, because they had never been companions on equal terms. But there must have been something between them in the past. She had trusted him – and, although she perfectly accepted his explanation now for his breach of that trust, at the time he had upset her in a way that a mere casual acquaintance would not have been able to do. She had missed him, in fact. His absence had made her miserable. Was that a kind of loving?

'Laura?'

In the end the choice was very simple. She had said 'No' to Alexis, she had said 'No' to Charles and, when she said 'Wait' to David, it had proved to be another 'No'. If she were not to spend the rest of her life alone, the moment had come when she must say 'Yes'. Although in fact there was no need for words. She turned her back towards him so that he could undo the buttons which fastened her dress.

He was gentle with her at first, as they lay together on the bed; stroking her naked body with an expression almost of awe on his face. Laura lay still, not knowing what was going to happen and whether there was something she should be doing. How ridiculous to be so ignorant at the age of twenty-seven! Most women, she supposed, were prepared for their wedding

144

night by mother or friends; but she had been given no time to ask questions.

Because she had not expected it, the pain as he entered her made her gasp aloud.

'Sorry!' he said. 'Sorry. Easy, Fred, easy, easy' — but with each repetition of the words he thrust down on her, again and again so that she was no longer able to lie passively but clung to him tightly, arching her body up with a movement which matched the rhythm of his own; the pain already overwhelmed by an excitement which made her want to shout aloud.

'Oh, Laura, Laura!' It was Fred who shouted — so that everyone in the villa must surely hear him — as he collapsed on top of her, his body shuddering. For a little while he lay without stirring, his face pressed between her breasts, his panting breath warming her skin. Then, sliding from the bed, he fetched the sponge which earlier she had used to check her tears and began to wipe her thighs. The coldness of the water made her shiver and shivering made her laugh. In a curious way the act of laughing seemed to bring the act of love to a satisfying conclusion: she felt drained, but very contented.

'You're lovely,' Fred told her, stroking her with a towel. 'Did you know that? Have you ever looked at yourself?'

Smiling, she shook her head.

'Look now, then.' He held out a hand to raise her from the bed and led her across the room to the cheval glass. Naked, she seemed in her own eyes to be too tall, her body stretched into an unnatural thinness. But as Fred stood behind her, with only his head to be seen above her shoulder, his smile was one of admiration and she was happy to have given him pleasure.

There was a moment, just a fleeting second, when the light dimmed in her eyes and she was aware of an unworthy longing. It should have been Alexis! She shook her head, dismissing the thought, but Fred had noticed the shadow.

'What are you thinking?'

'I'm ashamed to tell you.'

'Come on. No secrets.'

'I'm thinking that I'm hungry.' This more frivolous confession was true. She had slept through both breakfast and lunch, and had looked forward to being taken out to dinner.

Fred laughed and moved towards the door. 'I can deal with that.'

'Fred, stop. You can't . . .' He was still naked as he opened the door of her room. Didn't he realise how little privacy there was in the overcrowded villa? But he needed only a second to drag a wicker hamper inside the room.

145

'I left it on the landing,' he explained. 'Thought it might come in handy. All part of the Rolls-Royce service.'

It was Laura's turn to laugh again, and their light-heartedness brought them even closer together. Fred accused her of being a prude because she insisted on dressing for dinner, and she was confident enough to toss her head and do as she pleased.

There was more champagne, and for the second time in twenty-four hours Laura felt herself becoming light-headed as the picnic progressed.

'What did you mean by the Rolls-Royce service?' she asked.

'I've come to Paris to make my fortune,' Fred told her. 'Twice in my life I've thought I was set up for life, and twice I've seen it slip away. A nice little nest-egg I had in the Imperial bank after the old princess died. Not worth a penny now. And then, when his highness was trying to persuade me to help them all get to Finland, he filled two sacks with treasures. Jewels, snuff boxes, miniatures, gold spoons, silver medals. One sack was for me, he said. I could take my pick when I got there. I turned it down, Laura. I said I had to get back to you. Between you and that sort of fortune, you were going to win every time. Believe me?'

She nodded. From now on she was going to believe everything he said.

'But then afterwards, when there wasn't any choice any more and I had to go, I didn't see why I shouldn't have the wages I'd been promised. A whole sack! Just think of it, Laura, how rich I'd have been!'

'But you didn't get it.'

'When you're running for your life — with only one good leg — a sack full of treasure is a millstone, not a spur. I had to drop it and let the Reds have it, or they would have got me. But earlier, when we were loading up, one of the sacks came undone, because it was too full. I took a few things then and stuffed them in my greatcoat pockets to make it easier to tie up. I kept those, and when I got to England they brought in enough for me to buy an expensive car.'

'The Rolls-Royce! Irina mentioned it. But can you afford to run it, Fred?'

'I've bought it for business, not pleasure. That was all I ever wanted a bit of money for, to get myself started. You've seen for yourself how it is. You work for wages and you're a wage slave all your life. The Bolshies got that bit of it right. But then they went the wrong way. It's all very well taking capital away from people who've got too much of it, but what they want to do is to give some — enough — to

146

people who haven't got any. Let them set themselves up. That's what I've done.'

'How are you going to use the car?'

'Hire it out. Top of the market stuff. Special occasions sometimes, like weddings and race meetings. But mostly for people who are too grand to use taxis all the time. These rich Americans who come over, used to having their own limousines. They'll take it by the week, to make a splash. That's why I've come to Paris; it's where the money is. All I have to do is to get in with the head porters at one or two swish hotels, promise them a cut, and I'm off.'

Laura thought for a moment while she rolled up slices of smoked salmon and ate them in her fingers. 'One of the Ritz doormen is a friend of mine,' she said. 'He lives in the villa, so he's probably admiring the motor at this moment.'

'There you are then. It'll soon take off, you'll see. I'll do the driving myself to start with, and then get another car as soon as I can, and start hiring drivers. I don't intend to be a chauffeur for the rest of my life. We could be partners, Laura. I'll need to have some kind of an office and someone to take bookings while I'm out driving. And to find out who's arriving in Paris, that sort of thing. Will you help?'

'Of course I will.' Laura was excited by his plans and delighted at the prospect of sharing in them. They toasted the new venture in more champagne and settled down to bring each other up to date on the events of the past eighteen months.

Laura gave a detailed description of her journey from Moscow to England – including the loss of the diamonds – and told him also about her engagement to David. 'No secrets,' Fred had said, and she was glad to agree.

It was late in the night before they fell silent at last, still sitting on the floor with the hamper between them. Fred stretched out a hand and raised her to her feet.

'I told you it was a waste of time, putting all those clothes back on,' he said, taking them off again.

This time there was no pain, only pleasure. Laura lay on her back, smiling with happiness, as Fred slept beside her. What would Aunt Barbara say if she could see them now! She couldn't think and didn't care. At the back of her mind was a different small doubt, the awareness of a problem which would have to be solved. For the moment, though, she could not think what it might be, and before long gave up the attempt to bring it forward into her consciousness. Then she too fell asleep.

147

8

Laura was awakened by the creaking of metal springs. This time it was a single stealthy creak: a furtive note when compared with the urgent thumping of a few hours earlier. Trying not to wake her, Fred was getting out of bed.

She kept her eyes shut, not yet ready to face the day — not knowing either how she felt or how she ought to feel. Overnight she had become a different person. Should she be ashamed? Yes, she should: but the appropriate emotion eluded her. Instead she was at once exhilarated and content; glad to have been wanted and loved. But what was going to happen next? She heard the door of the room being opened cautiously in an attempt not to disturb her. Was Fred trying to creep silently away? And if he was, should she be relieved or upset?

A surge of panic flooded her body. She had survived bereavement, exile, revolution, danger and tragedy without flinching, because at any particular moment the best course of action in the circumstances had always seemed reasonably clear. But now life had picked her up and tossed her on to a new road, twisting her, blindfolded, round and round until she lost all sense of direction. Ought she first of all to decide what she would most like the future to hold, or would it be better to wait and see what was on offer? Frustrated by her own indecision, she continued to feign sleep.

Once again the door opened and shut — less quietly this time. Fred had perhaps only left her to go in search of a bathroom. A chair scraped. A finger touched her cheek. She opened her eyes at last to see him sitting close to her, wearing nothing but a towel round his waist. How thin he was! Shyly she reached out to touch each of his ribs in turn. He clutched at her hand and held it tightly.

'I ought to marry you,' he said abruptly. 'Well, not just ought to: want to. Nothing I'd like better. But I've got to tell you the truth.' There was a long pause. It seemed that the truth did not come easily. 'Fact is,' he blurted out at last, 'I'm married already.'

A barrier slammed down, closing one of the possible roads which a moment ago had seemed to lead towards happiness. Laura stared at him without speaking.

'Well, I suppose I didn't *have* to tell you,' he said. 'She's never likely to turn up here. Thinks I'm dead by now, I shouldn't wonder. But I want to have everything straight between you and me. Christ, those eyes of yours frighten me, Laura! Give me your other hand, there's a girl. No, don't hang on to the sheet like that. You're beautiful, d'you know that? Not just your face, I mean.' Pulling away the sheet which she had drawn up to cover herself, he stroked each breast in turn without speaking.

'Florrie, her name was,' he said at last. 'Before I ever met you, of course. She ran after me, you could say. It was the uniform. Girls like that were always fools for a uniform. I only went with her the once, but she fell.'

'Fell?'

'Fell for a baby. That's what she told me, any rate. So there were tears, and I must make an honest woman of her or she'd lose her place without a character. Well, I did it. I warned her that was the most I'd do, put my name to a marriage certificate, but I did do it.'

'And then left her?'

Fred nodded. 'That was why I took my chance to get away when His Nibs bought the Hispano-Suiza and asked me to go to Russia with it.'

'But what about the baby?'

'There isn't any baby. What she told my father, after I'd gone, was that she lost it at five months. Maybe she did, and maybe it was never there to be lost. I wouldn't have been the first chap to have been hooked by a fib. I don't owe her a thing. All the same, though, she's Mrs Fred Richards.'

Laura sat up in bed, clasping her arms around her knees.

'You ought to have told me before − before last night.'

'I know I ought. But then there might not have been a last night, might there? I couldn't risk it, Laura. I wanted you so much. Finding you like that, after I'd almost given up hope ...'

'So why are you telling me now?'

'I said before, I want to be straight with you. No secrets, no lies; not between the two of us. But to others we could pretend, you see. If you wanted to. We could have got married in Russia, for all anyone here could ever find out. We may not have papers, but neither have any of these others you're living with. And like I said, Florrie's never going to leave England. No danger of her turning up to upset the apple cart. You need to know the truth, but nobody else does.'

'They wouldn't believe the story about our being married, not my friends here in the villa. Or if they did, they'd be terribly hurt that I've told them so much about myself but left out the most important thing.' Irina for one was not likely to credit that her friend had mourned David's death while already someone else's wife.

'Well, there's another way of doing it. We could get married here. It would be bigamy for me, but *you* wouldn't be doing anything wrong. If anyone ever found out, they'd just be sorry for you. But

149

there's no way anyone *could* find out. It's a funny sort of proposal, this, but it's the best I can do.' He fell silent whilst Laura tried to collect her thoughts.

'I wasn't prepared for any of this,' she said. 'Not seeing you again, or what happened last night, or anything. I need time to think about – well, how we'd live, what we'd do.'

'We'll be partners.' Fred spoke with confidence about his plans. 'Partners in everything. We'll find an apartment, big enough to use as an office as well, and we'll set out to make our fortunes. I'm going to make a success of my life, Laura, and with you to help me there'll be no stopping us. I haven't had your sort of education, and maybe you think I'm not good enough for you – '

Laura interrupted vehemently. 'Of course I don't think that!'

'That aunt of yours would. And if I'd spent the rest of my life in England, I'd never have been more than someone to be given orders. I don't talk right, not the way I'd need to over there if I was to be the one giving the orders. But it'll be different in Paris. That's one reason why I came here. No one can tell for certain, when I speak French, what sort of chap I am. You gave me a good start, and His Nibs kept me going, and then the old princess, before she died, made me speak French all the time. I had to read to her even, and she'd correct me if I said it wrong. Anyone in France will know I'm not a Frenchman, because of my foreign accent – but they won't be sure whether it's an English accent or a Russian one, whether it's the accent of a toff or of a lackey. You won't need to be ashamed of me when we've made our pile, Laura, I'll promise you that.'

'Of course not. I never have, never would.' She flung her arms around him. She was speaking the truth. Even at their first meeting, when she had not known how a governess should behave to a chauffeur, she had recognised his practical good sense and had been glad that he was keen to make a good impression on her. He was good at his job, and that had inspired self-confidence in him and admiration on her part. When, later on, he had vowed always to be on her side, she had believed and cherished the promise. Only on the journey home from Russia had she doubted him; and the relief of having her doubts explained away formed a part of her happiness now. She had loved Sofiya and Tanya so dearly that in being loyal to them he had also in a way remained loyal to her.

'We can think about what we're going to tell people later on,' she said now. 'First of all, let's go and look for an apartment.' Dr Mainwaring's daughter in Oxford would not so casually have dismissed the need for a marriage certificate, but Paris was a city with

150

a different set of values and Laura had become a different person. A good deal of hugging and kissing took place to seal their new partnership before she was allowed to get dressed.

'I shan't be able to contribute much, though,' she admitted apologetically. 'I only earn – Oh!' She put her hand to her mouth.

'What's the matter?'

'I realised in the middle of the night that there was a problem, except that I couldn't think what it might be. I've just remembered. I've got a job. I'm going off to spend the winter in Nice.' She told Fred about Mrs Gillespie.

'You can forget about that. Now that I've found you again, I'm not going to let you go. And you're not going to be anyone's companion.'

'I promised though, only yesterday. Let me think.' She was silent for a moment, and then nodded her head in approval at her own decision.

'I can't just not turn up,' she said. 'But there are two possibilities. It could be that Mrs Gillespie only offered me the job because she was sorry for me and wanted to put some comfort and money in my way. If that's the case, she'll be glad that I've got somewhere else to go. If she really does want a companion, then I could find her someone else instead. Just hold on here a moment.'

She found Irina still in bed. Only when there was a job to go to and a taskmaster to enforce punctuality did the exiles rise early, and Irina had forfeited her post by being ill. Quickly Laura passed on the details of the offer which Mrs Gillespie had made.

'She may decide that she doesn't need a companion after all. But if she does, would you be interested? You met her at the party. She's very nice. Not a bully. She'd treat you as a friend, I'm sure.'

'But what have I to offer her? I know how to sell gloves now, but I have no other skills.'

'Nonsense. The main thing is, she needs someone to interpret for her. She's awfully self-conscious about not speaking French. And she likes to feel that she's in the swim of things. It's odd, really. She's very rich, and she's an important person, socially, in New York – but somehow out of her depth here, and rather shy about jumping in. Just arranging introductions and telling her where the fashionable place to have tea is, and little things like that: that's what she's hoping for. You'd be perfect for her. You're a countess, and she's a sucker for titles. Besides, you play the piano beautifully. Of course you have skills.'

'Why are you not taking the position yourself?'

Laura blushed. She could feel the hot blood flooding her neck as well as her face and her efforts to control it only made it worse. Irina, who had been lying lazily in bed during the earlier part of the conversation, could hardly fail to notice her friend's confusion, and sat up with a new interest.

'I saw that most handsome car still outside the villa when I went to bed at two o'clock,' she said. 'Who was your visitor, Laura?'

Laughingly, she shook her head. Before she revealed this new relationship to any of her friends, she must decide how it was to be described.

'There isn't time to tell you now. I'm going off to break it to Mrs Gillespie that I can't go with her. You must dress in your most elegant morning clothes. I suggest that you should arrive at the Ritz at twelve o'clock.'

Returning to her own room, she told Fred the arrangement.

'I'll drive you down in style,' he offered. 'Before you start introducing your countess to Mrs Gillespie, you can introduce me to your friend the prince/doorman, and he can introduce me to the head porter, and then I'll be off to a good start there. And just suppose Mrs Gillespie decides she'd like to take you and the countess out to lunch, you could tell her that a Rolls-Royce is at her disposal to take her to one of the best small restaurants on the Left Bank. I've got an arrangement going: I recommend them and they recommend me. The food's good. We'll all be happy.'

Laura was happy already. 'You don't miss a trick, do you?' she laughed.

'I'm feeling lucky. I've found you again, and everything on top of that is a bonus. We're going to be lucky together. Right?'

Laura danced with delight, twirling round the room until Fred checked her by taking her in his arms.

'Right,' she agreed.

9

'I think you care more about the Rolls-Royce's comfort than mine!' exclaimed Laura. She was laughing, but there was some truth in her accusation. It would not have been difficult to find an apartment in Paris had not Fred insisted that there must be a dry and secure place nearby for the motor car which was to be the foundation of his business.

She didn't mind too much. Although she looked forward to the time when she and Fred could set up a home of their own together, most of the rooms which they could afford proved to be small and

152

dark and at the top of innumerable stairs. And invariably near the bottom of the stairs sat a concierge, unfriendly and inquisitive, staring from her cubicle at the young couple as though suspecting that they were not married. Since these suspicions were correct, Laura sometimes found it hard to keep a pleasant smile on her face.

It had not taken her long to come to terms with Fred's married state. She was not prepared to make a bigamist of him, and yet very much wanted to be regarded as his wife. And so they had agreed on a date — the last day before Fred left Moscow for Petrograd — which they could claim to have been their wedding day. As he had pointed out earlier, no one in the rush to escape could be blamed for leaving papers as well as other possessions behind.

Laura didn't find it easy to lie. To her friends, she produced this story with an aggressiveness which dared them to contradict her but at the same time probably confirmed their suspicions that the ceremony was, at best, an unofficial one. It didn't matter. They were too fond of her to gossip unkindly, and on the subject of permits and certificates they all had their own battles to fight and were firmly on the side of the individual against officialdom.

While their search for more private accommodation continued, Laura and Fred were comfortable enough as they were. Irina had won acceptance from Mrs Gillespie, and Count Beretsky had agreed to let them have her room while she was away. They paid rent for it more regularly than Irina herself had been able to manage in the weeks since her illness, and had rearranged the two rooms to provide a sitting room and separate bedroom. Some of the exiles had grumbled at first, wishing to keep the villa as Russian as possible; but Fred's willingness to put up shelves, mend sash cords or clear blocked drains soon made him a popular member of the household. As for the Rolls-Royce, a home had been found for it in the stables in which Count Beretsky could no longer afford to keep any horses.

It was to the villa that a letter came one day from Mrs Gillespie, now comfortably settled in Nice. She described the pattern of her days, the new friends she was making and encounters with old acquaintances from the United States who were also wintering in the area. Only at the very end did it become apparent why the envelope was a bulky one.

'Finally, Laura dear, I enclose a small token of my appreciation for introducing me to Irina, whose company I so much enjoy that I have persuaded her to return to New York with me in the spring. Thank you for taking such pains to find someone so suitable to be my Social Secretary.'

'Social Secretary in capital letters!' exclaimed Laura, reading the

153

letter aloud. 'You know what really helped her to get the job, Fred? I set her a little exercise before she went off to the Ritz. Gave her a list of people. An English marquis, an American millionaire, a French writer, a Russian grand duke, a cardinal, an ambassador, a banker and a few more like that, with their wives. I told her to produce a seating plan as though Mrs Gillespie were having them all to dinner, in correct order of precedence. Just to show that she could do it. She drew it out all very neatly, and I really believe that for a moment Mrs Gillespie saw herself as hostess to exactly that group of people.'

'Well, she's certainly shown a proper appreciation.' Fred had been counting the dollars with a whistle of approval.

'Heavens, yes! Let's go Russian!'

'Going Russian' meant depositing the whole windfall with the owner of the Old Petersburg Club and letting a date become known when food and drink would be available free to all comers until the kitty was exhausted.

'We ought to build ourselves a nest-egg,' said Fred more cautiously.

'But we could have just one party. A kind of wedding reception. To serve as a public announcement that we're together.'

'D'you know something?' said Fred. 'First time I ever set eyes on you, you looked too young to be allowed out alone. Miserable and bewildered and trying terribly hard to look grown up; but still not much more than a schoolgirl. By the time you got on to the boat you were ten years older. Dignified, sensible, all ready to impress your pupils. When I last saw you in Moscow you were practically middle-aged with worry about the Kristovs. And now you're young again. Not twenty-six or twenty-seven or whatever it really is but, oh, about eighteen, I should say. No wonder I can't say no to anything you want.' He whirled her around the room until they were both breathless. 'Right, then, we'll go Russian. But only just this once.'

'You mean never again?'

'I mean,' Fred told her seriously, 'that all your Russian pals are delightful people, but they're not living in the real world. Cloud-cuckoo-land, more like. They think that they've only got to wait a bit and they'll get back, with everything just as it was before.'

'If they didn't hope, they'd have nothing to live for.'

'Anyone can have a dream, but you need to *know* that it's a dream. I sympathise with them, course I do, but sooner or later they'll have to take their heads out of the clouds. Get down to a bit of hard work. Make new lives for themselves. You and I, we've

154

learned that lesson, and we must hang on to it. We mustn't ever become charming spongers. That's what going Russian could mean if we weren't careful. Still . . .' He grinned. 'You're right. It can't do any harm to have a party and set ourselves up as a respectable married couple. You fix it, then.'

She arranged it for a date three weeks ahead, because part of the pleasure would lie in looking forward to it. Before that day came, a second letter arrived from Nice — and this one also contained money.

'A small present,' wrote Irina. 'My first week's salary — to thank you for your kindness, dearest Laura, in surrendering your post to me. I am in Heaven! Madame is kind, and I am instructed to order the best food and wine from the menu each evening and to share the meal with her. Before I left Paris the vendeuse at the House of Worth gave me a most elegant costume in which to make the promenade, in thanks for introducing Madame's custom — and in the hope, no doubt, that her friends would admire it! So both Madame and I are content with this arrangement, and I have agreed to travel in the spring to her house in New York. I see a new life opening for me and, although there is still sadness in my heart for the loss of the old one, I shall always be grateful to you, dear friend, for your great, great kindness.'

'I can't accept money from Irina!' Laura was horrified at the idea.

'You'll offend her if you try to send it back,' Fred pointed out. 'You've done her a big favour. You must let her say thank you.'

Reluctantly Laura agreed. She was sorry to think that she might never see Irina again, but glad that her friend was so happy. She might have given no further thought to the arrangement had a note not arrived from the Hotel Ritz at the end of January — addressed simply to 'Miss Laura' — asking if she would be good enough to call on Mr and Mrs Wasserman there?

'Who are they? What d'you think they want?' Laura turned the letter this way and that as though some explanation might emerge from its margins. 'Not English lessons, surely.'

'Only way to find out is to go. Best bib and tucker. Don't forget to mention the Rolls-Royce.'

What they wanted, it quickly emerged, was a princess. It was as simple as that. A princess. Mrs Gillespie had given a New Year's Eve dinner for all her acquaintances who were wintering on the Riviera, and the Wassermans had been charmed by her social secretary. So elegant. So poised. So well-connected. Irina had been able to recommend to them all the best restaurants and hotels and shops in the south of France. Now they needed the same kind of information in Paris.

'I'd like for Mrs Wasserman to have such a social secretary,' said Mr Wasserman. His accent was so thickly Germanic that he could indeed have done with a few of Laura's English lessons. 'But better. Higher in rank. I asked the countess, but she was embarrassed to mention any of her friends, because then they would know that she thinks them poor and needing work. But Miss Laura, she tells me, has the right connections. So I ask you for a princess.'

'May I sit down?' asked Laura. She had been left to stand as though she was herself being interviewed for a position.

'Ja, ja. Sit here, please.'

The movement gave her time to think. One name came immediately to mind. Prince and Princess Sokolov had been abroad at the time of the revolution and so had not had the opportunity to collect any of their treasures. Count Beretsky had given them shelter, but they were too proud to accept even an occasional meal at someone else's expense now that they were unable to return hospitality. They were fading away on a diet of bread and soup. Certainly they were in need of employment. But was the princess competent to hold down a job? Laura very much doubted it.

'You do understand, don't you, Mr Wasserman,' she said, 'that these Russian ladies of high rank have not been trained to work? They have very few practical skills. A social secretary may possibly be able to help you to enjoy the kind of society in which she is at ease herself, but she won't be able to work as an ordinary office secretary. No typewriting, I'm afraid. No taking dictation.'

'I understand this. You have a name to suggest, please?'

Laura continued to hesitate. So hopelessly impractical was Princess Sokolova that she might easily supervise the preparation of an elaborate meal for fifty guests but forget to send out the invitations — and just as easily invite the guests but forget to warn the servants. But she realised that this solid, ill-dressed couple wanted a princess as a possession, just as they might have set their hearts on a jewel or a puppy. It would probably be enough for them to be out-classing their dear friend Mrs Gillespie. Princess Sokolova could certainly interpret for them and give them social confidence; and for a few weeks she would feed well again and smuggle leftovers back to her husband. Why should she not have her chance?

'I can think of a possibility,' Laura said. 'But I must speak to her first, to see whether she is wiling. Tell me, please, how much you wish to pay, and for how many weeks.'

'Weeks, months, years, who knows?' Mrs Wasserman spoke for

156

the first time. 'We are here in Europe for eight weeks more. Then we return to America and our princess would naturally travel with us. Is this a difficulty?' For Laura was shaking her head.

'Yes. I shall have to think of someone else. The lady I had in mind is married, you see. She might be willing to leave her husband for a few weeks, but to cross the Atlantic without him would be a different matter. Impossible.'

'Perhaps we could employ him also? A Russian prince!' Mrs Wasserman looked hopefully at her husband; but he gave a grunt of doubt.

'What would he be able to do for us, this Russian prince?'

Laura thought quickly. Anyone running a regular employment agency would put Prince Sokolov's name straight into the no-hope file. He was older than his wife, and disaster had robbed him of none of his natural pomposity. He didn't even speak English very fluently. His only talent was to stand still and look impressive. 'A butler, perhaps?' she suggested with more hope than confidence.

'Butler? Explain to me, please, what a butler's duties are?'

'Not very onerous, I think.' Laura smiled to cover the fact that she was unable to answer the question. Her father had never needed or been able to afford male servants. But Fred had worked at a great house, although not as an indoor servant. Fred would know. 'I have a male colleague who would set out the duties in more detail than I can. But I know that a butler announces the guests and keeps the wine cellar book and looks after the silver and supervises the male staff. Mostly though, he just looks dignified. To show that his employers are able to afford him.'

There was a brief conversation in German. At the end of it, Laura was asked to arrange an interview for the couple.

'As for money, for our social secretary we pay ten per cent more than is given to Countess Irina, because for a princess. With all meals and accommodation, naturally. About the prince, we will talk later.'

'Perhaps I may make a suggestion? The prince comes from a very old family and he is a proud man. The thought of working for money may be uncongenial. But if he were to be offered board and lodging together with his wife, he would no doubt show his gratitude by appearing whenever you are entertaining guests.' That solution might ease the strains which would be bound to arise if the prince was offered a full-time post and tried to treat an American staff as though they were his own servants.

Mr Wasserman nodded his understanding.

'And for your agency, Miss Laura, what is your fee?'

Agency! Irina must have made it appear that this was a business. But Laura checked the impulse to shrug any payment away. All this was taking time which could have been devoted to English lessons. Agency? Fee? Why not?

'I shan't ask for any money from the princess,' she said firmly. 'So from the employer, the fee is the same as the first salary payment.'

'One month's salary.' Mr Wasserman nodded in agreement. 'In America is this arrangement also.'

Laura had been thinking of a week, not a month; but for a second time she managed to conceal her surprise. This interview was providing a good lesson in how to become a businesswoman. All she had to do now was to sell the offer to the Solokovs.

'I've just spent two hours with them,' she reported to Fred later. 'They didn't need much persuading to turn up for the interview. It will come easier to do that kind of work in America, where nobody knows them, I suppose. But when I tried to tell them how important it would be for them to be efficient and punctual and all that sort of thing, they didn't have the foggiest idea what I meant. They think that's how they are already. Well, this is an arrangement between adult people. They should be able to make their own decisions.'

'Seems to me you've got a nice little sideline here,' Fred suggested. 'Why not get people − the emigrés − to sign up with you in advance for what they're prepared to do? Then if all these rich Yanks pass the word amongst themselves, you'll have candidates ready.'

'That's a good idea. I think − don't you? − that I ought to write out some kind of contract for the Wassermans to sign if they decide to go ahead. I mean, suppose the novelty of having a butler wears off after they get back to New York. How would Prince and Princess Sokolov ever manage to return to their friends here?'

'If the Wassermans are rich enough to have a butler, they can afford to put down a deposit. The cost of two passages back to Europe. To be held by you, and used if the Sokolovs are dismissed without good reason.'

Laura was scribbling notes. This was what she liked: organising things to run smoothly. How marvellous it was that Fred should be not only so passionate by night but so capable by day! Like him, she sensed the makings of a small business: a satisfying arrangement of finding individuals to suit the most unlikely requirements. There would be mistakes, no doubt, and lessons to be learned through unfortunate experiences, but she could see the way ahead.

Superior Staff Supply: that's what she would call it − just like that, in English. She was a foreigner in both French and Russian

158

society, and there was no point in pretending otherwise. Besides, her best customers were likely to be the Americans who were increasingly being attracted to Europe now that the war was over and the strength of the dollar made living cheap: and they would be reassured to know that they could negotiate in English.

Perhaps she ought to consider providing some kind of training for all these unskilled aristocrats in need of employment. There was no time to help Prince Sokolov, but Fred must surely know someone in England − a retired butler or an ambitious footman − who could be persuaded to take a holiday in France and provide coaching in his duties. Here her thoughts were interrupted by Fred.

'Capital, that's what we need,' he said. 'We've got to get our hands on proper premises. And another car. Then I can train up a few more drivers and you can find chauffeur jobs for them. But I don't see how ...'

There was a long pause before he spoke again.

'Unless, of course, we were to sell the kokoshnik.'

10

Fred's mention of the kokoshnik dropped into a pool of silence.

Laura's reluctance to make any immediate comment was caused not by disagreement but by indecision. She had told him all about the jewels she had been asked to carry to France, and had confessed to the loss of the diamonds. He had made no comment at that time on the survival of the tiara, for the conversation took place soon after his reappearance, in an interlude between lovemaking. It was not clear at the time whether he had even been listening.

Six months earlier Laura would have refused even to consider such an idea. The kokoshnik was not theirs to sell. But now its owners were dead. It would never be wanted for the purpose which the princess had in mind. Laura herself had taken a considerable risk in smuggling it out of Russia and, as well as physical discomfort, it had caused her a great deal of anxiety. Did that now give her any kind of claim on it?

'It's doing no good to anyone, just sitting in a bank vault,' Fred reasoned. 'If Prince Kristov ever made any kind of will, we're never likely to find it − and anyway, he'd have left everything to his children and they're dead as well.'

'There's Alexis.'

'Even if His Nibs is still alive, which is a thousand to one against, the odds against him ever getting out of the country and finding his way to Paris must be even longer. And he's got no special right to this. It's not as if it's a family heirloom. Didn't you tell me that the princess was given it to mark Tanya's birth?'

'Yes. Yes, you're right. There's no reason why we shouldn't use it to raise money.'

'The snag's going to be proving ownership. When one of your Russian pals turns up to flog family jewels, I don't suppose too many questions are asked. But if *I* try it, the sort of people who give the best prices are likely to look sort of sideways.'

'Well, as a matter of fact,' said Laura slowly, 'there's a letter.' She described the authority which Princess Kristova had scribbled at her request. 'It was meant to refer to the emeralds which were a present to me. But I didn't need to produce the letter then, so I still have it.' On that first visit she had been accompanied by Count Beretsky, whose presence was a guarantee of her respectability. 'It doesn't actually specify what it is that I'm empowered to sell for my own benefit.'

She fetched the note for him to read. Whooping with approval, Fred clutched her waist and waltzed her round the room.

'I do like a girl with a head on her shoulders,' he exclaimed. 'Right. Let's go selling.'

Once again Laura asked Count Beretsky if he would come with her — not, on this occasion, to ensure that she was treated fairly, but because she was anxious that there should be no secrecy about the transaction. She made an appointment to see M. Cartier in person and Fred and the count acted as her bodyguard as she collected the jewels from the bank and carried them to the House of Cartier.

They were still wrapped in green baize which she had borrowed from her Aunt Barbara, and no attempt had been made to reconstruct them into one piece. She set each of the dismantled sections in turn on the velvet-covered tray in the centre of M. Cartier's desk. The jeweller looked down at them without speaking for a moment. Then he despatched his assistant to fetch the St Petersburg order books from the archives and to send up one of the craftsmen. None of the four spectators spoke as delicate tools and skilled fingers gradually restored the high tiara to its original shape.

At last it was complete. The Frenchman gently put out a finger to stroke one of the pearls, which quivered on its trembler.

'Beautiful,' he said. 'Beautiful. What can you tell me of its provenance, Madame?'

'It was commissioned by Prince Pavel Karlovich Kristov. As a gift to his wife in celebration of the birth of their second daughter. Princess Tanya was born in December 1908.

160

I don't know exactly when the order would have been placed.'

The assistant turned the pages of one of the order books and put a finger on one line.

'In that exact month, it appears. And how did it pass into your ownership, Madame?'

'I was a member of the Kristov household for five years. Princess Kristova gave the kokoshnik to me when I was about to leave Russia.' Laura produced the authority to sell from her handbag and laid it on the desk. M. Cartier gave a brief nod as he read it.

'There was a matching necklace, ordered at the same time as the kokoshnik,' he said.

'Yes. Little Princess Tanya was to carry that out of the country. The family planned to escape by a different route from mine. Unfortunately, they were all killed in the attempt.'

'So I have heard. Very sad. The two pieces ought not to have been separated into different ownership. They were complementary.'

'It was a time of great fear and confusion,' Laura reminded him. 'Princess Kristova had more important matters to think about: matters of life and death.'

'I suppose so. What is it that you have come to ask me, Madame?'

'I wish now to sell the kokoshnik. Directly to your firm, if you will buy it. But if not, I understand that with work that you recognise as coming from your House, you will sometimes agree to offer it to your clients, and take a commission on the sale. And this, as I'm sure you'll agree, is something of which you may feel proud.'

'It's a masterpiece,' said the designer simply. *'La Lachrymosa.* Created by our most brilliant designer, who was killed, alas, in the first months of the war. Like so many of our Russian clients, Prince Kristov demanded always the very best jewels, the most skilled workmanship. I have to tell you, though, that kokoshniks are out of fashion. They have never been worn in France. Here and in England this shape of tiara has always been considered too high. Now, with the new hair styles – like your own, Madame – there is a preference for a much simpler band, to lie across the forehead.'

Laura swallowed a lump in her throat as she realised that he was preparing to turn her request down. Her own short haircut had started as a matter of convenience rather than fashion, but she had come to enjoy the lightness of her bob and the ease with which she could brush it tidy. It was part of the fun of feeling young again after the years of dignity proper in a governess. But there was no

161

doubt that a kokoshnik would have looked ridiculous perched on top of her neat head.

'Put it on, Laura.' This was Fred's first contribution to the discussion.

Laura looked at M. Cartier, who nodded. One wall of his office consisted entirely of mirrored panels. She stood in front of them and lowered the tiara gently on to her head.

It did not look ridiculous at all. Certainly it was out of fashion and certainly it needed to rest on long hair elaborately dressed. But so beautiful was the design that nothing else seemed to matter. Laura felt herself straightening her back, standing taller. There was a moment, just a moment, when she looked like a princess.

'What about that, then!' exclaimed Fred in awe; but his next comment brought her back to earth. 'It could be broken up.'

'Indeed it could.' But the jeweller was staring at Laura's reflection as intently as Laura herself, as though he were better able now to visualise the piece as it had once been worn. Laura took it off and sat down in front of him again. 'To do that would be regrettable, however. Although the gems were the best of their kind, it is as a complete artifact that the adornment is most precious. The value of the stones separately is very much less — especially since the companion necklace is missing. There was another pearl identical to this.' He set the centrepiece once again trembling with his finger. 'Sold as a pair, they would fetch much more than twice the price of each separately.'

'That is true,' confirmed Count Beretsky sadly.

M. Cartier had not come to the end of his catalogue of gloom. 'Also the prices which may be obtained for jewellery of this kind fall with every day that passes. So much has come out of Russia, and the need to realise it is so great, that there are too many sellers and not enough buyers.'

'Are you saying . . . ?'

'I am saying that this is the wrong time to sell a kokoshnik. Whether we offered it on your behalf or bought it ourselves and looked for a buyer, you could expect only a fraction of the price it deserves. That won't always be the case. If you can wait . . .'

Laura's face must have revealed her disappointment.

'You have a special need of money now?' asked M. Cartier.

She nodded.

'Then I will make a proposal.' Once again the jeweller touched the kokoshnik, this time speading the fingers of both hands over its curved top. '*La Lachrymosa* is a special case. It represents the very peak of a certain fashion — of an era that has passed away.

M. Lamartine is dead and will never again design anything of such beauty. Prince Kristov and all his friends are either dead or impoverished and will never again give such lavish commissions. The Tsar is dead and there is no longer any society in Europe where jewellery of this kind would not appear out of place. *La Lachrymosa* has become a museum piece — and where better to display it than in the House of Cartier itself.'

'What are you suggesting to my friend, Monsieur?' asked the count.

'I will make Madame an offer. Of a sum to be determined by the value of the stones and the precious metals alone. In exchange, the House of Cartier will have the right for a certain number of years — ten years, we might say — to display the kokoshnik as an example of our workmanship. We would wish to exhibit it in other countries also. The contract would provide that at the end of the specified time you could, if you chose, buy the piece back from us at the same price. So that if the market improves during that period you will have the opportunity to obtain a better price; whereas if it continues to fall, you will have done well to take our offer now.'

Laura looked across at Fred, who took over the negotiations.

'Insurance?' he asked.

'We would take responsibility for insuring it.'

'We'd need to agree a figure for that. Higher than the offer you're proposing at the moment.'

'Of course.'

'And suppose, while it's on exhibition, a buyer appears who's willing to pay a proper price?'

'That also we can discuss. It would need the concurrence of all parties. Naturally we should have to deduct the payment already made. And we should take a commission of fifty per cent.'

'That's far too high!'

'You must reflect that what I propose will bring the kokoshnik to the attention of the whole world and authenticate it as a Cartier creation. Besides, the commission would be payable only during the term of the contract. If you buy the piece back afterwards, it would be yours to sell on your own terms.'

'Before we go any futher,' Laura interjected, 'it would be helpful to know how much you could offer under the arrangement you propose.'

It was agreed that she should leave the kokoshnik for a valuation to be made, and return the next day. Meanwhile, she and Fred and the count discussed the matter in a nearby café.

'What do you intend to do with the money if you accept this offer, my dear Laura?' asked the Russian.

'We hope to find a place of our own to live and work in,' Laura told him. 'I can't tell you, Ivan Viktorovich, how grateful I am for the shelter and friendship you've given me in the past year. But . . .'

The count interrupted her. 'Would the Villa des Cascades be a suitable property for your purpose?'

The two Britons stared at him: Fred in disbelief and Laura with some distress. She had always understood that her friend and one-time suitor was one of the more fortunate exiles. As a consequence of his racing interests he had not only owned valuable horses in France, England and the United States, but long before the Revolution had made investments in those countries to cover his training bills. Although by now he had sold most of the horses to cut down his expenses, he had given no hint before this that he might be under financial strain.

Realising what impression he had created, he was quick to dispel it.

'I don't believe that I shall ever return to the Motherland.' he said sadly. 'The civil war is almost over. General Denekin and his Cossacks will not, in my opinion, survive the withdrawal of British and French support, and that will happen soon. The Bolsheviks are secure in the centre. Besides, my country houses are burned. My land is confiscated. If I were ever to ask for it back, there would be more riots. And what pleasure is there to live amongst people who hate you?'

'That was what hurt Pavel Karlovich most of all,' Laura remembered. 'He had been so sure that his peasants and servants loved him. He was their father. It broke his spirit when they turned against him.'

'Well then, there's a choice to be made. I know that I'm almost alone in the decision I've reached. Most of my friends intend to wait and hope: they have faith that everything will be as it was before. There are some, like General Sablin, who keep their hopes alive by plotting and scheming, looking for support from other countries, planning a counter-revolution. I admire them for it, and it breaks my heart to think that I may never see my homeland again. But I have received a invitation from a friend in Arizona who owns a stud ranch. He offers me work, a home, a new life. If my child is not to be brought up in a world of impossible dreams, I must go.'

'Bully for you!' exclaimed Fred, speaking in English for the first time since leaving the villa. Although the count might not be familiar with the word, he understood the tone of approval.

164

'So the villa is for sale,' he continued. 'And it would give me especial pleasure if you − '

'That's impossible!' protested Laura. 'Cartier is not going to make a big offer and we shall have to keep some of the money to set ourselves up in business. We shan't be able to afford − '

Count Beretsky interrupted her kindly.

'Empty, the house might command a high price, yes. But I offer it only with encumbrances. It would be a condition that my friends be allowed to retain their rooms, at rents they can afford − or even no rents at all − until of their own choice they wish to leave. This may not be for many years. I would not countenance their being evicted. My honour would not permit it. No one would buy it under such a condition except perhaps yourself, nor would I sell it except to someone I could trust.' He stood up. 'You'll want to discuss it. At five o'clock, perhaps, over tea, we may talk again.'

Left alone, Laura and Fred looked at each other with sparkling eyes.

'It's a big responsibility.' Laura was trying to be cautious. She was referring to more than just the cost of maintaining a substantial property. The exiles who were still in residence would require emotional support as well as financial consideration, perhaps for many years.

'We can handle that. You've been running the household for a year already. And they'll drift away, the lodgers, a bit at a time. Irina and the Sokolovs have gone already, and now the Beretskys.'

'My agency could find residential jobs for some of the others,' suggested Laura. They giggled like children, although the idea was not in fact absurd.

'You and I could move into the Beretskys' suite. Spread ourselves a bit. Plenty of space in the stables for another motor. Irina's old room on the ground floor could be our office. That would leave our bedroom and the Sokolovs' free for lodgers paying a proper rent.'

'Or for people wanting to be trained for jobs. We could take a couple and let them practise on us to become a cook and butler so that we can find them work, with personal references.'

They were both laughing aloud. To the delight of the waiters they kissed each other across the small café table. Like Count Beretsky, but with none of his heartbreak, they were closing the door on their Russian experience as a new life beckoned.

'What style!' exclaimed Barisinova. 'How do you manage to live so well?'

All the other dinner guests had made their farewells. It was clear from the way in which the dancer lingered behind that she had something particular to discuss, but she was finding difficulty in introducing the subject. Smilingly, Laura suggested a nightcap.

'You've been away from Paris too long,' she said. It was 1923: three years since Count Beretsky had sold the villa to her and taken his family to America. 'Everyone else knows that they're only invited to the Villa des Cascades as guinea pigs, to be practised on.'

'But that magnificent dining room! The butler! The footmen! And the food! It was worthy of an Imperial banquet.'

'That's not too surprising,' Fred told her. 'We had one of the Tsar's chefs in the kitchen.'

'He cooks for you!'

'Not exactly,' Laura explained. 'He works at the Hotel Bristol. But on his day off each week he comes here. We have three young men who are training to become chefs. They produce the meal under his instruction and supervision.'

'Can be nerve-racking, I'll tell you,' added Fred. 'We're never quite sure whether the food will be a triumph or a disaster. What happened to the sorbet today, Laurie? It was on the menu.'

'I expect it melted. Nobody noticed but you.'

'And the butler and footmen?' asked Barisinova.

'All learners. Fred coaches them, and as soon as they're any good at the job they disappear. So we're not as pampered as we might seem. But you're right about the room, and at least that's a permanent fixture.'

One of the exiles whom Laura was trying to help was a grand duchess. Her former high station in society made her unwilling to work for a wage, but she had often in the old days advised the late Empress on interior decoration and now wanted to become known – and paid – as a consultant. So the Villa des Cascades boasted a dining room ornate in red and gold – a fitting setting for thne fine furniture which Count Beretsky had left behind. Rather less suitably for this particular house, the drawing room had been redecorated almost entirely in white and grey, with a few touches of yellow.

'Like a Maurice le Gris painting,' the grand duchess had explained when setting out her design. 'You should buy one to hang between the windows, here.'

She was referring to an artist who, although scorned by the critics, had within the past year become fashionable among American collectors. Turning his back on the sunburst light of the Impressionists and the angular picture puzzles of Picasso and Braque, he painted shadowy pictures of sad clowns and wistful children: subjects redeemed from sentimentality only by the narrow tonal range of his colour. It was generally assumed that he had adopted the name of Maurice le Gris as a deliberate link with his preference for confining his palette largely to different shades of grey.

Laura had not taken up the suggestion of buying one of his pictures, but was prepared to claim laughingly that her drawing room was a three-dimensional le Gris. She found it a little disconcerting to move from the drawing room to the dining room since they had become so different in style. However, she had agreed that the grand duchess might bring prospective clients to inspect the two rooms as samples of her versatile approach.

In return for this, the refurbishment came almost free. The emigrés existed in a world of barter, and the grand duchess had given promise of future professional success by triumphs of wheedling and fixing. Manufacturers provided materials without charge in exchange for discreet publicity and the expectation of valuable orders to come. Two of the non-paying lodgers had been provided with sewing machines and taught to use them. In return they made up curtains and covered sofas and cushions.

In the years since the count's departure, Laura's talent for organisation had been given full rein. She kept her vow to support those of the villa's original residents who were unable to look after themselves, but the number was diminishing. An elderly prince and princess, living at the top of the house, had become completely destitute and infirm, but Laura ensured that they were kept properly fed until they died − of homesickness as much as from any specific illness − within a week of each other, only a few days before the dinner party which had just ended.

This left General Sablin as the only one who failed to contribute in either work or rent. A man with a mission, he spent his time plotting; attempting to negotiate alliances with any country or party or organisation which might be persuaded to join in the overthrow of the Bolshevik regime.

He had plenty of supporters amongst the exiles, naturally, but by now most of them had exhausted whatever funds they were able to bring out of Russia and accepted the necessity of earning a living. Offering them training as well as work, Laura's agency had quickly grown into a thriving business. Paris, where the dollar went so far, became a Mecca for Americans and the news spread quickly by word of mouth — both in France and amongst the international set in New York — that for chefs or chauffeurs, manicurists or maids, governesses or glovemakers, Superior Staff Supply was the place to go.

Fred looked after the profits, investing much of the money in the purchase of taxis which the emigrés then hired from him by the week, keeping whatever they earned. His current pride, though, was a Bugatti, which had joined the Rolls-Royce for the highest class of hire.

It was no wonder that Barisinova sensed the prosperity of her host and hostess, for the success of their venture kept them light-hearted and adventurous, always willing to consider some new project. Even so, she must have realised the importance of what she was about to ask, for she approached the subject only with hesitation.

'I've been fortunate,' she told them as she took a seat on one of the white sofas. 'My talent was international. More easily brought out of Russia than money or jewels. But not with the same lasting value, I'm afraid.'

Laura and Fred waited to hear what she was about to propose.

'I'm thirty-five years old. Already the younger dancers are given the parts which used to be mine. Soon I shall be thought too old even for supporting roles. I decided not to wait any longer. I've applied for the post of ballet mistress. To stay with the company, supervising the daily exercise classes. And, of course, to work with the choreographers at rehearsals.'

'I think that's very sensible of you,' said Laura.

'It means that I shall still have to tour. To London, New York, Berlin, Monte Carlo ... And I'm becoming worried about Leon. He's nearly fourteen and hardly educated at all.'

'The experience of moving round the world ...'

'Oh yes, his languages are good and he's at home in restaurants and hotels. But there's no discipline in his life. And besides ...' Barisinova found the next words difficult to say. 'He's a very handsome boy. No, more than that: beautiful. With such fair hair, and skin like a young girl's. So many of the men in the company ... He's at risk, Laura. I don't want him to become like them. But if one of the principals were to make a pass at him and he rejected it, we might both find ourselves dismissed from the company. There's so much spite and jealousy. He doesn't realise the danger yet, but I'm afraid for him.'

'So what are you going to do?'

168

'It's a big thing to ask, but I must. You haven't any children of your own.'

Laura was silent. She knew that Fred would have liked to have children, and she had taken no steps to guard against pregnancy – indeed, she had no knowledge of how it happened that some women were able to limit their families to a single child, or two. But in a sense her involuntary childlessness came as a relief. In spite of the lack of any marriage certificate, she experienced no problems in pretending to be a wife, because she loved Fred so much. But to have children without being legally married would have proved harder for a woman of her upbringing to accept.

As a young girl, rehearsing the different roles which she might expect to play in the course of her life, she had taken it for granted that she would become a mother one day, and had tried to picture herself in the part. But the events of the past ten years had made her pragmatic. She was happy with things as they were: with Fred, with her work. Indeed, when she considered the life that her Aunt Barbara led – the kind of life which would have been her own mother's, had she lived – she found it impossible to think of anything more boring. Children were no longer on her agenda, let alone other people's children. In her silence now there was no encouragement for the dancer to continue.

'Would you accept Leon into your household while I'm away?' pleaded Barisinova. 'He must go to school, of course. So much to catch up. But he will need a home. Someone to care for him. Naturally I would pay for his keep. But I realise that to take such responsibility is a matter of more than money.

Fred and Laura looked at each other. Fred's eyes were bright with interest. He was going to say Yes. Quickly, before he could speak. Laura answered for both of them.

'We shall have to discuss this between ourselves.'

'Of course.'

'Bring him to tea tomorrow,' suggested Fred. 'Just for tea. No strings. Laura's seen him when she visits you, but I don't know him at all.'

'Yes, I will. Thank you very much.' As graceful and straight-backed as when she was fifteen years younger, Barisinova stood up. 'It's not just unsuitable lovers from whom I must protect him,' she said. 'Mixing all day with the exiles, his head is filled with romantic stories. He knows nothing of life in Russia, except for childish memories; but he dreams of a great crusade against the anti-Christ, a triumphant return, a life of – well, I don't know. I cannot make him understand that even if there were to be a new

Imperial court, I would be too old to take any part in it. He must make a life for himself, here, in today's world. This is a lesson that you've taught to many of my friends already. It's a more important lesson than anything he'll learn in school, and I can think of no better teachers. Till tomorrow, then?'

'What's the problem?' asked Fred after the visitor had left. 'We've got a room, since the old couple died.'

'I don't know that there is a problem.'

'You're not exactly bursting with enthusiasm.'

'He's a spoilt child, Fred. He's never had any discipline, except from one sadistic governess, and that probably made things worse. As a little boy he used to have the most terrible rages. I don't know that I could cope with them.'

'He's not a little boy now. When did you last see him fly off the handle?'

'He doesn't usually appear when his mother entertains.'

'Well, we'll give him the once-over tomorrow. It's not like you, Laurie, to say no to a friend.'

'This is different. We're being asked to let him be a third member of our family. I'm so happy as we are, Fred — just you and me and the house and the agency. I suppose I'm frightened of spoiling it.'

'You're a woman who's seen her life turned upside down three times running and come out smiling. You're not frightened of anything. Well, we'll talk about it again tomorrow, after we've had a dekko at this pretty boy.'

Barisinova had not exaggerated. Her son was indeed beautiful. His blond hair — the Kristov hair — shone like white gold. His pale complexion, which flushed with pink whenever he was addressed, was as translucent as his mother's had been in her younger days, and he moved with the same compact grace — very different from most gangling boys of his age. Only two details spoiled the effect. Although he had clearly been instructed to be on his best behaviour, his eyes were suspicious, as though nothing he heard could be believed before it was checked. And his fingernails were black.

'What have you been doing to put your fingers into mourning?' asked Fred at the end of an hour's over-polite conversation.

For the first time Leon's eyes showed signs of liveliness.

'The stage manager has a motor bicycle, but he's always crashing it,' he said. 'I help him mend it and then he lets me go for a ride. Have you got a motor car or bicycle, Mr Richards?'

Fred smiled. It was a question he loved to answer. 'Two. A Rolls-Royce and a Bugatti.'

'A Bugatti!' Leon sprang to his feet. 'May I see it?'

170

'Why not?' It was time for the tea party to end. When Fred led the way out to the converted stables, the two women followed.

'Leon is crazy about motor cars,' said Barisinova, smiling affectionately as her son stroked the gleaming brasswork.

'May I sit in it?'

Fred nodded smilingly. 'Would you like a run?'

'Oh, please! I suppose − I suppose you wouldn't let me drive?'

'How old are you: thirteen? You can't drive yet.'

'Oh yes. A lot of the company have cars, and they often let me.'

'Well, not today: not in Paris. Perhaps in some quiet place in the country. Why don't we invite this young man to spend a little holiday with us, Laurie? A week before school starts. He could help me to convert that old banger I've just bought into a roadworthy taxi.'

'I'd like that! May I, Mother?'

Barisinova turned towards Laura, waiting for the invitation to be confirmed.

'We'd be delighted,' said Laura. There was no choice. Everything was happening too fast − for she was under no illusions about Fred's intentions. He would no doubt go through the motions of asking for her agreement once they were alone again, but the proposed stay was likely to prove far longer than a week.

He wanted a son, she thought. This was a stronger and more specific urge than the earlier vague hope of having babies. Did he sometimes, she wondered, think about that earlier baby which might or might not ever have existed and wonder how it would have grown up had it survived the pregnancy? He would never have known, since he had so abruptly deserted its mother. Perhaps now he felt the need to atone for a young man's ruthlessness.

Well, after all, the situation was a simple one. Laura wanted for Fred whatever he wanted for himself. If it would make him happy to act as an adoptive father, it would be unkind to object. Leon himself had no father and Fred, practical and realistic, was exactly what Barisinova wished for her son. If it was to happen, it must be accepted with a good grace. She turned to Leon with her warmest smile.

'We have a room at the top of the house with a marvellous view,' she said. 'It's a bit dark and gloomy at the moment. I was going to have it painted more brightly before I invited anyone to stay in it. But perhaps you could help with the painting while you're staying with us?'

For a second time Leon's eyes brightened.

'I often help paint the backcloths,' he told her. 'I mean only

171

the plain bits, you know, like all the sky. I'm sure I could paint a room.'

'Why don't we go and have a look at it now then, before you leave? You could suggest what colour would suit it best.'

By pretending to be cheerful and welcoming, she managed within a few moments to convince herself that she was indeed pleased. Already, as Leon followed her back into the villa, she was slipping into her new role. As well as being a not-quite wife, from now on she would be a not-quite mother.

12

'Is it safe?' asked Laura. They had been sitting cosily in front of a log fire on a cold day early in 1930 when Fred broke the news of his intention to visit Leningrad.

'What's safe?' he asked in return. 'Is Leon safe when he hurtles round the race track at 120 miles an hour?' Leon had left school at the earliest opportunity to apprentice himself to a team of racing drivers. By now, at the age of twenty, he was an experienced racing mechanic and regularly tested the cars at high speed before each race. 'It's twelve years since the revolution,' Fred went on, squeezing Laura's hand. 'Things have settled down. I may not get what I want: that's a different matter. But I shall come back in one piece. You can rely on that.'

'Mind you do. I couldn't do without you. I love you so much, Fred.'

'Me you too.' There was a pause in the conversation while they kissed and hugged each other. A whole decade had passed since their passionate reunion after the war, but they were still deeply in love.

'All the same ...' Laura was still anxious. 'General Sablin says – '

'General Sablin is a conspirator,' Fred reminded her. 'I don't blame the emigrés for hanging on to the hope that they'll get back some day. If you're a waiter or a taxi driver and never likely to be anything better, well, naturally you dream of returning to the life in which you were a titled nob with a fortune. General Sablin hopes that he can weave some kind of diplomatic web which will involve half Europe in driving out the Bolsheviks. He doesn't seem to care that he might find himself responsible for a re-run of the Great War. So if General Sablin were to set off for Leningrad, *he* certainly wouldn't be safe.'

'Obviously you're different. But – '

'I'm not Russian. I haven't a drop of noble blood. I'm not trying to upset Soviet society. There's nothing about me that's a threat to the system. What's more, they need me. They're desperate to trade. I can understand the lingo a bit and I reckon I can arrange to supply them with engine parts.'

'You could do that from here.'

'Yes. But they've no foreign currency and their own is worthless. What I have to do is to go there and discover what they have to offer in the way of barter. It needs to be something that I know I can sell. The idea's as simple as that, Laurie.'

'It sounds dangerous and an awful lot of trouble. Do we really need the extra money?'

'There are two things to consider,' Fred pointed out. 'The ripples haven't reached us yet, but that stock market crash on Wall Street is going to have a bad effect on the agency. On the car hire business as well. The sort of American who used to employ staff is licking his wounds and washing his own car these days. Don't expect they'll be coming over to Paris so often, either.'

'There'll be other visitors.'

'Oh, sure, the British will keep coming. But they can bring their own cars on the ferries, and they don't take so kindly to foreign servants. We may be able to place the odd chef abroad, but in general we're likely to find ourselves stuck with the French market for a bit.'

Laura could not argue with any of that. 'You said two things.'

'Leon's twenty-first birthday's only six months away. I'd like to give him his own racing car. A Bugatti. Or a Maserati, if that's what he'd prefer. He was talking about Maseratis the other day: reckons they're the winners of the future. The Bentley boys have been good to him, letting him hang around; but — '

'He's very useful to them.' At this moment he was probably in Monte Carlo at the end of the rally after making his way through snow and ice from Paris. His patrons were two English gentlemen, Jack Graham and Harry Nelson, each of whom owned a Bentley. Their cars were really touring cars, although they had been successful at Le Mans. 'The fastest trucks' was what Ettore Bugatti had called them; and Laura knew that although Leon admired their sturdiness and was grateful for the kindness of their owners, what he really longed for was a car built for the racing circuit.

It was a rich man's hobby, though. The price of a car was only the start of the expenses, for running costs and living costs were both high; and there was no way in which the life of a racing driver could be combined with earning a living. If Laura frowned slightly at the

173

suggestion of such a generous birthday gift, it was only at the thought of Leon's later disappointment if he could not afford to run it.

But she held her peace, knowing that Fred would take as much pleasure in giving as would Leon in receiving. Fred adored the boy: nothing was too good for him. After handing him over, Leon's mother had withdrawn from his life. Letters arrived at Christmas and on his birthday; but even after Barisinova's marriage to a wealthy American she had never made any attempt to offer him a home again. 'A son of my age would make her seem too old,' he said laughingly on receiving news of the wedding only after it had taken place.

Laura didn't mind. She had taken it for granted from the start that the arrangement would become permanent. Although their lack of a marriage certificate had made them reluctant to become involved in any legal process, she and Fred regarded Leon as their adopted son.

The relationship had proved less disruptive than she had feared. To her surprise and relief, the haphazard way in which he had been brought up caused him to welcome, rather than rebel against, the firmness with which he was made to obey rules and go regularly and punctually to school. All that youthful wildness which might have proved alarming was channelled into the speed with which he drove anything on wheels.

Fred, who had earned his living by driving safely and decorously, loved to hear the screeching of someone else's tyres. He passed on hints about how to swing a car about to make up for the inadequacy of its brakes and how to get the maximum power out of an engine. As she had foreseen, Leon was the son whom Laura had not proved able to give him: and he wanted his son to live the life of a gentleman. All the same . . .

'It will have to be a pretty good barter deal to keep a Bugatti running,' she said — not raising an objection, but asking for reassurance.

'Well, as a matter of fact . . .' Fred paused for a long time. 'I wasn't going to mention it, in case I can't pull it off. But there is something else.'

Laura waited. It was unusual for him to be indecisive.

'I'm planning a kind of treasure hunt,' he told her at last. 'To add a little spice to the journey.'

'What kind of treasure?'

'When I was in Petrograd with Prince Kristov, that time when I let you down about the train, he got me to hide things away. Paintings, gold plates, jewels. I did a pretty good job on it. Chances are high that it's all still there.'

174

'But Fred!' Now Laura was indeed alarmed. 'You promised it would be safe!' she protested.

'Steady, old girl. Nothing to worry about. If I can't get at it, too bad. But nobody will know what I'm looking for, so there's no danger until the moment I find it.'

'That's the moment that worries me! And they're bound to search your luggage at the frontier.'

'This is the point about a barter arrangement. I'll be bringing some goods out with me legitimately. Could be just samples, could be a whole consignment. Either way, I should be able to get hold of the right sort of documents to give me a clear run. One thing I remember about the Russkies in the old days — and I don't reckon it'll have changed much. You have to have the proper papers. One wrong date, and you're in trouble. But if all the right stamps are there and someone at the top has said that I'm not to be interfered with, I shall sail straight through.'

He waited in vain for her acquiescence before continuing the attempt to reassure her.

'It doesn't belong to anyone any longer, all that hidden stuff. I've got as much right to it as anyone else. More, you could say. And a Rembrandt ought to be hanging on the walls of some gallery, so that everyone can see it, instead of mouldering away in a cellar. We could be really rich, Laurie: you and I and Leon. Monte Cristo rich. No more sitting in offices waiting for business.'

Laura didn't know what to say. She liked working, and was proud of the way in which together they had built up a prosperous business. But it could be argued that Leon had more right than anyone else to the hidden valuables. He was illegitimate, but nonetheless the only living descendant of Prince Kristov, although no one had ever told him so. But the cost might be too high. However casually Fred laughed it off, he would be taking a great risk.

'Damn it!' he said now. 'I shouldn't have told you. I knew I shouldn't. Now you're going to worry.'

'Yes,' she agreed, kissing him again. 'I'm going to worry. Please don't stay away too long. That treasure kept you away from me once before. Don't let it happen again.'

13

The painting by Maurice le Gris hung on the wall of Laura's office these days. Barisinova had bought it from the artist's first one-man exhibition in Paris, before he moved to live and work in the United

175

States; she gave it to Laura as a gesture of thanks for her generosity in taking responsibility for Leon.

The dancer was not the only one to have remarked that at that time, in 1923, the drawing room of the Villa des Cascades was decorated in exactly those shades of grey and white which were favoured by le Gris. That was the reason why she thought one of his paintings would enhance the room. But she was wrong. It had in a manner of speaking disappeared into the decor and become unnoticeable.

So Laura had moved it, after a year or two, to the room from which she ran her business. Against a dramatic background of dark maroon red, the picture came to life. She stared at it now, as she did at the start of every working day.

It was a large painting, much of it dark with the shadows characteristic of all this artist's work. Elegantly dressed in a gown of oyster satin, a woman stood at the foot of a wide, winding staircase, obviously on her way to a ball or party. At first glance she appeared to be the most important figure in the composition; but Laura always found her eyes straying to the upper landing at the top of the stairs.

A pale-faced girl with fair hair, thirteen or fourteen years old, wearing a nightgown of unbleached calico, looked down at the fashionable woman who was presumably her mother; another woman – perhaps a lady's maid – stood behind her, half invisible in the shadows. Almost certainly Laura was fulfilling the artist's intention in regarding the girl as the focus point of the work, for it was one of a series which he had entitled 'Woman in Waiting'.

The scene depicted was of no relevance to the work of the office, but Laura found it peculiarly satisfying to study the girl's face in an effort to penetrate its curious stillness – which had nothing to do with the fact that it was frozen for ever on canvas. The expression was not wistful, not envious, not excited or sad. She was quite simply – as the artist recognised – waiting.

On the day after Fred's departure for Leningrad in 1930 Laura went into the office earlier than usual, hoping to extinguish any feeling of loneliness in a bustle of work. The agency had been doing so well for so many years now that she employed assistants to make appointments, supervise the filling-in of forms, type out contracts and keep the books. But she still did all the preliminary interviewing of both staff and employers herself, and liked to look through the files at the beginning of each week to remind herself of anyone who was taking longer than usual to be suited. This she did now, taking advantage of the quietness before the agency officially opened and the telephone began to ring.

Beryl arrived punctually, to be greeted with a smile. Laura had chosen to have an English secretary because so many of her employer clients were Americans who preferred to have their calls received in an understandable language. Perhaps – remembering that conversation with Fred – this would not be true for very much longer.

They moved together into the inner office. Laura ran the agency from what was Irina's old room, but had originally been Count Beretsky's billiards room. It had proved quite large enough to divide into two. People who had jobs to offer were not expected to travel out to Passy; Laura either visited them in their homes or took advantage of an arrangement she had made to use a room at the Hotel Bristol. But those in search of work would first of all enter an office crowded with filing cabinets and busy with typewriters and telephones before being invited to pass through into the inner sanctum.

Here, everything was peaceful. One of the original long windows offered a view of the well-kept gardens; and the more recently built partition wall had panels of glass right across the room above the height of the door in order to admit more light from the other windows. The room was uncluttered, furnished only with a bookcase, a large, old-fashioned desk and three chairs.

There was the usual routine of appointments to be discussed, letters to be dictated, instructions to be given: then Beryl returned to her own desk. Laura, missing Fred more than was sensible when he had only been gone for a few hours, concentrated on what had to be done, and the morning passed quickly. She was almost ready to make her way to the dining room of the villa for lunch when Beryl came into the room.

'Someone's arrived without an appointment. But says she's sure you'll want to see her.'

'Buying or selling?' It was the phrase which they all used as shorthand for those who employed or offered service.

'Neither, I don't think. A personal call. This is her card.'

It was a curious card, designed to be read vertically. Up one side was a drawing. It consisted of only five bold black strokes delineating in almost caricature form a tall, willowy, elegant woman. Beside this, with the letters written from top to bottom, was printed the word ANASSA. Laura stared at it in bewilderment.

'What nationality is she?'

'She spoke French like a Frenchwoman to start with. When she realised I was English, she spoke English like an American. She says you know her.'

'I must just finish this letter. Ask her to take a seat for a moment, will you? I'll buzz you.'

177

There was no letter to be finished, but only curiosity to be indulged. Moving silently over the thick carpet, she followed Beryl across the room; but instead of going through the door, she stretched to look through the glass of the partition.

The visitor was standing by the window, looking out. She did not turn her head as the secretary spoke to her, but merely nodded and continued to stare out.

She was a tall woman, and very thin — so thin that her black coat, trimmed with fur at the collar and hem, seemed to be draped over a skeleton rather than a body. She held herself well, like a mannequin — and perhaps she was exactly that: an American model hoping to find work in Paris and supposing that to plead a personal acquaintance would give her some advantage; because Laura couldn't believe that they had really met before.

Why wouldn't the woman turn her head? Instead, she remained almost unnaturally still. Not as though there were anything particularly fascinating about the garden view. It seemed merely that, unlike the generality of people who fidgeted when they were kept waiting, she would move only when there was a reason for movement. Laura returned to her desk and pressed the buzzer.

She stood up again as the door opened, and stared questioningly at her visitor. The woman was younger than she had looked from behind. Her hair seemed almost unnaturally black. Her face powder was too pale for Laura's taste, and her lipstick too scarlet, giving her a mask-like expression. But beneath the paint was a beautiful woman.

There was a moment of awkward silence as the visitor waited to be greeted.

'You don't recognise me?' she asked, smiling. 'Well, I've changed the colour of my hair. Try to see me as a blonde.'

The words and the smile broke the mask and brought animation to her face — and now Laura did become aware that there was something familiar about her. What was it? Not the face or the voice or the body. But something about the stillness with which she had waited in the outer office. And the name on the card: Laura remembered that she had heard it before.

'Anassa!' she exclaimed. 'The girl Maurice le Gris uses for his model!' She turned to indicate with one hand the picture which she had been studying earlier that morning: the child in the nightdress.

'Yes, I am Anassa. So you have had a picture of me on your wall for all these years without realising!'

'Without realising what?'

There was a second silence. Was some other form of identification expected? Once again the smile warmed her visitor's face.

'I have been Anassa for ten years,' she said. 'But before that, my dear Miss Laura, I had another life. Before Anassa was born, I was Tanya. Tanya Pavlovna Kristov.'

There was a moment in which Laura was unable to breathe. She could feel the blood draining from her face with shock, and had to rest her hands on the edge of the desk to steady herself.

'It's not possible!' she exclaimed. 'For ten years I've believed – I was *assured* – that Tanya was dead.'

'Then I must be her ghost, for I am surely Tanya. But I'm no ghost. Not a con-girl, either. What can I do to prove myself to you?'

Hope began to swell in Laura's heart. No imposter, surely, would issue so confident a challenge when pupil and governess had spent so many hours together with no one to watch or overhear them.

'You can tell me,' she said slowly, 'the first words I ever spoke to Princess Tanya.'

'Right, I can tell you that. You spoke to me in the garden at Almyra. No one besides myself could have heard you except Sofiya – and Sofiya, alas, is certainly no longer alive. You said, dear Miss Laura, you said, "Shall I kiss it better?"'

She raised Laura's hand to her lips and kissed each finger joint in turn; her blue eyes meanwhile gazing steadily into Laura's. 'Am I right?' she asked.

'Yes.' Laura's voice was husky with emotion. It was true. No one else had heard those words spoken. Her body flooded with certainty and joy as she opened her arms to embrace her pupil. 'Oh Tanya, my dearest Tanya! I'm so sorry. I didn't recognise . . . you've changed so much.' They were both crying as they kissed.

'It was to be expected,' Tanya said. 'I was only a child.'

'But you haven't grown up to look like the woman that child was waiting to become. And I was told so positively that you had died. Fred – do you remember Fred?'

'I surely do. Such a bad conscience I had about Fred! He didn't want to come with us on the escape. He had a plan to travel with you, to look after you. I made him stay with us, because my father had been shot. Did you know about my father?'

'Yes.'

'So it was my fault that Fred was killed. He could have been safe with you. But instead . . .'

'Fred killed? What do you mean?' The hot excitement of the reunion faded, to be replaced by a cold lump in Laura's stomach. Was she about to be told a truth that she didn't want to hear?

179

'Fred promised to come back for me. After we were stopped by soldiers in the snow. He was going to lead them away from us all, and then return. He would have done it if he could, I know that. But I never saw him again. He must have been shot, as they shot my mother. I blame myself. He was a hero; our protector.'

There was a long silence. Laura should have been plying Tanya with excited questions, but instead she was filled with dismay. It had never before today occurred to her to doubt the truth of Fred's story, but now . . . It would be several months before she could expect to see him again. What would he say when confronted with the child he had left to her fate?

She must put all that out of her mind. This was a time for happiness.

'Come and have lunch. And then, my dearest Tanya, you must tell me all your adventures. Why you never managed to keep our rendezvous. And how you've suddenly found me now, after so long. I want to hear the whole story.'

Book Two

Anassa's story

1

'Bloody hell!' exclaimed Fred. 'Bloody, bloody hell!'

Tanya's blue eyes widened in anxiety as she looked up at him. Miss Laura had often told her that her English was very good, but she had never heard these words before. They were words of anger. But even though Tanya was only nine years old, she could tell the difference between someone who was cross with her because she had been naughty, and someone who was cross for quite a different reason.

Why was he so angry; and why did her mother and sister both look so pale and frightened? And where was Papa? Not understanding what was happening, and so not knowing what the right question was to ask, Tanya slid her small hand into Fred's large one, telling him silently that she needed to be looked after. She heard his breath expel itself in a huge sigh. Whatever it was that he didn't want to do, he had given in.

The next few hours passed in a flurry. Tanya had already had it explained to her that no one would call any of the family 'Your Highness' any longer, but even so she was surprised to see how meekly even her mother did what Fred told her. They all had to dress in their strongest boots and as many layers of clothes as they could manage. When Tanya protested that they made her look fat, she was told that she would be glad of them all before long. They would be glad of all the food they had as well, although it didn't look very inviting.

What a lot there was to be carried! Two bags of food and two much heavier sacks which Fred tied up without letting Tanya see inside; as well as four pairs of snow-shoes and several rolled-up bearskins to keep the travellers warm. It was Tanya who − very pleased with herself for remembering − told Fred that she had a toboggan which would slide the heaviest items along the frozen streets. 'Clever girl!' said Fred, not angry any more; and Tanya no longer felt that she wanted to cry.

They set off as soon as it was dark for the place where Fred promised that transport would be waiting. There were two sledges and teams of horses, because the men looking after them had expected seven people to be travelling. Although Fred could speak Russian when he wanted to, he asked Tanya's mother to translate his instructions.

'We only need a single troika. But one of these two is to come with us on horseback, riding ahead as a guide. Tell him you'll pay half now and the other half when we're within sight of the border. He can turn back then, if he's afraid of the Red Guards.'

The message was not a welcome one, and there was a good deal of argument before the arrangement was agreed. Tanya and Sofiya were settled down on either side of their mother, with Fred sitting in the coachman's seat. He flicked his whip at the shaft horse and, slowly at first but soon at a steady pace, the journey began.

'Where is Papa?' asked Tanya; but at the question her mother began silently to weep. Understanding what the answer must be, she did not ask again. Instead, she put another question. 'Where are we going?'

It was Sofiya who answered, with all the impatience of an older sister.

'To meet Miss Laura in Paris. Don't you remember?'

Yes, Tanya remembered. At the Café de la Victoire. How long, she wondered, would it take to arrive?

A very long time, she soon realised. All that night they jolted along. By dawn they had reached the bank of a river and Fred decided to stop at one of the many summer villas which were always closed up and unvisited at this time of year and which, since the revolution, might never be visited by their owners again.

'A little sleep for us and rest and food for the horses,' he said, lifting Tanya down. He had quite stopped being angry now, and was friendly and kind instead. It didn't seem right to Tanya to break down somebody else's door; but her mother reminded her that this was Princess Sokolova's dacha, which they had often visited for picnics, and that the princess would be glad to know that it was offering them shelter. Soon a fire was burning and they were able to melt snow and make tea to go with the dry black bread and salty sausage which was all they had to eat.

Tanya fell asleep in front of the fire as soon as she had finished the unappetising meal and did not awaken until they had already resumed their journey. Fred must have carried her outside and settled her comfortably to lie across Sofiya's lap with her head on her mother's knee. She was completely covered by one of the bearskins, so that the air she breathed was stuffy. But at least it was warm: even after her eyes opened she made no attempt to move.

On and on they went. They were following the course of a river now, or perhaps crossing a lake. Tanya could tell that from the high-pitched singing noise made by the metal runners cutting into ice. But still from time to time there was a sudden jolting as the horses failed to notice the rough places where snow had been blown into drifts and lumpily frozen. The stuffiness and darkness beneath the covers sent her back to sleep, so that a second night passed without her realising it.

The sound of an argument awoke her. Their guide was refusing to go any further. She heard the clink of money as he was paid off. Once again she slept.

Her next awakening was sudden and terrifying. There was a crackling sound, like the noise which her father and his friends used to make when they went out shooting. The bearskin slipped off her as one of the horses reared up into the air before crashing down on to its two team mates. The other horses swerved to avoid it, overturning the troika as they thrashed around in panic. Tanya was thrown into the snow, with Sofiya on top of her. So close were the thrashing hooves that neither of them dared to move. There was more gunfire; and Tanya heard her mother, a little way away, give a cry of pain.

The noise of whinnying came nearer and the snow and ice shuddered beneath the struggles of the horses to escape from each other. Amidst all the chaos, Tanya heard Fred's voice.

'Keep still, all of you. Absolutely still. Don't talk until I tell you. Don't move till I come back. If they find you, let them think you're dead. I'll try to draw them off.'

Almost smothered by Sofiya, who was lying above her, Tanya twisted her head in time to see Fred slash with a knife at the traces of the dying horse, which continued for a moment or two longer to raise its forelegs in agony before stamping them down again into the ice. The other two horses, freed of that burden, cantered away, dragging the overturned sleigh behind them and shedding a trail of sacks and rugs.

Sofiya gave a sudden jerk. For a second her weight lifted off Tanya's body before falling heavily down again. Tanya wanted to complain that she couldn't breathe, but Fred had told her not to talk. Instead, she jabbed upwards with an elbow, trying to persuade her sister to move: but with no result.

185

How heavy Sofiya was! Tanya wriggled, trying to free herself: but the sound of approaching voices made her freeze with fear and hold her breath for as long as she could. The men were shouting to each other in Russian. She couldn't hear what they said, but she could tell that they were coming nearer. Suddenly there was a chinking sound, and the shouting stopped, to be replaced by a softer murmur. They must have discovered one of the sacks which Fred had loaded. Perhaps now the men would go away.

By now her face and fingers and feet were so numb that she was unable to feel them. Yet the snow, which had seemed so cold when first she fell into it, was becoming almost as warm and cosy as the bearskin rug. Little by little Tanya allowed herself to sink into its embrace. Since she would have to lie still until Fred came back for her, she might as well have another sleep. The voices of the men who were hunting her — they must be the Red Guards of whom her mother had been so much afraid — gradually faded from her ears.

She awoke — it must have been a long time later — to hurt and bewilderment. Her body had been covered in grease and rolled tightly inside a rug or blanket; she seemed to be painfully crackling and prickling all over, with almost as much noise — to her own ears at least — as the thawing of the ice on the River Neva each spring. She was lying in a dim light with the roof of some building only a few inches above her head. Her back was too warm whilst her face and chest shivered with chill. Where was she? Was she dead? What was happening?

Some movement on her part must have attracted attention, for a woman appeared and lifted her down from her perch above a wood-burning stove. An older woman was called, and they were joined by three or four children: a jabbering began all around her. The women seemed friendly, as far as she could tell, and she guessed that they were asking her questions; but she didn't understand a word they said. It wasn't Russian — a language she knew although she rarely spoke it — and it certainly wasn't French or English.

Recognising the problem, the women resorted to sign language. Each in turn pointed to herself and said something: her name, almost certainly. Then they pointed to Tanya. She understood that she should tell them what she was called.

That at least should be easy enough. She was Princess Tanya Pavlovna Kristov. Yet should she confess to that? Her mother had told her ... But where was her mother? Where was Sofiya? Questions struggled with answers in her mind, making her unable to force even a single word past her lips. 'Tanya.' That was all she needed to say for the moment, but even that was impossible.

186

The women continued to fuss, but Tanya was no longer listening. Although her blood was no longer as icy as it had been a few hours earlier, her body was numbed by a different kind of chill. She was lost. There was nobody in the whole world who knew where she was and perhaps there was no longer anyone alive in the whole world who would ever try to find her. For the first time since her awakening a sound emerged from her mouth: a groan of hopelessness, so loud and despairing that the people in the hut were silenced by sympathy and bewilderment. They were doing their best to be kind, but she didn't know who they were. Still wrapped in the blanket, Tanya managed to roll over, turning her face away from them. She was trying to tell them that she wasn't really there.

2

The trapper who had rescued Tanya from the snow and carried her across the invisible frontier was not unkind. Although he expected her to work hard, her tasks were no more unpleasant than those allotted to his own daughters. He and his family thought she must be stupid because she could not understand anything they said to her, and they were certain that she was dumb because she was unable to speak even her own name aloud. Sometimes Tanya herself believed that she had become dumb, because what other reason could there be for her inability to say the words which battered inside her head? Could it be that something in her tongue had frozen as she lay on the ice with Sofiya's weight pressing her down?

She did her best to communicate with her rescuers, writing her name with a stick in the snow – but quickly realised that none of them could read. The wooden hut in which they lived contained no books, paper or pens.

The family was very poor. They cut wood from the forest which surrounded them, set traps for animals and owned just enough land to provide whatever vegetables would grow during the short summer season; but as winter ended and the river unfroze Tanya realised that they lived mainly on the fish which they caught and smoked. It was kind of them, she supposed, to accept another mouth to be fed but the tasks of chopping vegetables, sweeping floors, hoeing the earth or cleaning fish were cold and rough. Very often at night as she lay on a straw mattress between the two daughters of the house, she cried herself to sleep, pressing a fist into her mouth so that no one should hear her moaning. Was the whole of the rest of her life to be passed in such a way? Would she never be able to escape?

187

Nine months passed before a rescuer appeared. The nearest church — indeed, the nearest village — was a three-hour journey each way, and even the adult members of the household attended only the Easter and Christmas services, leaving the children behind with the old grandmother. If it was Christmas, Tanya realised, she must by now be ten years old, although her birthday had passed unrecognised even by herself. Certainly no one had offered her any birthday gifts but, even as she sadly remembered earlier and happier birthdays, an unusual Christmas present was making its way towards her.

When the fisherman and his wife returned from the service they were accompanied not only by the priest from the village but by another man: a huge man with a thick black beard and bright black eyes. Tanya could tell that he was a stranger to the family, for they had as little comprehension of his speech as she had of theirs.

'I am Father Ivan,' said the stranger. He sat down and lifted her on to his knee. 'Won't you tell me your name?' Although he was such a big man, his voice was gentle. But he was speaking Russian. The men who had shot at Tanya and her mother and sister had talked amongst themselves in Russian and she still felt frightened every time she remembered that long time of lying face downwards in the snow, listening to them and not daring to move. 'Don't talk until I tell you,' Fred had said; and the tone of his voice had convinced her that it was important to obey.

'I am Father Ivan,' said the strange priest again: and this time he spoke in French. Tanya's eyes lit up as she recognised one of the languages of her happy childhood — and the priest was quick to notice.

'God be praised!' he exclaimed, still speaking French. 'You understand me. So now, my little one, you will tell me your name.'

The word trembled on the tip of her tongue. She tried to say it. Tanya. I am Tanya. For almost a year she had prayed that someone would arrive who would know who she was; or at least who would want to find out. But during all those months she had not spoken a single word — because no one would have understood her — and now it seemed that she had forgotten how to talk.

There was a long silence while she struggled in vain to make the right sound. Still gently, the priest set her down on the floor.

'These good people call you God's innocent,' he said. 'Because you were dead, and came back to life. And because you lacked the wit to speak or understand. But now, even though you may not have the gift of speech, perhaps you can write your name for me.' He put

188

a piece of charcoal into her hand and gestured towards the kitchen table. As carefully as though she were writing an exercise for Miss Laura, Tanya drew the letters of her name on to its wooden surface for him to repeat aloud. T.A.N.Y.A.

The crowded kitchen buzzed with excitement. The other children, their parents, their grandmother, the village priest – everyone was repeating her name. Tanya, Tanya. The ten-year-old felt her heart thumping as though it were fighting to escape from her chest, just as she fought to escape from her silence. But there was a more important kind of escape in prospect. She was a prisoner who could hear the key turning to unlock her cell. She had been forgotten and now was found. Soon, surely, she would be replaced in her proper life.

It was not as simple as that. The priest continued to ask questions and she drew the answers, letter by letter, in the palm of his hand with one finger. Patiently she listened to what he had to tell her, nodding her head to show that she understood. From him she learned that the family of river fishermen with whom she had lived for the past nine months was Finnish. A recent civil war had liberated their country from Russian rule, but they had always spoken only their own language. She heard, too, that Petrograd was starving and that the churches were closed. Father Ivan, in peril of his life, had been forced to flee from the sacrilegious Bolsheviks.

'Did you also come from Petrograd, Tanya?' he asked.

Tanya nodded, and slowly answered other questions. What was her family name? Where did she live before her escape? Who was travelling with her?

After she had traced out the answer to that last question there was a long silence. Then the priest's broad hand stretched out to cover her own. From him she learned that her mother and sister were dead. Tanya found that to cry was as hard as to speak; as though her heart as well as her tongue had been frozen for ever on that icy winter's night.

During another session of questions and answers Father Ivan tried to discover what destination the family had in mind when making its escape; and here Tanya could answer confidently. 'Paris,' she wrote. 'I have to meet Miss Laura in Paris as soon as the war is over.'

The war, she learned, had already ended in most of Europe. Only in Russia did the fighting still continue, with foreign troops supporting the White Army which hoped to overthrow the revolution. It was too difficult for her to understand. The only important thing was that she should go to Paris.

She took it for granted that her new friend would help her. While she waited, her life in the fisherman's wooden hut continued as

189

usual. Now that the family knew her name, it was frequently on their lips, making her feel welcome. And when Father Ivan returned for a third visit, she was given practical proof of their goodness.

'There have been many families like yours who fled from Russia,' he told her. 'Most of them reached the border much further south. That's why these kind people had no idea where you had come from or who you might be. You must have taken a longer route, across the lake. I have found a Russian lady, Countess Balakin, who also hopes to reach Paris. She has agreed to take you with her. Collect your things now, and we will leave at once.'

What things? She watched in amazement as a bundle was pulled down from the rafters of the roof which acted as a storehouse. On the day she left Moscow, she remembered, she had been made to wear so many clothes that she had looked fat and horrid. Two of her dresses had been worn to rags with all the work she had to do; but here were the rest of them, unspoiled. Even her boots had been kept for her whilst she, like the other children, had been wearing roughly made moccasins tied on with straps of skin. The boots had become too tight to be comfortable, but she forced her feet into them for the pleasure of looking properly dressed again.

The other children admired her transformed appearance with no trace of jealousy. She was ready to go when one more article was held out to her. It looked like a belt made out of felt; except that it had no fastening. Tanya remembered that her mother had sewn it round her waist. The Russian priest looked puzzled for a moment before taking a knife and slitting it open.

Hidden inside was a necklace fit for an empress. Circles of tiny diamonds fell in three tiers, and inside each circle hung a pearl.

A silence fell in the smoky kitchen as all its occupants stared in amazement at the treasure: even Tanya had not known what it was that she had been wearing.

'You are a fortunate girl to have been brought back to life by such honest folk,' said the priest at last. 'This means that you can make them a little present in gratitude for their care. And also a donation to Mother Church in thanks that you are found and given protection. Shall I tell them that?'

Without understanding what he meant, she nodded — but as he took hold of the large pearl in the centre of the necklace and twisted the thin wire which held it until it broke, she instinctively put out a hand in protest. It wasn't right that her mother's jewellery should be spoiled like that.

'This is no use to them as it is,' said the priest. 'I will sell it

190

and send them some money. Come then, Tanya. Say goodbye and thank you.'

There was a flurry of embraces as each member of the family rubbed cheeks roughly against her own — chattering away as though they had still not recognised her inability to understand more than a few words of their language. And then this interlude in her life was over. Just for a moment, as she took her seat in the sleigh, she shivered at the memory of the last disastrous journey over the snow: but that sadness was soon overwhelmed by the excitement of the new adventure.

Countess Balakin was not nice at all. 'She smells!' was her first comment as she was introduced to her young charge. Father Ivan hurried to explain the primitive conditions under which Tanya had been living, but it did not make for a good start to the journey. It seemed that the countess was poor, because she explained immediately that their railway fare to Paris was being paid out of a special fund set up to help the refugees, and that she hoped that the Miss Laura who was expected to take charge of Tanya in Paris would be prepared to repay the cost of food during the journey.

None of that mattered to Tanya as she was taken to the station the next day. She was going to Paris at last: well-scrubbed and with her hair clean and tidy for the first time in a year. She skipped happily along, holding Father Ivan's hand. But as the time of departure approached, there was something he seemed to have overlooked. For a farewell gift he had given her a notebook and pencil so that she could write down anything she needed to communicate. She used its first page to ask for the return of the necklace.

He put on a show of having forgotten all about it, but Tanya could tell that really he had hoped she would be the one to forget. At least, though, he had brought it with him. The countess's eyes opened wide at the sight of such jewels and she snatched the piece from the priest's hands.

'I'll take charge of that. There are thieves everywhere. A child . . .'

Tanya put out a hand — not to stop her stowing it away but because she wanted to look at the necklace before it disappeared from sight. She studied it for a moment before staring up into the priest's eyes. One of the three tiers of the necklace had been cut away so neatly that there was no trace of its previous existence. But Tanya knew what had happened. If disappointment and scorn could have melted the heart of a greedy man, he would have returned what he had stolen; but instead he stared her out.

191

'Come along,' said the countess briskly. Whistles were blowing, the train was about to move. Tanya didn't know what she could do. And, after all, her mother was dead and would never wear the necklace again. Perhaps it wasn't important. But she must make sure that she was given what was left as soon as they arrived in Paris, because Miss Laura would need money to look after her.

The journey was long and bewildering, with many changes of trains and long interrogations at each frontier they crossed. Tanya had been issued with a Nansen passport before she left Finland, to show that she was a stateless refugee; but not every border official was familiar with the document and Countess Balakin grew impatient with the need to repeat that no, she was not a relation of the child herself, but was merely escorting her into the care of a guardian.

At last, though, the moment arrived. 'This is Paris,' said the countess as the train drew to a halt.

Yes, it was Paris. Everyone on the crowded platform was speaking French as they greeted the alighting passengers emotionally. There was no one to meet Tanya, but nevertheless she shared in the mood of excitement.

'Stay here and look after your luggage while I go and find a taxi,' said the countess, showing her a place on a wooden bench. Neither of the two travellers was carrying very much luggage. Tanya had only a single change of clothing inside the grip which Father Ivan had given her, and could easily have carried it to a taxi rank. But she did what she was told and sat patiently while the other passengers dispersed.

A long time passed. Now the platform was empty except for two porters who were unloading goods from the end of the train. Was it so difficult to find a taxi in Paris? Or had Countess Balakin perhaps forgotten the number of the platform to which she should return. Increasingly worried, Tanya stood up and walked towards the main concourse. Here there were more people moving briskly to and fro, but no sign of the countess. And through the doors which continually swung open Tanya could see a line of taxis waiting for passengers. The countess was not there either.

Without any real hope of being collected, Tanya walked back towards the seat on which she had been abandoned and waited there for a little longer. She was so angry that for a few moments she forgot to be frightened. Instead, her whole body trembled with rage as she understood what had happened. Father Ivan had robbed her, and now Countess Balakin had stolen from her as well, disappearing with what was left of Princess Kristova's necklace. She had never intended to return. Was there no one in the world who could be trusted?

Yes. There was Miss Laura. Tanya took out her notebook and wrote a question in clear letters. 'If you please, which is the way to the Café de la Victoire?' Returning to the concourse, she showed the page to the first person she saw in uniform. He must have assumed that she was deaf as well as dumb, for he responded in sign language, pointing out a starting direction and then indicating the left and right turns she must take. Tanya couldn't remember them all, but she could ask again later. Summoning all her courage, she walked out into the city.

Two hours later she knew that she was lost. The pavements bustled with people who all knew where they were going and the streets were busy with carriages and motor cars which were all trying to arrive somewhere faster than anyone else, but Tanya didn't know where she was. Her feet hurt in the boots which were too small for her, but she continued to trudge along because to stop would be to admit that for a second time in a year she had been completely abandoned. The last person she had asked for directions had tried to send her back across the river she had only just crossed, which couldn't be right. Did the Café de la Victoire really exist?

Tears swelled behind her eyes, but were not allowed to escape. Had she been able to speak, she would have stood still on a corner and shouted aloud, 'I need someone to look after me!' But the nearest street corner was already occupied by a man with only one leg who was selling matches as a way of begging. At least he couldn't hurry away if she asked him for help. Gripping the notebook in her hand, Tanya made her weary way towards him.

3

The light was fading. Maurice Jardinais swore under his breath as he wiped his hands on his smock and began to clean his brushes. If only he could afford a proper studio with a north skylight! But he knew that he was lucky to be able to rent a cheap room in the artists' colony which was known as The Warren. The rooms were called 'coffins' by the residents because the way in which they were arranged round a central staircase left them wedge-shaped. There was no heating, no means of cooking, and only one tap for each building. In the twenty years since the hands of Puccini's Mimi had first frozen with the cold, not very much had changed in the Latin Quarter.

Stepping back, Maurice considered his day's work and sighed. His ideas were exciting as long as they remained fluid inside his head, but no one ever wanted to buy them after he had expressed them on canvas. He was out of step with other artists and also with possible customers.

Maurice was a man of obsessions. Before the war, painting only as a hobby while working as a teacher of Latin and Greek, he had invariably chosen as a subject his mother in the sunny setting of her farm. But the horrors he experienced as a soldier banished sunshine from his palette. Since coming to live in Paris at the age of thirty-eight with injuries to his head and abdomen which left him unfit for further service and of little interest to the woman he had hoped to marry, he had become interested only in shadows. He was fascinated by the colour which was called simply grey but which was made up of so many subtle and different shades. His paintings these days were titled by numbers: Shadows 1, Shadows 2. All his work was stacked at the back of the coffin: no gallery would show it. An invalidity pension covered his rent, and the money needed for food was earned by sketching instant portraits between the book stalls on the banks of the Seine every Sunday; for although he refused to value it, he had a talent for portraiture.

It was time to think about food now. Every day at this time he and his friends assembled at a *cantine* which had once been called Chez Victor but was now, since the end of the war, more grandly named La Victoire. Here for only fifty centimes he would be given a bowl of thick vegetable soup, the entrée of the day, a glass of wine and a single cigarette. In addition, his half franc would entitle him to four or five hours of lively company and warmth, for Victor was a kind-hearted host.

The hot, smoky, noisy atmosphere beat against his face as he pushed open the door and at once all the tension of the solitary day and the concentration needed for his work fell away. He shouted greetings to announce his arrival and was drawn into a rowdy group of other artists who, like himself, needed to let off steam.

'Who's the kid?' he asked Victor half an hour later. He had noticed her as soon as he arrived. Almost all Victor's customers came from either the Warren or the Sorbonne. There was no prohibition against females, but in practice neither women nor children were ever seen in the *cantine*.

The *patron* shrugged his shoulders. 'Waiting for someone, apparently. She's not giving any trouble.'

The subject was not pursued; but the girl's stillness held Maurice's attention. She was sitting in one of the low window seats, leaning slightly forward so that she could see the door. Every time it opened the shape of her face changed very slightly,

194

expressing hope, but after the briefest second froze again into disappointment.

She was an oddly old-fashioned figure, wearing clothes which did not quite fit and boots which she had unlaced for comfort. They were clothes of good quality, though, which didn't quite blend with the untidiness of her hair and the roughness of her hands. But what fascinated Maurice was the colour of her eyes. Anyone else would have described them as blue but he saw them as a marvellous blend of shades: several different blues, with a little mauve, a fleck or two of green, all merging into a neutral coolness.

Yet she was not cool. She was struggling not to cry and struggling not to fall asleep: a brave child, only just controlling panic. Waiting! thought Maurice to himself. It was the subject of a picture. He took out the sketching notebook which was always in his pocket and began to draw her.

Charcoal was not the right medium. He needed colour. Not very much; just a few touches to brighten a subject which, like his Shadows, could be depicted mainly in shades of grey. But for twenty minute his fingers moved over the paper, concentrating as hard on the child as she was concentrating on the door.

'Are you hungry?' he asked her when he had finished the sketch. She was startled; for although he had sat down close to her, she had not been aware of what he was doing. Without speaking she nodded her head.

'Come on, then.' He took her hand and led her to one of the smallest tables.

'Two dinners tonight, Victor,' he shouted. 'I have a guest.'

'She can share your meal,' said Victor gruffly, ladling out two generous bowls of soup. 'But don't expect an extra cigarette.'

Her table manners were good. In spite of her hunger, she did not attack the meal greedily. Nor did she set all her attention on the food, for her eyes stared into his even as she dipped her spoon and raised it to her lips. There was gratitude in those eyes, and tiredness, and uncertainty. Oh, what expressive eyes they were! He must paint her. It was time to emerge from the shadows.

'What's your name?' he asked, lighting his cigarette when the meal had been consumed. For answer she pulled a notebook from her pocket and opened it at the first page, where the words were already written − in French, although the name she gave sounded foreign. 'I am called Tanya.'

'Can't you talk?'

She shook her head. Perhaps that was why her eyes were so expressive, if she needed to use them for communication.

195

'How old are you?'

She held up both hands with fingers outstretched.

'Ten years old? Where do you live?'

This time she could only shrug her shoulders sadly, and the tears which she was so bravely controlling came nearer to falling.

'So why have you come here?'

She turned the pages of her notebook and pointed to a sentence which perhaps she had written when Victor asked her the same question. 'I have to meet Miss Laura. She will come to look for me here.'

Maurice frowned to himself. It was too unlikely a meeting place for a woman and a ten-year-old girl. Perhaps the police should be informed that there was a lost child. He left her for a moment and pushed his way across the smoky room. Victor was busy serving and, while he waited to have a word, Maurice glanced back. Tanya had fallen asleep at the table, her head lying on her outstreched arms. He changed his mind about what he had intended to say. For her to find herself being questioned in a police station would be frightening. And he needed a day, two days, to paint her. Because of the meal, she would think of him as a friend and would not be afraid.

'The kid,' he said abruptly. 'She's been told to meet someone she calls Miss Laura here. But she's whacked. I'm going to take her home with me to sleep. If the woman turns up, you know where I am.' He turned back and picked Tanya up. She weighed almost nothing. He was able to carry her in his arms back to his room.

Next morning he went out early to buy bread. An under-nourished child should have milk as well, he supposed, although it was not something to which his budget usually ran.

'I'm an artist,' he said when the simple breakfast was finished. He showed her two of his paintings. She was not interested in Shadows, but a picture of his mother feeding the hens brought a smile to her face. 'I'd like to paint a picture of you. Will you sit still for me for a little while?'

Anxiety flickered in her talking eyes. 'I have to wait for Miss Laura,' she wrote in her book.

'Victor – the man who gave you the soup last night – knows where you are. He'll bring Miss Laura here if she comes. I'd like you to sit just here, with your outdoor coat on, and watch the door so that you'll see her the minute she walks in. Just as you were watching the door last night.'

Perhaps it was unkind to make the child hope when there seemed so little chance of her hopes being fulfilled. But Maurice quickly realised that although she was experiencing rather than acting the

196

emotions which he hoped to capture on canvas, she was already prepared for disappointment.

How still she kept! It seemed unnatural that someone so young should not fidget or grow impatient. She didn't even seem to feel the cold. No adult model would have allowed Maurice to continue for so long without a break as he set to work on the picture which was already clear in his head. There would still be shadows, but now a recognisable figure would emerge from them. And as soon as he had finished this painting, he would need to begin another. Maurice recognised that he had a new obsession.

'You must be cold,' he said when at last he recognised that he was asking too much of his young model. 'Shall we go for a walk to warm ourselves up? And to look for something to eat.' He had trained himself to survive on one meal a day, but Tanya would need more than that. To buy more food meant that he must earn more money. He took with him on the walk the large sketch pad which he used for his Sunday portraits.

Although the January day was frosty, the Luxembourg gardens were, as usual on a Saturday afternoon, crowded with families taking the air. Children chased balls or hoops or each other, but Tanya showed no sign of wishing to join in their games. Instead, she took hold of his hand. She was frightened of getting lost again. He squeezed it reassuringly.

'I've had an idea,' he said. 'Sit down here and let me draw you again. As soon as somebody comes, I'll draw them instead and you can go off and play. I'd like a smiling face this time.' He propped up the notice which announced instant portraits and set to work. Almost at once a small crowd gathered round him, admiring the speed with which he caught a likeness, and he was able to release Tanya and portray other children instead. At the end of two hours he had earned enough to buy not only food but new shoes to replace those uncomfortable boots.

'What have you been doing?' he asked as he packed away his materials. She had made no attempt to run about and join in the other children's games, but instead had sketched one of the statues which lined the avenue.

'That's very good!' he exclaimed sincerely. The proportions were right and she had used shading to give the figure a three-dimensional appearance. Only the face had defeated her, perhaps because the statue's nose was broken. 'So, we're both artists! Hungry artists, yes?'

They went skipping down the avenue together; but although he laughed as happily as she, Maurice's emotions were in turmoil. It was a long time since he wanted to marry or to have babies. But this ten-year-old who had arrived so unexpectedly in his life could, he felt sure, inspire him to great things. He saw the years ahead filled with her image, changing gradually as she grew into womanhood. He couldn't let her go.

And yet she had the right to her own life and he was not a thief, to steal it from her. That evening, in his tiny room, he encouraged her to tell him her history.

Although she wrote perfectly in French, and understood everything he said, he had already guessed that she was Russian. Miss Laura, it seemed, had been her English governess, but Tanya had never known her surname.

'That will make it more difficult to find her,' said Maurice. 'Tell me exactly the words in which your mother arranged the meeting place.'

Reading over her shoulder as she wrote it down, he realised that — as he already suspected — Victor's renamed *cantine* could not possibly be the intended place. She had presumably been misdirected only after wandering into the neighbourhood.

'Now write down your full name.' Again he watched as she wrote. 'A princess!' he exclaimed, swinging her up to sit on the table so that he could bow in laughing obeisance before her. 'I shall call you Anassa. My own special name for you, which nobody else may use.' He read the question in her eyes. 'It means princess. Now then, my little Anassa, listen to me. It's time for you to go to sleep. But I shall go out and ask some questions. There are a great many Russians in Paris. Perhaps I can find one who knows something about Miss Laura. If not, I shall take you next week to stay with my mother. It was her picture you saw, feeding the hens. She will send you to school and feed you well and keep you warm and comfortable and love you like a granddaughter. And I shall live there as well and paint you and teach you to paint as well as you draw. We shall be a very happy family. Will you like that?'

Her smile was uncertain as she opened the notebook at the page on which she had written of her need to meet Miss Laura.

'Tomorrow,' Maurice promised her, 'we will eat another meal at the Victoire, like last night. And you will see me give Victor the address of my mother, so that he can tell anyone who asks for you. It may be that, like your mother and sister, Miss Laura didn't succeed in escaping from Russia. Paris isn't a good place for you to wait.' He waved his hand round the tiny bleak room. 'But Victor, will tell her if she comes.'

He tucked her into his own bed again and set off to walk to

198

the other side of the river. He had never been inside the Café de la Victoire, but knew it to be tucked away somewhere near to the Bourse. He walked past it once without noticing, and had to return; for so expensive and exclusive was the restaurant that its windows were curtained and it identified itself only by the single letter V above the entrance. This must certainly be the rendezvous intended by Tanya's mother.

Stepping inside, he was made conscious of his shabbiness by the unwelcoming stares of the waiters. The hour was late, and most of the tables − set back into semi-private alcoves − were occupied by large parties who were well on the way to inebriation. At least one group was Russian, but Maurice's already uncertain intentions were stifled by the loud drunken shouts and the crash of breaking glass. This was not the right setting for his little princess. His mother would offer her a far more wholesome life. As the head waiter stepped towards him, Maurice turned away and went out without speaking.

4

It was a matter of some bewilderment to Tanya that she had suddenly become Anassa Jardinais. Maurice had said that Anassa would be his special name for her, but when they arrived in the country it was the name by which he introduced her to his mother. And when his mother in turn took her along to the village school, she told the curé, who was also the schoolteacher, 'This is Anassa Jardinais. She can't speak, but she's not a fool. She understands everything you say, and if you let her write her answers down she'll learn as well as the rest.' From that moment on it was as though Tanya had ceased to exist and a quite new person had been born.

She − Anassa now − knew that it was kindness which prompted the change. Madame Jardinais had hugged her in welcome as soon as she arrived at the farm; and had asked to be called 'Grandmother'. For the first time in two years Anassa found herself warm and well-fed. She had a home: she was loved and looked after. The business of the name was probably because Maurice and his mother wanted her to forget the unhappiness of the escape from Russia. Her mother and father, sister and governess were all dead, she supposed, but she was being offered the chance to put her old life behind her and start again. However difficult it might be to understand, she recognised that the offer was made in love.

And perhaps it was what she really wanted. If she tried to think back to the old days, the happy days, she had first to cross the frontier of the escape. Whenever she moved her memory towards laughing lessons with Miss Laura in the garden, or the exciting moments of seeing her parents dressed for some glittering occasion, she was always abruptly checked by the sound of her mother's cry, the crashing of the horses' hooves, the weight of Sofiya's dead body pressing her down, the cold, cold snow which had so unexpectedly become warm and sheltering as she slipped into unconsciousness. Many times in the night the reliving of that moment in nightmare jerked her awake, on the point of screaming – but she wasn't allowed to scream, because Fred had told her to keep quiet.

So it was not long before she accepted that she had no choice but to be Anassa. There was nowhere else to go: no one else who could be expected to befriend her. She was lucky to have found such a happy home. The farm, in Normandy, was mainly devoted to the growing of apples as a cash crop; but in the yard outside the farmhouse a collection of livestock helped the family towards self-sufficiency: hens and ducks and geese, a cow and a goat, pigs and rabbits, and two cats to keep down the rats and mice. Anassa made it her business to care for the animals. She loved them all – but especially the cats, who would never be killed and who cuddled up to her out of affection and not merely because they associated her with food.

Going to school was a new experience, and not a pleasant one: but the nervousness she felt at first did not last for long. It was a small school of only a single class. The other children soon ceased to tease her when they found that she did not react. Instead, they ignored her; and because she understood the reason, she did not find it hurtful. By now she had ceased even to try to speak. She wrote answers to questions on the slate, and earned as much praise as anyone else, but at the end of each day she hurried straight back to the farm without wishing to play.

There was a routine to be followed there. As well as looking after the animals, Anassa was expected to spend two hours each day being painted. Maurice spent almost all his time at the farm, and Anassa guessed that this was one reason why his mother was so pleased to have her there. When he went to Paris now, it was only for short visits – and very often he returned, pleased and excited, to say that he had sold one of his pictures.

'It's all because of you, Anassa,' he told her. 'Nobody cares about the way I paint, but they all like looking at you.' He could make her smile with that, although smiles did not come easily to her face. She was glad to be useful.

So the days, the months, the years passed in a peaceful country life. She grew too old for the village class and moved to a different school. One of the new subjects there was English. In the three years since she last spoke that language she had almost forgotten that she ever knew it; but at the very first lesson her understanding flooded back. She was not regarded as particularly clever, but did so well in this subject that her marks improved at once.

Her other good marks were for drawing, for Maurice had kept his promise to teach her. She was no good at handling paint, though. It seemed that she could only see things clearly in black and white and she was happiest when she was allowed to use black Indian ink.

She was thirteen when Maurice returned from the capital with great news.

'It seems that Americans like my paintings of you. Someone has taken one back to New York, and now other visitors have made enquiries about me. So a gallery in Paris has promised to give me a one-man exhibition in the autumn. What I've been wanting for years. I must have as many paintings as possible ready to hang and sell. I am to have three rooms. And I have this idea. I shall call one of the rooms "Woman in Waiting".'

To show what he meant, he carried in from the hallway a picture − painted three years earlier − which his mother had liked so much that he had never tried to sell it. It was a picture of a woman making an apple pie in a farmhouse kitchen. But although Maurice's mother stood in the centre of the painting, it was the figure of Anassa which caught the eye. She had been given careful instructions before he started to paint.

'Maman will give you some of the pastry to roll out yourself and then you'll very carefully cut it into circles for tarts. That's when I want you to stop and keep still − looking towards her just before you cut, to make sure that you're doing it right.'

Anassa was good at keeping still in exactly that way, and other domestic scenes had been set along the same lines. Although she had never heard him use the phrase 'Woman in Waiting' before, she understood immediately what Maurice meant, for she could recognise in her own face on canvas the blend of admiration and wistfulness which he had encouraged her to act.

In his excitement now he could not wait to get started, and sent her − still wearing her navy blue school dress and white smock − up to the top of the stairs, with instructions to lean over the wooden banister. The farmhouse was a large stone building with high, spacious rooms and a wide staircase which turned a corner, but she was told to pretend that it was something very much grander.

201

'You're looking down right to the bottom,' he instructed her. 'As though you were two floors up, not one. And what you can see is your mother just going off to a grand party. You're thinking how very beautiful she looks, and you're wondering whether one day you'll have a beautiful dress like that and go to a ball. You wish you were old enough now.'

It was too close to home. Anassa had indeed watched her mother in just such a way on many occasions. The wistful regret for which he asked was replaced by sadness — but because to start with he was only blocking out the composition of the picture, he did not for the moment attempt to change her expression. It was Anassa herself who indicated that the picture needed to be altered, when at last she was allowed to come downstairs again and look at his work.

As usual, he had sketched his own mother in the centre of the canvas, as the party-goer. This time it wasn't right. Mme Jardinais in real life wore black all the time, and her figure was comfortably plump. It was impossible to imagine her even considering the idea of going to a ball. Anassa went in search of her own sketch pad.

The woman she drew was tall and slim and elegantly dressed in a low-cut gown. The style was out of fashion by now, but Anassa did not know that. She sketched in the necklace which Father Ivan and Countess Balakin had stolen from her, and on the woman's head she set a kokoshnik. Because she was working quickly she used few lines, not trying to include the features of a face or to produce a detailed picture but only to give an impression. When she had finished, she held the drawing out to Maurice.

He stared at it for a long time before turning his head to look at her.

'Your mother?'

She nodded her head as tears ran down her cheeks. The scene which Maurice had set was a real one in her memory, but the emotion he was demanding was false. Often and often in the old days she had watched her parents leave the palace for some imperial function — not with any feeling of regret, but with pride and excitement because her father looked so handsome in the uniform of the nobility, her mother so beautiful in her court dress. She had never at the time doubted for a moment that she would grow up to wear silks and diamonds and dance with grand dukes in the Winter Palace. Her sadness now was not on her own behalf, but because her mother would never again attend such a ball.

'I'm sorry,' said Maurice — but so great was his excitement in the new project that he could not tear himself away from the painting to comfort her. She watched as he smudged out his mother and replaced

202

her with a fashionable woman. The fashion was that of Paris in 1923, not St Petersburg in 1914; but Anassa was not dismayed by the change. It was enough that he had understood his mistake — and she preferred to feel that the partygoer was a fiction.

'Yes, yes!' he exclaimed, working as though the whole exhibition had to be completed that evening. 'Not Maman all the time. A different woman in each picture; a different form of waiting. The next one can be of an artist, with you holding out your drawing, just as you did a moment ago. An artist painting one of my Shadows, perhaps, to keep the picture grey and link two of the rooms in the gallery. Oh, well done, Anassa! What would I do without my little muse?'

5

Anassa arrived in New York in 1925 as a shy sixteen-year-old. The success of Maurice's exhibition in Paris had prompted an invitation from a gallery in Manhattan to show there as soon as he had a sufficient body of work prepared. Maurice could not bear to let a day pass without painting, and for the past six years he had felt unable to work without Anassa to inspire him. And so it happened that she stood at his side as the *Mauretania* glided past the Statue of Liberty on a cold January morning.

The black cloak she wore had a fur-edged hood which fastened tightly under her chin. It concealed her fair hair and framed her face, showing to advantage her wide, high cheekbones, clear blue eyes and pale, perfect skin. She was a tall girl, and now looked older than her true age — and strikingly beautiful.

Photographers lined the dockside, for there were always celebrities on board when the great ocean liners came in. Maurice's name, on the list of passengers, was hardly yet known in the United States, but the policy of the newspapermen was to take the photographs first and only afterwards find out whom they had captured.

A young reporter came to identify Maurice and discover his business and degree of fame. But the artist spoke little English. Anassa, who understood it perfectly, answered all the questions in writing without thinking there to be anything odd about the process. It was this young reporter, describing the artist's companion as a stunning beauty, who first used in print the phrase 'the silent Anassa'.

Within a year she was the talk of New York. Tony Steed, the gallery owner, saw the publicity potential the moment that first photograph appeared in the evening paper. He instructed his wife to take the child shopping for a fashionable – and adult – outfit to grace the private view, and was delighted when Anassa herself expressed the wish to have her hair dyed black.

He fed hints of a mysterious background to the gossip columns – and, indeed, there could be no doubt that she was mysterious. It appeared that she had been brought up as a simple country girl on a farm in Normandy; yet she understood and wrote two languages fluently. Her dress style was sophisticated for a young woman who until recently had worn clothes made at home by her grandmother: she chose fashions almost exclusively of black and white, with just a single splash of some bright colour. Her beauty was not of a French kind, and her natural dignity hardly accorded with stories that a month earlier she had been milking her grandmother's cows.

What was certain was that her image in photographs was invariably dramatic. She had the knack of freezing into stillness at a photographer's command whilst retaining the impression of movement. Before long she began to earn her own living as a photographic model; wearing first of all furs, but very soon choosing to specialise in jewellery. The ease and elegance with which she displayed creations which were each worth a small fortune earned her a second soubriquet. As well as 'the silent Anassa', she was known simply as 'the princess'.

By the time she was nineteen she was being employed by Tiffany's to wear its creations to the grandest social events. There was no secret about her commercial role, but this did not prevent society hostesses from inviting her – and her bodyguard – to their parties and balls, or young men from escorting her to the opera. Far from proving a social disadvantage, her silence made other women seem trivial chatterers, for the intelligence in her eyes proved her to be a perfect listener, and her presence at any party provided a talking point for others.

Nor did her dumbness prove a deterrent to suitors. The sons of those society hostesses clustered around as though one of them could make a fairy tale come true, unlocking her tongue with a kiss. But none of these admirers ever succeeded in becoming more than an escort. Anassa would rest a hand lightly on a companion's arm or accept the necessary clasp of a dancing partner, but she shrank from any touch which expressed affection or love. A third label attached itself to her. The silent Anassa, the princess, was also the ice maiden.

It was as the ice maiden that she became famous outside New York, across the whole continent, when her photograph appeared on the cover of a magazine. Her hair – still raven black – was strained back from her pale face in the style of a ballerina. She wore a diamond choker round her neck. A diamond bracelet encircled the wrist of the one bare arm which emerged from a sable cloak to give the impression – whilst revealing nothing – that she was naked beneath it. The pose, against a background of snow, was a dramatic one: the picture was a work of art.

It was this cover which was the cause of her first serious quarrel with Maurice. He had raised no objection to her glittering social life, because much of the publicity she attracted attached itself also to his work. By now he had come to the end of his 'Woman in Waiting' period and had embarked on another which he called 'Listening'. Once again, Anassa served as his muse and willingly devoted four hours of each day to posing for him. The paintings sold almost as soon as they were dry. If Maurice sometimes wondered whether their popularity was due as much to the model as to the artist, he kept his doubts to himself. For whatever reason, his reputation was growing and he showed no signs of wishing to return to France.

Because he wanted her to be happy, he had wished her well when she began to earn her own living by posing for commercial fashion photographers. But the magazine cover was a different matter. New York was full of young men who believed that photography could be considered an art and that film was a tool which one day would out-rank paint. They held exhibitions to which so-called critics came. Maurice regarded the pretensions of these camera-holders as bogus, and forbade Anassa to have any more to do with them.

In the quarrel which followed her refusal, she was bound to win. The need to use pencil and paper made it impossible for her to express any loss of temper. She needed only to point over and over again to the page which reminded him that she was now almost twenty-one years old, and able to support herself. She would always be grateful to Maurice for his care, she wrote, and would continue to sit for him; but it was time for her to make a life of her own.

The quarrel was made up before too long, because the two of them needed each other. Mme Jardinais had died before they left France, so that Maurice was Anassa's only family; and she herself had become the essential inspiration behind his obsessive urge to paint. But the tie which bound them together was in some ways loosened by the disagreement; and this perhaps contributed to the event which sent the gossip columns into their blackest type, their largest size of headline.

'ANASSA SPEAKS!'

It happened on the first day – the private view – of an exhibition

205

of jewellery. M. Pierre Cartier invited his most valued clients to inspect a special display of pieces created in Europe during the past fifty years and recently exhibited in Paris and London. In an attempt to steal her from Tiffany, he invited Anassa to wear some of the House of Cartier's modern pieces whilst posing for photographs near the showcases. So closely was she identified with the most exclusive jewellery that such a picture would prove a far better advertisement than any paid insertion.

The private view was a society occasion, for no one could afford to have it thought that she had not been considered worthy of an invitation. The gentlemen of the press − less interested in the jewels than in tittle-tattle about the guests − were early arrivals. Anassa also arrived early in order to tour the exhibition before the gallery became too crowded for photographs to be taken. She moved slowly round the showcases on the walls, admiring their contents with a knowledgeable eye. But the most important exhibits were individually displayed on pillars in the centre of the rooms. Reaching the first of these, she looked down to read the label.

'*La Lachrymosa*. Kokoshnik (Russian tiara), created St Petersburg 1908 (with matching necklace, whereabouts now unknown). Designed by M.Pierre Lamartine. Central pearl one of a pair presented to Marie Antoinette by the Emperor of Austria. Present owner: Miss L. Mainwaring.'

The words were of no particular significance to her. But then she raised her eyes.

The kokoshnik was set on the model of a head which had been created out of black velvet: a featureless head, more in keeping with the Art Deco craze than with Tsarist St Petersburg. Even the hair style was created from ripples of the same black velvet. But none of this was of any significance to Anassa as she stared in recognition at the hanging teardrop pearl.

'Oh!' she cried aloud. 'Oh, Mama, Mama!'

The words, issuing from a throat which had been closed to sound for so many years, could hardly be distinguished. All that emerged was a hoarse scream of anguish − but that was enough to draw the attention of everyone in the room. There was a moment of stunned silence, followed by the beginnings of an excited chatter − but this too was interrupted by a new distraction. Anassa, overcome by the emotion of remembering the kokoshnik on the head of her living mother, had flung herself towards the showcase, rocking it sufficiently to set off the alarm which guarded it. And as bells rang and guards came running, she herself slid to the floor in a faint.

She opened her eyes to find herself lying on a couch in a small room. A bearded man in his thirties was holding her wrist and looking down at her.

'They called out to see if there was a doctor in the room,' he said. His accent was European: German perhaps, or Austrian. 'I was the nearest approach to that at hand. Don't be alarmed. You're not ill. But you have suffered a shock, I think.'

Anassa nodded.

'You called for your mother. Was there an association between your mother and something in the exhibition?'

Once again she nodded. She was feeling stronger now, and with the stranger's help was able to sit up.

'My name is Eli Gutzman. I know yours. You are the silent Anassa.' He paused for a moment as though considering whether it was ethical for him to continue. 'I have the right to call myself Doctor, but I'm not a doctor of medicine,' he told her at last. 'A psycho-therapist. Do you know what that is?'

This time she shook her head.

'The silent Anassa who for the first time has been heard to speak. Can you speak again now? To say, perhaps, "How do you do, Dr Gutzman".'

Her lips moved, but no sound emerged. He nodded his head as though he had expected this.

'It may be,' he said slowly, 'that you've chosen silence as a refuge. Retreated into it to escape from something, some memory perhaps, which you never wish to recall. It would be wrong of me to offer to help you without warning you that the road could be a painful one. But I think I must make the offer in case there is a desire within you which is struggling to escape. I believe that I could, if you wished it, help you to talk again.'

Anassa stared into his eyes for a long time without moving her head. The little girl whom she could remember as chattering happily away to her parents, her sister, her governess, had been dead for ten years − and perhaps it was despair at her inability either to understand or to make herself understood which had killed her. But that was a long time ago. Anassa, who had taken her place inside the same body, had had plenty of time to grow into a new and different personality.

Maurice had never wanted to change her. Her silence was part of his inspiration and he had been angry when one of the teachers at her second school had taken her to be examined at a clinic. But the doctor there had shrugged his shoulders, announcing that he could find no physical cause for her dumbness; and there had been no further attempt at examination. Her life had continued as before, in a manner which seemed so natural that she shivered with fear at the thought of changing it.

And yet — and yet the image of the kokoshnik swam before her eyes, making her for a second time feel dizzy. It brought to her mind memories which came from the further side of the nightmare of screams and heaviness and cold. Was it possible that this man could somehow take that nightmare away? It didn't seem likely, because after all what she remembered was not a dream but a true happening.

Dr Gutzman's eyes were grey and steady. They could perhaps be kind, but at the moment were serious and neutral. The decision was to be her own. Taking a deep breath, she nodded her head three times.

6

'Cough, if you please,' said Dr Gutzman. He began each session in the same manner. It was to prove to his client that she was capable of making noises. For the first fifteen minutes of every hour he made her exercise her tongue and lips and throat, in order that they should be ready to obey her will when after so many years of disuse they were ordered to produce meaningful sounds. For the moment, however, no meaning was allowed, but only grunts and groans and the imitation of animals.

Nor was any reference to Anassa admitted to the consulting room. As soon as he learned that she had been born as Tanya, Dr Gutzman had insisted that Anassa was to be regarded only as a kind of stage name. For the time being the person who used that name could continue with her life, but it was Tanya who would learn to speak again.

He had shown no surprise at learning of Tanya's real name and background, but had taken her steadily through her babyhood and childhood, asking questions about the most trivial details and waiting patiently as she wrote the answers. There had been times when she felt as though she were a baby or a small child still, wishing that her interrogator would sit her on his knee, or toss her in the air; but little by little she was allowed to grow older. Until now all her recollections had been happy ones, but they were approaching the time of her father's death and her own flight from Petrograd. For the whole of the past week she had been strained and nervous, knowing what was coming; unable to eat or to concentrate. Always slender, she had since the start of the therapy become too thin.

208

Maurice was angry about the new development. Not only had the shape of her face changed, but he was conscious of her mind wandering as she sat for him. It had always been her ability to express emotion in her eyes and his skill at depicting that emotion which had made his reputation, and no doubt he could see this slipping away.

And now, in the consulting room, the moment of the escape had arrived.

'Did you understand why you had to go?'

'There wasn't enough to eat,' she wrote. 'Only fish soup and a sort of gruel. We were hungry all the time. That was the first thing. And Papa said that people had started to hate us. I didn't know why. But it must have been true, because he was shot. And Mama was frightened. We would all have been shot if we'd stayed.'

'So now write all about it. Everything you can remember about the journey.'

He turned his chair so that he could read the words as she wrote them and sometimes interrupted in order to make the picture more vivid to both of them. 'What were you wearing? What colour were the horses? When you sheltered at night, did you sleep in a bed? What did you eat?'

The questions disturbed her, holding her up. After worrying for a week, she wanted nothing more now than to reach the heart of the nightmare as quickly as possible. She hurried towards the moment of the first shot, the dying horse rearing into the air, the second fusillade and her mother's scream. Dr Gutzman no longer interrupted, but read her almost illegible scribbles as she poured the words on to the paper. Now Sofiya was lying on top of her, heavy and uncomfortable. She herself was face down in the snow. It was unbearably cold – and then suddenly it was warm.

'I fell asleep,' she wrote. 'But I thought I was dead.' She was crying, now; the tears pouring silently down her cheeks. But after a pause she took up the pencil again.

'You're trying to make me remember things. I realise that. But I haven't ever forgotten any of this.'

'Then there's something missing,' said Dr Gutzman. 'Something or someone that you *have* forgotten.' He read through the pages again. 'Who was driving the troika?' he asked.

At first she didn't understand the question, so he spelt it out patiently. 'Three horses, you said. A shaft horse and two off-horses. Pulling a heavy sleigh with three passengers and several sacks. You and Sofiya couldn't have controlled it. Even your mother – and anyway, you said you were lying across her lap. And your father

209

was dead. So there must have been a coachman. What happened to the coachman?'

Yes, there must have been a coachman. Why had she forgotten all about him? Puzzled, she searched her memory; and little by little it all came back to her.

She was lying in the snow, unable to move, when a voice whispered in her ear. 'Keep still. Absolutely still. Don't talk until I come back. Don't move. Let them think you're dead.'

It was the voice of a friend; someone who was on her side. Who was it, then? And why had he never come back?

Because he had been killed, like her mother and Sofiya. It had to be that. And now she began to picture him. A man she didn't know very well, because he had never been part of her own household. He had worked first for Uncle Alexis and then for her grandmother.

'You're beginning to remember.' Dr Gutzman's voice was soft and encouraging: he was holding her hand.

It was too simple. If she described that whisper, it would seem as if she had not spoken since then only because she had been told to keep quiet and the prohibition had never yet been lifted. But it was not, surely, as straightforward as that. She gripped the therapist's hand convulsively and her brain felt as though it were bursting with the effort to remember and understand.

The explosion, when it came, was a physical pain; as though an abcess in her head had burst, allowing a ten-year accumulation of foul matter to pour out. She knew what it was that she had not wished to remember.

He had not wanted to go with them at all, the man who had told her to keep quiet. He had already promised to look after Miss Laura and was anxious to return to Moscow. Even after her father's death he had tried to say no. It was she, Tanya, who had taken his hand and forced him to understand how helpless she was. She was the one whom the soldiers were trying to shoot, but he was the one whose body had taken the bullets. It must have been so, for otherwise he would have come back to save her. His death was all her fault. He could have been safe on the train with Miss Laura, but she, Tanya, had enticed him to his death.

'Fred!' she cried out, startling herself by the sound of her own voice. 'Fred, I'm so sorry. Oh, Fred!'

She was crying again now − not silently, as before, but with a noisy harshness. Sitting up on the couch, she flung her arms round the therapist's waist, forcing him to hold her, comfort her. For ten years she had endured only half a nightmare. Now it was complete.

'Say the words again.' Dr Gutzman was still holding her steady, his hand rubbing her back. 'Remember the exercises we've been doing. Move your lips, your tongue, and let me hear it clearly.'

'Fred. It was Fred.'

'And who was Fred?'

Automatically she reached for her notepad; but the therapist pushed it out of reach. He loosened his grasp, easing her back into her usual half-sitting position on the couch.

'The barrier is down,' he said gently. 'I'm going to suggest that for a little while you should keep both your two selves alive. Let the silent Anassa remain mute in the outside world until you feel safe and confident. But here, in this room, you are Tanya; and you and I will talk about the past – and the future as well. Do you agree?'

She nodded her head; but he tutted laughingly. 'No more of that. Do you agree?'

'Yes,' she said.

'Well, our time is up, and you are tired. Take a cab home, and rest for an hour or two. Can you come tomorrow? We can move faster now.'

'Yes.' The sound was hoarse and croaky, emerging from her throat rather than her mouth; but it didn't matter. The lock had been broken. Her voice was free to emerge. She would have liked to kiss her liberator, to feel him hold her again as he had held her when she cried. If only he would lean over her now, whilst she lay on the couch, and tell her that she was special to him, something more than a client for an hour. Surely that was love that she could see in his eyes. But as though he could read her thoughts, he was shaking his head.

'It's not I who have opened the door for you,' he said. 'It's you yourself. Your own courage. You must be very clear about that. And you are going to need more courage yet, when the world begins to talk to you and wait for your answers. But for the moment, you must go home and rest.'

She smiled, pretending to agree, but did not in fact obey. Instead, she returned to the Cartier exhibition. Ignoring everything else, she stood in front of the kokoshnik, mourning her dead mother. Not until some time had passed did it occur to her to wonder how the kokoshnik had once again become the property of the House of Cartier. Or rather ... She bent her head to read the label at which she had only glanced on her first visit. Present owner: Miss L. Mainwaring. Who was this Miss Mainwaring, and how had she come to acquire any of the Kristov family jewels?

The answer stared her in the face. Not Miss Mainwaring, but Miss

L. L for Laura? Was it possible? Miss Laura? Anassa turned away and approached one of the attendants. Dr Gutzman had told her to remain dumb, and she had intended to obey; but the words, although still husky, emerged before she had time to think.

'I would like to speak to M. Cartier.'

Two hours later she returned to the studio apartment which she shared with Maurice.

'You're late,' he said without turning his head. He was working on one of his 'Listening' paintings, and she had been expected to take up her pose as soon as the session with Dr Gutzman came to an end. Although she would only appear as an indistinct figure in the shadowed alcove behind a pillar — and although he had painted her so often before in just such a way — he still needed her presence to bring the picture to life.

She stared at the picture — little more than a rough sketch — before answering.

'No,' she said in her unpractised voice. 'I'm not late. I've finished.'

He spun round to face her, so much amazed by the sound of the words that for the first moment he did not take in their meaning.

'You're talking! He's done it, that shrink!' As always, they were conversing in French, but he used the American word for someone whose pretensions he had regarded with disdain.

'Yes,' she agreed. 'I can speak. I can ask questions.'

'What questions? What do you mean?' His eyes narrowed in anxiety as he related the coldness of her tone to the earlier announcement that she had finished.

'There's a restaurant in Paris called the Café de la Victoire,' she said. She had elicited the information in the course of her conversation with the head of Cartier's New York establishment. 'A very expensive restaurant. It has an international reputation. People from all over Europe dine there. It's so exclusive that it doesn't need to advertise itself. There's no name sprawled along the façade. Just the single letter V, I'm told.' She picked up a tube of crimson paint and squeezed it out over the canvas in the bold shape: V.

Instinctively Maurice's hand jerked forward to stop her, although too late. Anassa clutched his wrist and pressed his fingers into the shining snake of paint, dragging them down from it until the canvas appeared to be dripping with blood.

'A ten-year-old girl, a foreigner, newly arrived in Paris for the first time and distressed by being robbed and abandoned, might walk past such a restaurant without recognising it, even supposing that she was correctly directed there.' Anassa's voice was bitter with anger. She

212

picked up a second tube of paint – this time it was black – and squeezed it downwards and across into a grid, the bars of a prison cell, in the centre of the canvas. 'But you. You lived in Paris. You must have known. Or you could have found out. You must have realised that a *cantine* in the Latin Quarter wasn't likely to be the only Café de la Victoire, so soon after the end of the war. That's why you took me to your mother in the country. Not to give me a home, but to rob me of one. You stole ten years of my life just so that you could become famous.'

'You were destitute.' Maurice found his voice at last. 'No money, no voice, nowhere to sleep, nothing to eat, nothing. You didn't even know if the woman you hoped to meet was alive.'

'Well, I know now. She's alive and living in Paris. By now she must believe me to be dead. But when she first came there, she would have looked for me. I know she would.'

'Anassa,' said Maurice. 'My little princess.' He stretched his arms towards her; but gave a rueful laugh at the sight of his fingers, red with paint. 'Well, I mustn't touch you and spoil your dress. But admit this. They've been happy years for you. And if I've become famous, you've been part of my fame. Everyone knows that my paintings are yours as much as mine.'

'Not any longer. I'm going to Paris. You'll have to find some new inspiration. Or shall I do you that last good turn?' She picked up every other tube of paint which lay opened on the table and squeezed the colours on to the canvas in circles and crosses, ticks and squiggles. 'This is how artists create new work these days. Perhaps you should start to move with the times.'

'Anassa!' Maurice had made no attempt to stop the ruin of his painting. 'Don't destroy the memory of this time we've had together. Yes, you must go to Paris. I understand that. And I must do the best I can without you. But for these ten years I've loved you as though you were my daughter. No, much more than a daughter. Don't turn your back on all that. You're angry now. But later – when you remember how desperate your situation was and how much you needed a protector – think of me more kindly. Let us be friends again.'

She had talked too much in that newly discovered voice; her throat was suddenly too dry to continue. Instead she sighed, shrugging her shoulders in a gesture which Maurice could interpret either as a helpless inability to control her own emotions or as a promise of forgiveness one day. Then she went to her own room and washed the paint off her hands before packing her clothes.

It was time for Princess Tanya Pavlovna Kristov to return to her interrupted life.

213

Book Three

Part One

Secrets and Searches
1930–1933

1

The reunion should have been an occasion for joy but, long before the story was finished, Laura was weeping.

'I can't bear to think of it. So young and so completely alone in the world. And not even a familiar world. Oh, my dearest . . .' She checked herself, half laughing through her tears. 'Do I call you Tanya or Anassa?'

'I am Anassa. Tanya only in my memories, and yours. I've made a new person of myself. A career, and a character. Besides, there's something I have to do. Unfinished business.' She paused, but was apparently not ready to explain. 'I don't want anyone to discover my birth name yet. Maurice knows, of course, and Dr Gutzman. But Maurice would be ashamed, and I can trust Dr Gutzman to be discreet. I guess a touch of mystery won't do any harm in my working life.'

Again she paused, before taking Laura's hand and squeezing it.

'Don't cry, Miss Laura. You could say – '

Laura interrupted her. 'You mustn't call me "Miss Laura" now. I'm not your governess any longer. Just your friend, Laura.'

Anassa's painted lips parted in a smile.

'With my mother and father both dead, those two words, Miss Laura, have been the only lifeline to my childhood all these years. It may not be easy to change. But I'll try. I was saying, though, that I was lucky in some ways. Those Finns on the border were kind – and Maurice as well, although he chose a way which suited himself. I was mad with him when I left the States, because he'd robbed me of you. But until I found out about that, I was okay.'

'And all the time there was a message waiting for you at the Café de la Victoire! I used to go in every two or three months,

217

to make sure that it hadn't been forgotten.'

'What a difference it would have made if that woman had hung around just long enough to get me to the right rendez-vous, instead of leaving me at the station. It wouldn't have cost her much in time, and she could still have made off with the necklace. But I suppose she needed me to be without a protector, to keep her safe from being tracked down.'

'Who was she?' In the account of her sufferings Anassa had referred to the villainess of the story only as 'the countess'. From the way in which she now shook her head, it seemed that she was not prepared to be more specific, and Laura did not press the question.

'Maurice ought to have taken you to the police,' she said.

'There were a lot of things that ought to have happened but didn't. But when you're only ten years old you tend to go along with what other people do as long as they seem helpful. And I guess the biggest problem was that I'd never known your surname.'

'Did you think that I'd abandoned you?'

Anassa shook her head again, this time more forcefully.

'I'd had a pretty good education in the difficulties of getting out of Russia and into other countries. I just assumed you hadn't made it, as I nearly hadn't myself. It was only when I recognised the kokoshnik, and saw the name of the owner . . .'

'That's wrong, of course. The kokoshnik is yours. I can buy it back from Cartier's.' She explained the arrangement which she had made with the jeweller – an arrangement which had now come to an end with the expiry of the ten-year period of loan.

Only a few days earlier, shortly before he left for Russia, she had been discussing with Fred what it would be best to do. Until a few months ago it had been their intention to sell it; but the Wall Street collapse in October had ruined so many potential customers that it now seemed wiser to wait for better times to return. There would be no problem about raising the money to redeem the head-dress, for Fred's luxury car hire business was as thriving as Laura's employment agency – and his second string was equally successful. It was by now taken for granted by Parisians that almost every taxi driver in the city was a Russian nobleman: less well known was the fact that many of them leased their taxis from Fred Richards.

Laura's conversation with Anassa, which had extended itself over luncheon and through the afternoon, was interrupted by a tap at the door. Janine, apologising for the intrusion, was anxious that the *placement* for tonight's dinner party should be approved.

Janine was the housekeeper. The days were long past when Laura herself was responsible for nagging the lodgers into sweeping cor-

218

ridors or leaving the bathroom tidy. Only two of the exiles were still living in the villa: General Sablin and Grand Duke Viktor. True to her promise to Count Beretsky, Laura charged them no rent and made sure that each was served one good meal a day in his room; but she no longer expected them to provide any domestic service.

Janine was employed by the agency. One of her duties was to provide training for domestic staff who wished to better themselves. As had been the case right from the start, they learned on the job, so maids and under-cooks and butlers came and went at a dizzying speed. But the housekeeper herself was always there and always responsible for the smooth running of the villa.

'There'll be one more for dinner tonight,' Laura told her now. 'You'll join us, won't you, Anassa?'

'Sure, if it's not inconvenient at such short notice. Thank you.'

'Mademoiselle? Madame? And the surname?' Janine's pencil was poised to write the full and correct form of the additional guest's name.

Anassa handed her one of the printed cards which earlier she had sent in to Laura.

'Just Anassa, nothing else,' she said. 'It's an affectation, I guess, but I'll stick with it. Professionally useful.'

Laura meanwhile was adjusting the table plan to include her. 'And will you get the blue suite made up, please?' she said. Again she turned to Anassa for confirmation. 'I hope you'll regard this as your home as long as you're in Paris.'

'Thank you,' said Anassa again. 'I left all my things at the studio just in case you weren't in when I called. But I certainly did hope ...' Once again they squeezed hands.

'Tonight's dinner,' Laura told her after Janine had left the room, 'is in honour of an English friend of mine, Mr Charles Vereker, and his wife, Lady Daphne, whom I don't know so well. I'm not going to sit you next to him, though, because he was a close friend of your Uncle Alexis. They were at Oxford together. You could find it awkward concealing your name if that subject were to come up. You'll find it easier to control a conversation with him before or after the meal.'

'Right. Has there been any news of him? Uncle Alexis, I mean?'

Laura shook her head sadly.

'I haven't made any enquiries recently, but for a couple of years after I came here I asked everyone I could. No one had heard what had happened to him.'

'That's another thing, then,' said Anassa mysteriously. Laura

219

waited for her to explain what she meant, but in vain. 'What is your English friend doing in Paris?'

'He's just been appointed Minister at the embassy here. I fixed this dinner for tonight because – ' She stopped, appalled by a memory which in the excitement of hearing Anassa's story she had managed to push to the back of her mind. Now it was Anassa's turn to wait for an explanation, but in this case also none was forthcoming.

There were two reasons why Laura had chosen this evening for her dinner party. The first was that she had expected to feel lonely after Fred's departure and had prescribed a social evening for herself as the best palliative.

Her motive for choosing Charles as the guest of honour was more complicated. It was some time since she had last seen her friend. Contrary to what she had feared when he left Paris soon after her rejection of his proposal, he had not severed contact with her, but continued to write friendly letters from wherever he happened to be working. His diplomatic postings had not, until now, brought him back to France. It was natural that she should wish to welcome him without delay. But as a rule, naturally, she and Fred entertained together, as husband and wife, host and hostess. Did the timing of her invitation have anything to do with the fear that for an English aristocrat – albeit only a second son – to be asked to dine with his ex-chauffeur might cause embarrassment?

Earlier, worrying about the propriety of the invitation, she had asked herself whether she was ashamed of presenting herself to Charles as Fred's wife. No, of course she wasn't. She was proud of Fred, who had raised himself from a poor childhood with no prospects to become a prosperous businessman. And she loved him. But, but, but. This was the moment when she recalled the first doubt raised in her mind by the discovery that Tanya had survived.

'I went back and they were all dead.' That was what Fred had said. Could he really have believed that to be true? Or had he lied? If so, why?

Perhaps it was a simple matter of cowardice. He had been afraid to return; and, later, afraid to admit it. She had a right to feel angry and let down about the lie; but not, perhaps about his earlier fear. Wounded and hunted, in unknown territory and in the middle of a snowfield offering little chance to hide, the temptation to save his skin by escape must have been very great – and who was she, who had taken a safe train journey out, to hope that she would have been braver herself?

But there was that less excusable alternative which had flashed instinctively into her mind at the moment of the princess's reappearance and which would not quite go away. Fred had never made any secret of his wish to better himself; to rise above his humble beginnings and become rich. His ambitions had spurred him on to work hard, and Laura had respected him for that. But in 1918 he could not have foreseen his future success as a businessman. Might greed have caused him to leave a ten-year-old girl to her fate?

No. Laura could not believe such a thing. And yet the very survival of the princess proved that Fred had not been honest in his description of the tragedy. At the time of their reunion in Paris, she remembered, he had told her of the sack of treasure which Prince Kristov had offered him as an incentive to accompany the family on the dangerous journey. The few pieces with which he managed to escape had been a part of that gift, stuffed in his pockets before they set off because the sack was too full to tie up.

That was Fred's story and, overwhelmed by love after their first passionate night together, Laura had believed it. Now an insidious suspicion began to scratch at the back of her mind. Might he have been worried lest his right to this booty should be challenged?

Since he had only just left for Leningrad, it would be two or three months before she could confront him with the new situation and demand to know the truth. Until then she must put her suspicions out of her mind. But this was more easily said than done; and for that reason she was not yet ready to mention to her guest Fred's survival, and her relationship to him. It was not a matter which could be long concealed if Anassa was going to live in the same house. But one more night, while she worked out how best to approach a subject which might cause distress, could do no harm. She was glad when Anassa, controlling her curiosity, stood up.

'If I'm to dress for your dinner tonight, I must go and fetch my clothes.'

'I'll get the chauffeur to bring round the car.' Laura rang the bell before she too rose to her feet. Drivers, like maids, tended to disappear almost as soon as she had learned their names, but there was always one attached to the staff while he studied the streets of Paris and the geography of France in preparation for being entrusted with one of Fred's expensive motor cars.

As they waited, the two women stared affectionately at each other. Laura had wept as she listened to her pupil's sad story, but this was the first time that tears had appeared in Anassa's eyes. Yet there was a smile forcing its way through those tears.

'Oh, my dear Miss Laura!' she exclaimed. 'It's just great to have found you again! I'm so happy!'

221

2

It was time to go down for the dinner party, but Anassa lingered in her bedroom for a few more moments, checking her appearance in the mirror.

She had asked for an advance introduction to tonight's guests. The occasion promised to be a middle-aged one. To meet the English diplomat who was the guest of honour would come a poet, a financier, a couturier, the owner of a bookshop, the headmistress of a school, and their no doubt unexciting spouses. The conversation would be about books which she hadn't read and people she didn't know and plays she hadn't yet had time to see. It could have made for a dull prospect had it not been for that mention of a couturier.

M. Fournier was not young, and it was rumoured that although he devoted his life to the adornment of beautiful women, it was with a beautiful young man that he shared his apartment. Anassa didn't care about that. It was in his honour that she had chosen the gown which showed her figure to its best advantage. The bodice was cut low, but she had put on no jewellery to distract his eye from the perfect skin of her neck and shoulders. Like a ballerina she had strained her hair back from her face and into a chignon; but the severity of that style — at a time when most women were fluffy with curls and waves — served to accentuate the strong framework of her face: the smooth forehead, high cheekbones, slender nose and small, neat chin. Her blue eyes appraised what they saw in the glass, and approved.

Three separate threads had drawn her to Paris. To find Laura was by far the most important, but as well as that she hoped if it was at all possible to discover what had happened to her Uncle Alexis. And she had every intention of tracking down Countess Balakin and making her suffer for the suffering she had once inflicted. But in the meantime she would need to earn a living, and it was the couture houses of Paris which would provide it, she hoped. Her work as a photographer's model in New York had provided her with a portfolio to show to anyone who was interested, but her best selling point was her body itself. With any luck she would be able to arouse the first flicker of interest this very night.

The evening was a success. Anassa rightly guessed that she would do well to appear remote. She spoke little, content to observe her fellow-guests. Lady Daphne Vereker in particular repaid study. She was beautifully dressed and perfectly groomed, and at some pains to explain why she was titled when her husband was a commoner. But it seemed to Anassa that there was little warmth between the

Verekers – and it was interesting to realise that Laura appeared to be coming to the same conclusion.

As the guests began to move out of the drawing room at the end of the evening, Anassa chose her moment to hold the couturier back, pressing her qualifications for employment on him and asking him for an appointment. He could hardly in politeness refuse. She felt herself flushing with triumph. It was at that moment that there was an unexpected disturbance.

A young man had appeared in the hall. He was not dressed for a dinner party. Indeed, he was not dressed for polite company of any kind, for his clothes were crumpled and his fair hair was tousled. Anassa, looking from the doorway of the drawing room, was able to watch the little scene without at first being observed.

'Hello, Mum!' he said in English. He was addressing Laura.

Anassa listened to the greeting with astonishment. It had taken her so long that morning to recount her own adventures that, to her shame, she had made no enquiries about Laura's life; not even to ask whether she was married. But certainly the governess had been unattached in 1917. How could she possibly have a son who looked to be about Anassa's own age?

Mr Vereker looked equally incredulous, as though he were mentally counting off the years in the opposite direction and calculating that Laura could only have been about sixteen when this young man was born.

'Leon, darling!' Laura kissed him in welcome before turning specifically to the Verekers to perform the first introduction. 'I don't think you've ever met Leon. My adopted son.'

The slight emphasis which she placed on the word 'adopted' suggested that she was well aware of the surprise which Leon's greeting had caused. 'He only calls me "Mum" when he wants to tease and make me feel old. Don't you, Leon?'

'Yes, Laura. Sorry!' Politely changing to speak French, he shook hands with the other guests in a manner which suggested that he had met them before. Anassa stepped forward to join the group and to be introduced.

Leon turned towards her in response to Laura's gesture, and his eyes widened in surprise. Amused, Anassa watched him struggling for words. No doubt he had taken it for granted that all the evening's diners would be in their forties.

There was nothing to surprise her in her effect upon Leon. She knew that she looked good, and she was well used to the admiration of young men. What was unusual was her own reaction to the meeting.

It was not just his looks which bowled her over, although she had never in her life before seen a man so pleasing to the eye. He was handsome in very much the same way that she herself was beautiful. Naturally there were differences: his body was sturdy where hers was slender, and his neck in particular was thick and strong, while Anassa's was exceptionally long and thin. But his hair was as golden as her own had been before she began to dye it black. His eyes were as blue as hers, and, like hers, his cheekbones were wide and high. And there was something extra to such resemblances: an instant bond of interest and sympathy, as though they had known each other all their lives.

That was nonsense, of course. Laura was only just performing the first introduction. The young man bowed over Anassa's hand, raising it to his lips. Still speaking in French, he began to murmur a compliment.

'Hi!' she said.

The admiration in his eyes changed to surprise. 'American?'

'Just in from New York.'

'I don't believe it. When I was eleven years old I toured America with my mother. My real mother. The continent was full of gum chewers and baseball players and large ladies wearing too many large pearls. There was absolutely no one like you there at all.'

'Perhaps I was only eleven as well.' They grinned at each other. The attraction between them was not only immediate but mutual.

'Anassa will be staying here,' Laura told Leon. 'So if you were to break the habit of a lifetime and come down punctually for breakfast tomorrow, you would have more time to talk to her then.'

'Better and better.' Still smiling, he retreated, leaving Anassa to say her farewells to the rest of the departing guests.

Next morning Anassa rose early as usual. Over the coffee which was all she ever had for breakfast, she discussed with Laura a plan for the day.

'Cartier first,' Laura said. 'I shall have to give notice of my intention to repay the loan and end the agreement as soon as the exhibition tour is over. After that, here's a list of the couture houses in which I have contacts. All we can expect today is to make appointments; but if you're with me when I ask, there might be someone who'd take a look at you on the spot. So dress for that.'

'Furs,' murmured Anassa. 'I look great in furs.'

Laura thought for a moment before adding another name to the list.

'Right,' she said, standing up. 'I'm sorry we can't start this morning, but I have appointments I mustn't break. At two o'clock, then.'

Anassa was glad that she would have the morning free to make plans; but she was not left alone at the breakfast table for long.

'A penny for your thoughts!' said Leon.

She had not heard him approach, and looked up with a smile.

'I'm deciding whether − no, I have definitely decided. I'm going to be a blonde again.'

'No wonder you looked so far away, with such a serious matter on your mind. So you're going to dye your hair?'

'No. To stop dyeing it. In New York to be a blue-eyed blonde was − well, ordinary. I chose to look older, to wear a disguise. But my hair is as fair as yours. I have only to take away the dye. To be a blonde in Paris will be elegant, right?'

'You would be elegant anywhere, with any colour.' Leon helped himself to coffee and a croissant before sitting opposite her. 'Laura didn't introduce you properly last night,' he added casually. 'Just "Anassa", she said, as though you were only a child. What's the rest of your name?'

'Just Anassa was right,' she told him. 'In New York I have some reputation under that name − that name by itself − and I intend to build one here as well.'

'But your family . . .?'

'Isn't important. You must think of me as a woman with a great future, but without a past.'

'That all sounds very mysterious.'

'A little mystery is no bad thing.'

'So what's your connection with Laura? How did you come to meet her, when she's never been to America?'

Anassa hesitated for a second before answering. She was anxious not to lie, but it was too early to tell the full truth. 'She was a friend of my mother's. One of the only two people whose names I know in Paris. So when I decided to come here, naturally, I looked her up. And she, very generously − '

'What *did* make you decide to visit Paris?'

'You ask a lot of questions!'

'I'm not getting many answers.'

She laughed in acknowledgement. 'Well, I've come to live, not just to visit. For three separate reasons. One is already accomplished. The second is to find work.'

'What kind of work?'

'In New York I was a model for photographers and artists; I'll do that here as well. The second person I know in Paris is a

225

photographer. But I reckon I'd be good at modelling clothes. As a mannequin. Laura says she has contacts in some of the couture houses. That's where we're going this afternoon.'

'And the third reason?'

'I guess I shouldn't tell you that.'

'Oh, come on. If you're going to live here and be part of the family, we can't have secrets.'

He was putting on the charm now, and Anassa was duly charmed.

'I might also want to pay off an old score,' she said. The smile faded from her eyes. 'Many years ago, when I was only a child, someone did me a great wickedness. Although I was so young, I knew what was happening as it happened, so I remember the name.'

'What are you proposing to do?'

'I don't know yet. But now that I've mentioned it, you must forget it again. Otherwise you could be accused of conspiring.'

'I'd love to be a fellow-conspirator of yours. Nothing I like better than a little adventure. What can I do to help?'

Anassa looked across the table, considering his offer. It would not be right to involve him in any revenge which she might plan, but there was a way in which his help could save her a lot of time.

'Well,' she said at last, 'since you're so good at asking questions, it's certainly true that you could ask one or two on my behalf. Nobody could possibly be suspicious about why you wanted to know. Whereas if I ask myself, people might begin to wonder.'

'What is it you want to find out?'

'The whereabouts of a Russian emigrée. In 1919 she called herself Countess Balakin. She may have married and changed her name since then, of course.'

'Should be easy. Laura and her staff do a lot of unpaid work for the exiles. Things like organising the annual New Year's Ball. She's bound to have an address list.'

'I don't want Laura herself to be involved,' said Anassa hastily. In describing her childhood adventures, she had been careful never to mention the countess's name.

'Well, I can probably get a peek at her lists. If not, Fred's bound to know. I can ask him as soon as he gets back. He's a great one for keeping up with who's marrying whom.'

'Fred?' Anassa rose slowly to her feet. 'Who is this Fred?' In the whole of her life she had only met one man with that name, and it was a name which she had forgotten during the years of her silence. Dr Gutzman had pulled the name out of her memory, and the pain she had felt at that moment attacked her again now. She felt her heart pounding as though it were about to burst out of her chest. This could not possibly be the same man: and yet ...

'I have to look after Miss Laura,' Fred the coachman had said in the conversation which was so indelibly engraved on her memory that for ten years she had suppressed memory itself. That Laura's adopted son should know someone called Fred had to be more than a coincidence.

Leon gave her a curious look. 'Fred is my sort-of dad. Laura's husband.'

Shock had made Anassa stand up; faintness now made her collapse back into her seat again.

'But Laura is Miss Mainwaring. The bureau ...'

'She uses her maiden name for business, yes. But she's Mrs Fred Richards at home.'

'Laura is married! Why didn't she tell me? Where did they meet, she and Fred? Do you know that?'

'In Russia, when they were both working there. They lost touch in the chaos of getting out of the country. Ran into each other in Paris a year later. A romantic story.'

'Yes. Yes, sure. That they should both manage to escape! Laura alive, and Fred too!'

By now Leon's curiosity had changed to anxiety.

'Anassa, are you all right? Have I said something ...?'

Anassa was not all right. Dr Gutzman had taught her that her long period of trauma was the result of suppressed guilt because she had unconsciously blamed herself for Fred's death. She ought to have felt relief, even delight, that she did not after all bear that responsibility. Instead, though, she was overcome by anger. It had all been for nothing, the time of silence and loneliness. She tried to persuade herself that Fred was not to blame for her misconception, but the effort brought a second wave of fury flooding through her whole body.

'Excuse me,' she said, and ran from the room to Laura's office.

A secretary was taking dictation, but she was gestured to leave as Anassa burst through the door. Laura stood up, pale-faced, as though already guessing what she was about to hear.

'So Fred is alive!' Anassa said, keeping her voice down in an attempt to control her emotions. 'He left me to die, but he is alive!'

'He thought you were dead. It was the first thing I asked him. He told me that he had to hide while the soldiers were about, but he went back after they'd left and found that he was too late.

227

He was quite sure you were dead.'

'If I'm not dead now, I can hardly have been dead then,' Anassa pointed out bitterly. 'I'm prepared to accept that he came back, but I guess it was for something more attractive than a small girl. We were carrying sacks of family treasures.'

'They were taken by the soldiers who shot your mother.' But Laura did not speak with the same certainty as before, and Anassa was quick to notice it.

'Please believe me, Laura, I'm not angry with *you*. But you came out of Russia with nothing but the kokoshnik, you said yesterday, and I can see for myself that you didn't sell that. Yet you're living in this grand house, running your own business, waited on by servants. Was it Fred who set you up in such style?'

'No. I was the one who set *him* up. All Fred had when he arrived in Paris was a single car. He did buy that with one or two Kristov pieces, I admit − but they were given him by your father as an inducement to help in your escape.'

'You're just telling me what he's told you. I can understand that you believed what he said when he first arrived. Do you still believe him now?'

'Yes. Yes, I do.' But Laura's voice trembled as she spoke. It was natural that she should express loyalty to her husband, but Anassa guessed that she was not as confident as she tried to sound.

'Well,' she said, 'there's only one person who can tell us the truth. When can I meet Fred?'

'Not for three or four months, I'm afraid. He's just left for Russia.'

'Russia! What's he doing there?'

'Setting up a barter trade deal. And perhaps − '

'Perhaps what?'

Laura shook her head. Whatever it was that she had been about to say, she must have decided that Anassa was not to hear it. Anassa felt not only her curiosity but also her anger rising again, bringing a bitter taste into her throat. She was being kept in the dark about something she ought to know. But she had spoken sincerely in claiming to attribute no blame to Laura and, for the rest, it seemed that she must be patient.

'Guess I shall have to wait till he gets back, then,' she said. 'But then your Fred's going to have a lot of explaining to do.'

3

In the summer of 1914, untroubled by any presentiment of war, Laura had spent a few weeks in Carlsbad with Sofiya and Tanya, to provide company for their grandmother while she took the cure. Alexis had been there too, claiming it to be his favourite spa. It was no wonder that she remembered it as an idyllic spot.

Returning for a business visit in 1930 she found few changes in the little town except for its name and nationality. It was Karlovy Vary now: no longer Austrian, but Czechoslovakian. But its inhabitants still spoke German, its tea rooms still offered the cream-piled cakes beloved of the Viennese and, beneath the stately Colonnades, visitors strolled up and down just as they had done sixteen years earlier, sipping the mineral-laden waters through the slender pipette spouts of the resort's distinctive drinking vessels.

One difference — because this time she had arrived in the spring — was that snow was still lying on the mountain peaks and over the highest of the firs which clothed them. But the spa itself was warm at any time of the year. Its hot thermal water bubbled down the centre of the narrow valley; it filled pipes and pools and rose as steam through gratings.

Allowing herself an hour's relaxation after the journey from Paris, Laura left her hotel and walked up the winding path through the forest. There were wooden seats at intervals all along the path for the benefit of invalids taking their constitutionals, but the air was cold, and for the moment she had the mountainside to herself.

Pausing at a gazebo she stared down at the rows of tall, substantial houses which climbed the steep cliff between the river and the forest. Once upon a time, in the fashionable season of the year, more than half of them would have been taken by members of the Russian nobility; but that was something which must certainly have changed. She wondered who among the surviving or newly rich had taken their place.

This was not idle speculation. Laura had come to Karlovy Vary with a purpose. A letter from an elderly Frenchman requesting the services of a nursing companion while he took the waters had stimulated an idea which had been in the back of her mind for some time. Now that the agency was doing so well in Paris, why should she not open branches elsewhere in Europe? Nothing more elaborate would be needed in each than an office, a secretary and a manager, who could make use of the Paris files as well as developing local lists of would-be employers and employees. The mere fact of having an address in a place like this would bring in new business.

The decision should have been a straightforward one. Why, then, did she feel uneasy as she stared down at the prettily painted façades and elegant iron balconies of the tall villas and hotels? The agency was her own. She had the right to develop it in any way she pleased. In practice, however, she had always in the past asked for Fred's advice on important matters. She was pretending to herself now that her reason for going ahead without consulting him was simply that he wasn't there to be consulted. But of course the decision could have awaited his return. The truth was that after believing for more than sixteen years that Fred had always been honest with her, she wasn't sure about it any longer.

It was curious that Anassa had not, in the weeks which had passed since their reunion, wanted to talk any more about the circumstances of her escape. After her first flare of anger at the news of Fred's survival, she had made no further reference to the way she had been left in the snow, presumably realising that any questions which needed to be asked must wait until Fred himself could answer them.

Laura told herself the same thing — but it was almost as though she had decided in advance that she wouldn't be able to believe him. Anassa's story had upset her; this visit was in a sense a gesture of independence. She thrust the uneasiness to the back of her mind and began to make plans. Appointments must be made with the managers of the various bath houses, the biggest hotels and a property agency. But before embarking on any of that she decided to explore the various thermal establishments to see how they were organised.

If temporary staff were needed to provide care, it would probably be in the hotels and lodgings. As she had expected, there were attendants on the staff of each bath house to look after the visitors in their cubicles, in the treatment rooms and in the pools; whilst others worked outside, pushing crippled clients in chairs to and from the hotels. Buying a day ticket to one of the bath houses, she wandered around, studying the visitors and trying to assess whether their needs would be for nurses or for maids and valets. She stood on the edge of a large enclosed pool of the brown bubbling water, watching as a grossly overweight man whose legs seemed unable to bear him was helped out of the water and into a waiting chair.

For this exercise three attendants were needed. The one in the water was white-haired, although his broad shoulders suggested the strength of a younger man. The uniform bathing costume which he wore had a high back; but in the effort of raising his patient one of the shoulder straps was tugged down over his arm, revealing three deeply-puckered scars across his back. Laura shuddered to think what a vicious slashing must have caused this.

230

She watched as he stepped out of the water, his spell of duty finished, and pulled on a white towelling robe. Moving quickly, he turned in Laura's direction, and might have walked into her had she not put out her hands to stop him.

They both – one in German and one in French – began to say sorry; and both fell silent at the same moment. A throbbing which began in Laura's heart rose to her head, making her giddy first with disbelief and then with joy, so that she would have fallen into the pool if he had not grasped her wrists.

'Larisha!' he said in a voice quiet with awe.

'Alexis!' Now that she could see his face, her recognition was as fast and as certain as his. 'I can't believe it! Alexis, you're alive!' She flung herself into his arms. Once before, in a Crimean pine forest, they had kissed like this; but then, prudish child that she was, she had torn herself away, rejecting love. This time she pressed herself against his body, as though to assure him that she would never let him go again. He was kissing her lips, her cheeks, her neck – until a peremptory command in German came across the pool. This was not, presumably, how the attendants were allowed to behave.

'I have a room here,' Alexis told her, putting a hand under her arm to hurry her away from the bath and up four flights of stairs. They were both panting by the time they arrived, but that did not prevent them from falling into each other's arms once more.

'I'm making your clothes wet,' said Alexis at last; and it was true that the dampness from his bathing costume was seeping through the towelling robe – and bringing with it the unpleasantly metallic smell of the spa water. 'Stay here while I shower.'

He clutched a pile of clothes which had been thrown over a chair and disappeared at a run. Left to herself, Laura looked round the tiny, uncarpeted room. Was this all the living accommodation he had? A narrow iron bed, with a rail for clothes above its foot. A table and chair, and an icon and candle in the corner. Laura had seen many of the exiles in Paris reduced to just this kind of bleak poverty; but that it should happen to Alexis was unbearable.

She was still examining the room when he returned.

'A little primitive, you think?' he said, reading her thoughts. 'I remember that my bedroom in my first year at Oxford was even smaller, so I'm used to it.'

But then he had had a large sitting room – and apartments in five or six palaces for vacation living. Laura could only shake her head unhappily.

'We can talk more comfortably in my hotel,' she said, and they made their way there together, holding hands like young lovers. She

231

had chosen to stay in the Hotel Central and not in one of the grander establishments on the mountain slopes, because it could easily be reached by the potential managers whom she intended to interview during her visit. With those interviews in mind she had booked a suite rather than a room. So many of her clients paid their fees in dollars that she could afford to live well.

As the door closed behind them, Alexis took her into his arms again. Now that the emotional shock of the encounter was over, they were both able to laugh happily as they kissed.

'Oh, Alexis, there are so many questions,' Laura said when at last he gave her a moment to speak.

'And I will answer them all; but not yet. I have only one question to put to you. Are you still Miss Laura?' He saw that she did not understand. 'I'm asking: are you married?'

He must have thought it a simple question to answer: either she was married or she wasn't. But to Laura it was not as clear-cut as that. She could say 'No' — which in legal terms would be truthful, but which would give a false impression. Or she could say 'Yes', which was strictly speaking a lie but one which expressed a truth.

And so she hesitated, until realising that it was the question, not the answer, which was not as simple as it seemed. Alexis came to the same conclusion at the same moment.

'I withdraw that question,' he said quickly. 'I don't care whether you're married or not. You're how old now? Thirty-seven? Thirty-eight? I could hardly have expected you to wait for me all this time — especially since you thought I was dead. And it doesn't matter. All that matters is that I love you and you love me and here we are, together at last.'

He was wrong. That was not all that mattered. It was not surprising that she should feel emotional about this unexpected encounter with the man who had been her first love. Not surprising, either, that she should long to go to bed with him, now, this moment, to consummate a love affair which until now had existed only in her imagination. But his question had given her pause; and she was using the pause to think through the situation.

There was Fred. Legally married or not, she was bound to Fred. She had loved him and had been faithful to him for ten years. Only once — on the very first occasion — had the thought come into her mind that it should have been Alexis to whom she offered her body. It was unfortunate, in a way, that today's reunion had occurred so soon after Anassa's reappearance had aroused doubts about Fred, shaking her faith in him. The temptation to surrender was very great.

For the moment, at least, she managed to resist it, stepping back from Alexis's embrace. What was it that Fred had said to her once, many years ago? 'I'll always be on your side.' That was it. He had been loyal to her, and she must be loyal as well.

'You're right to remind me,' she said faintly. 'I do love you, yes, but of course it's true that I have my own life. Someone to whom I must be faithful. I'm sorry. I shouldn't ... I was just overwhelmed by seeing you, but ...'

'I'll have to see if I can overwhelm you a little more.' Alexis grinned at her. It was the same wide smile which had thrilled her when she was a schoolgirl. But that was a long time ago. She shook her head.

'I'm sorry,' she repeated. 'But I hope ... We were friends before, weren't we? I was so worried when we lost touch, when there was no news. I want to hear all about what happened to you. We could have dinner tonight here in the hotel, and talk.'

'Talk!' Alexis's voice was incredulous and angry. Now that he was no longer smiling, she realised how much the years had changed him. He was forty now, a middle-aged man with white hair and a lined forehead. As he brought his disappointment under control and forced himself to look cheerful again, it was easy to read his thoughts. He was poor and probably hungry and she was offering him food. After the meal he would renew his campaign, and probably was already taking success for granted. It would be wise, she decided, not to telephone for a meal to be sent up to the suite but to go down to the dining room.

She left the ordering to Alexis and noticed how his eyes brightened as first of all vodka and then champagne were brought to the table. He waved the wine waiter away, saying that he would pour them himself, and within only a short time was calling for a second bottle.

Over the meal she asked him about the scars she had seen on his back.

'Not a pleasant story,' he told her. 'My regiment joined the White Army in the civil war. You probably guessed that. I was taken prisoner. Lucky not to be executed on the spot. Sent to a labour camp in the east. We each had a quota of work to do each day. With a choice of punishment if we failed. Five days without food, or the lash. Starvation might have seemed the easy option — but without food there was no hope of filling the next day's work quota. So those of us who wanted to survive took the beatings.'

'Oh, Alexis! How did you get out?'

'There was an amnesty for Civil War prisoners about three years ago. God knows why. An administrative slip-up, I expect. It didn't

233

last long. Most of my friends were re-arrested within six months. I was lucky then as well. I've always been lucky. I had friends who helped me to keep out of sight. When the heat came on again I made my way across the High Tatras into Czechoslovakia. And have been here ever since.'

'Why didn't you come to Paris like so many of the others?'

'I would have arrived too late. I heard on the grape-vine. By the time I got out of Russia — only two years ago — people had stopped feeling sorry for refugees like me, I was told, and were beginning to think of us as spongers. If I'd found friends there, they would have spent all their money by that time. And when I asked about my family, I learned that they were all dead. So I thought it best to stay where I'd found a job. And the spa does as much good for me as for the people I heave in and out of the water. So many beatings: so many broken bones. Without the heat, my body would protest even more than it does now.'

Laura was silent. Was this the moment to tell him that one member of his family had in fact survived? Without understanding the reason, she had promised Anassa faithfully never to divulge her real name to anyone — but of course Anassa had extracted that promise without knowing that her uncle was alive. To reveal the information would almost certainly tempt Alexis to Paris. But no: a promise was a promise. She must do it the other way round. On her return home she would make the happy announcement of Alexis's survival and then Anassa could get in touch in whatever manner she chose.

Alexis seemed not to have noticed the length of the pause.

'Besides,' he added, 'I have another interest in staying here, as well as the thermal waters. We have a scheme, a group of us, which will take us back to Russia one day.'

Laura groaned inwardly. She already knew about so many conspiracies which had the same purpose. They were all quite impossible — and they were all, sooner or later, infiltrated by Bolshevik spies. There had been unexplained murders amongst the emigrés, as well as kidnappings whose purpose was so obvious as to need no explanation. But she could see that Alexis was longing to tell her about his plot.

'One of the great Bohemian crafts is engraving. We have a man who has made perfect plates for printing rouble notes. When we have enough — millions of them — we shall introduce them into Russia. The economy will collapse. There will be a revolution. The people have had years of starvation already, because of the blockade. They'll remember the time, under the Tsars, when prices were steady and there was

234

enough food for everyone. The Bolsheviks will be overthrown. Hurrah!'

'Do you really believe that, Alexis?'

He shrugged his shoulders, and for a second time she recognised the insouciant smile of twenty years earlier. But in answering her question he was serious again.

'Whether I believe it or not isn't of much importance. Am I to accept that I have nothing more to look forward to than standing in four feet of stinking brown water until I'm no longer strong enough to be of any use? A man has to have a dream. Perhaps I have enough sense to understand that it's better to make plans and sustain a hope than to carry them out and recognise a failure. I shall extend the dream for as long as I can, because I'm frightened of waking up.' He refilled her glass, and his own. 'And now that I've found you again, my dearest Larisha, I can have a second dream. With this one, I hope I shan't need to wait so long for fulfilment.'

He raised his glass before draining its contents down. Automatically Laura lifted her own glass to her lips, but took only a sip. He was hoping to make her drunk: she had realised that from the start of the meal. But he was the one who was no longer completely sober.

There was a moment in which love and compassion almost weakened her resolve. She had to speak quickly, for it seemed important that she should not allow his hopes to rise.

'I meant what I said upstairs,' she told him. 'I'm sorry, Alexis, but I can't just turn my back on ...'

He reached forward to take hold of her hand. Laying it on the table, he stroked it gently.

'Paris is a long way away,' he suggested. 'I don't believe there's a woman alive who doesn't dream of a little adventure, a secret lover.'

'You're looking at one now.' Laura's voice trembled as she spoke, for the words were not completely true. But she managed to keep her eyes steady with determination. Attempting to turn the conversation, she began to talk about old times, old friends; but Alexis's questioning gaze made her throat dry and caused her hands to tremble.

'Who is it, Larisha?' he asked as they came to the end of the meal. 'Who is this man who is even luckier than myself, because he has you?'

It was tempting not to answer. Laura had never allowed herself to scorn Fred's humble origins, but she could tell in advance how Alexis would react.

'You know him,' she said, refusing to be ashamed. 'Fred Richards.'

'Richards! Are you telling me that you've married my *chauffeur*? I don't believe it. You're teasing me.'

'He's a good man. Someone I can rely on. I love him. And he's earned my loyalty. So . . .'

'Oh yes, yes. I quite see that if your taste is for servants, you have no time for princes. You disappoint me. So.' The brightness of expectation faded from his eyes, to be replaced by sullenness as he rose unsteadily to his feet. 'You promised that we should talk, and we have talked. And now you will go back to Paris, to your Fred Richards.' He pronounced the words contemptuously. 'And you will pretend to yourself, I suppose, that there was never a time when the name of Alexis Karlovich Kristov brought a flush to those pale cheeks. Well, it's true: you're no longer a young, romantic girl. And I'm no longer a rich man. I see that I have nothing to offer that a chauffeur can't match. My coat is in your suite.'

They went up together without speaking again. Laura watched as Alexis put on a greatcoat which had seen better days and probably many owners.

How shabby he was! She was used to the poverty of the emigrés and admired the care which most of them took of their appearance, doing their best to conceal the inadequacy of their clothing. But there was a kind of seediness about Alexis which went deeper than poverty. He had always worn his hair long, but now it was white and wild instead of smooth and bright. His skin as a young man had been soft and now was weathered and in need of a shave. His collar and cuffs were frayed and his shoes scuffed. That such a golden young man should come to this! Her eyes filled with tears of distress.

Drunk though he might be, he was quick to notice how emotional she felt and pulled her roughly into his arms again. This time, though, there was no tenderness in the embrace. The fingers of one hand gripped her arm with bruising tightness while the other tore at her clothing. Laura struggled to free herself, twisting her face aside to prevent him from kissing it. Surely, when he became convinced of her unwillingness, he would leave her alone. But instead he grew more frenzied, more violent.

They fought in a silence broken only by their panting. Becoming frightened, she opened her mouth to scream. His hand moved to gag her and in desperation she bit it. Instinctively he pulled away for a second and, steadier on her feet than he, she was able at last to give a violent push which sent him staggering towards the door.

With his back against the wall he stared angrily across the

room. Then he gave a deep bow and left the room in silence.

Shuddering with shock and relief, Laura locked the door behind him. At last she could allow her tears to flow. Not any longer for Alexis. It was he, an hour earlier, who had spoken of the danger of putting a dream to the test. Whether she had always been conscious of it or not, Laura for more than twenty years had cherished the memory of a beautiful young man smiling up at a bedroom window and had dreamed of becoming his lover one day. Now the romantic prince was dead, replaced by a bitter and disillusioned exile. Her dream was dead as well, and its death had been an ugly one.

When at last her sobbing ceased, she stood up and began to pack her clothes ready for a departure next day. Wherever she might eventually decide to open a branch office, it would not be in Karlovy Vary.

4

'There they go!'

Standing beside her, Leon felt Anassa's grip tighten on his hand, but she made no other movement to betray her excitement. For the past hour they had been lingering on a piece of ground levelled to offer drivers the chance to pause and enjoy a panoramic view. On either side were terraces of vines and orange trees. A little lower were the perfumed plains of Grasse, although it was still too early in the year for the best of the scents which had made the little town famous. More distantly, the land fell away to reveal a coastline of rocky headlands and bays and the shimmer of the sea. It was a beautiful scene — but the only part of it which interested the two watchers was a stretch of road immediately below. A car had just emerged through the gates of a country house to drive in the direction of Cannes.

Anxious, after their first meeting, to impress Anassa with his wish to help her, Leon had thrown himself into the role of a detective and before long was able to report that Countess Balakin had married a M. Delacroix, lived in the hills above Cannes and was, like her husband, a fanatical bridge player.

Even after Anassa enlisted his help she had refused to tell him why she was anxious to track the countess down. Leon was not too pleased about this. He could sympathise with her decision to promote a new career in Paris by presenting herself as a woman with a mysterious and secret past, but felt that he should be entitled

237

to special treatment. As it was, the best he could do to tease her in return was to refrain from any attempt to probe the mystery. He asked no questions, expressed no interest.

He had, however, offered to take her to the house. As it happened he had already made an arrangement to drive a car from Paris to the south coast. Jack, one of the Bentley racing drivers for whom he acted as racing mechanic and test driver, was sailing his yacht round from Southampton to the Mediterranean and they had agreed to rendez-vous in Cannes.

That plan, although enabling him to make the offer sound casual, was only an excuse to keep Anassa company. The true reason was that he had fallen in love with her at their first meeting. He was fascinated by the subtle changes in her face and body: she was an actress who needed no words to express herself. Sometimes her beauty was calm, almost dignified; but five minutes later she might reveal the mischievous sparkle of a kitten. Sometimes she was a mature, sophisticated woman, but within seconds her eyes could be dancing like a child's. It made no difference: he loved her at every age, in every mood.

The two of them had much in common. Unlike Laura, who was conscientiously hard-working and well-ordered, they were both untidy and high-spirited. To an outsider they might have appeared impulsive, even wild; but Leon was able to recognise in Anassa one of his own traits. They would both pause for long enough to weigh up the risks of any course of action and were less cautious than most people only in following whatever course of action they decided upon without much regard to laws or conventions – or danger.

That was why, after making a reconnaisance of the house from a safe distance, he had been standing next to Anassa on the viewing terrace for the past hour, whilst other drivers paused briefly to stretch their legs and passed on. There was nothing about the two of them to attract particular attention. Although her hair was once again its natural colour – a silky gold which caught the eye of anyone who saw it – Anassa had today tucked it inside a black turban. Leon's own hair was an even more unusual colour, so fair as to be almost white, but it was cut short enough to be concealed by his motoring cap.

'Let's go, then,' said Anassa as the Delacroix' car disappeared down the hill.

'Not yet.'

'Why not?'

'They might come back for something they've forgotten. The

238

servants will allow for that. Give it twenty minutes and they'll all have disappeared for a siesta.'

She nodded, reluctantly acknowledging the good sense of his suggestion. While they waited they could afford to relax.

'Tell me, do you often commit burglary?' Leon asked. It was only while they were driving south that he had discovered the purpose of her journey.

'This won't be burglary. Restoration of stolen property to its rightful owner.'

'I will amend my question. Do you often restore stolen property to its rightful owner?'

'This will be the first time.'

'Oh dear. An amateur! I'd better come in with you and keep you out of trouble.'

'You've already done enough. Offering to be my getaway driver. I don't want to involve you in a break-in.'

'Don't be an idiot,' he said. 'You may need to force open some kind of strong box. I have tools. I have strength. If the worst comes to the worst I can hold people off while you dash for it. I practise sprinting in readiness for the day when I drive my own car at Le Mans and have to make the running start. I promise I could catch you up.'

He could tell that she was hesitating, and grinned at her to clinch it.

'Well, thanks,' she said. There was a pause. 'Tell me more about yourself, Leon. Laura told me that you were adopted, and that you were born in Russia. Who are your real parents?'

She was only making small talk, of course, to pass the time of waiting; but Leon found the question interesting. Had something about their present adventure caused her to think about her own childhood, that she should suddenly express interest in his?

'My mother is Russian by birth and American by marriage,' he told her. 'She used to be a dancer. I have a photograph of her in the year before I was born. Very beautiful. The whole of St Petersburg was at her feet, she claims, and it may have been true. It's five years since I last saw her, though.'

'And your father?'

Leon gave a rueful laugh. 'That's a trickier question. Certainly not my mother's husband. I used to ask, when I was younger, but I never got a proper answer. Only dramatic hints about my high birth. The impression I got — that I was intended to get, I'm sure — was that the blood of the Romanovs flows in my veins. That the secret must be kept for my own sake, in case an assassin is sent to eliminate the last representative of a hated dynasty. But that perhaps one day, bastard though I am, I may be able to claim an imperial heritage. Tsar of all the Russias. Father of his people.'

'Do you believe that? The Romanov thing?'

'Not the inheritance bit, no. Quite apart from the fact that there are plenty of legitimate Romanovs around, the Tsar himself, from all I've ever heard, was a thoroughly upright and uxorious gentleman. Not at all the type to pay court to ballerinas. But there were one or two grand dukes who might fit the bill. And you see, if I turn that hypothesis down, I have to consider the possibility that my mother couldn't actually be sure who my father was. That's not a comfortable thought for a son. So! Kindly show proper respect in future, mademoiselle.'

'Sure, Your Excellency. Do you wish that you were a proper grandee? Title? Fortune?'

'I'd like to see the people who stole the country kicked out, certainly. For the sake of the others, not for myself.' Living in the Villa des Cascades he had been able to see at close quarters the increasing destitution and misery of the Russian aristocrats as they gradually accepted that they would never see their homeland again. 'What would there ever be in Russia for the illegitimate son of a faded dancer? I'm just a humble racing mechanic whose dreams are all of racing a car of my own one day. I think we could risk moving now.'

'Right. Listen, Leon. If anything goes wrong, you must run for it. Don't worry about me. Even if I'm caught red-handed, they won't dare send for the police. I could make too much of a scandal. But they might try to take it out on you, so they mustn't catch you. Promise.'

'This is all very mysterious.'

'Mystery is my speciality. I'll explain one day. But in the meantime − let's go!'

They had already worked out the safest way to approach the house, and had noted with relief that many of its windows were open, for the day was warm and the household unsuspicious. It had been built into the slope of the hill, in order that all the main rooms might enjoy the magnificent views over the flowering fields and down towards the sea. As a result, the wide first-floor balconies were more like roof terraces, easily reached from the side by the two fit young people. Within only a few minutes they were inside one of the bedrooms.

The object of their search was a piece of jewellery which Anassa claimed to be her own. They were luckier than they deserved. Mme Delacroix's jewel box was strong and it was locked: but it was not kept in a safe. Leon had no lock-picking skills, but he needed only a short time to force it open.

His success was marked with a snap which sounded, on that silent afternoon, like a clap of thunder. The two burglars froze, listening, for what seemed an age, but could hear nothing except the thumping of their hearts. Cautiously Anassa opened the lid. She lifted off the top tray of ear-rings and rings and a second layer of diamond and emerald bracelets. Beneath that was a catch which released four shallow drawers lined in velvet. She pulled them out one at a time and stared for a long time at the contents of the bottom drawer.

The necklace which lay there was clearly valuable, but in an old-fashioned style which Leon found hard to associate with a modern young woman like Anassa. From a curving line of diamonds set in platinum were suspended seven circles of smaller diamonds in the same setting, increasing in size towards the central one. Six of the circles contained pearls which hung from wire so thin as to be almost invisible. In the largest circle − completely out of keeping with the rest − was a gold locket. Anassa tut-tutted at the sight of it and made a scissor gesture with her fingers, asking Leon to cut it away.

He did so quickly. She laid the locket back in the drawer and fastened the necklace around her own neck, winding her motoring scarf round and round over it. A moment earlier, looking down, she had seemed sad, but now her eyes danced with mischievous pleasure as she nodded to show that she was ready to go.

'If there's something connecting this to you, and you don't want it to be traced, we ought to steal some of the other stuff as well,' he said quietly. 'Make it look like an ordinary jewel theft.'

Anassa shook her head. 'That would make me feel like a criminal.' She closed the box and returned it to the wardrobe in which they had found it. It was a walk-in wardrobe extending from floor to ceiling for the whole width of the room, and she needed to step inside and stand on tiptoe to push it to the back of the highest shelf. Leon was watching her when, for a second time, they both froze. Someone, after approaching silently, was opening the bedroom door.

There was no time to reach the terrace. Hastily Leon moved into the wardrobe and had just time to close the door before a maid came into the room with a pile of newly ironed underwear to be put away.

It all happened so quickly that for a moment he was confused by the sudden darkness and his own lack of balance. There was room to stand, but the floor of the wardrobe was fitted with rails on which dozens of pairs of shoes lay in sloping lines. He stumbled and grabbed at Anassa for support. Not daring to move, they held each other so tightly that he could feel her breath on his face, and her heart was beating loudly against his chest. Although she had claimed not to fear discovery, it was clear that she did not wish for a confrontation at this moment.

Commonsense told Leon that he ought not to move, but Anassa's closeness made it impossible for him to restrain himself. She was so soft, so slender: her skin was so smooth. Breathing in the sweet smell of her body, he was unable to control himself. His lips pressed hers in the darkness. This was the first time he had kissed her, but there was nothing tentative about it. His tongue explored her mouth whilst one arm tightened its grip around her, pulling her body even closer to his own. With his free hand he undid her blouse and then felt for the fastening of her skirt. So urgent was his need that there would hardly be time to unbutton his trousers. His lips left hers only so that he could whisper into her ear: 'Now. Here.'

'No.' Anassa's whisper, like his, was almost soundless. He could feel that she was as excited as he was, but she attempted to wriggle out of his grasp, pushing him away by the shoulders. Neither of them dared to move their feet while the maid was still opening and closing drawers. As though in a silent movie they began to wrestle with each other: Leon trying to make love and Anassa determined to resist, but each of them equally anxious to avoid discovery.

In the end it was laughter which almost betrayed them. Anassa seemed overcome by the inappropriateness of such behaviour on the part of amateur burglars: he could feel her chest heaving with the attempt to stifle giggles. Just in time, the maid completed her task and left the room, closing the door behind her. Anassa allowed herself to relax into Leon's arms, burrowing her mouth into his shoulders to suppress the sound of her mirth. It was less easy for Leon to curb his desire, but the need to escape while the going was good had just enough of a sobering effect. He relaxed his grip sufficiently for her to button up her blouse again and cautiously opened the wardrobe door. Hand in hand, they stole out of the room.

Once they were out of the grounds, Leon insisted that they should stroll back to the car in a casual manner, in order not to attract notice.

'But why wouldn't you?' he asked as he steered the Bentley back on the road again. 'I love you. You love me. I could feel it.'

'It wasn't the right place.'

'How fussy you are! The most commodious wardrobe in the south of France, I should think! And full of the most expensive clothes! You do love me, don't you, Anassa? Say it.'

'I love you.' She put her hand on his thigh: he felt something like an electric charge pass between them.

'Well then?'

'When I'm an old lady, looking back on my life,' said Anassa dreamily, 'I don't want to remember that I lost my virginity in a wardrobe.' She began to giggle again.

'Really?' Leon glanced at her in surprise. Although since their first meeting he had discovered that she was only a few months older than himself, she was so poised and sophisticated that he would have expected her to be already experienced in love.

'Really. I've been waiting for Prince Charming to turn up on a white horse − or in a 4½-litre Bentley, of course. This is a big thing in a girl's life. It needs to be tackled in style.'

'I think I could arrange that.' Happiness bubbled through Leon's body. It was going to happen! How delightful it was that the passion which would soon unite them should be light-hearted and carefree rather than sultry and ashamed.

The prospect went to his head. They had left the flower-filled plain and were zig-zagging steeply downhill towards Cannes. It was a road which demanded caution, but instead he increased his speed until he was taking the hairpin bends at a racetrack speed.

'Am I frightening you?' Even though he asked the question, Leon made no attempt to brake, instead screaming round corners with little regard for any vehicle which might be coming in the opposite direction. It was perhaps a side effect of ecstasy: the unexpressed feeling that to die at a moment when the future promised such perfect, almost unbearable, happiness would be to preserve that happiness for ever, untouched by time. But it was surprising that his passenger should show no anxiety.

'I can't be frightened.' Anassa made the statement simply, without drama. 'Not of death, at least. I expect there are a good many worse things to fear. But I died once, when I was a child. Well, as near died as makes little difference. I was frightened before it, but the dying itself was warm. Peaceful, somehow. Simply a matter of letting go.'

'Just as well you're not a racing driver, then. Fear is the only thing that keeps you alive when you're hurtling round corners at ninety miles an hour.'

'That suggests that a racing driver is what I ought to be. Without fear, I could take them at a hundred.'

'Obviously I must keep you away from the race track. I want you to stay alive for ever and ever.'

243

'And you reckon this is the best way to make sure that happens?' She was laughing, not protesting.

'Sorry.' Leon did now slow down. His earlier feeling that he couldn't wait was replaced by the calmer pleasure of anticipation. He didn't speak again until they had completed the descent and wound their way through Cannes towards the sea.

'A yacht,' he suggested, bringing the Bentley to a halt beside an inner harbour. 'Would a night on a yacht meet your demand for style?'

Anassa's pencilled eyebrows rose as she looked out at the small boats which tossed their heads and strained at the ropes of their mooring buoys.

'Certainly not. Narrow little bunks!'

'Not one of these. Let's walk a little.' He put his arm round her waist as they strolled. Jack's yacht, the *Esmeralda*, dazzling with white paint and cheerful with fluttering flags, was moored to a jetty on the further side of a small headland. Jack was a millionaire whose pleasure it was to entertain kings and queens, and his motor-racing friends, on a craft the size of a small liner. As well as his own accommodation and that of the numerous crew, there were twelve luxurious guest suites; and unless they were all occupied he would certainly be willing to offer hospitality. Although Leon was employed only in the lowly role of a mechanic, the drivers who relied on his skills recognised him as a young apprentice who might one day become their equal. He was not as rich and well-connected as they were; but he was a member of a team, and all the members of the team were friends.

'What about this?' he asked, bringing Anassa to a halt.

'*This* is the yacht?'

'This is the yacht.'

Stretching herself with contentment like a cat, Anassa turned to face him and linked her arms around his neck, kissing him with no trace of self-consciousness. Their embrace extended itself, becoming more passionate with every second, until it was interrupted by a shout from the highest deck of the yacht.

'Ahoy there! Come aboard! The Widow is waiting!' Dressed in a peaked cap, navy blazer and white trousers, Jack waved a bottle of champagne above his head. Leon took off his own cap and waved it back before looking questioningly at Anassa.

'I love you,' he said. 'Will this do?'

'Oh yes,' agreed Anassa. 'This will do.'

244

5

'Anyone home?'

Fred shouted cheerfully as he took the steps up to the Villas des Cascades two at a time. His spirits were high. It was great to be back in Paris again, but simply to be safely out of Russia was reason enough to celebrate.

Every moment of his stay there had been a strain. The problems of trying to do business were bad enough. Everything needed forms and papers and official stamps, and none of these were easy to come by. Permission to travel outside Leningrad in order to inspect the factory with which he was negotiating? Three and a half weeks. Permission to test a sample? Ten days. Permission to import goods? Twenty days. Permission to export goods in exchange for the said imports? Twelve weeks. Twelve bloody weeks! And yet they needed the machinery he was offering to supply and hadn't a hope in hell of acquiring the foreign currency to buy it in any normal fashion.

Well, he had known all that, more or less, before he embarked on the operation. It was in the Russian nature to be both suspicious and bureaucratic, and a revolution hadn't proved strong enough to change that. What he hadn't reckoned on was the atmosphere of fear.

Before the revolution Fred had mixed easily with all the members of the Kristov households. Granted, he was a foreigner and therefore an outsider, especially while he was still learning the language. Granted too that as a skilled mechanic he had always reckoned himself to be a cut above the ordinary domestic staff. But that hadn't stopped him drinking and chatting with them; and he had found them pleasant people. Easy-going to the point of irresponsibility, unpunctual to the degree of having no sense of time at all, and with a lack of deference to their superiors which in any other country would be regarded as impudence. But friendly and jolly and glad of a drink; taking the world as it came.

Not any longer. No doubt there had always been spies, just as there had always been rebels, but now it seemed that everyone was a spy – and frightened of being spied on in turn. No one spoke frankly and even the most casual remark was examined for hidden traps. Almost everyone he spoke to knew somebody who had been sent off to Siberia for some unguarded comment. The whole country had the shivers.

Had a legitimate trade contact been Fred's only business in Leningrad, no doubt he could have shrugged off the feeling of being perpetually watched. But he had set himself the goal of getting

245

his hands on some of the Kristov treasure, and the knowledge that he was qualifying himself for one of those trips to Siberia gave him the shivers as well. He had been successful, up to a point. But — not daring to smuggle out anything too bulky when the risks were so high — he had left a great fortune behind, and that was where it was going to stay.

What he had brought out would be enough to set Leon up in the motor racing game. Although for a time Fred himself had flirted with the idea of being a millionaire gentleman of leisure, the truth was that he liked running his own business. He and Laura were both successful and their joint incomes allowed them to live in comfort. That would have to be good enough. Nothing, but nothing, would persuade him ever to set foot in Leningrad again.

Where was Laura? He shouted her name as he stood in the hall. Two of the servants came running, and he sent them out to help carry in his heavy luggage.

Someone was coming down the curving stairs. He didn't know who she was, but that was not surprising. More than four months had passed since he was last in the villa and he was naturally aware of the speed with which maids and secretaries changed as they ended their periods of training.

Not that this woman looked like a maid. She was very tall and unnaturally thin; with long blonde hair and a carefully made-up face. Although Fred had been out of Paris for a whole season and therefore didn't know the details of the latest fashion, he could tell just by the way she wore her clothes that they represented the style of the moment. A friend of Laura's, then, and not a servant.

'Good morning,' he said cheerfully. 'I'm Fred Richards. Do you happen to know where Laura is?'

'Fred Richards?' The woman put out a hand to touch the banister, as though she needed to steady herself, and did not answer at once. Then, unsmiling, she nodded towards what had once been the billiards room. 'In her office, I guess.'

'Thanks.' Excited by the prospect of embracing Laura after the long separation, he made for the door at a run. With any luck she would let him take her straight up to bed.

Half an hour later, with all the bounce gone out of him, Fred made his way slowly back to the living quarters of the house. Laura's pleasure in the reunion had been genuine but brief. After only a few minutes she had brought him up to date with what had happened during his absence.

She was longing to trust him; that was easy enough to see. If he could persuade the girl to accept his story, then Laura would be happy as well. She had said so almost in so many words, leaving him in no doubt of the importance of the interview to come.

Anassa was waiting for him in the morning room. Neither of them tried to pretend that this was a chance encounter.

'Tanya,' he began, but she interrupted him at once.

'You are to call me Anassa. I wish no one to know about my past.'

'Anassa, then. But I have to think of you as Tanya. I didn't recognise you. Not surprising, after ten years. And when I'd never expected to see you again.'

'No.' Anassa's voice was cold.

'T— Anassa, I went back to find you that day. You have to believe me. I want to tell you exactly what happened.'

She waited in silence. It took Fred a moment to marshal his thoughts. He had done his best to put the terror of those events out of his mind, but for many months after he reached safety they had continued to run through his head in pictures like a film on a loop, over and over again. He was determined now to be honest, but it was not easy to be sure whether or not he had imperceptibly edited the film in an attempt to justify himself.

'Your mother was killed by one of the first bullets fired by the frontier patrol,' he said. 'And I was shot in the leg. One of the horses was killed at the same time. The other two panicked. They were rearing up. Perhaps you remember that.'

She nodded without speaking. If it was hard for him to give this account, it must be unbearable for her to hear it.

'The sledge tipped over on top of the three of you. I went to help you up. I could see at once that your mother was dead. You and your sister were alive, but Sofiya had the whole weight of the sledge on her legs, and you were beneath her. All the time the patrol was getting closer. I could tell that I wouldn't be able to get you free in time, so I told you both to keep still and pretend to be dead.'

'I remember that as well.'

'I thought, if I made a run for it, I might draw them off. There didn't seem any hope of actually escaping. Even ordinary footprints are easy to follow in a snowfield, and I was bleeding as well. You won't believe this, Tanya – Anassa – but I really thought that I was playing the little hero; giving you a chance. But they didn't follow me. They found the sacks which your father had loaded with silver and gold and jewels, ready to set you all up in a new life. They weren't interested in me any longer. I stopped running after a bit. I could see them dividing up the loot; stuffing their pockets.'

247

He looked at Anassa to see whether she had been aware of this as well, but this time she shook her head.

'It took a long time. They couldn't carry it all, and I suppose if they'd taken the sacks back to their barracks their officers would have confiscated the lot. They wrapped up what was left of the stuff in one of the furs from the sledge and buried it a little way away. All this time I was hiding in the snow and losing blood. I wonder whether you remember this, Anassa. Lying in snow is very cold at first. It chills you right through. But then there comes a moment when your body is so cold that the snow feels warm by comparison. A friendly, comforting sort of warmth. You want to go to sleep. Just for a few moments, to rest.'

Almost reluctantly Anassa nodded her agreement. Yes, she too had slipped into that comfortable sleep.

'It was lucky for me that my leg began to give me hell. Hadn't hurt too much when I was first hit. Just a kind of punch and then a numbness. But when the pain really got going, it was enough to pull me out of that sleep. And that was when I went back to get you out.'

'And what did you find?'

'Sofiya was dead. One of the horses had reared up and crashed down on to her head. No possible doubt about it.' He paused for a second. Even after so many years, the memory of that smashed skull still made him feel sick. But he must hurry on. This was the hard part.

'You were lying beneath her, pressed into the snow. There was blood all over your hair. Your eyes were closed. Your lips were blue. Your face was white: a bluish sort of white. I couldn't get at your wrists, but I felt your neck where there should have been a pulse and there was nothing. Nothing. Tanya — Anassa, you have to believe me. You were dead.'

'I suppose you saw what you expected to see.'

'I didn't see what I *wanted* to see. I'd sacrificed a lot to get you out of Russia, and I wanted to succeed. If I'd believed that there was any possibility at all ... When I think about it now, seeing you here, and try to understand where I went wrong, I suppose that my own fingers may have been so numb with cold that I wouldn't have been able to feel even my own pulse if I'd tried. And I was frightened. No point in pretending I wasn't. I knew those soldiers would be coming back, and they wouldn't want to leave any witnesses of their looting. All the same, if I'd thought there was anything to be gained by digging you out, I'd have done it.'

248

'And the sack that the soldiers had buried? You helped yourself, I imagine?'

That was a nasty one. But he couldn't expect her to believe that he had been telling the truth so far unless he went on to the bitter end.

'Yes,' he confessed. 'When your father was trying to persuade me to help him, he offered me as much as I could carry. I turned that down, because I never meant to go out that way. It was only later, when you asked me yourself ... Well, I reckoned that your father would rather I had his things than a bunch of bloodthirsty revolutionaries. I only took a few bits. Just what would go in my pockets.'

'So what did you do with them?'

'Sold them in France later on. Didn't get as much as I'd expected. There were so many Russian exiles trying to keep afloat in Paris that the market was swamped. But it was enough to set me up in a chauffeuring business. I'd be happy to make you an allowance out of the business, to keep you afloat. It's doing well.'

Nothing in her expression changed as she considered his offer. Was there no way in which he could make her smile and tell him that of course she understood?

'So it's all gone?' she said. 'Except for the kokoshnik which Laura has returned to me. Everything my family owned, all gone?'

It was a long time before Fred could force himself to speak. The temptation to agree with her was very great indeed — but if he succumbed to it, he would never be able to offer Leon the life on which he had set his heart, because this woman would surely discover how it had been funded. He took a deep breath.

'There is some Kristov property hidden in Leningrad,' he told her. 'I hid it there myself, at your father's request. In what used to be your palace. It's a museum now, so it's possible for anyone to get inside. And someone who knows his way around the building can hide.'

In the middle of the night he had switched on a torch and found his own initials, scribbled on a wall twelve years earlier. The cellars had long ago been cleared of all the wine and stores they had once held and, to judge by the cobwebs, no one had been down there for years. If the museum had a guard or caretaker, he was almost certainly asleep on a higher level. All the same, it had been a moment terrifying enough to rival the escape to Finland, that moment when he eased away the ceiling-high wine rack and began to prise away the plaster from the concealed doorway behind it.

'I managed to bring out part of a gold dinner service,' he said

249

unhappily. 'I suppose really it should be yours. But ... Have you met Leon?'

'Yes.' For the first time in the conversation her expression softened.

'He wants to be a racing driver.'

'Yes, he told me.'

'It's not a way of earning a living. Spending a fortune, more like. I took those risks because I wanted to see his dreams come true.'

'Yes, of course. Give him the gold.' Everything about Anassa had changed. She had listened to the earlier part of his story stony-faced, but suddenly now her eyes were sympathetic and her body relaxed. She was no longer a painted dummy but an animated and beautiful woman — a true Russian in her changes of mood. She was even smiling, as though with some secret happiness. It was that smile, seeming to embrace Fred with its warmth, which seduced him into uttering words which he regretted even before they had passed his lips.

'I could go back. Not straightaway, but in a couple of years, when there's more business to be done. I could bring some of the Kristov treasure out for you.'

'Yes. Yes, that would be very kind. Thank you, Fred.' She spoke so lightly that she couldn't possibly realise the risk she was expecting him to take. Well, perhaps he would be able to dodge out of the offer before the time came. In the meantime, he must make the most of the softening of her mood.

'So can you forgive me now for running out on you? Laura told me —'

'I was angry, yes, when I discovered that you'd been living comfortably here for years. But it was a complicated sort of anger.' He waited patiently while she worked out what to say. 'If you had died in the snow that day — and I thought you must have done — it would have been my fault, because I was the one who made you come with us. So I felt guilty about it and then I tried to forget the guilt; and the effect — oh, it's all too difficult to explain. Not important any longer. Yes, all is forgiven. Well, more than that. Not really anything to forgive. All very understandable, and if it hadn't been for you I would never have got even as far as I did. I do realise that. Thank you, Fred.'

So now he could make his peace with Laura. Relief and desire flooded his body as he stood up and prepared to hurry to her; but Anassa held him back for a moment longer.

'Laura did tell you, didn't she, that I want my real name to be

250

kept a secret just for the time being? I'm planning a surprise for someone, and I don't want it spoiled.'

'Right. And in that case ...' Fred had to think the situation through. If there was even the slightest chance that he might return to the cellar of the Kristov palace, then no one must know what had happened on this first occasion. Not even Leon, who would have to be persuaded that his father could afford to be generous because he was a brilliant businessman.

'We'll have to swap secrets,' he said. 'I keep yours and you keep mine. Not a word to anyone, ever, about where the money for Leon came from. If even a whisper about a Kristov treasurehouse leaks out, I can't ever go back there.'

'Understood.' They shook hands in a friendly fashion. Anassa was the first to leave the room, leaving Fred sweating with anxiety. He had solved his first problem, but at what a cost! He must have been crazy to make such an offer.

Well, he had warned her that any return visit must be at least two years ahead. Anything could happen in two years. The regime might crumble. The Kristov palace might burn down. Anassa might marry, move away, forget all about his promise. Not likely, that last one, but never mind. It would be time enough to worry when she began to nag at him. In the meantime, Laura would be waiting to hear how the confrontation had gone.

6

The social highspot of the exiles' year was the New Year Ball: a date for which they continued to use the old calendar. Laura and Fred were regular attenders. They were regarded as honorary Russians because of the hospitality and employment which they had provided for so many members of the community.

Leon, who was known to be the son of Barisinova, was naturally welcome, but Anassa was less obviously qualified to attend. The circumstances of her birth had been the subject of gossip and speculation ever since she appeared on the Paris social scene. Although some assumed her to be American, the more widely held view was that she had been born in France in conditions so humble that she did not wish to acknowledge them. Certainly no one suspected that she might have Russian ancestry.

Laura, knowing the truth, invited Anassa to join her party on the occasion of this year's ball: it would offer her a glimpse of the life she might have led if her family had escaped from Russia.

251

'You'll need some kind of fancy dress,' she warned her guest in advance. This had been the rule for some years already. Older revellers might sigh nostalgically at the memory of glittering occasions in the Winter Palace of St Petersburg; but the reality was that their jewels were sold and their grand gowns tattered beyond repair. Dressing up allowed poverty to be disguised — if necessary by a pretence of poverty: to come as a ragged goose girl or a sandalled friar was so amusing, my dears.

'If Leon and I are to be partners, we should dress as a couple,' suggested Anassa.

'You might find that a little unglamorous. I believe he plans to go as an aviator. Orville Wright, he suggested. Do you see yourself with smears of oil on your face?'

Anassa laughed. 'I shall talk him out of that.' She went off to do it on the spot.

Whatever they decided together was to be a secret. Over the next few days Laura several times caught sight of them whispering and laughing together, and looked forward to whatever surprise they were preparing.

But the surprise, when it came, was an unwelcome one.

Leon was the first of the two to appear on the night of the ball. He was dressed in the court uniform of the old Russian nobility: tight white trousers and a black frock coat richly ornamented with gold braid. He looked both handsome and genuinely aristocratic, but Laura, who had chosen medieval costume for herself, stared at him uneasily as he paraded for her inspection. Presumably the outfit had been bought from some nobleman who was no longer slim enough to wear it and who needed whatever price it would fetch. If the seller were to attend the ball, he would surely be offended to see the clothes he had once been proud to wear paraded now as fancy dress.

Any unease caused by Leon's appearance was overwhelmed by a more profound shock when his partner appeared in the doorway of the drawing room.

She was dressed as a princess.

Laura knew that after the success of her first season as a mannequin, Anassa was often employed on grand occasions to wear gowns created by one or two of the greatest couture houses. Not that the emigrés' ball ranked high in the social calendar, but it invariably attracted photographers and gossip writers. So she had probably had little trouble in persuading the House of Worth to part with one of its masterpieces for a night.

The dress was white, cut low at both the front and the back. The diamonds of the necklace which curved around her neck sparkled against Anassa's fair skin, and between her elbow-length white gloves and the tiny cap sleeves which supported the bodice, her slender arms were bare. The front of the dress was embroidered in fine silver thread with a cobweb design which had a pearl attached in the centre of each web. Its skirt fitted tightly over her slim hips but flared out below the knee, the intricately cut panels extending at the back to form a train. It was a gown designed for royalty; and Anassa did not disgrace it.

She stood without moving, her back straight and her head held high. With the help of a hairpiece she had dressed her blonde hair in the high style of twenty years earlier; and on it, like a crown, she had set the Kristov kokoshnik.

Laura's gasp of disapproval had nothing to do with the ownership of the kokoshnik, which she had handed over to Anassa, its rightful owner, soon after their reunion. The young woman was entitled to wear it whenever she pleased — but this was not the right occasion. What could be in worse taste than to appear as a princess in a ballroom which would be filled with princesses who could not afford such finery themselves? Laura blamed herself for not making the nature of the occasion more clear.

Fred, standing behind her, apparently felt no such doubts.

'By God, you're a beauty!' he exclaimed. 'I remember when I first saw . . .' He checked himself as Laura gave him a warning glance: Anassa's request for the details of her birth to be kept secret presumably included Leon amongst those who should not be allowed to know the truth. 'Well, you're a handsome couple, the two of you. You'll be the belle and beau of the ball.'

'Yes, indeed.' Laura smiled, to make up for the lack of enthusiasm in her first reaction, and kissed each of them in turn.

'Am I allowed to kiss the princess as well?' asked Leon softly. 'Since just for one night I share her rank.'

He kissed her cheeks three times in the Russian style, but then drew her a little closer in order to touch her lips with his own. Anassa's pale face flushed and her eyes glinted with excitement as she declared herself impatient for the ball to begin.

There was something unusual about her mood. Laura couldn't help noticing how Anassa's flush deepened as the evening progressed and how her eyes continuously searched the ballroom as though there was always someone other than her current partner whom she was more anxious to see. Yet she was surely too sophisticated a young woman to be thrilled merely by the occasion. Between her own dances, Laura watched her curiously: something unexpected, she felt certain, was about to happen.

Time passed. Perhaps she was wrong. Anassa was behaving as any beautiful woman might: revelling in the crowd of young men who pressed to fill her programme and dancing the old-fashioned waltzes and polkas with healthy energy and grace.

She had allowed Leon the supper dance, and when the time came to move towards the buffet, Laura and Fred happened to be close behind the young people, in a good position to see what happened next. Anassa was standing back, waiting politely for an older woman in front of her to finish loading her plate.

The woman — dressed as Pierrette — turned away from the table. Laura, who of course was well acquainted with all the guests, recognised her as Countess Balakin, who had continued to use her title even after marrying a French commoner. Chatting to her husband, in his Harlequin costume, she caught sight of Anassa, who was standing very still in a place which prevented her from passing. The countess's face paled as she stared incredulously.

'Where — ?' She thrust her plate into her partner's hand and waved at him to put it down, but did not take her eyes off Anassa. 'Where did you get that necklace?'

'It's a very beautiful one, isn't it?' Anassa smiled pleasantly, but already there was an intensity about the exchange which caught the attention of those nearby. Gradually the buzz of conversation faded. Laura was particularly puzzled. She had not immediately recognised the necklace when Anassa first appeared that evening, perhaps because the distinctive teardrop pearl was missing from it. But now that her attention was drawn to it, she realised that this was the piece of jewellery which she herself had sewn into a felt belt for little Princess Tanya to wear during the escape. There could be no possible doubt about Anassa's right to it — but how had it come into her possession again?

'It may be beautiful, but it doesn't belong to you.' Then, as though recognising several possible explanations, the countess's voice became less sharp. 'Well, of course, if you bought it, you may not have known who its rightful owner was. I shall have to ask my lawyer to investigate the situation. But whether you realised it or not, you are wearing a piece of stolen property and I must request — '

'Oh, yes, I do know who its rightful owner is.' Anassa's voice remained soft. 'If you think it doesn't belong to me, you must find it curious that it complements my kokoshnik so perfectly. It seems to have had an unfortunate history, this necklace. It is certainly stolen property — it was stolen from me, as well as from you. I'm quite prepared to describe how it first came

254

into my possession. Are you willing to explain how it came into yours?'

Laura held her breath, beginning to guess at the reason for this confrontation. Anassa had described to her how, as a little girl, she had been robbed of the necklace; but had not mentioned the name of the thief. Could it really be true that this apparently respectable woman had once, for her own profit, abandoned a child entrusted to her care?

'I hardly consider that to be your business.' The countess, uneasy, showed signs of regretting that she had started the conversation, and was about to turn away when Anassa put herself in her path.

'Then perhaps you'd like me to begin.' By now the room was quiet, the food neglected – and the grand duke who was president of this year's ball had approached to find out what was happening. 'This necklace was my mother's, given to me for safe keeping when I was nine years old. It was stolen from me when I was ten: a child who needed protection and was betrayed by the woman who promised to provide it. Do you wish me to continue, madame? Because the thief did more than steal a few precious stones. She hoped to rob me of my identity, my future. Shall I go on? Or shall I pause for a moment while you describe your own claim to the necklace?'

'You're talking a pack of lies,' exclaimed the countess, but the bright red flush of her cheeks was caused by more than simple anger. 'I know who you are. I've seen your pictures in the papers often enough. French, American, I don't know what you're supposed to be, but we are talking about a Russian necklace and this is a Russian occasion and you have absolutely no right – '

'I am not French and I am not American,' said Anassa calmly. 'I was born in St Petersburg and I am wearing the Kristov jewels because I am the Princess Tanya Pavlovna Kristova.'

The silence which followed this statement was broken by the flash of a camera. No doubt Anassa had dropped a hint to one of the photographers whom she knew so well that he might find it worthwhile to keep her in view. Already he had taken one photograph of her and Leon together as they waited to be received by the grand duke; and another of Anassa by herself, a princess from the peak of the kokoshnik to the tip of her satin shoes. This one, the princess and Pierrette, would be different: a picture to tell a story. And he was only just in time, for at the sound of the Kristov name the countess hurried from the room.

The buzz of chatter resumed at a higher pitch than before. Anassa was surrounded by an excited crowd. Her contemporaries were delighted to discover she was one of themselves, but it was the

255

emotional kisses of the older generation which reduced her almost to tears. One by one they expressed their relief at her survival and added personal memories of her parents. At the beginning of the evening she must have wondered whether she would be ostracised for behaviour which would be condemned in any book of etiquette; but instead she was overwhelmed by affection.

'Did you know?' Laura was startled by the tone of Leon's question. He sounded both angry and upset.

'That she was planning a confrontation of this kind? No, I certainly didn't. If I'd known, I would have tried to stop her. This isn't the right occasion – '

'I mean, did you know that she was Princess Kristova?'

'Yes. Yes, I did. That was why she came to Paris, to find me, because I was her governess once.'

'You should have told me.'

'I was particularly asked not to tell anyone at all except Fred. I didn't realise, of course, that her reason for asking was presumably just so that she could spring this sort of surprise. But why should her name be important to you?'

'*She* should have told me,' said Leon vehemently. 'It's not just a name. It's a whole life. You think you're getting to know someone, and then you discover that she's a completely different person. If she trusted you, she could have trusted me. She said she'd marry me. Only an hour ago, when she must have known that she was going to tell the whole world who she was, she said she'd marry me. There oughtn't to have been any secrets between us. She should have – '

'She said *what*? Oh, God!' Laura came near to fainting with shock, and Leon needed to help her to a chair. Supper was forgotten as they stared at each other; Laura aghast and Leon puzzled.

'Are you saying that you want to get married?' she checked, hoping that she had misheard.

'That's right.' It was easy to see that Leon's distress had already passed, overwhelmed by his delight that his proposal had been accepted.

'I didn't realise . . .'

'How could you? It's only just happened. You'd have been the first to know. But at home; not in such a public place, I thought.'

'What I mean is, I didn't even realise that you were interested in each other in that sort of way.'

'In love, you mean? Well, we are. Head over heels. Can you blame me? She's the most beautiful woman in the world, and I'm the luckiest man.'

256

'Leon, my darling, I'm so sorry, but you can't.'

'Can't what?'

'You can't marry Anassa. She's your sister. Half-sister, at least.'

He stared at her unbelievingly. Even Anassa's revelation of her parentage would not have put any doubts in his mind, of course, because no one had ever told him who his father was. Laura told him now.

'I don't believe it. Mother always said – or at least, hinted . . .'

'Yes, I know. That's why I felt I had to keep quiet. It was her business to decide what you should or shouldn't be told, not mine.' So deep was Laura's sympathy for her adopted son at this moment that she wanted to touch him, to hug him. But there had been enough secrets revealed to the photographer already this evening, without allowing him to suspect more.

'Does Anassa know?' Leon asked quietly.

'No. There was no reason . . . Well, at least, I didn't realise that there was any reason. You didn't behave, the two of you, as though you were in love.' But when she came to think about it, she had not often during the past few months seen them together; and it was natural enough that Leon should not expose his emotions until he was sure that his love was reciprocated. She sighed unhappily, feeling guilt that she should have allowed such a situation to develop.

'I don't believe it,' said Leon for a second time, and this time his voice was firm. 'You can't possibly know. No one can know except Mother. I shall write to her and tell her why I need to know the truth. There were dozens of men who adored her when she was young. She told me that herself. It might have been any of them.'

'She wasn't a promiscuous woman, your mother, Leon. There were conventions of a sort.' But this was not the time to deliver a lecture on the habits of the Tsarist nobility. 'Yes, you ask her. But until you hear – '

'Until I hear, you're to say nothing to Anassa. Will you promise? I'll tell her anything that has to be told, in my own good time. But this is my life that's got messed up, and I reckon I have the right to sort out the mess.'

Fred appeared in front of them, carrying two well-stocked plates.

'Leon, my lad, if you don't rescue your partner soon, the two of you are going to starve.'

Leon stood up and helped Laura to her feet. Looking intently into her eyes, he spoke almost too softly to hear.

'Promise? That you'll leave it to me.'

How handsome he was — and how vulnerable at this moment as he struggled to control the battle between love and the fear of losing his love. Laura wanted to protect him; but there was nothing she could do. She nodded helplessly.

'I promise.'

7

'When are you going to make that trip to Leningrad that you promised me?' asked Anassa. She had chosen a moment when Fred was alone to make the request, since Laura would certainly be upset by it.

Fred himself did not look too happy about the suggestion. Perhaps he had hoped that she would forget about his offer. For her own part, Anassa had originally intended to let more time pass before raising the subject; but her mind had been changed by the extraordinary way in which Leon was behaving.

The night of the Russian New Year Ball had marked the highest point of her life. She was at the peak of her beauty, she was wearing a dress more magnificent than anything she would ever be able to buy for herself, she had taken an exquisite revenge on the woman who had wronged her, and the man she adored had asked her to marry him.

Naturally a triumph on such a scale could not be expected to last for ever. Although she might hope that her beauty would endure for a few years longer, the gown had to be returned the next day. Laura, from whom she had expected praise, had seemed first of all disconcerted by the way she had chosen to dress and later positively disapproving of her confrontation with the countess.

That reaction ought only to have been a temporary one, but Laura had continued to behave in an oddly restrained way ever since that night, as though she were holding back something she wanted to say. Since Anassa had no wish to endure a lecture on her behaviour, she in turn had held herself slightly aloof, avoiding any opportunities for intimate chats. It was an unsatisfactory situation.

Far more worrying, however, was the change in Leon's behaviour. Naturally Anassa had wanted the whole world to know that she was engaged to be married, but he had insisted that it must for the moment be kept a secret. The reason he gave was that his real mother, Barisinova, must be the first to hear the news. Such consideration was not, in Anassa's secret opinion, deserved by someone who was eventually discovered to have changed both her address and her married name for a fourth time without informing her only son, and it was the last straw when the middle-aged bride proved to be on a world cruise, leaving no forwarding address.

Surely it was enough that Leon should have written the required letter! But he had shaken his head unhappily, claiming that he must wait for her blessing.

None of this would have mattered too much if they could have gone on as before, joyfully making love whenever Leon returned to Paris between races or rallies. But the really incomprehensible thing was that he no longer wanted to go to bed with her. Or rather, he did want to − she could tell that easily enough − but he wasn't going to give into his desires again until they were married.

It didn't make sense. Either they should have the wedding straightaway, without waiting any longer to hear from a mother who had shown no interest in her son for years; or else they should forget that the proposal had ever been spoken, and continue their love affair without commitment. As she gradually realised that Leon was not prepared to adopt either course, Anassa had worked out her own explanation. It must be that Leon was worried because he had no income on which to support a wife. Fred had given him a Maserati and enough funds to support him for five years while he raced it; but motor racing could never be a means of earning a living.

What Leon needed was a rich wife: so that was what Anassa intended to offer him.

By now she was in regular employment as a mannequin and also much in demand as a *mannequin mondaine*. The public disclosure that she was a Russian princess had brought her many invitations into high society, to add to those within the artistic circles where she was already at home. As in New York, she wore the clothes of the most fashionable designers for the cost merely of murmuring the name on the label to her fellow-guests. All this earned her a good living, although she was sensible enough to realise that it would not continue for ever; but Leon would be too proud to exist on a wife's wages. What she wanted was capital: a fortune of her own, to be shared with the man she loved.

And the fortune, the Kristov fortune, was there in Leningrad, only waiting for someone to bring it out. That was why she was now face to face with Fred, determined not to be the first to blink.

'It's too soon to go back,' he said. 'They haven't completed the last contract yet.'

'All the more reason, surely, for you to check what's holding it up.'

259

'There won't be any special obstacle. Just general slowness. I told you before, it's a barter deal. Carpets, that's what I'm waiting for. They're probably still being woven.'

'There's a special reason why I need some money. A lot of money. All those things you hid in the palace, they belong to me. I didn't mind you giving the first batch to Leon.' She had genuinely not minded, because she was in love with Leon; but Fred, who did not know that, would be made to feel guilty by the reminder. 'But now it's my turn. And you did promise.'

'I don't think you realise what a dangerous country it is. The risks ...'

'There seem to be journalists going there every day, from what I read.'

'Yes, well, they're not trying to smuggle out gold plates, are they?' Fred had begun to sweat with anxiety already, even before she had persuaded him to agree.

'What else did you hide?' A single diamond, if it were large enough, might be worth a fortune.

But Fred had no memory of diamonds. 'Your father packed the small stuff to go with you.' He began to list the contents of the concealed store room. It was true that most of what he described was heavy and in some cases bulky. But one item caught Anassa's attention.

'Pictures? What sort of pictures?'

Fred thought for a moment. 'There were a couple of Rembrandts. Two or three other pictures as well. I was told at the time who painted them, but I can't remember the names: only Rembrandt, because I'd heard of him.'

'I'm surprised you didn't bring those out first. Out of their frames, the canvases would be the easiest to conceal, wouldn't they? Especially in a load of carpets.' Anassa could feel success rising in her throat. He was going to agree. If she could just keep him talking long enough for his guilt to grow as he remembered how he had once left her to die, she would have him.

'Simple answer to that one. Gold and silver you can melt down and no one can ever tell where they came from. But these Rembrandts ... I went along to the Louvre before my last trip; asked someone for advice on the best way to protect the surface. He got excited straightaway. There's a book; a kind of catalogue, tells anyone who needs to know where every important picture in the world was last seen. The moment the Kristov Rembrandts come up for auction, there'll be little men in Moscow working out how they got there. It wouldn't be a good idea for Fred Richards ever to show his face in the country again.'

'Sure, I can see that. Well, of course *I* wouldn't ever ask you to go back again after this, not if you managed to bring something like that out. That's a promise in return for your promise. And I'd tell Laura – '

She was about to say that Laura, who had been upset to learn how her husband had abandoned little Tanya in the snow, would be glad to feel that the slate was wiped clean; but Fred interrupted her.

'No. Not a word to Laura till I'm back. She'd worry herself sick. Not a word to anyone else either. Too dangerous. It only needs a rumour, a whisper of suspicion, and I'm in real trouble.'

'Of course. Thank you, Fred.'

She was tempted to skip out of the room in delight at her success. It couldn't really be as risky as he pretended, when no one else in the world knew where the treasures were stored. Fred was obviously a bit of a coward. He had proved that when he hurried away from the sledge without trying to pull her out, so she didn't feel guilty about giving him the chance to make up for it. It would clear his conscience as well as setting her up financially.

She might have expected that he would invent excuses for delay, but it seemed that he had decided to act quickly, before his nerve went – as quickly, at least, as was possible when each letter in which he tried to arrange a business meeting went unanswered for several weeks.

At last the day of his departure arrived. Anassa felt a twinge of guilt as she noticed Laura's strained expression. Was she being selfish? The answer was probably yes; but Fred was a survivor. He would be back, safe and sound, within a few weeks.

Once he had left, Laura took the opportunity to visit her aunt and cousins in England. Her absence opened a different opportunity for Anassa. For the first time since they fell in love, Leon and she could be alone in the villa. She sent him a cable to announce the good news.

He would not be able to come at once. She knew that, because he was just about to compete in the Mille Miglia in the Maserati which Fred had given him. If he did well, he hoped that he might be invited to become a member of the official Maserati team. She waited impatiently, looking forward to the excitement of an unannounced arrival.

All that arrived was a letter. It was as affectionate as ever, but its content dismayed her. He had come second in his class, he announced proudly, and as a result had been invited to

261

Berlin to discuss the possibility of joining the Mercedes team. Mercedes might prove to be the car of the future, so this was a suggestion to be taken seriously. He was sure she would understand that he could not return to Paris just for the moment.

No, she did not understand. It was almost as though he were deliberately avoiding her company. Ever since she became a woman she had needed to fend off the attentions of men who claimed to adore her. It was perfectly ridiculous that the one man she loved should keep his distance in such a way. After consulting her diary, Anassa cancelled a clutch of appointments and took the train to Berlin.

'Of course I love you,' said Leon unhappily when she bearded him in his hotel room. 'It's just that I think we ought to wait now until after we're married.'

'Why?'

'Well, there might be a baby.'

'That never worried you before.' Anassa had assured him from the start that there would be no unwished-for consequences of their lovemaking: all the professional mannequins knew the importance of preserving their slim figures, and had shared their secrets with her. 'But if that's really what's worrying you, why don't we just get married. Today. Here.'

'I'm waiting to hear from my mother.'

'You're never going to hear from your mother. Your mother is not important. Only you and me. Oh Leon, my darling — '

As she spoke, she began to undress; not in the matter-of-fact manner of the salon changing room, but slowly and sensuously, deliberately exciting him.

'Don't!' he cried, but she took no notice, pressing herself against him as, wearing by now only a camisole, she began to undo the buttons of his clothing. She was right in believing that he would not be able to resist for long. Within seconds they had tumbled together on to the bed. Never before had he seemed so strong or so loving, as all the pent-up desire of the long period of self-denial was released. And yet, when at last they lay panting but unmoving in each other's arms, it looked almost as though he had been crying.

'I was frightened,' she said softly. 'It seemed as though you didn't want to marry me after all.'

'Of course I want to marry you. More than anything else in the world.'

'Good. I love you so much.'

'And I — ' A moment earlier he had seemed exhausted, but now he moved towards her again. It was a night to remember.

262

By the time she left Berlin Anassa had no fears about the future. It was for that reason that she decided not to return to Paris by the direct route. Instead, she travelled to Karlovy Vary. If Leon could tell his mother about the engagement, there was no reason why she should not announce it to her own only surviving relative.

She had visited Alexis as soon as Laura brought the news of his survival, but had found herself not altogether easy in her uncle's company. It was the difference of generation, she supposed, which made him so bitter, so determined not to forget the privileged life he had once led. Anassa had no sentimental feeling for the land of her birth, which she associated more with the deaths of her parents and sister than with the happiness of her early years. She had made a life for herself and even if she were offered a chance to go back, she would not take it. They country had changed. Everything she heard about it made it hateful to her, and there seemed no way in which the old days could ever return.

So she found it hard to listen as Alexis now greeted her with yet another diatribe about the murderers in Moscow. On her first visit to Karlovy Vary she had been so shocked by the bleakness of his living conditions that she had sent him as generous a gift of money as she could afford. She was dismayed now to discover that he was still occupying the same bleak room and had put all the money she had given him into what seemed to her a hare-brained scheme for toppling the Bolsheviks by wrecking their economy.

'It's an investment, you see,' he tried to persuade her. 'Once that lot are out, we can go back and restore order and prosperity.'

'But in the meantime, I wanted you to live more comfortably. If I were to buy an apartment here for you, Uncle Alexis, would you move into it? I should keep the ownership myself, to make sure you couldn't give it away again, but would you use it?'

'My dear child, you can't possibly be earning enough to go around buying property.'

'This wouldn't come out of my earnings. I'm expecting to get a generous present from Fred before long, as soon as he gets back from Russia.'

'Fred? You expect me to accept hand-outs from a chauffeur!'

'He's not a chauffeur any longer.' Anassa tried to be patient, although she had encountered this prejudice before. 'And it's Kristov money really, so it would be quite right for you to have a share of it. But only if you'll promise — '

'What do you mean, it's Kristov money?'

'Well, he rescued some things from the palace in Leningrad and sold them.'

263

'By "rescued", do you mean "stole"?'

'Not unless you count getting things away from the Bolsheviks as stealing, and I don't suppose you do. My father asked him to hide some valuable property: pictures and jewels and so on.'

'If he's bringing that sort of thing out, some of it should have come to me as part of the Kristov fortune.'

Anassa was silent, not liking to point out that Alexis was not necessarily his brother's heir. As though reading her thoughts, he continued to grumble.

'There were a couple of Rembrandts, for example. They must be worth a fortune. But they're family heirlooms. The property of my father before they came to my brother. It would be quite wrong for Fred Richards to think that he has any claim on them. Are the Rembrandts amongst the things he's brought out?'

'Not yet.'

As soon as she spoke the words, Anassa could have bitten off her tongue. How had she allowed herself to get into this conversation, when Fred had been so adamant that no word about his mission must get out? But Alexis could keep a secret. At her very first visit she had asked him not to let anyone know that his niece, Princess Tanya, was still alive; and he had promised and kept the promise.

'Uncle Alexis, I shouldn't have mentioned this to you. It's terribly secret. You won't say anything, will you, to anyone at all?'

'Not if that's what you want.'

'Promise?'

'Certainly I'll promise. It's not my habit to gossip about the affairs of chauffeurs.'

'When you were in Russia, Fred said, you and he were — well, friendly. Why have you taken against him now?'

'I haven't taken against him, as you call it. I no longer have any kind of relationship with him, that's all.'

Anassa sighed at the difficulty of establishing any subject on which they could be in sympathy. But of course the sight of her uncle still living in poverty had distracted her from the true reason for her visit.

'I have another secret to tell you, Uncle Alexis. It's only secret for a little while, though: just till I've had time to tell Laura.' She had intended to add Fred's name, but decided that it might be tactless. 'I'm engaged to be married.'

'Bless you, my dear.' In one of his swings of mood, Alexis embraced her joyfully. 'I was worried that you were becoming rather old for finding a husband. In my days, girls were always married before they were twenty. But then, not many

264

of them were as beautiful as you. Who is the fortunate young man?'

'I've mentioned Leon to you before, haven't I?'

'The motor racer; is that the one? Tell me more about him. Didn't you say once that he was born in Russia, like you? What is his family? Is he of the nobility?'

'Well.' Anassa hesitated. She didn't believe the story of his possible Romanov connections any more than Leon himself did. It was better to stick to facts. 'His mother, Barisinova, was a dancer with the Imperial Ballet.'

'Barisinova.' Alexis gave her a look which she did not understand. 'Tell me, Tanya Pavlovna, does Laura know that you love the son of Barisinova; that you plan to marry him?'

'Not yet. We shall announce our engagement as soon as she gets back from England.' Anassa was not prepared to waste any more time in waiting for Barisinova's blessing. 'Is something wrong, Uncle Alexis?'

'There is a difficulty,' he said. 'But it's not for me to interfere. Laura will tell you. Laura should have told you years ago.'

Nothing she could say would persuade him to explain what he meant, causing her to feel worried as she made the journey back to Paris. The first thing she saw as she stepped inside the villa was a letter to Leon from his mother; she recognised the handwriting. Anassa gave a smile of relief. At last Barisinova was writing to say how pleased she was at Leon's news, and that would mean that Anassa could set about arranging the wedding at once. She had no hesitation in opening the letter.

'To answer your question,' wrote the former ballet dancer to her son, after a page of chat about her cruise. 'Your father was Prince Pavel Karlovich Kristov, who was also the father of the Princess Tanya Pavlovna Kristova. I am very sorry to have to give you this news. It will, of course, make your proposed marriage impossible.'

If Leon had asked the question, it must mean that he had already suspected what the answer would be. This was why he had done his best to keep away from his fiancée instead of revelling in their engagement. He must have known. Laura must have known as well. She should have told them both months ago, years ago. How dare she keep such a thing secret!

As she read the letter for the first time, Anassa had been incredulous. Now, reading it over and over again, she became furiously angry. Why should it make any difference that they were half-brother and sister? It would affect any children of their union,

265

but they could be careful never to have any. Why shouldn't they just get married quietly, somewhere where nobody knew them? But Leon could have suggested that already if he had wanted to, instead of insisting that he must know the truth. Although Anassa told herself that she could fight, in her heart she already knew that she would be defeated.

Little by little her fury turned to misery. Dragging herself up the stairs, she locked her bedroom door behind her and flung herself on to the bed in tears. She would never be able to marry Leon: but she would never love anyone else.

8

'Any letters?'

It was a ridiculous question. Dozens of letters arrived for the agency every morning. But Beryl knew what her employer meant.

'I'm afraid not.'

Laura went through to her own office with a heavy heart. The fact that so many months had passed since Fred's departure, when he had expected six or seven weeks to be enough, was not sinister in itself. Laura was well aware of the delays which could be caused by Russian bureaucracy or inefficiency. But why had he not warned her that he might have to stay longer? For the first month he had written every week. The letters often took a long time to arrive, but they came in the end. The last of them, dated in October, had given the impression that he was almost ready to leave. It had reached her only in November, and in the seven weeks since then she had heard nothing.

Beryl, bringing in a batch of personal correspondence, tried to be optimistic.

'Didn't he say that he was going to be travelling back with that load of carpets he's bought? Perhaps he's gone off to wherever it is they're made, to make sure that the quality is all right. Probably communications go to pot once you get outside the big cities.'

'Yes, I expect you're right.' Laura expected nothing of the kind, but did her best to smile. For a little while she stared down at her desk without moving, unable to raise enough energy even to take her letters out of their envelopes.

She was lonely as well as worried. This was the longest period which she had spent apart from Fred, and during his earlier trip to Leningrad both Leon and Anassa had been living in the villa, keeping her company. But Anassa had moved out in a tantrum

266

after discovering that Leon was her half-brother, and had not yet forgiven what she saw as a deception. Laura was able to learn of her doings through the newspapers, but every attempt at a reconciliation was met with silence.

Even more upsetting, although less stormy, was Leon's departure from the villa. When he came to pack up his possessions he had shown no anger, but made clear his regret that the truth of his parentage had been concealed for so long. It was clear, too, that he was under pressure from Anassa to continue his affair with her even though they could not legally marry. Although he had decided it was not right that she should be prevented from having a normal married life, with children, he was still so much in love with her that he could not bear to see her while knowing she could never be his.

So he had moved to Berlin to be near his new Mercedes teammates, and showed every sign of settling there permanently. His mother, after failing to take part in the Kristovs' flight from Russia in 1918, had taken him as a young boy to the Crimea, hoping to escape by sea. When the Germans invaded the area she had used her beauty to obtain the protection of their commanding officer and was able to retreat with his army to the safety of western Europe. It must have been during that period that Leon, as a boy, had not only learned to speak German fluently, but had grown to like the nation which most Frenchmen and Russians still thought of as the enemy. It was clear to Laura that he would never return to Paris.

Lethargically now she began to read this morning's mail and found one note to lift her spirits. During the period when he was in the British Embassy in Paris she had seen a good deal of her old friend from Oxford days, Charles Vereker. The slight awkwardness caused by her earlier rejection of his proposal was easily overcome, and when after two years he was posted home to work for a time in the Foreign Office itself, she had happily agreed to become his 'Paris correspondent'.

They wrote regularly and at length to each other. As a rule Laura's letters were devoted to plays and books and exhibitions and social gossip, to keep him in touch with Parisian society. But recently her anxiety had prompted an appeal to him in his professional capacity. Could he, she asked, approach the embassy in Moscow for news of Fred?

His brief answer made no reference to her enquiry. 'I have to come to Paris on personal business and will call on you, if I may, on the evening of the 20th.'

She glanced at the calendar on her desk. This same evening, then. But even as she was registering this, the door opened.

267

'Mr Vereker to see you,' said Beryl.

Laura had only a second in which to wish that she had put on a little make-up that morning, to disguise the anxiety which showed in the lines of her face. And then he was walking towards her – and he too looked haggard. She had never seen him anything but well-dressed, but today his clothes, smelling of smoke, had a crumpled look and his hair was tousled. Like her, he was in his forties, and he was showing his age.

'I couldn't wait,' he said. 'I took the overnight boat train instead. Oh, my dear Laura, it's good to see you.'

Stepping forward, he took her in his arms. Although he made no attempt to kiss her, the fierceness of his embrace was quite different from the usual friendly manner in which they greeted each other on their irregular meetings.

'I'll shut up shop here.' Laura, breathless, tried to speak normally as she went into the outer office and handed the day's business over to her assistants. She led the way into her drawing room and asked Janine for coffee.

'What's wrong, Charles?' she asked when they were alone. She expected the answer to relate to her own enquiry; but it seemed that he could think of nothing but his own problem.

'It's Daphne,' he said unhappily, lighting a cigarette and pulling on it for a moment before he could continue. 'We're going through a sticky patch. When we were in Vienna, she fell for a chap there, in the French Embassy. Had an affair with him. I knew about it, but I didn't expect it to last. Every diplomatic corps has the same rules. No scandals. In particular, no divorces. And he was a Catholic. I sat it out, and we were posted away, and everything seemed all right.'

'So what . . .?'

'A few months ago he turned up in London. No collusion, I don't think; just a normal appointment for him. But they started up again. Too obviously this time. Our chaps dropped hints to their chaps and he was recalled to Paris. Should have faded away. But Daphne's taken it into her head that he's the love of her life and she can't live without him. She's done a bolt and taken a flat over here. I've got to get her to come back.'

'Do you still love her?'

'No.' The answer was matter-of-fact. 'But I can't afford to let her go, not if I want to keep my job. It's my whole career. The only thing I know. A divorce would finish me. And for my wife to be having a blatant affair with a foreigner is almost as bad. She knew the form when she married me.'

'Will you be able to persuade her, d'you think?'

'God knows.' He sighed and once again drew deeply on his cigarette. 'I've got three good cards to play. The first one is that he'll never marry her. And she's had the experience, with me, of moving in good society in Paris. She may not like it when she feels shoulders grow cold. The second thing is that I'm coming up for an embassy of my own. Only if she behaves herself, of course. But to be His Excellency's wife should be worth something to her.'

'Would a knighthood go with it?'

'Might do. She's always had a title, of course, from being born her father's daughter, but Sir Charles and Lady Daphne Vereker would certainly sound more impressive than Mr and Lady Daphne. And on top of that ...' He paused, stubbing out the cigarette before continuing. 'My elder brother isn't what you'd call a good life,' he said at last. 'He's had one heart attack already and he's not the sort of chap to let a doctor teach him how to dodge the next one. He's a good bit older than me. No wife or children. I hope it will be a long time yet, but Daphne must realise that she could be Lady Knaresborough one of these days if she sticks around. So yes, I may win; but even if I do, it's not going to be much fun. What sort of marriage is it if your wife has to be bribed with titles to stay? I was thinking on the boat coming over, Laura. If David Hughes had died a few months earlier, it could have been you.'

Laura remembered − with shame − that the same thought had once entered her own mind. She was silent, not prepared to confess it, because by now there was Fred to be considered.

Charles's mind ran along the same lines.

'Rotten timing I always had with you,' he said. 'At Oxford we were both too young − and you were in love with Kristov, weren't you? And then you were engaged to Hughes. And now you're married to Fred.'

'What about Fred?' Laura had been patient for long enough. 'Did you get my letter, Charles?'

'Yes. Sorry. I shouldn't have been burbling on about my own affairs.' His voice changed to a more businesslike tone. 'I've been in touch with our chaps in Moscow, asking them to look into it. I'll contact them again from the embassy here to see what they've found out. What precisely was he doing there, Laura?'

In as much detail as she could, she described the trading company which Fred had set up separately from his taxi and car-hire business.

'There was a lot of barter involved. They never have enough foreign currency to pay for everything they want. But he'd been there before and there wasn't any trouble. Well, nothing that a bribe or two couldn't solve.'

'And that's all? Straightforward business deals?'

Laura didn't answer at once. Fred had emphasised that the treasure hidden in the Kristov palace must never be mentioned to anyone. But she could not expect Charles to help unless he knew all the facts. Reluctantly she told him about the gold which he had brought out as a gift to Leon.

'He must be mad!' exclaimed Charles. 'If he tried anything like that again and they caught him ...' He checked himself apologetically. 'Sorry, Laura. The Daphne business has left me edgy. What you want is my soothing diplomatic voice, isn't it?'

'No. What I want is to find out the truth about what's happening. And then to know what can be done about it, if it's bad.'

'I'm going to make one more undiplomatic suggestion. Have you considered the possibility that Fred might have decided to pick up a handful of diamonds and run? Live the life of a millionaire in some quiet paradise.'

'I remember there was an occasion a long time ago when you told me that he'd probably run off with a sackful of Kristov valuables. And in fact he nearly got himself killed trying to get the family out of the country. You don't really know him, Charles. He's — he's *responsible*. He wouldn't desert me.' She paused, wondering whether Fred had in fact planned to return to the treasure storehouse. He had not mentioned any such possibility, but that could have been merely in order that she should not worry. 'He can be rich here as well as anywhere else,' she cried. 'He's rich already. There's no possible reason ...' She began to weep.

'What a brute I am.' Charles moved to sit on the sofa beside her, his arm round her shoulders. 'It's jealousy, Laura. Or envy, at least. Here you are, in love with your chap and absolutely confident that he'd never do the dirty on you; and here am I ... Well, I'm sorry. I'll come back to you as soon as I have some news.'

It was two days before he returned: two of the longest days of Laura's life.

'How's Daphne?' she asked, frightened to ask the only question which truly concerned her.

'A treaty has been negotiated. I'd hoped to ask you out to dinner last night, but we had to make a formal public appearance together. And there'll be another one tonight. To still the wagging tongues. If I get the embassy, she promises to behave impeccably in public and discreetly in private. I don't know whether to laugh or cry. Now, Fred. I'm afraid the news isn't good, Laura.'

Pale-faced, she waited for him to continue.

'He was arrested in October, when he was on the point of leaving.

There was a Customs search of a load of rugs and they found five paintings and half a gold dinner service. Sounds as though there must have been a tip-off.'

'But who could have known?'

'Presumably he employed some kind of helper in Leningrad. He may have been an informer. Or a drunkard. Anyway, Fred has been charged with theft and smuggling.'

'He was only returning private property to its proper owner.'

'Oh Laura, Laura, you know better than that! The Kristovs have no right to anything they may have owned once. It's the property of the people, the state. And unfortunately the theft and smuggling charge is only part of the trouble. He paid for the rugs — and offered a bribe to get them shipped out by an unapproved route — in what turned out to be counterfeit roubles.'

'But that's ridiculous!' Laura exclaimed. 'He doesn't work that way round. He wouldn't have paid for them in money at all. I mean, he's not in the business of importing Russian goods into France. He went there originally to sell engines, not to buy carpets. He didn't *want* the carpets. It was just, as I said, that the people he was dealing with didn't have foreign currency to pay and so he had to accept goods in exchange. If he *had* been buying merchandise, they'd have made him settle the bill in dollars or pounds; certainly not roubles. And anyway, where — ?' She stopped dead, struck by an unpleasant thought. She had heard mention of forged roubles once before.

Charles waited for her to finish the sentence. 'You were going to say?'

'It doesn't matter now. The important thing is, what can we do? How much can they prove? What ought I to do about his defence?'

'No easy answers. I'm afraid, Laura. The paintings and the gold prove themselves. There may have been a tip-off, but from what you told me earlier, there hasn't been any sort of plant. And the business with the roubles may turn out to be even more serious.'

'I'm quite sure that they won't be able to show any connection between him and counterfeit money,' Laura told him.

'Unless someone else landed him in it. Someone who knew about what was hidden, perhaps, and tried to divert the consignment — the whole wagon-load — by offering a price for it behind his back but in his name. Well, we can send an observer when he comes up for trial, of course, but I'm afraid their system is that the defence lawyer will be provided by the state. And there is a danger — ' He sighed. 'It does sometimes look as though the purpose of these trials isn't so much justice as public education. "This is what will happen to all

271

of you if you behave in this way." I'm sorry to upset you like this, my dear, but if I paint the blackest possible picture to start with, any change that shows itself should be for the good.'

Laura could hardly bring herself to speak.

'So what can be done? Should I go − '

'Christ, no! No, the best hope is some kind of trade. Another treaty. What − or whom − have we got that they would like back? And if we aren't holding anyone at the moment, who can we find? I'll set to work on it as soon as I get back to London. To be going on with, it will be helpful simply to let them know that we're watching. That will stop them from putting him against a wall and shooting him without a trial.'

'Shooting him!' Shuddering with terror, Laura leapt to her feet. For a second time Charles took her into his arms; this time gently comforting her.

'It won't come to that. I'll do my best. Trust me, Laura.'

'Yes, of course. Thank you, Charles.'

After he had left, she continued to shiver. She had been anxious enough before, but subconsciously she must have believed that everything would turn out well, for that anxiety could not compare with the emotion she felt now.

There came a moment, much later in the day, when she could keep still no longer. She must talk to someone, and it must be someone who already knew at least part of the story. Leon was too far away but Anassa, surely, would not allow resentment to inhibit her from providing comfort. The question, rather, was whether Laura herself could be brave enough to confess the whole truth. For as she rang to order a car to be brought round, her errand was prompted not only by fear but by guilt.

9

The diplomatic reception was a glittering affair. It was somebody's national day: Anassa was not sure whose. She had been asked to go as the partner of a young French diplomat who thought he was in love with her, and she had accepted because it was exactly the kind of occasion for which she was employed as a *mannequin mondaine*.

There was no secret about the fact that she was a walking clothes horse, paid to display a product. This evening, indeed, Lady Daphne Vereker − whom Anassa had met some years earlier through Mr Vereker's friendship with Laura − made an almost embarrassing fuss about how she had come over to Paris specially to shop for

272

clothes: the evening dress Anassa was wearing was a design she simply must have. Her husband, standing beside her, had agreed politely that it would certainly suit her. So tomorrow Lady Daphne would call at the salon to buy it – and would be tempted with a dozen or more other garments – and Anassa would have earned her fee.

What made Anassa all the more in demand was that she had once again become the ice princess. During the course of her affair with Leon, happiness had made her animated. He belonged to the wild set of young Parisian society and she had joined with delight in its frenetic round of parties. But now Leon had left her. He had wept as bitterly as she at their last meeting, after the arrival of the letter from his mother; but there was a streak of determination in his character which she had never encountered before. They must make a clean break, he told her, to make it clear that she was free to marry and to have children. Only after she was happily settled with someone else could they attempt to develop a new relationship as brother and sister.

It was no good. No one else could replace him in her heart. The young diplomat who kissed her in the taxi – one of Fred's taxis – on the way home from the reception was not invited to cross the threshold.

Her maid greeted her with a babble of apology. There was a caller who had insisted on entering, insisted on staying. She had cried for an hour, two hours, and had then fallen asleep in the drawing room.

Anassa silenced the maid by putting a finger to her lips and looked through the doorway. The visitor was Laura, who must have been sitting upright on the sofa to start with but whose head had now fallen sideways on to the arm.

Anassa's heart jerked with alarm. If Laura was upset and had braved the likelihood of a chilly reception to call here, it could only mean that something had happened to Leon. An accident! Instinctively she stepped forward, but was checked by professionalism. The shimmering golden gown was not her own property and must not be spoiled by tears.

It took her only a moment to exchange it for a house-robe and return to the drawing room.

'Laura!'

Awaking abruptly, Laura looked dazed, as though trying to remember where she was and why she had come. She staggered a little as she rose to her feet. Anassa stepped forward, but did not need to steady her.

'Leon. Has something happened to Leon?'

273

'No, it's not him. It's Fred.'

'Oh.' Fred as much as Laura had been party to the secrecy which had allowed her to fall in love with her half-brother. But any chilliness in her expression disappeared as the story poured out of Fred's arrest and the prospect of a trial and the danger that he might be executed.

'They wouldn't do that. Not just for what they're calling theft.' Anassa, their quarrel forgotten, hugged the weeping Laura in an attempt at consolation.

'Charles — Charles Vereker, you know — seemed to think it wasn't impossible. And you see, there's this business of the forged roubles as well. This is why I had to talk to you, because I can't say it to anyone else. I can't help wondering whether Alexis might be involved somehow.'

'Uncle Alexis? Oh no, that's unthinkable.'

'He has been involved in some kind of plot. I don't remember the details, but I know forgery came into it.'

Anassa remembered that this was true. She too had heard mention of an economic conspiracy, but had not taken it seriously. It would require a powerful secret organisation to make it work, and she did not credit her uncle and his emigré friends with that kind of efficiency. And there was another, more compelling argument.

'But he's on our side, Laura. None of them would do anything to help the Bolsheviks.'

'That's what I'd have thought. But if it were a matter of personal spite . . .' Laura was working herself up to tell some difficult truth. 'I feel so guilty. It may be all my fault.'

'Nonsense. How could it be?'

'When I was a young girl — really young, I mean: sixteen, seventeen — I was in love with your uncle. A romantic schoolgirl's love for a glamorous man who was out of reach. The sort of thing that you believe at the time is more important than anything else in the world; but you grow older and you learn better. Alexis knew how I felt. There was one occasion, before the revolution, when he tried to seduce me. When I said no, he probably recognised that I was simply too young and too prudish. There were no hard feelings. He had plenty of other women, I'm sure. But then, the second time . . .'

'He tried again?'

'Yes. In Karlovy Vary. That was where I discovered he was still alive and — well, I was so glad about that that I gave the wrong impression at first. I blame myself entirely. So when — almost too late — I said no again, he was angry. And he turned the anger against Fred. Quite rightly, in a way: it was because I loved Fred

274

that I wouldn't, couldn't ... I don't think Alexis will ever forgive me, Anassa. All his troubles, all those years in prison, have left him bitter. I almost believe it would give him pleasure to see me in mourning for a man he thinks of as just a jumped-up chauffeur.'

'So what are you suggesting?'

'Well, he couldn't have known anything about the smuggling. I didn't even know myself what Fred was planning. But suppose Alexis discovered somehow that Fred was in Russia. He and his White Russian friends must have contacts in the country. They may not have realised that the carpets were part of a barter deal. Suppose they made a cash offer for the consignment. Some corrupt official would see the chance of getting two payments for a single shipment. It could have been a try-out to see whether the forgery would be detected. Not caring what might happen to Fred.'

'That's a lot of supposes. It doesn't sound very likely, Laura. Why should they try to buy a load of rugs?' Thoughtful, and a little worried, Anassa tried to recall her own visit to Alexis that summer. Had she mentioned that Fred was about to return to Moscow? She couldn't remember, but it was not impossible. The journey was not a secret one. For the moment, she did her best to rid Laura of any feeling of personal guilt.

'If Uncle Alexis *did* deliberately put Fred at risk, I'm sure it wouldn't be because of you,' she said soothingly. 'I suppose he might have felt that anyone trading with the Bolsheviks was giving comfort to the enemy, so to speak, but it wouldn't be in his own interest to get Fred arrested.'

'Why not?'

'Because last time I saw him I promised to buy him somewhere decent to live. To get him out of that awful room. I told him I should do it as soon as I got the money from – ' She stopped dead. 'Oh, my God!' she exclaimed.

'What is it? What's the matter, dear?'

Unable to speak, Anassa groaned aloud. The conversation which she had tried to recall a few moments earlier now flowed through her mind as clearly as though she and her uncle were speaking the words aloud. She would have enough money soon, she had told him, because Fred was planning to bring the Kristov Rembrandts out of Leningrad.

How could she have been such a fool? Laura had aroused her anger by keeping secrets, but how much worse it was to betray other people's confidences!

Alexis would have known the true value of that wagon-load of carpets. Perhaps he had told his associates about the pictures and they had decided to get them away from Fred and sell them to finance their operations. How like them to have bungled the attempt by using counterfeit money! Instead of leaving Fred to smuggle the valuable Rembrandts to the west, they had made a present of them to the communists instead. And whoever had made it possible for Fred to be linked to the forged rouble notes was heartless indeed, even if he hoped that the deception would not be discovered.

Nothing was proved, and maybe it never would be. But if Fred's predicament were indeed the result of some action of her uncle's, there was no one to blame but herself.

'Oh, Laura!' she exclaimed. Tears began to run down her cheeks as she knelt on the floor at Laura's feet and confessed.

10

Days, weeks, months passed; there was no pleasure to be found in them. Leon had made his home in Berlin. Laura rarely saw him, but needed little imagination to tell her that he was unhappy. Not only from his own letters but from newspaper gossip columns she realised that he was driving too fast, too dangerously. It was the way to win races, and he was rapidly building a reputation for himself on the motor racing circuit; but it was not the way to stay alive. Sometimes she wondered whether he was deliberately trying to kill himself.

All she could hope was that before too long he would meet some other woman who would help him to forget his love for his sister. He was young and good-looking — and motor racing had always attracted glamorous girls to hang about the pits, idolising the drivers. Sooner or later, surely, he would fall in love again. Until then, Laura recognised helplessly that there was nothing she could do to release him from his despair.

Anassa, meanwhile, living in an apartment of her own in Paris, was equally affected by the separation. The radiance of love had disappeared from her face, taking with it the healthy exuberance with which she had applied herself to building a new life in Paris. She had become once again the remote and painfully thin woman whom Laura had first glimpsed through the glass partition of her office. Her name, like Leon's, was often to be found in the gossip columns, each time linked with a different escort, but Laura knew better than to believe that she was behaving promiscuously. It was because she allowed no one to come near her that so many made the attempt.

The two women had made up their quarrel on that tearful night

276

when each of them accepted some of the responsibility for Fred's predicament. Although Anassa still wished that the truth about Leon's birth had been revealed to her as soon as they first met, she had ceased to blame Laura for a situation created by Barisinova.

'If I could fall in love with someone else, then perhaps Leon and I could at least be friends and see each other again,' she confided once. 'That's what he told me when we parted, and so I try. But all the time I know that he's the only man I shall ever love. And if I were to see him again, I should want more than friendship. How can this ever end, Laura?'

Laura had no answer. To suggest that time would heal the wound would probably be true, but not of much comfort. In any case, she had greater worries on her mind. An unhappy love affair, however tragic it might seem to the couple involved, could not compare with what was happening to Fred.

What *was* happening? Sometimes she clung to the lack of news as a sign of hope, while at other times it made her fear the worst. She flung herself into her work as a way of making the time pass, and tried not to nag at Charles for information, knowing that he was doing the best he could. He had been given the embassy he hoped for, as well as the knighthood which went with it and which had persuaded Daphne to behave herself. So he was no longer based in the Foreign Office itself; but from his frequent letters she learned of all the efforts which were being made to secure Fred's release.

Wearily one day she returned from a week spent moving along the resorts of the Riviera, where she had been inspecting the agency's branches. Beryl gave her no time to read the pile of messages which had accumulated on her desk.

'Sir Charles Vereker is anxious to see you,' she said. 'I told him when he telephoned that you were expected back this afternoon and he arrived here half an hour ago. I suggested that he should wait in the drawing room rather than the office; was that right?'

For a moment Laura's heart ceased to beat and it seemed that she had forgotten how to breathe. If Charles had come in person, it could only mean that the news was bad. She stood still, willing herself not to faint, while Beryl watched her anxiously. By the time she was able to make her way to the drawing room, she had forced herself to accept in advance what she was about to hear.

First of all she had to endure a moment of small talk. Charles, stubbing out his cigarette before kissing her in greeting, was not willing to come straight to the point.

'You work too hard, Laura. You're looking tired.'

277

'That's because I've been on the move for six days and I'm only just off the train.'

'Do you need to push yourself to that extent?'

'What else have I to do? I'm running a business and I like to run it well. It helps me to keep my mind off — off what you're just about to tell me. What have you heard, Charles?'

'Sit down,' he said — and that in itself was enough to chill her heart still further. He sat on the sofa, holding her hand. 'There's some bad news. And some other news which isn't quite so bad; but not good either.'

She waited until he could bring himself to go on.

'Fred's trial has taken place. He was accused of bribery, theft and attempting to destabilise the economy. Bribery hardly rates as a crime at all in Russia, and theft is an ordinary criminal matter. But the business of the forged roubles ranked as a political offence. It was considered a form of espionage. He was sentenced to death. No, wait, I haven't finished.' His grip on her hand by now was painfully tight. 'There was a party of left-wing big-wigs just about to go over from England to meet Stalin so that they could come back and tell us all how marvellous communism was. We gave all the details about Fred's case to one of them and asked her to intercede on his behalf and see if Stalin would agree to deport him as a friendly gesture.'

'And did he?'

'No. But he did make a gesture of sorts. Commuted the death sentence to hard labour in Siberia for life.'

'For life!'

'Think of it this way. While there's life there's hope.'

'What hope?' asked Laura.

He put his arms around her and held her tightly. 'There could be another revolution one day. A change of policy. He might escape. I remember saying to you once, Fred is a survivor. He's survived execution. He's been given a gift of more time, and he may survive that as well.'

'What hope?' asked Laura again. 'Tell me truly, Charles. What hope?'

Too honest to continue with a false reassurance, Charles released her gently, stood up, and began to pace up and down the room. Leaning against the mantelpiece, he stared compassionately down at her.

'I remember speaking once to a political refugee. A Trotskyite. He'd been on the run inside Russia for two years before he managed to get out. He told me what had happened to his friends, and what he'd feared for himself. If you're arrested for a political crime, he said, there comes a moment, in the building they call the Lubyanka, when you're led in front of an examining officer, and in that moment you must tell yourself that you are a dead man. You may live for ten more years, even twenty, but your old life has come to an end, and you will only be able to survive what comes next if you think of it as borrowed time.'

'Is that so good?' Laura asked. 'If you had told me now that Fred was already dead, at least I could know that he would never be frightened again, would never feel any more pain. I could be glad about that much as I mourned for him. But now − if it terrifies me, how much more must it terrify him to think what lies ahead. I feel so helpless, Charles. Surely there must be something I can do. Could I send money for comforts?'

'It won't reach him. They won't even let him have any letters you write. I'll keep my ears open, and if any kind of treaty or trade pact comes up for discussion in the next few years I'll see if it's possible to get some kind of amnesty included in it. But for you − this isn't an easy thing for you to hear, Laura, but the best thing would be to say to yourself now that Fred is dead to you, even though he may still be alive somewhere. You'll never see him again. It would be better for you − and it will make no difference to him − if you mourn him now as though you were a widow.'

It was too much to bear. Laura groaned aloud and for a second time Charles took her in his arms, kissing her cheek and neck as he attempted to comfort her.

'Oh Laura, darling Laura, I'm so sorry. Terribly sorry.'

'You've been very kind, Charles. I'm grateful for all your help. But now, I think − '

She wanted only to be alone and, diplomat that he was, he was quick to understand.

After he had left, Laura went slowly upstairs and sat down in the bedroom which had been hers when she first came to live in the Villa des Cascades. As though it were yesterday she recalled how Fred had arrived in that room, leaving a picnic hamper in the corridor outside. She remembered the gentleness with which he had undressed her, the intensity of his lovemaking, the unexpected softness of his skin.

'You're beautiful,' he had said afterwards, and made her stand naked in front of the cheval mirror, staring at her own body as though she had never seen it before − while he, looking over her shoulder, had stared as well before cupping his hands under her breasts and twisting her back towards the bed again.

The excitement was real, not simply remembered. Charles, she suspected, had never quite understood how she could be happy with a man who was so much her inferior in education and breeding. But Fred had been a marvellous lover − and, in spite of what she knew about his love life as a young man, she didn't believe that he had ever been unfaithful to her. 'I'll always be on your side,' he had promised her once, when they were still almost strangers; and he had kept his promise. The only element lacking in their time together had been a child of their own, and Leon's arrival had given him the opportunity to show what a loving and generous father he could be.

There was nothing to regret in her memories of their relationship. It had proved to be tragic that she should have made such a bitter enemy of Alexis, but even that had happened because of her determination to remain faithful to Fred.

There was still a looking glass in the room, although now it was an antique in an elaborately carved Florentine frame. She stared at herself unblinkingly. Her travelling clothes were crumpled, her hair was tousled where Charles had run his fingers through it and her face was ravaged by tears. She had passed her fortieth birthday some time ago, but good grooming and smart dressing usually succeeded in making her look attractive. With those lacking, as they were now, she saw herself as a middle-aged businesswoman: unloved, undesirable, as much alone in the world as any widow.

Another memory intruded, of another mirror. In the office of the House of Cartier, thirteen, fourteen years ago, she had set the kokoshnik on her head and saw herself briefly transformed into a princess. It had seemed at the time as though the kokoshnik brought nothing but good fortune. It had helped them to raise the capital needed to buy the villa and establish their businesses; and later it had been responsible for the reunion with her one-time pupil.

Anassa herself had no good feelings about it. She had worn it in public only once, and the evening which began as her triumph was also the evening on which Leon discovered that they could not marry. She had returned it to the strong room of the bank, saying bitterly that if she could not wear it on the day of her wedding to Leon, she never wanted to see it again.

For Laura as well the jewelled headdress seemed to have led her to her present misery. *La Lachrymosa*, it had been called. The tiara of tears.

If she had not been asked to carry some of the Kristov jewels out of Russia, there would have been no need for her to keep a rendez-vous in Paris in order to hand the kokoshnik back. She could have married David when he first asked her. She might as a result have been a widow within a year; but perhaps she would have been able to nurse him successfully through his illness. In either case, she would probably have settled down to an uneventful life in England. The kokoshnik had made all that impossible, and so was responsible for her present sadness as well as for the happiness of the earlier years in Paris.

Well, she was never likely to see it again, and she could bear that well enough. But she would never see Fred again either. Would she ever be able to accept that? She stood for a long time without moving, still staring into the glass, but a curtain of tears obscured any reflection.

What was it that Charles had quoted to her? In that moment you must tell yourself that you are dead. The Villa des Cascades was far from being the Lubyanka, and Charles himself bore no resemblance to an interrogating officer, but what he had told her was just as decisive. Once upon a time she had told herself that her years in Russia were over and done with and could have no effect on her future life. She had been wrong then, because all her years in Paris had been influenced by the Revolution and its victims. But she could say it again now with more certainty. A new life, a lonely life, was about to begin.

Part 2

Absent Friends
1939–1947

1

'Sir Charles Vereker to see you, madame.'

On a hot Sunday afternoon in 1939 Laura was relaxing in the garden, cooled by the faint splashing of the water which gave the Villa des Cascades its name. Delighted, she leapt to her feet.

'Charles! How marvellous! But you should have told me you were coming and given me all the pleasure of looking forward to your visit.'

They embraced each other warmly as they kissed in greeting, but moved quickly apart to stroll together round the garden. During the past few years Laura had grown to love the man who was her oldest friend, but she knew that it was a love which must never be revealed in words or expressed in actions.

When Charles had first fallen in love with her, twenty years earlier, it had been her engagement to David which proved to be an obstacle. Now, when she was alone, Charles was the one who was tied. Although Laura knew that he no longer felt any affection for Daphne, she was well aware of the Diplomatic Service rules which linked the success of his career to the permanence of his marriage. Sometimes she was tempted to test him and to find out whether his feelings for her were as deep as her own; but for his own sake she had never yet succumbed to the temptation.

Their friendship had been sustained mainly by letters. He had asked her to continue acting as his Paris correspondent, keeping him in touch with all the social gossip and cultural activity of the French capital. Whether or not this had been his deliberate intention, the request had forced Laura to emerge from her period of mourning for Fred. Little by little, in order to have something to write about,

282

she had begun to accept invitations again and to entertain, to attend theatres and opera houses and exhibitions.

How handsome he was, she thought to herself as they sat down opposite each other in the shade. Charles was so tall that as a young man he had appeared lanky; but years of diplomatic banquets had filled him out, giving him an imposing presence. Always well-groomed and wearing the most expensively tailored suits and shirts, as a rule he exuded a decisive self-confidence. But now his fingers fidgeted with a cigarette case and he seemed unsure of what he wanted to say.

It was unusual for him not to light up immediately, for he was a chain-smoker. Laura sometimes suspected that he used cigarettes deliberately as a barrier between the two of them — as though the temptation to kiss her could only be resisted with the help of a smoke barrier. Today's self-restraint was uncharacteristic; she wondered briefly whether it had any significance.

'Daphne's come for a fitting, I suppose,' she said. It was Daphne's custom to visit Paris twice a year, using the spring and autumn collections of Schiaparelli and Chanel as an excuse for discreet meetings with her lover. Charles accompanied her on these occasions whenever he could, in the interest of damping down any gossip. Summer was not such a usual time for ordering clothes, but no doubt an ambassador's lady could plead the need for a new ball gown at any season of the year.

'No. I've come on my own this time,' he told her. 'Ostensibly for discussions with the Paris embassy. But actually to persuade you to sell up and return to England.'

'Charles! Why on earth should I do that?'

'Because there's going to be another war. Very soon.'

'Yes, I know. For Poland. But not here.'

'Just think about the last one,' he reminded her. 'It began as an incident in Serbia, but almost the whole of Europe was drawn in. That will happen again. And it's not by any means certain that we shall win. Russia may come in on either side, or else hold off to see what she can gain from other countries' defeats. Italy is Fascist and more likely to back Germany. Britain has been shilly-shallying and is still not prepared for war. France is a civilian country which may not have the stomach for a fight: she's already trying to repudiate her alliance with Poland. And Germany is an aggressive and well-organised totalitarian state, a military machine. We have to hope that Britain will be protected by the Channel, but I can't see anything that will save Paris.'

'The Germans in Paris? Oh come, Charles. That's impossible!'

'This is my profession, Laura. You know all about employment. Well, what I know about is foreign affairs.'

'Surely America — '

'The United States isn't going to let itself become involved in any European war again. I believe that France will quickly be defeated. Paris won't be a safe place for long. If you were French, you might not have any choice but to stay. Since you do have the choice, I want you to come back to England.'

Laura was silent for a long time. Save for a few months at the end of the war, she had not lived in England since 1913. Paris had been her home for twenty years and — except for Charles — all her friends were here, as well as the work which provided her livelihood.

'I've no home in England any more,' she said slowly. 'I don't know anyone. I wouldn't know what to do with myself.'

It was Charles's turn to be silent. When at last he spoke again, it seemed that he had changed the subject.

'Fred,' he said abruptly. 'I take it you've had no news.'

Laura shook her head. 'Nothing.' By now she had managed — as Charles himself had once advised — to convince herself that Fred must be dead.

It had not been easy at first. For months after hearing of his sentence she had suffered from nightmares, both sleeping and waiting. At night she awoke screaming; by day she was sick. Over and over again she relived the discomforts of her own long journey across Russia in 1918. It had been hellish enough even for someone who was escaping to freedom. How much worse must such a journey have been for someone who was being carried against his will towards deprivation and pain! From Alexis she had learned of the beatings and malnutrition which Fred would certainly suffer, and this too had fed her imagination. In the end, the only argument which provided the comfort of believing that he was no longer suffering was the belief — the hope, even — that he must be dead.

'After seven years it would be possible to apply for certificate of presumption of death,' Charles went on. 'I'm not sure that you'd get it, though. The camps don't keep records of their inmates. But there's another way in which you could gain your freedom if you wanted to. You could divorce him for desertion. Oh, I realise that it would be involutary desertion. But the courts will give a decree to a wife whose husband is in a British prison for life, so I'm sure there'd be no trouble in your case. If you were willing to try.'

Laura frowned in puzzlement. What did her marital situation have to do with a possible return to England? She still held a British passport. The obstacles to any return were practical, not legal. 'I wouldn't need a divorce. In fact, I wouldn't be entitled to get one. I've never been married, not properly.'

'What!' Astounded, Charles sprang to his feet. 'Are you saying that you and Fred were never married?'

'There was an impediment in Fred's case. A wife. He didn't want her to know that he was still alive. So it was easier to pretend that we'd got married in Russia and lost our papers in the chaos of escaping. But actually it never mattered. I kept my own name anyway.'

'Oh Laura, Laura!' Charles pulled her to her feet and took her into his arms, kissing her neck, her cheek, her lips. 'Why didn't you ever tell me, you little goose? I've been waiting so patiently, and all the time ...' He kissed her again and again; but then a new doubt seemed to strike him and he drew a little way away from her. 'I'm talking about legalities, but there's more to it than that, I do realise. Have you — what's the right word? Have you recovered?'

'Yes, I have.' Laura could feel her heart thumping ecstatically, but did her best to keep calm. 'The legalities, as you call them, Charles, were on your side, not mine. Daphne.'

'Do you love me, Laura? Just tell me that you love me.'

There was no point in pretending when her eyes, her smile, the whole of her body proclaimed the truth.

'Yes, I love you. But — '

'There are no buts. This is what I came to tell you anyway. Daphne and I have agreed on a divorce.'

'But your career!' Laura was startled. Yet why was she still expressing doubts when she could feel hope and expectation surging through her body? 'You told me once — '

'I'm nearly fifty,' he said. 'I've done reasonably well, had two good embassies. There'd be nothing ahead except more of the same. Anyway, once the war begins, all these petty rules about divorce will be thrown overboard. Either I can be useful to my country or else I can't. If the foreign service doesn't want me, there'll be something else. Daphne's already making a run for it. She sailed for New York last week. To get away from bombs and blockades, she claims — but there's someone waiting for her there. Not the chap I told you about before: a new one. She wants to be free, and I shall be glad to be rid of her. So.'

'So what?'

'So I want to marry you. I've spent a good deal of my life wishing I were married to you. Just never managed to get the timing right, that's all. Will you come back to England with me,

Laura, and do me the honour – the great honour – of being my wife?'

She couldn't help smiling as she remembered how the conversation had begun. 'Did you really think that the political situation was more likely to budge me than an offer of marriage?'

'If I'd done it the other way round and you'd turned me down, you'd have stayed on here to spare my feelings, wouldn't you? Just to pretend that you couldn't leave Paris. I've loved you for years, Laura. Please say you'll marry me?'

In the years since Fred's disappearance, Charles's friendship had been the most important element in her life. She had forced herself never to expect anything more than friendship; but now that the offer had been made she knew at once that it was exactly right for both of them.

Charles knew it as well, and gave her no time to answer. Instead, taking hold of her hand as though they were children, he made her run with him across the garden, into the villa, up the stairs to her bedroom.

'Just for the record, though,' he said as he pulled her sun dress down over her shoulders. 'The one word "Yes".'

'Oh, Charles! Of course I'll marry you! I love you so much. I just never thought – '

She was not allowed to finish the sentence. He kissed her again, spinning her round and round the room until they collapsed, breathless with laughter and desire, on the four-poster bed. They had both been starved of love, and it was a long time before their appetites were satisfied. Only when the low evening sun flooded the room with gold did Laura turn to lie on her back, breathing deeply with happiness.

'Now then,' murmured Charles, burying his head between her breasts. 'Time to be businesslike. Everything I said about the situation in Europe was true. How soon can you extricate yourself from here?'

'It shouldn't take too long.' Laura had to force herself back to the world of financial affairs. 'There's already a manager running Fred's business. I still own all the cars and taxis but he leases them and pays me a percentage of the profits. He's asked once or twice already if I'd sell out to him. My agency, though . . .'

She paused to consider. Since the office premises were part of her private house, they could not be included in any deal, and the files of those seeking work were likely to become thin as soon as the war started. But then, few people in Paris now were likely to accept the possibility that the city might one day be occupied by Germans. 'Well, it will be a question of goodwill, I suppose. I'll see what I can do.'

'Don't waste time haggling on money. I may be only a second son, but my father set me up generously after Oxford so that I'd always have a private income. And in any case – ' But he stopped without completing that thought. 'I'm simply asking you to clear the decks so that you won't have anything left here to worry about.'

She nodded happily without bothering to argue. This was not the moment to discuss balance sheets. In fact, although Charles might not realise it, Fred's business activities alone had made her a wealthy woman and she could have given up the agency long ago had she not felt a need to work.

'How long can you stay?' she asked.

'Only till crack of dawn tomorrow. The wires are buzzing in the diplomatic world, as you can imagine, and playing hookey from the office even for a day is frowned upon. But I'm hoping you're going to offer me dinner and a bed for the night.'

'Of course. Oh, Charles!'

It was a second honeymoon night, which left her in the morning tired but contented as he leant over the bed to kiss her goodbye.

'Come as soon as you can, my darling,' he said.

Her slender arms encircled his neck in a final, lingering embrace. After he had left, she continued to lie in a state of drowsy happiness. Everything at last had come together to offer a completely satisfying relationship. She had been infatuated with Alexis, but had never been able to respect him. David had been a good friend, yet even if they had married she was not sure that he would ever have aroused her passionately. It was Fred who had done that, but Fred had never shared any of her intellectual or cultural tastes.

Charles, though, would satisfy every side of her nature. How odd it was, she thought, snuggling down into the bedclothes as though Monday morning was for sleep rather than work; how odd it was that her life should have been so greatly affected by a single tea-party which three young men had politely but unwillingly attended when she was sixteen.

So much had happened since that day when she watched from an upstairs window as they approached her father's house. She was forty-seven years old now – but she felt almost as though she were still sixteen. Except that in the intervening thirty years she had learned how to be a romantic and a realist at the same time: she had discovered the path to happiness.

287

2

'Lady Vereker!' exclaimed Anassa. 'Oh Laura, I'm so glad for you. How grand you will be. Champagne! We must celebrate your news with champagne.' She rang for her maid to put a bottle on ice. 'So I suppose you'll be leaving Paris. Will you sell the villa?'

'Yes. Everything. And I might have decided to do that in any case.' Laura passed on Charles's warning and suggested to Anassa that she too should consider going to live in England.

'There won't be a war.' The younger woman refused even to consider the possibility. 'Anyway, what would I do in England?'

'New York, then. You must still have friends there.'

Anassa shook her head. 'I've been uprooted often enough,' she said. 'I can't go through it all again. And the Germans will never take Paris. Tell me about your wedding, Laura. Are you going to have a magnificent reception, stuffed with ambassadors all wearing sashes and stars? And waited on by the best butlers in Paris — all trained in the Villa des Cascades?'

'No, nothing like that. I know it's supposed to take place on the bride's home ground. But we shall have to wait until Charles's decree is made absolute, and by then I shall have packed up everything here. Besides, I think he hopes that if he's as discreet as possible about his divorce and re-marriage, he may still be allowed to be useful on the international scene. So we plan to be married by a registrar and then have a small reception in his family home. You'll come over for that, won't you?'

The maid brought in the ice bucket and set it down near her mistress. Instead of answering Laura's invitation at once, Anassa began to turn the bottle round and round in a nervous manner, setting the ice cubes rattling.

'Leon will be there, I suppose,' she said after a few moments.

'I hope so. I've written to him, but I haven't had time for a reply yet.'

There was another long pause.

'I can't do it, Laura. I'm ashamed to say it, when you've done so much for me and I love you like a daughter. But to be in the same room as Leon and see him not daring to come near me ... Or me not daring to go near him. I couldn't bear it, Laura. I'm desperately sorry, but I can't.'

'You still love him, after all this time?'

'I shall be in love with Leon until the day I die,' Anassa said simply. 'And if he were to die first ...' She shook her head vigorously and applied herself with a trembling hand to opening the champagne. 'Well, he won't. I shan't let him. A life of its own: wasn't that the phrase you used once for a true love? But in this case, of course, it's an illegitimate life. Of course Leon must be the one to go to your wedding, because he's your family. And so – ' Her eyes were brimming with tears as she filled their glasses. 'I shall think of you on the day. But to be going on with, a toast! To the future, to happiness, to Laura and Charles!'

For a moment Laura hesitated, wondering if there was anything she could say to make Anassa change her mind. But she could think of nothing. Smiling, she raised her glass.

'To all our futures.'

She was disappointed that Anassa would not come, but it was true that if she had to choose one of the two star-crossed lovers, it would be Leon, her adopted son. She waited confidently for his reply and was delighted when he promised to come.

However, by the time the necessary six months had elapsed before Charles's decree nisi could become absolute, the war of which he had warned her had started in earnest – and Leon was on the wrong side.

It was a bitter pill for Laura to swallow. After thinking of him as a son for so many years, she had assumed he would feel himself to be British by adoption. It was necessary to remind herself that he was not British, but Russian; and that he was not even formally adopted. Because she and Fred lacked the marriage certificate which would be needed to make any arrangement legal, they had let the matter slide. They were happy to act as Leon's parents and it was what both he and his real mother wanted, so there were never likely to be any problems. But it meant that he was still travelling on the Nansen passport which had originally been issued to refugees who had become stateless, and for a long time it had been clear that he found his companions in the Mercedes team congenial and enjoyed living in Berlin. In a hurried letter as the frontiers of Europe began to close or to be broken down, he assured her of his continuing affection, but recognised that it might be a long time before they could meet again.

So the November wedding was quiet indeed, and the reception at Knaresborough Hall was little more than a family tea party with champagne added to give it extra sparkle. Charles's brother, able at last to make it clear how much he had always disliked Daphne, drew Laura aside.

'Are you planning to go back to that poky place of Charles's in London?' he asked.

Laura couldn't help smiling. Compared to Knaresborough Hall, it was true that the Mayfair house was small; and because he had spent so much of his working life overseas Charles himself tended to refer to it as a pied-à-terre. But by any normal standards it would provide a spacious home for two people. She agreed that that was the plan.

'Not a good idea,' said Lord Knaresborough. 'Bombing and all that. Why don't you settle yourselves down here. It'll be yours one day.'

The statement startled her. True, her new brother-in-law was white-haired and overweight, and his complexion was coloured as much by a steady consumption of port and whisky as by the time he spent in the open air, hunting and shooting and fishing; but he looked healthy enough to run his own estate for a good many years yet.

'Natural course of events,' he grunted in explanation. 'I'm thirteen years older than Charles, and he hasn't fallen off as many horses as I have. Besides, had a couple of scares already. Heart attacks. They say it's the third one that kills. If I listened to the doctors, I'd be giving up everything I enjoy in life, but I've no use for that sort of business. If a man can't have a drink or two in his own home ... So that's how it is. And I've no plans to marry again.' His wife, Laura knew, had died twenty years earlier, in the same influenza epidemic which had killed David, and they had had no children.

'Mrs Kennedy reckons she's queen bee here,' he continued. Mrs Kennedy was the housekeeper. 'You'll have to fight her for your place, and you'll find it easier if I'm still around to back you up. Plenty of room here, what? You can have a wing to yourselves if you like; but to tell you the truth I'd like the company. Wouldn't ever have asked that tart Daphne, but you and I and Charles, I reckon we could rub along together. Have a word with him. Tell him what you think.'

It was a double-edged offer. Laura was experienced in managing a houseful of servants, but the sheer size of Knaresborough Hall was daunting — and there were enough new wartime restrictions already in place to indicate that housekeeping of any kind was likely to become more and more difficult. But if what seemed like a generous invitation was in reality a plea for help, it was all the more important that she should take it seriously. She promised to discuss the suggestion with her new husband while they were on their honeymoon. There was not much doubt, though, about what he would say; she knew how much affection he felt for the house in which he had grown up.

It was the house in which Fred had spent four years of his youth, as well — she had remembered that when the present family chauffeur was driving them in Lord Knaresborough's Rolls-Royce from the marriage ceremony to Knaresborough Hall. It was not the right time to think of Fred, but her thoughts could not be controlled. It seemed terrible that she should be so happy while he — but he could not possibly be still alive, not after so many Siberian winters.

Nevertheless, his name returned to her mind once more as the champagne flowed and one toast followed another.

'To Absent Friends!' called Charles, and Laura, smiling, raised her glass. Too often already in the course of her forty-seven years she had told herself that one life was ending for ever and a new life was beginning in which the whole of the past would be put behind her. This moment, more than any of those others, would seem to promise just such a break. But she had been wrong before and did not intend to make the same mistake again. She would never see Fred at Knaresborough Hall; but this war could not last for long and surely, surely, she would one day be reunited with Leon and Anassa.

'To Absent Friends!' she repeated.

3

It was to be a long time before any of the reunions for which Laura on her wedding day had prayed became even remotely possible. She had certainly not expected that the war would last for six years.

For most of that time no news reached her from Paris. Had Anassa remained in the city after the Germans marched in or had she escaped to the unoccupied zone? To wonder was to worry: Laura used hard work to put these anxieties out of her head as much as she could.

Lord Knaresborough died in 1943 and Charles succeeded to the title and the estate, but for three years before that Laura had already been running the household. It was not easy to manage a large property through the years when fuel and food and petrol were rationed and domestic help scarce; but she was a good organiser. The skills she had learned in running Count Beretsky's villa and her own agency enabled her to solve the problems posed both by shortages and by evacuees.

The inevitable difficulties of life in wartime were all made bearable by the happiness of her marriage, although Charles was often absent.

As he had expected, a man of his experience was so useful when it came to drafting treaties or writing briefing papers for conferences that such an unimportant matter as a divorce ceased to be relevant. The length of his working day meant that he spent four nights a week in his London house even when the bombing was at its heaviest, making his weekends with Laura at Knaresborough Hall precious to them both. Although too old for active service, he was frequently sent on missions to the United States to influence opinion and plead for material aid. Whether by air or sea, crossing the Atlantic was hazardous, and each reunion was made more passionate by relief.

By contrast, Laura's reunion with Anassa, when it came at last, silenced her for a moment with its unexpectedness. She had written as soon as the Allies entered Paris, but received no answer. It was without any warning that Anassa arrived at Knaresborough Hall in the spring of 1945.

Laura, who was a WVS County Organiser, had just returned home from a meeting and was on her way upstairs to change out of uniform when she heard the unmistakeable sound of the delivery van coming up the drive. Since the introduction of petrol rationing, five of the shopkeepers who had once made separate daily rounds as a matter of course had agreed to combine their deliveries — but the van had already called at the Hall once that day. Laura paused at the great window above the main door to see what was happening.

Because it was so unexpected, she did not immediately recognise her visitor from above. The tall, thin woman who climbed out of the van as it came to a halt wore a close-fitting turban hat which concealed all her hair; and, although the spring day was warm, she had wound a scarf not only round her neck but across her chin. Recognition came only when the baker, who had been driving, began to pull out piece after piece of luggage. Much of it was large and looked heavy, but there was one box which she was able to identify at once. It was the case which had been specially made for the kokoshnik.

'Anassa!' Laura rushed down the stairs and across the stone-flagged hall and down the curving steps. 'Anassa, dearest, is it really you? Why didn't you tell me? How good to see you. How are you?'

Her questions carried her into Anassa's arms and for a few moments Laura was content to hug her enthusiastically. But the scarf prevented them from kissing. She tugged it away. That was when she discovered that Anassa was no longer beautiful.

Laura drew in a hissing breath, shocked by what she saw. Up one side of Anassa's neck and chin and cheek was a streak of bright red shiny skin, puckered at the edges. 'Oh, dearest, what's happened? Was it a fire?'

Anassa shook her head. 'A long story. I'll tell you later. Did you get my letter?'

'No. No letters. Not for years.'

'Damn that concierge. I'm sorry then, Laura. Arriving like this without warning. But I didn't have anywhere else to go.'

'But of course this was the right place to come, dearest. I wanted you here six years ago. Let me just get some money for Mr Wootton. And someone to carry in your luggage.'

She returned quickly, and was thanking the baker for coming to her guest's rescue at the railway station when she became aware that Anassa, leaning through the back doors of the van, was speaking French to someone there.

'Are you not alone?'

'No. Not alone.' When Anassa straightened herself again she was holding a small child in her arms: a sleepy two-year old with hair as fair as Anassa's own. 'This is my daughter.'

'Oh, Anassa! What a beauty she is.' Laura had never expected that Anassa would have any children and was now able to feel in a proprietorial manner almost as though she herself had become a grandmother. She stroked the little girl's cheek with her finger. 'What's her name?'

Anassa looked straight into Laura's eyes, and her back seemed to stiffen with a refusal to be apologetic as she answered.

'Her name is Leonie.'

It was the second shock of the afternoon, and the greater one. Laura stared wordlessly at Anassa. Was she saying . . .? Yes, almost certainly she was; but this was not the moment to discuss it.

Until she could ask the question and be helped to understand the answer, Laura felt that all the pleasure and excitement had gone out of the unexpected reunion. She busied herself with the normal household arrangements of having rooms prepared for the visitors and ordering tea.

Leonie woke up at the sight of milk and biscuits and revealed herself as bright-eyed and alert. When she had finished, she asked for her book and was settled down with it in a deep armchair. It was a picture book of animals, and the conversation between the two adults which followed was punctuated with the sounds of mewing and quacking and mooing.

'She doesn't understand English,' said Anassa. 'You don't need to ask. Leon is her father.'

293

'How did it happen?'

'You knew he was fighting for the Germans?'

'I knew that he wasn't prepared to come to England. I didn't know that he was actually fighting.'

'He didn't enlist straightaway. But from the moment when Germany invaded the Soviet Union he knew who his enemies were: the men who had killed both his fathers: Prince Kristov and Fred.'

Laura nodded her understanding. There were others all over Europe, she knew, who would have felt the same way. All the White Russians whom she had known in Paris had made their attitude clear: the enemies of communism, whoever they might be, were their friends.

'I could sympathise with it,' Anassa said. 'To have the Soviets as allies in war is a cynical thing. I wouldn't ever want to go back to Russia myself, but I sympathised with those who wanted to see it free.'

'By free, do you mean occupied? Like Paris?' Laura spoke more sharply than she intended at this time of reunion and was glad when Anassa avoided a political argument.

'We were talking about Leon. I hadn't heard anything from him for a long time. But I came home to my apartment one day and he was waiting in the street outside. You know, during the occupation, we learned how to ignore Germans. If you caught sight of a uniform, you dropped your eyes, refusing to look at their faces, only their boots. So I didn't recognise him at first; walked straight past. He caught me up, put a hand on my shoulder. I was frightened for a moment, until he spoke my name.'

'Was he part of the occupying force?'

'No. On leave. It was a special privilege for them, to take leave in Paris. To see how a proud city had fallen. In all those years of occupation, Laura, I never socialised with Germans. I walked out of a dinner party once when I saw that two of the guests were officers. I never invited any German soldier into my home. Except Leon.'

'Well, of course he would be different.'

'Different, yes. Special. Because I still loved him, you see. And I knew that he loved me. It was for my sake that he went away, so that I'd be free to find someone else. But I didn't want anyone else. Seeing him like that, so suddenly, how could I have turned him away just because ... because ...? To me, he wasn't a German soldier. He was the man I loved. Nothing different about him, except the uniform. But of course it was the uniform that people noticed.'

She fell silent and Laura waited patiently.

294

'The scars on my face. The day after the liberation I was beaten up in the street as a collaborator. They cut my hair. And someone threw acid.' Her fingers went up to touch her chin.

'Paris was full of collaborators, Laura,' she said bitterly. 'There were women who denounced Jews and betrayed Resistance workers. There were militiamen who did all the dirty work, arresting people and handing them over to be tortured. There were small-time whores who sold themselves for a packet of cigarettes or a pair of stockings and there were expensive whores who were kept in requisitioned mansions. All I did was to invite the man I loved to stay with me for a few days. But there were eyes everywhere. Eyes and notebooks.'

'Could you not have explained . . .?' But no, it would not have helped to have claimed that the enemy soldier was her brother.

'I'd slept with Leon before, you know,' Anassa went on. 'Before you told him about the relationship. I was always careful not to risk having a baby. But when he turned up so unexpectedly, I wasn't prepared. I think that's what made people so angry. They had all those months of pregnancy in which I must have seemed to be rubbing in what had happened. If I'd been raped, I expect they would have helped me to get rid of the baby. But I wanted to have it. It was a part of Leon inside my body.'

There was a long pause before she spoke again.

'After we parted, Leon and I, all those years ago, it affected us in different ways, I didn't want to sleep with anyone else. But Leon — I used to read about him in the papers. With a new woman every time. A playboy, I suppose you could call him. But as long as he didn't settle down with any of them, I could feel that I was still the one. And after that leave in Paris, I knew. So it's been a kind of happiness. And I love Leonie very much.'

'And is she — ? I mean, sometimes when people marry who are only cousins, not even as closely related as you and Leon are — '

'Are you asking me whether she's an idiot?' For the first time since her arrival Anassa laughed aloud — and the little girl looked up from her book and laughed with her. 'Bright as two buttons, she is. That's enough about me. Unless you want to say that you can't have a fallen woman under your roof?'

'Of course not. I'm so delighted to have you both here. And so sorry about all the unhappiness you've had.' It was the whole unfortunate situation which Laura regretted. To make moral judgements would be out of place, since much of the blame lay with herself. It was a relief when Anassa changed the subject.

'Are you happy, Laura? With Charles, I mean.'

295

'Oh, yes. Very happy indeed. And now that the war's coming to an end, it's all going to be perfect. He's going to resign from the Foreign Service.'

'Why? I should have thought this was an important time for people like him, with the whole map of Europe to be re-drawn.'

Laura knew the real reason why her husband had decided to abandon his career, but it was a matter to be kept between themselves. There had been too many decisions taken with which he disagreed. He could understand how military requirements and pressure from allies had proved to be irresistible, but would have found no pleasure in negotiating arrangements which he considered to be fundamentally flawed. His private income offered an escape which was not open to many of his colleagues.

'He's got a seat in the House of Lords now, of course,' she said instead. 'It will give him a platform to put forward his views — and people will listen, because he knows what he's talking about. Anyway, he'll be home tonight for the weekend. You'll be able to talk to him then.'

Over dinner that night Anassa repeated to Charles the news which she had already given to Laura.

'What are your plans now?' he asked.

'I don't ever want to live in Paris again. New York, perhaps, or London. I've been trying to turn myself into an artist.'

'I remember how good your drawing was as a child!' exclaimed Laura enthusiastically.

'Maurice used to teach me as well. While I was sitting for him, he'd explain what he was doing, and why. And then let me practise. So I'm not a complete duffer.'

'Have you sold anything?'

'No. I've been living on the money Fred gave me. I sold the necklace — you know, the one I stole back — last year. That brought in enough to keep me afloat for a time. And I still have the kokoshnik. Not that I ever intend to part with that.'

Laura glanced across the dinner table at her husband and was delighted to see him nod.

'Well, you must stay on here while you sort yourself out. There's plenty of room.'

'You're very kind, both of you, and to rest for a little while would be wonderful. But I must find a home of my own. What I would like, though, is to use you as a contact address, if I may. It's so easy for people to get lost in Europe. So many refugees; so many buildings destroyed. If Leon writes to me at my apartment, I can't trust the concierge to forward the letter, or even keep it. But sooner or later he'll get in touch with you, and then you can tell him where I am. Will you do that?'

'Of course,' said Laura. It was Charles who asked the question she had not dared to put.

'Do you know that he's still alive?'

'He was last October. Since then ... how can anyone be sure? But − ' She gave a wry laugh. 'They enlisted, almost all of the emigrés of military age, because they wanted to fight the Russians on the eastern front. But they never went near it. Perhaps the Germans thought they would desert if they were sent anywhere near their homeland. Leon was upset about that. But it may have helped to keep him alive. I expect he's a prisoner of war by now; and if he is, he'll be safe.'

She looked at her host and hostess, expecting their agreement. Laura smiled reassuringly, sharing Anassa's relief; but Charles did not respond in the same way.

'Is something wrong?' Anassa asked.

'No. Except that of course it does depend on where his regiment surrendered, and to whom. If they gave themselves up to the Soviet army, they're liable to be regarded as traitors rather than PoWs.'

'They wouldn't do that. They'd know. After all, some of them fought for the Whites in the Civil War. They'd only surrender to the British or Americans.'

'Yes, of course.' But there was a note of restraint in Charles's voice which Anassa was quick to interpret.

'What's the difficulty?' she asked. 'If Leon surrenders to the British army, surely he'll be treated well. The Geneva Convention −'

'I'm not in a position to − '

'Please tell me,' Anassa said quietly. 'If I'm living in a fool's paradise, I'd rather know.'

'Well, it's a messy time. This isn't the sort of thing I ought to say, but Stalin made rings round us at Yalta. A lot of people don't realise yet just what was agreed. One of the problems is that the Russians have liberated some of our men: British PoWs who were held in German camps in eastern Europe. No one actually uses the word hostages, but ... Uncle Joe wants to get his hands on any Russians who fought for the Germans, and it won't be to give them a heroes' welcome.'

'Surely we haven't agreed,' protested Laura.

'We've tried to negotiate conditions. I can't tell you the details off the top of my head. A German subject wearing a German uniform

297

will have the benefit of the Convention, yes. But the Soviet Union has never recognised it, and those who are or who have been Soviet citizens may have to be repatriated.'

'That can't possibly apply to Leon. He was only about ten when he left the country. He's never had a Russian passport.'

'He should be all right, then. But what's going to happen out there is a bit different from an orderly queue at a passport office in Dover, say. There'll be a small number of British troops who have been fighting for six years and want nothing more than to tie up the loose ends and get home as soon as possible. They've got to do something with a large number of men who have been their enemies, trying to kill them, until a few days ago. What do they know about the history of the White Russians? They may not have much incentive to begin splitting the categories and looking for exceptions.'

'Is there anything you can do, Charles?'

'I'll make some enquiries on Monday,' he promised. 'But one man out of so many thousands ... Well, I'll do my best.'

'Thank you.' Anassa, although very pale, spoke calmly. 'If you can find out where he might possibly be ... I'll write down for you all the details I know.'

Laura read through her notes next day and paused on one line. 'Adopted by Fred and Laura Richards in 1925. British citizen? British passport?' She made no comment, but was glad when Charles produced a good reason for not investigating this possibility.

'If he ever did have a British passport he would have destroyed it long ago. He couldn't afford the discovery of any links with the country he was fighting against. And remember that a British citizen taking up arms against his king would be a traitor.'

'He still used his Nansen passport when he was living with me,' Laura remembered.

Charles nodded. 'Leave it to me. I'll find out what I can.'

He returned to London as usual on Monday morning and for once Laura took the train with him, apologising to her guest for the fact that she had to attend an important meeting for WVS County Organisers. Anassa expressed herself happy to spend the day relaxing in the garden. So it came as a surprise to Laura when she returned in the evening to find no sign of her. She ran upstairs to the suite of rooms which had been placed at Anassa's disposal.

A note was propped against the dressing-table mirror, as if by an absconding wife.

Charles has just phoned to say where Leon's regiment is being held. The men in the camp are scheduled for repatriation to Russia. Of course I realise that he may not be there. He may not even be alive. But I have to go and find him. I know that you must disapprove of our love, dearest Laura, but you will realise how I feel. I can't live without him. You love him too, so I shall be doing the best I can for the two of us. It may make all the difference if there's someone — his sister — to prove that he's never had a Russian passport. It would be death for him to be sent back. We both know that.

I've borrowed a haversack from your luggage room: easier for travelling. I hope it's all right to leave my things here. If I fail to find him in Austria, this will be our rendez-vous, Leon's and mine.

The big thing is: will you look after Leonie for me until I get back? I know it's far too much to ask when you've done so much for me already, but there's no one else I could trust to be a grandmother to her and she is Leon's daughter as well as mine. Please. Please. Your cook promised to put her to bed tonight if you were late getting back.

With all my love, my dearest Laura,

from Your Tanya

Tanya. Why had she used that name after so many years of being Anassa? Had the prospect of a desperate journey at the end of a horrifying war reminded her that this had happened before?

Poor little Leonie, to be abandoned amongst strangers in an unfamiliar place. It did not occur to Laura for as much as a second to abandon a responsibility of which she had been given no warning. Looking after refugees and evacuees was the kind of crisis with which she was most qualified to deal. She must hurry down to the kitchen and reassure the little girl that she was amongst friends.

Before turning to go, she looked around the bedroom. The pieces of luggage which had arrived with Anassa on Friday were neatly stacked in a corner, except for one. The wooden box made by Cartier at the time of the touring exhibition had been left on the dressing table. Curious to see the Kristov jewels again for the first time in thirteen years, Laura lifted the lid.

The box was empty. Anassa had taken the kokoshnik with her.

Before the war the journey across Europe might have taken forty-eight hours, but after ten chaotic days Anassa had still not reached her destination. Roads were clogged with refugees: some fleeing and others attempting to return to their homes. Trains were so overcrowded that it was often physically impossible to force a way inside. There were no timetables, and to start a journey was no guarantee of completing it if some military authority should decide that the track or the engine was needed for a troop movement. And at every moment of the day or night, whether she was fending off hunger by bartering cigarettes, hitch-hiking on the back of a cart or lorry, waiting for endless hours on a station platform, fighting to board a train or attempting to sleep on her feet in a filthy corridor, she had to fight a constant feeling of panic. What if she should be too late!

At Lienz, in the south of Austria, the train was commandeered by the military and all passengers were turned off. Searching for somewhere to spend the night, Anassa found herself unexpectedly on the outskirts of a Cossack encampment. Was this the kind of camp in which Leon was being held?

She quickly realised that its inmates represented a tribal migration rather than a corps of volunteers from inside Germany. The Cossacks had never accepted the Bolshevik revolution in Russia and had welcomed the German invaders as liberators. As the Germans retreated, the inhabitants had moved with them, knowing all too well what fate would await them when Soviet troops reconquered their territory.

There were thousands of them here: men, women and children, together with their horses. Happy to have surrendered to the British, they needed no guards. The scene was a peaceful one, and Anassa's spirits rose for the first time since leaving England. It was impossible to think that so many thousand families could be forced to return to Russia. Charles might be right about diplomatic agreements, but the men on the spot were not villains, to march children at gunpoint towards execution or slavery. That night, for the first time since leaving England, her sleep was not disturbed by nightmares.

Early next morning she began to move eastward along the line of the railway, conscious that every mile was taking her nearer to the Soviet zone. When at last she reached the area which Charles had suggested as a possibility, she found a camp where a very different atmosphere prevailed.

The prisoners here belonged to a Cossack cavalry corps to which

Leon, she knew, had been attached at one time as part of a motorised wireless and communications unit. He was not a cavalryman himself, but the corps had been staffed with German officers and allotted various support facilities.

It was not easy to ask questions here, for the area was wired off. But at the sight of a civilian face half a dozen men ran towards the fence and began a panic-stricken appeal for help. They were to be returned to the Soviet Union against their will — although a British officer had promised them that this would not happen. If he found out, they were sure that he would stop it. Someone must tell him, for they were all convinced that once in Soviet hands, they would either be tortured and executed on the spot or else condemned to life servitude in the Siberian labour camps.

It was many years since Anassa had spoken Russian, but she understood it well enough, and their panic infected her when she mentioned Leon's name and found that they recognised it: yes, he had been one of those who surrendered with them. He was somewhere in the camp. Her heart began to thump with hope and anxiety at the same time. Although her feet were blistered and her legs aching, she ran towards a group of huts, outside the wired compound, where she could see men in British uniforms.

'Where would I find the camp commandant?' she panted to the first officer she met.

'He's got no time to talk to civilians now. Unless you have a permit you shouldn't be here. There's a spot of bother going on at the moment. Best report to the guardroom.'

He pointed towards a hut which was set apart from the others. It was empty; and on its further side was pandemonium. A group of several hundred prisoners, all wearing German uniform, had formed themselves into a solid square, clinging to each other in an attempt not to be moved. One row at a time they were being beaten with rifle butts and dragged towards a line of lorries. They shouted curses as they went, whilst those waiting emitted an unearthly moaning sound which turned Anassa's blood cold.

A single prisoner had broken loose and was pleading with a senior British officer, tugging at his sleeve in an attempt to make him understand. The officer shook his head impatiently to indicate his lack of comprehension. He wore a red band round his hat, and Anassa saw her chance. This must be the commandant.

'He's trying to tell you that his friend has killed himself. He wants permission to bury him decently.'

The colonel looked at her in astonishment. 'Who the devil are you?'

'An interpreter,' said Anassa boldly.

'You mean you understand their lingo?'

'Yes.'

'Then tell him to get back in line. We'll send a burial party out at sunset.'

Anassa did the simple translation and was ordered to accompany the commandant to his office.

Seated behind the wooden table which served as his desk, he demanded to know who had sent her. When she confessed the real purpose of her mission, he exploded with anger.

'This is a restricted zone, closed to the public,' he pointed out. 'And I've got a riot on my hands, as you can see. Personal visits are strictly forbidden. Every man in this camp is somebody's brother or son or husband. Do you expect me to release them all?'

'I don't expect you to release anyone. But to keep him in British custody, not to hand him over. I am a French citizen, but my brother was recruited into the German Army. He's surrendered to the British Army, and you have a responsibility under the Geneva Convention – '

'I've already screened out all those who have German papers. If your brother is still here, he's not a German.'

'He's in German uniform.'

'That has nothing to do with it. If he's a Soviet citizen who has been fighting against his own country – which happens to be an ally of ours – I'm under orders to hand him back to his government.'

'But he's *not* a Soviet citizen. That's what I'm trying to tell you.'

'Where are you saying that he was born, then?'

'He was born in Russia, but before the revolution. He left the country when he was a boy of ten, in 1918, and he's never been back.' Anassa found it hard to decide whether the officer was being obstructive or merely stupid. Did he know nothing about Russian history? And had he no idea how an emigré would be treated when he fell into Bolshevik hands? 'He has a Nansen passport. Do you know what that means? He was a Displaced Person. Specifically not Russian.'

'Oh yes? Half the men in this camp have spent the last three weeks forging papers to show that they're DPs or Poles or Balts or what have you?'

'Doesn't it occur to you that half the men in the camp may be telling the truth?' said Anassa desperately. 'Surely you can check their papers, divide them up, only send back the ones who want to go.'

'Our Soviet allies are well aware of how many thousand Russians we are holding and they want them all back. It's my responsibility to see that they get them. We can't spend weeks investigating every individual case.'

'What were you fighting the war for then?' By now tears were streaming down Anassa's face. 'To protect democracy and defeat facism, I thought. Democracy is all about individual cases. Mine wouldn't take a minute, I'd only have to call my brother's name and he'd show you his passport.'

'I'm sorry.' The colonel rose to his feet, not sounding sorry in the least. 'I don't know how you got in here, madam, but I must ask you to leave immediately. I have a very complicated operation to complete. The first batch should be aboard by now and it's too late to call a halt and deal with interruptions.'

Too late! It was surely not possible that the end of her search should fail by a matter of hours – or perhaps only minutes. As the officer strode out of the hut she hurried after him. He raised his arm and shouted out a command and, at the signal, a long line of trucks began to move slowly forward. The officer turned back into his office, ordering Anassa to remove herself from the camp immediately.

'Yes, sir,' she replied, and began to run.

At the tail of the convoy was a young lieutenant in an open jeep. The last of the closed lorries was beginning to move and, as he switched on his engine, Anassa flung herself in beside him.

'Interpreter!' she gasped.

He looked surprised and briefly doubtful, but was anxious to keep his place in the line.

'For the handover?' he asked as he let in the clutch.

'Yes.' There were so many questions she wanted to ask, but was afraid of revealing ignorance where he would expect her to have had instructions. There was one question, though, which could not be restrained. 'Will it be from these vehicles?'

'No. They'll do the last stretch by train. There are some wagons waiting. They'll be loaded tonight and move off tomorrow. Have you got a billet for the night?'

'Someone's dealing with it,' she said. Thank goodness he had accepted her description of herself. He seemed glad to have company.

'What are your languages?' he asked.

'English, French, Russian, a little German.'

He whistled appreciatively. 'I'm going to read languages at university when I'm demobbed,' he told her. 'I've got a place waiting. If we can get all this tidied up quickly, I might make it by September. They've promised to give priority to people who've got scholarships.'

Anassa would have liked to scream aloud at his haste to 'tidy up'. What possible interest could she have in his plans, when Leon's life was at stake? She had to grit her teeth in determination to be pleasant to him.

After an hour and a half the convoy came to a halt not at a station but in a deserted spot where the road ran for half a mile beside a railway line and a stream. It was a gloomy hollow at the foot of a valley, with conifers pressing close to the track and the mountains to the south cutting out much of the daylight. Anassa said goodbye to the young lieutenant and set off as though making towards the head of the convoy. As soon as she was out of his sight, she stepped off the road casually, as though to answer a call of nature, and concealed herself in the forest. Watching from the shadows, she strained her eyes to see the one man who mattered.

The transfer was efficiently organised. One truck at a time backed towards one of the goods wagons which were waiting on the track. Out of the escort of British troops, a dozen, with bayonets fixed, formed a corridor along which their prisoners had to walk when the doors were opened. Others, armed with Sten guns, took up positions in a circle round the whole area.

The very first prisoner to appear twisted himself away from the train as he was in the process of hauling himself into the wagon and made a dash for freedom. He was shot before he had covered more than a few feet. To Anassa, gazing in horror, it seemed clear that the man's intention was to commit suicide. What if that should prove infectious! The idea that Leon might die in front of her eyes was unbearable.

She studied the faces of the British soldiers after the shooting. At least one of them looked satisfied by the opportunity to demonstrate that they meant business. A few stared stolidly, not allowing themselves any reaction. But others could not conceal their distaste for the operation in which they had found themselves involved. That was a hopeful sign. Anassa knew that she could not rescue Leon on her own. She was going to need help.

The sad parade continued. Then suddenly she saw Leon! His hair had been cut close, but its fairness distinguished him from all the others. Her heart leapt at the sight of him, but there was no time to indulge her emotions. She watched to see which wagon he entered and fixed her gaze on it so intently that it began to swim before her eyes. When forty men had been loaded into it ration packs and a bucket of water from the stream were handed in after them. Then the door was closed and a metal bolt slid into place with a clank which spelt doom. But there was no padlock. Perhaps, perhaps . . .

There were still hundreds of men to be loaded. Night had fallen by the time the last wagon was closed and a new batch of guards came on duty. Anassa listened from her hiding place as they were given their orders. Since there was no risk of the prisoners breaking out unaided, a single guard on each side of the train was deemed to be enough, with the rest keeping watch over the engine.

The soldier on Anassa's side of the wagons did not appear to be taking his responsibilities too seriously. But fate had decreed a full moon and she would be clearly visible if she approached the railway track. Besides, she might not have the strength to shift the bolt herself. Trembling, she stepped out of the forest and walked slowly towards the sentry.

'Who's there?' He spun round, aiming his rifle at her.

'I'm the interpreter,' Anassa claimed for the third time that day. 'Nothing to do till they move off. Cigarette? Have the pack.'

'Thanks.' He put it in his pocket and lowered the rifle.

'Do you know what's going to happen to them when they're handed over?' asked Anassa.

'I know what they bloody think will happen, poor sods. Asking us to bloody shoot them, they were, rather than send them back to Uncle Joe.'

'My brother's in there,' Anassa said softly. 'He ought not to be. He's not Russian. He has a Nansen passport.'

'I don't know anything about that. You'd better talk to the officer.' The soldier was at once scared and suspicious.

'It's too late for that. They won't listen. Will you help me get him out? I can make it worth your while.'

'How?' He was still wary, but she caught a glint of greed in his eyes.

'With money.'

'It would need to be a lot.'

'I don't have much with me, but I could get − '

'No.' He shook his head abruptly. 'It could land me in front of a court martial. I could get bloody shot myself.'

'Then there's something else that I do have with me.' She felt in the bag which was slung over her shoulder and took out the scarf in which the kokoshnik was wrapped. 'It's a family treasure. Worth a fortune. Yours if my brother gets away.'

It was the last card she had to play and she waited breathlessly as the diamonds sparkled in the moonlight. Raising the tiara, she settled it on her head and stood up straight, like a princess. The last time she had worn it was at the New Year's Ball for the confrontation with Countess Balakin. How happy she had been that day, with Leon at her side and no suspicion that there could be any impediment to their love. She felt tears flooding her eyes at the memory.

'Bloody hell! Is it real?' The soldier was hooked.

'Yes, you can see it is.' She took it off again and let him examine it. 'Diamonds and pearls. You could be rich for the rest of your life.'

He was holding it now. 'What d'you want?'

'The fourth wagon.' She pointed. 'Slip the bolt. Let them get into the forest. After that it will be up to them. If you bolt it back again, no one here will realise.'

'Won't be my bloody fault if it goes wrong.'

'No. But give them the chance. Oh, please, please.' As if in answer to her prayer, a cloud moved across the face of the moon. 'Quickly, quickly,' she urged.

With a furtive look around him he stuffed the kokoshnik inside his clothes. She would have preferred to give him his reward after the job had been done; but there was no choice. Stepping back into the darkness of the trees she watched as he stood for a moment by the door of the wagon, looking round, and then hit the bolt hard with the butt of his rifle. Bending low, he ran along the railway track to distance himself from whatever might happen next.

The pause which followed was unbearable. Had the men inside not realised that they were free? But at last she saw the door sliding quietly open. One man lowered himself to the ground, looked round and waved to the others. Two at a time they followed him out and ran towards the trees.

Where was Leon? Oh, Leon, quick, quick! He was the last of them all to jump down and ran quickly over the open ground to catch the others up. He was not wearing a cap and his blond hair shone in the moonlight as the cloud passed.

Anassa felt herself choking with emotion. If only she could join him! If only she could let him know that she was here! But she would only be a hindrance, for it might be weeks or months before he was out of danger. All she could do was to hope that the intensity of her love would somehow reach into his own mind. I love you, Leon. Even if we never meet again, it will be enough for me to know that you're still alive. I shall love you till the day I die.

The guard hurried back to close the door and shoot the bolt. He had just resumed a steady patrol when there was a shout from further up the line. An officer came running.

'Did you see that?'

'No, sir. See what, sir?'

'Someone moving around in the woods. Looked like a blonde. Have you had a woman here?'

'No, sir.'

The officer shouted for the rest of the guards to come and search the forest. Anassa's eyes widened in alarm. Leon would need to have a longer start than this. Instinctively she knew what she must do. Running between the trees she made her way to the part of the forest into which Leon had disappeared and then began to walk back towards the track as calmly as she could. When the officer caught sight of her, he would be satisfied that the golden hair which had caught his eye must be hers.

It was not, however, the officer whom she first encountered, but her accomplice. With his rifle at the ready he was moving cautiously through the darkness, for only a dappling of moonlight penetrated the trees. When he caught sight of her he brought the rifle up to point straight at her heart, and steadied himself with legs apart.

Anassa smiled reassuringly.

'It's okay. You can arrest me, and your officer will believe it was me he saw running away.'

The soldier did not smile back. Instead, his finger moved and Anassa's smile froze on her face as she realised his intention. He was going to kill her. Surely it wasn't possible! Was he afraid that she would betray the story of the bribe he had accepted? Yes, that must be it. Her mind was unable to accept what was going to happen; but her body knew. She found that she had stopped breathing as she waited.

Once, long ago, she had told Leon that she could never be frightened of dying because she had died once already. This was the moment which confirmed that she had been telling the truth. She stared steadily into the eyes of her murderer, making no attempt to run away.

The sound of the shot which was about to kill her would bring all the other searchers running to this spot. They would see her blonde hair and be satisfied that there was no need to look for anyone else in the forest. If by her death she could give her lover time to escape, it would be worthwhile. In the long last second of her life she remembered her conviction that she would love Leon until she died, and knew that it was true.

5

Charles had something to say, and Laura suspected that it was not good news. Three times since his return from London that day he

307

had lit a cigarette, although he was trying to cut down on the habit, and three times, impatient with himself, he had stubbed it out. It was clear that he was waiting until the two of them were alone.

'Bedtime,' said Laura to Leonie, bringing to an end the hour which they usually spent together. 'Let's go and find Nanny.'

Finding Nanny was a game of hide-and-seek and as a rule the three-year-old was allowed to run into four or five of the Hall's many rooms before being steered towards the night nursery; but tonight Laura cut the game short.

'Come up and kiss me!' ordered Leonie, after she had been chased and caught. Laura had spoken English to her right from the start, because someone had told her once that the best way to help a child become bi-lingual was for each language to be linked to one specific person. She had expected Anassa to take over the French side again before too long; but Anassa had never returned.

Until now Laura had not quite given up hope. She tried to persuade herself that perhaps Anassa had penetrated into the Soviet Union in her attempt to find Leon. It would be a desperately dangerous thing to do, for Russian had never been her first language, and twenty-seven years had passed since she had last used it to chat with servants. Nor did she have any of the right papers, in a country where credentials were for ever being demanded. But until something was definitely known, it was possible to hope that one day she would walk into Knaresborough Hall as unexpectedly as she had done nine months earlier.

'There's some news,' said Charles when she returned to the library which they used instead of the drawing room in winter, because it was easier to heat. 'The last name you produced did the trick.'

It had been one of the problems, when they first became seriously worried, that it would be nobody's business to notify Lord or Lady Knaresborough of anything which might have happened to Anassa, since there was unlikely to be anything on her person to suggest a link. And neither of them knew what name she had on her passport. The single word which she used in her professional and social life would hardly be acceptable to officialdom, and so Charles's first enquiries had been made in respect of Anassa or Tanya Kristova. He had drawn a blank with that. Only later did Laura realise that all her official identification was probably still in the name which her childhood protector had arbitrarily bestowed on her. Even then, because the artist – now dead – had been professionally known always as Maurice le Gris, it had taken a while to discover his true surname. Not until January 1946 had Charles been able to use his old contacts to instigate another search, this time into the fate of Anassa Jardinais.

'Is she still alive?' There was a grimness about Charles's expression which gave the answer even before Laura had asked the question.

'I'm afraid not, Laura.' He put his arm round her shoulders to comfort her, and for a long time they sat in silence. There were no tears, perhaps because for so many months already it had seemed almost certain that nothing but death could have kept the mother from returning to her child.

'She was such a pretty little girl,' Laura said, sighing as she remembered her first sight of five-year-old Princess Tanya. 'And such a sweet, loving nature. No one could possibly have foreseen then what a sad life she would have. Seeing everyone she loved die or disappear. And that she should die herself just when she had something, someone, to live for ... What happened, Charles? Do you know?'

'She was accidentally shot by a British soldier. There was an enquiry at the time. He was one of a squad who were searching for escaped prisoners. There weren't supposed to be any civilians in the area. According to the chap who killed her, she sneaked up on him from behind, startling him. The forest was full of partisans, who had presumably been responsible for helping the prisoners to escape. He thought it must be one of them. So he wheeled round and fired before he had time to see who it was.'

Laura frowned to herself. Something didn't ring true.

'It might just as easily have been one of his own comrades. Wouldn't he have paused just long enough to look? And a woman seeing an armed soldier might sneak away; but if she did decide to approach him, she'd draw attention to herself, surely.'

'You're right,' said Charles. 'I don't think we've got the whole story here. But it was an itchy time. The soldiers were doing a job they didn't like and they'd no means of knowing how many men were prowling round the forest, or what they might be planning. I don't think we can blame the chap too much. The enquiry exonerated him. Accidental death.'

He moved away and lit another cigarette, this time drawing deeply on it instead of stubbing it out.

'Dr Morgan told you – ' said Laura automatically, but her mind was still on Anassa, and she did not press the reminder. Another thought had occurred to her, but before she had time to express it, the nurse appeared in the doorway to remind her that Leonie was waiting for her goodnight kiss.

By the time Laura reached the nursery, the little golden-haired

309

girl was already asleep. As sweet and as pretty as her mother; was she too doomed by her birth to a life of sadness? No, not if Laura herself could help it.

Charles had followed her up and was looking over her shoulder at the sleeping child. He stretched out a hand and gently pulled her thumb from her mouth.

'Charles, Anassa took the kokoshnik with her when she went. Was there any mention of that in the report?'

It must have seemed an odd question at such a time, and it would be too complicated to explain her feeling that the kokoshnik had brought unhappiness wherever it went. It was a relief in a sense when he shook his head.

'No. Nothing about that. Stolen on her journey, I expect. It was crazy to carry something like that about under such conditions.'

So it was gone: the last material treasure of the Kristovs. Little Leonie would inherit nothing from her family but her double dose of Kristov blood. Laura told herself that she was being superstitious, but could not help being glad.

'She can stay here?' By the inflection of her voice Laura made it sound like a question, but she was so sure of what the answer would be that she was really making a statement. Charles had delighted in Leonie's company from the moment of her arrival. It was easy to tell how much he, like Fred, had longed for children of his own. In Laura's case infertility had been accidental, but Daphne had deliberately refused to ruin her figure by becoming a mother: it was one of the things for which Charles could not forgive her. There was probably a special poignancy in the lack of an heir for a man who had a title and an estate to bequeath.

'Of course. As long as it's not too much for you?'

'We could adopt her.'

She expected an immediate agreement to the suggestion, and was surprised when he received it in silence.

'I haven't come to the end of all my news yet,' he said.

Puzzled, she followed him downstairs again and watched, trying not to nag, as he lit yet another cigarette.

'I actually found out about Anassa several weeks ago,' he said. 'Almost as soon as you gave me the Jardinais name.'

'Why didn't you tell me at once?'

'Partly because I was waiting to see the report of the enquiry, so that I could give you the whole story at one time. But there was something else. Why was Anassa in that particular forest? What was going on there at the time? The answer turned out to be

310

exactly what I'd expected. It was an entraining point for Russian prisoners being repatriated. She must have found out about that. She might just have been scouting round on spec, but it seemed possible that she'd tracked Leon to that spot. Worth investigating, anyway.'

'And you said that some of the prisoners had escaped?' Laura's eyes opened wide as she realised the importance of what Charles was suggesting.

'Yes. That could well have been down to the partisans, of course, as the military enquiry assumed. The mountains were swarming with refugees, deserters, men of all nationalities who weren't at all sure that their particular war was over. But just suppose that it wasn't entirely a coincidence that there should be an escape on the night when Anassa happened to be around.'

'You mean that Leon might have been one of the batch who got away?'

'I've been asking around. It hasn't been easy to get anyone to talk. Escapes like this were all covered up at the time, in case the Russians accused us of losing the men deliberately. But thanks to good old British bureaucracy, all the rosters were kept even when people were lying through their teeth about who was or wasn't on them.'

'Have you found him, Charles?' Laura clutched his hand as her throat tightened, making her feel almost physically sick with hope. 'Are you telling me that Leon is still alive?'

'No, I'm not saying that. I'm as sure as I can be that he was on that train and that he escaped from it. Since I don't believe in coincidences, I'm also pretty sure that Anassa was responsible for his escape. But what happened after that, I have no idea at all. He's simply disappeared. The most sensible thing for him to do, in the circumstances. I doubt whether we have any chance of finding him. But he could find us. You told him that you were going to marry me: you told him the address. We shall have to wait and see.'

'Oh, if it could be true!'

Charles, kissing the top of her head in affectionate understanding, felt it necessary to repeat his warning.

'It's only a thin chance, Laura. You mustn't pin too many hopes on it. In the meantime, I shall be happy to apply with you to adopt Leonie, and since her mother is now known to be dead, there oughtn't to be any problems. But we ought to keep in mind, you and I, that she may not actually be an orphan.'

311

6

Yes, Leon was alive.

The news arrived in the shape of a blotchy duplicated form issued from a Displaced Persons Camp, with personal details filled in almost illegibly by hand. Laura gasped with relief and delight; but Charles, reading the form with more attention, sounded a note of warning.

'I'm glad for you, Laura. But this isn't entirely straightforward.'

'What do you mean?'

'Well, it says that Leon has no identity papers. That's not surprising: he'd have thrown away anything which showed that he'd been fighting on the wrong side. He's claiming to be British, the son of Lady Knaresborough by her first marriage. They're asking you for his birth certificate.'

'Well, I can't provide that, of course, but I don't mind making a statement to back him up.'

Charles shook his head. 'How old were you, darling, when Leon was born? Fifteen or sixteen? I'm not going to let you commit perjury. And if he gets into England under false pretences, he could be kicked out again if anyone finds out the truth. But you could send the certificate of adoption instead.'

'There's a problem about that,' said Laura. Since Charles already knew that she had never been legally married to Fred, he was quick to understand why they had not made the adoption official either.

'I'll draft a statement for you,' he promised. 'As long as we're prepared to guarantee his support, there's no reason why he shouldn't be admitted to the country.'

'He has a daughter here. That should count for something.'

'If you remember, Anassa had more sense than to put the name of a soldier in the German Army down on the birth certificate. "Father unknown".' Charles laughed, though the laughter turned into coughing and he was forced to pant for a moment before regaining his breath. 'There's a remarkable lack of documentation amongst your associates, my darling. Makes me feel quite smug, having a proper marriage certificate to prove you're mine. Anyway, I'll do whatever I can to help.'

His voice was affectionate; but Laura, sensitive to every nuance of tone, recognised a certain lack of enthusiasm.

'You don't really want him to come here, do you, Charles?'

'I want anything that makes you happy.' He took out his cigarette case but put it away again unopened; his recent bout of coughing must have reminded him of Dr Morgan's warnings. 'If I'm not gushing about Leon, you must remember that I don't know him well. What

312

I do know is that he's been voluntarily fighting for the Nazis against us and now he's telling lies to cover that fact up. It does make me wonder how suitable a father he is for Leonie.'

So that was it! Laura reproached herself for not being more understanding. Leonie's adoption had been approved six months after Anassa's death was confirmed. Laura was anxious that Leonie, as she grew up, should be shown pictures of her beautiful mother and told that only death could have parted her from her beloved daughter; but legally Laura and Charles were now her parents.

In practice, however, they regarded themselves as grandparents and Charles doted on the little girl who called him Grandfather. He had bought her a pony, although her legs were hardly long enough to straddle its back, and patiently led it round and round the paddock. He made up stories about the pictures which hung on the walls of Knaresborough Hall, and he took her for walks in the grounds, telling her about the games he had played there as a boy.

The title would become extinct when he died, but he could do what he liked with his estate, and it was clear that he took pleasure in thinking of Leonie as its mistress one day. Into this relationship Leon would come as an intruder. Charles was jealous.

Laura knew that, whatever his feelings, he would keep his promise, and six weeks later Leon arrived at Knaresborough Hall. She stared aghast as he was helped out of an ambulance. Was this the golden boy who had spent so many happy hours learning from Fred how to repair and tune his cars; the handsome young man who had squired Anassa to the New Year Ball; the popular racing driver with his following of adoring women?

Although he was only thirty-seven, he looked years older. His face was haggard, his body emaciated, and he was suffering from a skin disease which had made it impossible for him to shave, leaving him with something between a beard and a stubble. Almost too weak to climb the steps into the great hall, he agreed as soon as he had tearfully greeted Laura that he had better go straight to bed.

She had decided to keep Leonie out of the way until there had been time to tell him of his daughter's existence, and was glad of that decision now; the little girl would have been frightened to find herself being kissed by such a gaunt and prickly figure. Leon proved in fact to be suffering from a serious bowel infection and remained in his room for three weeks while the family doctor treated him with medicines and diet recommendations.

More worrying than his physical condition was his state of mental confusion. He had concocted an account of the past ten years of his life which would gain him admittance to Britain. Perhaps in an effort to ensure that he would never contradict himself by mistake, he had managed to persuade himself that his fiction was a correct account and insisted on repeating it even to someone who was well aware of the truth.

Charles would be angry if expected to swallow such a farrago of lies; so Laura, sitting at the side of the bed, did her best to assure Leon that he was safe and could dismiss the more fantastic stories from his mind. She coaxed out details of his wanderings since the end of the war, although it was difficult to piece them together in the right order.

Most particularly she asked him how he had managed to escape repatriation to the Soviet Union; but this was something which still mystified him.

'There were British guards,' he told her. 'They didn't like what they were doing. We'd all shouted to tell them what would happen to us on the other side. One of them slipped the bolt of the railway wagon I was in. It was just enough to give us a chance. We were lucky. There was a camp in the mountains. Deserters, were they, or partisans? I don't remember.'

Even this small effort of memory had tired him. Laura allowed him to slip back into sleep.

While he recovered, his meals were taken up to his room, so Laura was surprised when she came down early one morning to find him sitting in the library. On the table beside him was a decanter of whisky.

'I need a drink.' The slurring of his voice made it clear that he had already had more than one. Had Dr Morgan said anything about alcohol for the invalid? Laura couldn't remember, but she was alarmed by the pallor of Leon's face and the shaking of his hand.

'What's wrong, Leon? What's happened?'

'I've seen a ghost. Wearing a long white shroud. It just appeared in the doorway and stood there. It was Anassa, Laura. But Anassa as a child. As though she'd been growing backwards.' He shuddered, and poured himself another whisky.

'No more, Leon. You've had enough.' Laura guessed what had happened. She had wanted him to be the first to mention Anassa's name; she would have told him after that about the existence of his daughter and the fact that Anassa was dead. But in the course of all his wanderings through an imperfect memory, this was the one person whom he seemed to have obliterated from his mind.

'Anassa's daughter lives here,' Laura told him now. 'She loves wandering into different rooms. What she was wearing was just her nightdress. No ghosts.'

314

'Are you telling me that you've seen Anassa? Are you hiding her from me? Where is she?'

'I'm afraid she's dead. She died as the war was ending.'

'Oh God!' He groaned and once again reached for the whisky, fighting off Laura's attempt to take the decanter away. 'My beautiful Anassa.' His voice was thickening and his eyes were bleary when, after burying his head in his hands for a few minutes, he looked up at Laura. 'A daughter, you said? How old? No, it doesn't matter. My daughter. Anassa told me, in Paris, that she'd never had anyone but me. It has to be mine. I want to see her, Laura.'

'Yes, you shall, but not while you're drunk. Come back to bed. When you've slept it off you can have a bath and make yourself look smart.'

She managed to get him to his feet, but was glad when Charles appeared, looking disapprovingly at the half empty decanter and the young man who had now become maudlin.

'Anassa. What happened to Anassa?' He turned to face Charles. 'Where did she die, my darling Anassa?'

'In a forest in Austria, trying — '

'No, Charles!' Laura interrupted him urgently. For Leon to discover that the woman he loved might at one time have been within only a few yards of him and had probably been killed while helping him to escape was likely to unbalance still further his already unstable mind.

Charles saw the question differently. Perhaps he hoped that Leon would find comfort in the sacrifice which his lover had made for him; or perhaps he was merely unsympathetic to an uncongenial guest. Laura listened helplessly as he described what was known about Anassa's death.

Leon groaned again and did at last allow himself to be helped upstairs. Laura went to look for Leonie and found her having breakfast. It was time to tell the little girl that she had a Daddy.

The conversation was interrupted by a shout from Charles.

'Damn the man, he's stolen my car!'

Even as Laura hurried to join him in the hall, she could hear the spinnning of gravel and the fierce acceleration of an engine. By the time they reached the door, Leon was halfway down the drive, swerving from side to side.

'Not really stolen.' Laura did her best to calm her husband. 'He'll bring it back.'

Charles was fighting for breath. To run even such a short distance seemed to be more than his lungs could cope with these days. She looked at him anxiously.

315

'He's drunk,' Charles said baldly when he could speak again. 'He could kill someone in that state. He could certainly smash up the car. And he doesn't seem to realise that petrol's rationed.'

That last anti-climatic statement might at any other time have made Laura smile, but she was equally worried lest Leon should have an accident. She was worried too about Charles's health; but a third anxiety could be more easily put to rest. If her husband found Leon an uncongenial guest, then Leon must go as soon as he had recovered. She could afford to set him up in a home of his own and to buy him a small business — a garage, perhaps.

She suggested this now to Charles, in the hope of calming down his fury; but, hunched over the balustrade of the outside staircase as though in pain, he did not seem to hear her at once. At last he turned towards her, smiling.

'Thank you, darling,' he said. 'Yes, that would be the best plan. And then we can be happy here with each other again. Just the three of us.'

It was Laura's turn to feel a pain in her chest: a stab of anxiety. True, she and Charles and Leonie could be happy together; but it might not be as simple as that.

7

In the February of 1947 England lay in the grip of its coldest winter for a century. A shortage of fuel made it impossible to heat homes or trains adequately, forcing the whole population, indoors as well as out, to wrap itself in layers of rationed clothing and still to shiver. Throughout the countryside, roads were rendered hazardous by snow which, after falling in blizzards, had frozen into a rough surface with all the slipperiness of an ice rink, making the riding of a bicycle or horse an act of foolhardiness. In newspapers and public house bars there was general agreement that the country was enduring a Siberian winter.

To Fred Richards, however, who had survived so many actual Siberian winters, this minor cold snap was nothing to worry about. As he limped from the bus stop towards Knaresborough Parish Church he could not be described as in good shape. The leg which had been wounded in 1918 had not taken kindly to the cold, nor to the cramped conditions of the mines, and his other foot had been badly crushed in an accident. His hair, although as thick as ever, was white and what could be seen of his face above his beard was gaunt. The scars left by beatings and accidents were covered by the

316

clothes he had been given at the reception centre, but still pulled his shoulders down in an old man's stoop. Nobody who met him in the street now would recognise him as the cocky young man who had once turned the heads of so many girls in the village.

None of that worried Fred in the least. If anyone had asked him, at that heart-stopping moment when he had been confronted with a display of the paintings and the gold plates which he had hoped to smuggle out of Leningrad, whether he would still be alive as his sixtieth birthday approached, the question wouldn't even have been worth considering. He had never understood how his plans had been discovered; nor did he really understand why an order should have arrived in Ufa in the autumn of 1946 authorising the release of all political prisoners of foreign extraction. Bad luck, good luck: all that was out of his control. His job had been simply to survive the years in between, and he had managed it; he had come through.

It had been a touch-and-go matter for the first three nightmare years. Working down a lead mine, on a daily diet of a quart of cabbage soup and a pound of bread, had brought him near to death through sheer exhaustion. He was saved by a transfer to a forestry camp much further west. When the lorry carrying twenty-five prisoners from a train depot to their new home broke down in the middle of the forest, twenty-four of the prisoners took their chance to escape. But Fred did not give much for his chances of survival in an area inhabited only by prisoners and their guards and hundreds of miles from any possible sanctuary. Instead, he was able to repair the lorry – and, on his arrival at the camp, was rewarded by being let loose on a whole yard of vehicles which had been abandoned because no one had the skill to keep them running.

By the end of his time there he was the camp commandant's personal driver, all the more trusted because he was not a Russian and the crime of smuggling carried no great stigma. Not only was the work easy, but left-overs of food came his way and by passing some of them on he was able to placate the camp bandits who were far more dangerous than the guards.

So he had survived his imprisonment; now he must survive his freedom. He had been repatriated to England without having the chance to discover whether Laura was still alive and in Paris and whether his business was still in existence. Neither of those two things seemed very likely. Before he could find out, he needed both money and a passport; and before he could obtain a passport he needed proof of birth. That was why he was at this moment on his way to Knaresborough Parish Church to copy the necessary details from the parish register.

317

A funeral was about to begin. The mourners, dressed in black, were just filing into the church as he arrived. Fred recognised that he would have to wait; he was used to waiting.

'Who's dead?' he asked the driver of the hearse. English felt almost like a foreign language to him: he had to think about the words and mentally check that they were correct.

'Lord Knaresborough.'

Yes, he could see now that the large family vault had been opened. Considering the frozen state of the ground, it was probably just as well that there was no need to dig a grave. The Lord Knaresborough for whom Fred had worked once would be dead long ago. 'That's what used to be the Honourable Edward, I suppose,' he said.

The hearse driver shook his head.

'No, he died getting on for four years ago. This is his younger brother, Charles.'

Fred was surprised by the news. Charles — younger than himself and born to a decidedly softer life — was the member of the family he had known best. Fred had taught him to drive and had acted as his chauffeur, delivering him to Oxford in the Hispano-Suiza which he still remembered with affection. That was the car which had caught His Nibs' fancy. If it hadn't been for that car Fred himself would never have gone to Russia, never have met Laura, never — but was what the point of thinking like that? What had happened had happened.

The Honourable Charles had been a friend of Laura's, he remembered — and as though the mere thought of her name was enough to conjure up her presence, at that very moment Laura emerged from the church to stand in the porch.

It was a moment which almost stopped his heart with its unexpectedness. He stared at her so intently that she must surely have felt the force of his gaze. But although her eyes might have glanced towards the hearse and the two men standing beside it, they found nothing to interest them there. She was looking for somebody else: presumably somebody who was expected but late.

It came as a blow to Fred that she should not recognise him; but then, he had hardly recognised himself when he looked in a glass for the first time after his release. The white hair, the beard, the clothes which looked exactly like the charity handouts which they were. How could she possibly have seen beneath all this a man whom she must believe to be dead?

Well, this was not the moment to make himself known as a living ghost. As a little girl ran out of the church and took Laura by the hand, Fred moved away, behind the patient horses, and asked

318

a second question of the hearse driver.

'That tall woman standing in the porch, holding the little girl's hand. Do you know who she is?'

'That's the widow, Lady Knaresborough. And her grand-daughter.'

'Ah. Thanks.'

Fred took another look. The little girl was so much like Princess Tanya as he remembered her from long ago that she must certainly be Anassa's daughter. Not a real granddaughter, certainly. It had been one of the sadnesses of his life with Laura that she had proved unable to have children.

His heart, which had temporarily frozen, began to beat faster than normal as he watched Laura from a distance. She had been wearing black, he remembered, on the day he first met her, because her father had died. It hadn't suited her then, but now she looked well in it. She was a handsome woman still; he had never ceased to admire her. He didn't blame her for giving up on him and finding herself a husband; there must have seemed no chance that she would ever see him again. He had accepted that possibility even while he was in the camps and day-dreaming about her; making love in his imagination in ways which he had never dared to try in practice.

With a look of disappointment on her face, Laura turned and took a first step back into the church. But just at that moment the sound of a car in the distance broke the silence. One of things which had startled Fred after his return to England was the emptiness of the roads. Petrol rationing and the harsh weather conditions were combining to keep drivers at home. What was more surprising now was Laura's reaction to the sound. She hurried back to the porch entrance and stared along the road with eyes which were both expectant and angry.

The car — it was an elderly Morris with a Midwife On Call card propped against the windscreen — approached and drove sedately past the church. For a second time Laura, disappointed, turned away into the church, and this time she did not reappear. Within a few seconds the mournful meanderings of the organist were replaced by the vigorous singing of a hymn.

Fred had to cope with a disappointment of his own. It should have been a romantic episode, this unexpected encounter after so many years of separation. But it was necessary to be realistic — and the future suddenly seemed much brighter than he could have anticipated when he set out that morning.

Just as he bore no grudge against Laura, so she had no reason

319

to feel ashamed of meeting him. Perhaps he would even be able to bring her some comfort in her bereavement. But to stage a public confrontation would be wrong; there was no point in hanging about near the church. The funeral service would take at least half an hour, and then there would be the business of interment, and after that again the shaking of hands and murmuring of condolences. Slowly, because with his gammy legs he could only manage a short distance at a time without stopping, he began to make his way towards Knaresborough Hall.

There was a private footpath which provided a short cut from the church to the Hall; but the door might be locked and he was not confident of remembering the way. Instead, he went along the road, towards the lodge gates.

The park, silent with snow, was smaller than he remembered it. As a boy he had thought it enormous — but that was before he had become acquainted with the wastes of Siberia! Stepping towards the gates, he heard for a second time the sound of a car. But this one was approaching very much faster and had a much more powerful engine. Turning his head, he found it almost upon him, and was only just able to flatten himself against one of the pillars in time to get out of the way. The movement landed him on his bad foot, which slipped to leave him sprawling on the ground. As he picked himself up, cursing, he saw the lodgekeeper looking out of a window, making a face which suggested that he had seen this sort of thing before.

Indicating that he was not hurt, Fred stared after the car. He was too much out of touch to recognise the marque, but it was surprising that anyone should choose to drive an open-top sports car in this weather. The driver had swerved and skidded after taking the entrance to the park too fast, and now was continuing to swerve as he continued up the drive.

He's drunk, thought Fred, and watched with interest as the car swung across on to the flat ground of the deer park and began to roar round and round in a circle. As though the driver were on a race-track. Once again, as at the church, he was startled by the unexpectedness of what he saw. It was unbelievable; and yet it must be true. That blond hair. That way of swinging the rear of the car round in a situation when braking would be useless. He had taught that trick to Leon, blond-headed Leon. As fast as his feet would carry him, Fred hurried up the drive.

The car changed its pattern. Now, like a skater, it was describing a figure of eight on the frozen ground. This was a reckless act, for the park was dotted with substantial trees. Fred stood still near the crossing point of the figure as the car approached again. There could be no doubt about it, for the driver was not wearing goggles. It was indeed Leon.

Never in his most hopeful dreams after his release had Fred expected to find the two people he loved most in the world so quickly, and in the same place. He waved his scarf up and down as though it were the chequered flag which marked the end of a race.

'Leon! It's your dad!'

The car screamed past, but Leon had heard the shout. He looked back, his face incredulous, and pulled the car round in a tighter circle than before. It came towards Fred in a sideways slide, out of control, unable to get any grip on the ice. For a second time he attempted to move out of the way. For a second time, he slipped.

8

The snow began to fall again as Laura came out of the church and moved with the other mourners towards the Knaresboroughs' family tomb. Earlier in the day there had been a light cascade of sparkling flakes which danced and glistened in the sunshine, but now it descended heavily in a silent sheet, settling on the hats of the women and the bare heads of the men and obliterating the shape of the single wreath which still lay on the top of the coffin. It cut them off from the rest of the world, as though nothing were happening anywhere except the sad ceremony of saying goodbye to Charles.

How cold it was! The church had been icy, and by the time she took her place beside the entrance to the vault, staring down at the coffin and not even pretending to listen to the vicar's muffled words, her body was too frozen even to shiver. Inside, however, inappropriate emotions burned and raged.

For four days she had mourned, and this moment, above all, was the occasion for grief, for sadly letting go. But she was unable to weep, or even to feel bereft, because she was so furious with Leon.

How dare he be late for the funeral! Had it not been for Charles's efforts, he would still be languishing in some Displaced Persons' Camp. He owed respect and gratitude on his own account, quite aside from Laura's need for support.

Even while she asked herself the question, Laura knew the answer. Leon could not bring himself to attend the funeral because he blamed himself for Charles's death — and in a second burst of inward anger, Laura blamed him as well.

321

Dr Morgan, hurrying – too late – to the Hall after Charles's fatal collapse, had shrugged aside any idea that fury could have been responsible for his patient's death.

'I've been telling him for years that he ought to stop smoking. If you could look inside his lungs now, you'd find that there was no room for air. Just a spongy mess, which has drowned him in the end. He died because there wasn't space for him to breathe.'

There had seemed no point in arguing, and in any case she was at that moment too shocked and distressed to ask questions. But she knew, as Dr Morgan did not, what had led to her husband's last gasping attempt to draw a breath.

Leon, realising that there were limits to Charles's hospitality, had gratefully accepted Laura's offer to set him up in a small business. He was well aware that he was too old and too unfit ever to return to the motor racing circuit and had agreed without any trace of arrogance that a vehicle repair workshop would probably give him the best chance of making a living. He would look out for something himself, he said. And he would probably need a little time to settle down before he was able to send for Leonie to live with him.

It was the statement which Laura had feared. She had all the arguments ready to deploy in a gently persuasive manner. She and Charles were officially Leonie's adoptive parents. Leon himself had no legal claim, since his name was not on the birth certificate. He had no experience of bringing up children, or even of family life, and would find it impossible to look after a little girl and earn a living at the same time.

She had felt confident that she could persuade him – and that, indeed, he had probably only mentioned the possibility of taking his daughter away as a bargaining ploy, designed to ensure that he should be allowed to see her as often as he wanted. But Charles, forgetting all his skills as a diplomat, had allowed her no chance to negotiate. Instead, he flatly and indignantly refused to entertain any idea that Leonie should leave Knaresborough Hall.

The argument grew personal. Leon was a drunkard. Charles was a selfish old man. Leon was unfit to be a parent. Charles had never been a parent himself; probably couldn't manage it. Distressed by the quarrel, Laura did her best to mediate, but was not allowed to interfere. She could see Charles's colour rising and could tell that he was having to snatch for breath; but even so the abruptness and finality of his collapse had taken her by surprise.

For her it had caused heartbreak, but the effect upon Leon was different. Horrified by what had happened, he saw himself as a murderer. No one was likely to punish him, and so for these past four

322

days he had punished himself – drinking even more than before and then driving around in a frenzied fashion as though inviting death to visit him by accident. But he ought to have come to the funeral. He owed Charles that much.

It was still not too late for him to make an appearance. For the second time that afternoon Laura heard through the snow the muffled sound of a vehicle approaching. Looking up, she saw that this time it was an ambulance, no doubt on its way to the lodge. Earlier that day Collins had told her that the baby was expected at any moment. He had been expecting the midwife to perform the delivery, but perhaps there had been complications.

The vicar came to an end and closed his book. There were a few moments of silence before the coffin was carried into the ornate Victorian tomb and placed on a shelf beside his brother's. Laura felt a tug at her hand.

'I'm cold, Grandmother.'

'We're all cold. But we're going home now. You've been very good, darling.'

She expressed her thanks to the vicar and began to move amongst the mourners, thanking them for coming and inviting them up to the Hall. It had always seemed odd to her that a funeral should be the occasion for a party; but it was the thing to do. She was almost ready to leave when there was a disturbance in the churchyard.

It was Collins, the lodgekeeper, who was dashing towards her. In spite of the cold he wore only a leather waistcoat above his shirt, and his boots were unlaced. Laura could think of only one emergency which would have brought him out into the bitter weather in such a state. She crossed quickly to meet him.

'Has the baby arrived? Is everything all right?'

'Coming along nicely, Mrs Timpkins says. It's not that. There's been an accident. A car accident. In the park.'

It had to be Leon. Laura was unable to speak, but the lodgekeeper answered her unspoken question with a nod.

'Nanny, will you take Leonie home, please? Through the church gate.' If Leonie went back along the private footpath she could avoid seeing whatever had happened on the drive. Laura herself hurried along the road towards the park gates.

'How was he driving?'

'Well, erratically, you could say, milady. He almost killed the old gentleman once before, just here.'

'What old gentleman?'

'Well, I couldn't be saying who he was. White hair and white beard and a greatcoat longer than usual. I suppose he might have been a tramp, but that greatcoat had a sort of foreign look to it, so I reckoned as how he was one of his lordship's friends from abroad, walking up from the church after the service.'

Probably that meant that the man had indeed been a tramp and Collins was making excuses for not having intercepted him. But Laura was hardly listening. As she turned into the drive, trying to keep her balance on the frozen snow, she saw the ambulance coming towards her. She wanted to stop it and ask if she could get in; but if Leon was badly hurt she ought not to hold it up for even a second. It would be better to get her own car out and follow to the hospital. She pressed on up the winding drive at a speed which brought a stitch to her chest.

Even from a distance it was easy to see the scene of the accident, for the tyres of a car had cut circles into the snow. And now she could see the vehicle itself, on its side and smashed against the trunk of a beech tree. Here the snow was in different places black with oil and red with blood.

An ambulanceman, who had been leaning over the wreckage, straightened himself as she approached.

'I've given him a shot of morphine to keep the pain down,' he said. 'He'll be out cold in a moment.'

'You mean — ' Laura pushed past him. 'I thought he was in the ambulance.'

She looked down at Leon's crushed body and had to fight her impulse to scream. He had never had a serious accident in a motor race or rally. How was it possible that he could have done so much damage to himself in the safety of an English park? His head was hanging over the edge of the car at an impossible angle: his neck must certainly be broken. Blood was dripping from the back of his skull, but there was no mark on his face. Indeed, as she watched, even the lines which had been etched on his forehead by hardship seemed to be smoothing themselves away — but perhaps it was the effect of the tears clouding her eyes which made him look once again like the handsome young man he had been in his twenties.

'Oh Leon!' She put out a finger to touch his cheek.

His eyes opened. 'Mum!' He had not called her Mum for years. She could tell that he was trying to move his head, and told him quickly that he must be still. His eyes began to close again, but he forced them to look at her again. There was something he was trying to say. 'Dad.'

'Keep still,' she repeated, and this time his eyes did close as he slid into unconsciousness. The ambulanceman, behind her, was talking about the need to wait for the fire brigade to arrive with tools to cut the victim out.

'The ambulance will be back again by then, ma'am, don't you worry. We thought it best to take the old gentleman away at once, although I don't think the hospital will be able to do anything for him. According to the people in the lodge, he was run down before the crash.'

Laura had no attention to spare for the fate of an elderly tramp. What frightened her was Leon's sudden stillness. Was it only the effect of the morphine, or was it − ? 'Can you find a pulse?' she asked.

He took her place beside Leon and moved his fingers over that stretched and unmoving neck. The search took longer than it should have done.

'I'm very sorry, ma'am,' he said at last. 'I'm afraid he's gone.'

She had no more tears left to shed. White-faced but dry-eyed, she made her way back to the Hall. The other mourners had been invited to take tea, but the housekeeper would have to deal with that; she could not face a social occasion.

Upstairs in her bedroom she flung herself down on the bed she had shared with Charles, and allowed loneliness to overwhelm her. It was hard to feel sorry on Leon's behalf, because almost certainly he had willed his own death. Poor Leon. He had made wrong decisions, but the seeds of his unhappiness had been sown in Barisinova's bedroom thirty-eight years earlier. To be the son of a prince might have brought him a life of privilege, but instead it was that heritage which had spoiled his life.

She resolved to forget the unstable and difficult man who had emerged from the wreckage of Europe and to remember only the eager, affectionate lad who had so patiently absorbed all Fred's skill with engines. In the last moment of his life perhaps Leon himself had been remembering that happier time of his life, when Laura and Fred were Mum and Dad.

Briefly she wondered whether she ought to enquire about the man Leon had run down, and compensate his dependants. But a tramp was unlikely to have any family − and Laura had enough to worry about at home.

'There's a lovely tea downstairs with gingerbread men.' Leonie had appeared at the side of the bed.

'I'm not very hungry. You go and have a gobble.'

'What's the matter, Grandmother?'

Laura hesitated only for a moment. The little girl would have to know sooner or later. She had been told only a short time ago that

Leon was her father and the news had made her anxious rather than delighted; she was wary of this strange and often rough man, and frightened lest he should take her away.

'There's been an accident, darling. Your daddy's dead.'

'Like Grandfather?'

'Yes.'

'Are you going to die as well, Grandmother? Who's going to look after me?'

Laura lifted the little girl on to the bed and hugged her.

'No,' she said. 'I'm not going to die for years and years. I shall look after you until you're grown up. And by that time I shall be very old, so you'll have to look after me.'

'So we'll stay here and look after each other. I'm glad.'

She leaned forward to give her grandmother a kiss and for a moment Laura gripped her almost too tightly. Unless Alexis had found someone to console him in Karlovy Vary, this child was the last of the Kristovs. Some people might argue that she ought to be told about her heritage, but Laura intended to keep quiet. To be descended from the Russian nobility might make for an interesting life, but not for a happy one; and even a child might feel the stigma of her parents' incestuous love.

How much better it would be for Leonie to grow up in the peaceful English countryside as an ordinary English girl. Laura could teach her for a year or two, just as she had once taught her mother. Then there would be ordinary school, ordinary holidays, a safe, unthreatening existence.

Leon and Anassa had been ambitious and talented, so Leonie might grow to be ambitious and talented as well: there would be nothing wrong with that. But Laura intended to make sure that they were English ambitions, English talents. Leonie Jardinais, who had really been Leonie Kristova, was now Leonie Vereker; and Leonie Vereker was going to have a happy life.

Part Three

The Tiara of Tears
1970

1

'Are you ready for something really big, Mr Sampson?'

For security reasons, the catalogue entries were being drafted in the strongroom, three floors beneath the suite of auction rooms in London's West End. Kathy Walters, five years out of college with a degree in Fine Arts, watched as the old man snapped the case shut on a bracelet which had once belonged to Anna Neagle. She slid it along the table to join the ruby-studded belt of a nineteenth-century maharajah, the diamond earrings of an exiled queen and the unfashionable and unappreciated legacies of a dozen anonymous grandmothers.

William Sampson, London's leading authority on jewellery, was no longer a regular member of the auction house's staff. Now well over seventy, he came in only on one day a month to advise what should go into the regular jewellery auctions and what should be held back for the annual sale of Important Antique Jewellery. So far today he hadn't found anything Important. The pile of yellow cards for the next ordinary sale was growing, but he hadn't yet reached for a green one.

Kathy, who had been his apprentice and then assistant until he retired, carried on a continuous appraisal of her own as she watched him. She was still learning, still needing to absorb his expertise, to develop instincts as sharp as his — although her working methods were different.

The yellow cards, for example. All the catalogue details would eventually have to be put down again, this time on special printed forms. But he seemed to need the physical act of shuffling the cards around, arranging their order as though it was not his brain but his fingers which knew how to space the plums in the pudding;

how to lead a roomful of dealers and socialites towards the dramatic climax of any sale.

It was not merely the colour of the cards which told her that he had not yet been excited by anything she had produced. Would the next piece cause his fingers to tap the table with the only sign of interest he permitted himself? She pulled the box out of the safe and laid it, opened, in front of him.

'My goodness!' exclaimed Mr Sampson. 'A kokoshnik!'

'A what?' This was not a term which Kathy had heard from any of her tutors.

'A kokoshnik. A Russian tiara. Do you see, it's a completely different shape from anything that was worn in France or England or America. Higher in the crown. Allowing, as you see here, for a monstrous degree of ostentation.'

'I'm glad you think it's monstrous too. I didn't like to say ...'

Her voice faded away as she stared into the open box. The kokoshnik — she must remember that word — was formed from seven overlapping circles of platinum lavishly set with diamonds. In the middle of each segment formed by the overlap was a large pearl; and suspended from the top of the central circle, which was higher and wider than the others, was a pearl which was not just large but enormous.

It was of the first quality — all the gemstones to be auctioned were appraised for weight and cut and grade before they appeared in front of Mr Sampson. And it was of unusual shape. Not round, but long; and swelling towards the bottom like a teardrop. Mounted alone, to hang as a pendant from a neat silver collar, it would be a beautiful object. But here ...

'An unfortunate choice of word.' Mr Sampson withdrew his charge of monstrosity. 'Ostentation, the flaunting of wealth, is one of the justifications for jewellery. The other is beautification, and beauty is a matter of fashion. I was startled, that's all. I didn't think I'd ever see one of these again, outside the Hermitage. Not untouched like this. Most of them were sold off stone by stone in the Twenties.'

'By the White Russians?'

'Yes. It's sad, when you think of it. The woman who first wore this must have been unimaginably rich when it was made, and may well have been starving ten years later.'

'There are people starving all over the world who have never been rich.'

'That doesn't diminish the pain one individual must have felt. You're allowed to be sentimental, Miss Walters.' Mr Sampson had not adopted the modern fashion of using Christian names. 'After

328

all, sentiment affects the price. We have to ask ourselves: is the value of this piece simply the value of all its stones? And if not, how much does it gain from the knowledge that it may have made its first appearance at an Imperial ball in the Winter Palace in St Petersburg?'

For the first time that day he pulled a green card towards him and wrote KOKOSHNIK in the top left-hand corner.

'Cartier,' he said with confidence, writing as he spoke. 'Between 1905 and 1910. Probably by Lamartine.' He put his magnifier into his eye, picked up the tiara and peered at the back. 'Did you get that?'

It was part of Kathy's continuing training that before each session she should make her own judgements, to be tested against those of the expert. That was the way she would learn.

'Cartier I got. Where do you look for Lamartine?'

Her eyes were good. Once he pointed it out she could see the tiny shape of a bird impressed in the tiara's gallery.

'Have you the values?' Mr Sampson asked next.

Kathy passed over the list of appraisals and watched as he copied the details down. What a waste of effort, she thought, when it would all have to be typed out again.

'It gives me time,' he said, reading her thoughts. 'Instinct and experience are my only tools. *Your* instinct, no doubt, will develop at an electronic speed. Mine has to swirl around a little, absorbing information, asking questions, coming up with answers. Now then. What about the history?'

This was what he asked about every piece and it was really two separate questions. Answering them was the main part of Kathy's job. She had to check title: to be sure that the seller had the right to sell. If there was any doubt, the lot would be handed to a lawyer for investigation, but it was Kathy's responsibility to realise that the doubt existed.

Her second duty was to arouse interest in the lots. Mr Sampson knew that this had to be done, but was not involved in the publicity process himself. It was left to her to decide whether the best approach was a general one, through stories to the press, or an individual one, alerting three or four potential buyers to the existence of an article which would exactly fill a gap in their collections.

This item had proved tricky. She was going to need more time to work on its history. Luckily the important auction was still several months away.

She wasn't even sure that there was good title. Although the word kokoshnik was new to her, she had recognised the piece as

329

being Russian. But the vendor had appeared to have no Russian connections; nor the sort of family money which could have bought something so valuable.

She had written as tactful a letter as she could, giving the impression that she needed background information in order to attract publicity. The answer, from Mr Alan Edwards, though obviously sincere, had not been reassuring.

The headdress came into my father's possession in 1945, *he wrote*. According to what he told my mother, he was given it for saving someone's life. In 1947 he tried to sell it by showing it round in a pub to see what anyone would offer. Two nights later, a couple of men broke into the flat and my father was killed trying to fight them off.

I was a year old at the time and my mother was pregnant with my younger sister. She took us to live with her parents. She always reckoned that my father had been killed for the headdress and so she never let anyone know of its existence and never tried to sell it. I don't know where she hid it to start with, but later on she padded out a box to keep it in and put the box with our dressing-up clothes because she thought no burglars would look there. She was terrified of burglars.

My sister Margaret, as a little girl, was sometimes allowed to wear the headdress for pretending to be a queen. Our mother said that the jewels weren't real, but had come from Woolie's. But Margaret always felt there was something special about it; even when she was quite small she took care not to damage it.

Margaret was killed in a bicycle accident when she was sixteen. When my mother died last year I inherited her property. I took the headdress to an antiques road show for valuation. They told me what I ought to insure it for. I couldn't afford it, and that is why I want to sell. I hope this information is helpful.

No, it was not helpful. It sounded to Kathy suspiciously like a case of looting. The previous owner, after twenty-five years, might well be dead, but one could never be sure − and there were always heirs. Once in a while, disputed ownership could provide the perfect breeze to fan the flame of publicity. But although it might be helpful if newspapers took up the story, it was essential that Kathy should be armed with at least some of the facts.

Until she discovered exactly how Robert Edwards, now deceased, had come into possession of the kokoshnik she had no hope of reaching back into its history. Except that

330

from a reference book she had made one important identification.

'The teardrop pearl in the centre,' she said. 'I'm almost sure. The weight checks. It's one of a pair given to Marie Antoinette to celebrate the birth of her first child. I imagine it was either appropriated by the revolutionary government after her execution or else stolen when she tried to escape.'

'I don't think you need pursue the quest of sound title as far back as that.' Smiling, Mr Sampson put a finger under the teardrop pearl. It was not fixed, but suspended from the top of the central circle of diamonds; he was able to move it gently.

'Marie Antoinette ... yes. Yes, well done. Just a minute and I shall have it.'

Kathy waited. She was familiar with these silences. Any minute now he would come out with something she couldn't have found in her books if she'd searched for a hundred years. It was depressing to think that she might have to be seventy herself before she would be able to rival his knowledge.

'Kristov,' he said at last, allowing himself a small smile of triumph. 'Yes, that's it. The Kristov kokoshnik. If I remember aright, it had a name.' He thought again before nodding with satisfaction. '*La Lachrymosa*, yes. The tiara of tears. Exhibited by Cartier in London and Paris and New York in the 1920s. There'll be an exhibition catalogue. With any luck, there should be an illustration.'

'Would that mean that Cartier themselves owned it then?'

'Not necessarily. They *might* have bought it back. But they could have borrowed it especially for an exhibition. Either way, they'll have an owner's name for that period. That will help you to go both backwards and forwards in the provenance.'

It was time to move on to the next piece, but his finger still moved gently over the kokoshnik.

'Has it made you happy, Mr Sampson?' Kathy checked herself, realising that the question was impertinent. But curiosity drove her on, because she was treading the same path herself. 'Have you found it satisfying, devoting the whole of your life to the study of objects? Inanimate objects, however beautiful they may be.'

'Instead of the study of human beings, do you mean?' The old man did not take offence. 'Two answers I could give you to that. One is that an object like this brings me into contact with all the people who have owned it. I can share the delight they felt in their own beauty when they first wore it, or their sadness when the time came to part with it. Don't you feel that. Touch it, stroke it. Open your imagination.'

331

Kathy touched, trying to imagine; but there was no one there.

'The other thing to remember,' Mr Sampson told her, 'is that an object has a life of its own. Its owners die. Who knows now what may have happened to the Princess Kristova who first set it on her head? But its creator continues to live in his creation. This kokoshnik bestows immortality on M. Pierre Lamartine, who has been dead for nearly sixty years. That's what inspires all creators. Babies or artifacts, it's the same urge. Something to endure after they themselves are dead. If created objects are not valued, the desire to create is stifled. We'll talk about *La Lachrymosa* again next month. What is next?'

Next was something easy: an emerald ring which had once belonged to the Shah of Iran. The remaining items were run-of-the-mill, allowing Kathy plenty of time after Mr Sampson left to transfer the handwritten information from his cards on to the standard forms.

She worked swiftly in the cubicle which passed for an office. Only when she reached the green card did she pause. The kokoshnik had been locked away, but she attempted the exercise recommended by Mr Sampson, visualising the piece as though it lay in front of her, and opening her imagination.

Who were the Kristovs? What triumphs and tragedies had they known? What had happened to them after the collapse of their society? The Cartier catalogue did indeed provide the name of the kokoshnik's owner in 1929, but that only raised another question. Who was Miss L. Mainwaring?

2

'Eleven more days and eight more hours!'

Laura smiled affectionately as her granddaughter came singing down to breakfast. In eleven more days and eight more hours Leonie would be standing at the altar of the parish church and making her wedding vows to Peter Cardew.

Laura herself was counting the days to the wedding just as eagerly as Laura. Two months earlier she had been told by a surgeon that the only operation which might prolong her life would itself be life-threatening to a woman of seventy-eight. The clot which would kill her one day very soon was already lodged in her veins. Although she was perfectly well aware that some movement as simple as that of lacing up her shoes might prove enough to send it on its way towards her heart, she was determined to survive at least until after

332

the wedding. Her posture had always been good, but in recent weeks she had adopted a new way of moving around, keeping the upper part of her body steady. Leonie, quick to note any change, had exclaimed with delight that her grandmother had become stately.

'What are you doing today, dear?'

'I'll exercise Uncle Tom first. After that, I'm going to take Marco Polo down to the jumps. I've got him used to continuous noise now, but Peter's promised to come and turn a radio on and off to make sure he can cope with sudden roars.'

Leonie Vereker, at the age of twenty-seven, was an equestrian star. Already she had won an Olympic bronze medal, and her first words when she woke up each morning were: 'Gold next time.' It was Charles who had started her on her love affair with horses; Laura's part had been only to find her a good trainer and offer encouragement and the considerable amounts of money required to buy good eventing horses before the first offers of sponsorship arrived.

Luckily Peter, her future husband, was as horse-mad as herself – though perhaps there was no luck about it, since she only mixed with people who shared her own enthusiasms. After the wedding Peter would move into Knaresborough Hall and together they would establish their own stud.

The Kristov pedigree, about which Leonie knew nothing, had given her the golden hair and blue eyes and fair skin which led newspaper reporters to describe her as an English rose. She was sturdier than her mother, and not as tall; it was her father's muscular strength which had proved useful in her career. She had inherited Leon's will to win and Anassa's confidence in her own ability, but her nature was far more down-to-earth than theirs. Leonie was not interested in the world of social and cultural gossip which her mother had inhabited, and had no time at all for dressing up in beautiful clothes.

Except, of course, on her wedding day. Laura gave her a reminder now.

'You haven't forgotten that the last fitting for your dress is this afternoon?'

'Of course not. Four o'clock. I'll leave time to have a shower first, in case you're worrying whether I intend to step into the dress all sweaty and smelly.'

'And put your hair up, the way you're going to wear it.' For the greater part of most days, Leonie fastened her long hair into a pony tail with a rubber band, letting it hang straight over her shoulders in the evenings.

'Will you come in and look?' she asked her grandmother. 'All through the service everyone will be staring at my back, which is the bit I can't really see. I'd like to be sure that it's all right.'

'I've got an appointment myself at the same time, I'm afraid. But you can interrupt. Come in and show yourself.'

The appointment was with someone from a London auction house. Laura had no idea why a Miss Kathy Walters should wish to call on her. She supposed it was because she had sent a picture to be auctioned eight years earlier, when it first became clear that if Leonie was to realise her ambitions she must be given a really good horse. Perhaps they hoped that she might have more business for them. If so, she would go away disappointed. It would be for Leonie and Peter to decide what they might want to sell in order to set themselves up as breeders.

The first surprise when her visitor arrived that afternoon was that she was not alone. A man whom Laura at first assumed to be a driver accompanied her into the drawing room.

'I have to have an escort,' said Kathy apologetically after she had introduced herself and shaken hands. 'This is Mort Hall. A bodyguard, sort of. I could have brought you just a photograph to see, but I wanted to show you the real thing.'

'What real thing is this?' Laura was pouring out tea. The bodyguard, whose role was clearly a non-speaking one, stepped forward politely to hand round.

Kathy had arrived carrying a small square suitcase. She knelt down on the floor to open it, and there was a rustling of tissue paper. Then, on the polished top of an eighteenth-century wine table, she set down the Kristov kokoshnik.

The shock of seeing it again after so many years set Laura's heart racing. She put a hand on her chest, as though by pressing down she could somehow will that tiny clot, that unexploded bomb, to stay where it was. There were still eleven more days to be survived before the wedding.

'Lady Knaresborough! Are you all right?'

It should have been clear enough that she was not all right. The china cup which she had been on the point of handing to the bodyguard rattled on its saucer and tipped over, spilling the contents on to the Persian carpet. Looking reproachfully at Kathy, the guard took a handful of the tissue paper and mopped it up.

'I'm terribly sorry,' said Kathy. 'I didn't realise – '

Laura interrupted her. 'You are not sorry at all, Miss Walters. You came here to see whether I would react to the sight of this object, and you have seen.' Oh dear, she thought to herself, now I'm talking like a stately old lady as well as moving like one.

334

'May I explain? I know that this kokoshnik once belonged to you.'

Kathy paused, as though hoping for a nod of agreement. Laura could have interrupted to say that she had never in fact been the owner; but she was anxious to listen before she spoke, and after a moment's hesitation the young woman continued.

'It's now been sent to us for auction. Just as a matter of interest, to get some publicity, it would be a great help if I could find out how it came to leave Russia. But what's more important is that it's not at all clear how it came into the possession of the family which wants to sell it. I'm hoping that you might be able to help with some information.'

'This family.' Laura's voice emerged as a croak. She took a sip of tea to clear her throat. 'The sellers. How do they explain their possession of it?'

'The present owner's father was in the army in 1945. He claimed to have been given the kokoshnik as a bribe. To save someone's life, apparently. That may or may not be true. It's not easy to check. But I thought, if you would be willing to tell me something of the history . . .'

She was interrupted by the opening of the drawing room door.

'Tarra!' exclaimed Leonie cheerfully, parading herself in her wedding dress. 'Oh, sorry, Grandmother. I forgot you had someone coming.'

'That's all right. Come in darling. This is Miss Walters. And Mr Hall. My granddaughter, Leonie Vereker.'

'How do you do? How do I look, Grandmother?'

There were no words to tell her how she looked. Or rather, there was only one. 'You look like a princess,' said Laura faintly. 'Come here and kiss me.'

How odd it was that clothes could make such a difference! Never before had Laura realised quite how lovely she was. Lovelier even than her mother, who had always been too thin.

Kathy Walters seemed equally impressed by her beauty.

'Miss Vereker, would you do something for me? Would you wear the kokoshnik for a moment?'

'The what?'

'The kokoshnik.' Kathy indicated the jewelled headdress.

Leonie brushed it aside with a laugh.

'Not my sort of thing, I'm afraid. Distinctly too fancy. Little white rosebuds are more my line.'

'I'm not trying to sell it to you,' said Kathy — a statement whose truthfulness Laura doubted. 'Although if you'd let

335

me take a photograph ... Your hair is exactly right. May I?'

She lifted the kokoshnik off the table and held it high in both hands, like an archbishop preparing to crown a queen. Leonie raised her eyebrows in amusement, but stood politely still, inclining her head slightly as though the coveted gold medal was about to be hung round her neck.

Although a hairdresser would come to Knaresborough Hall on the wedding morning, she had already taught Leonie how to put her hair up herself, pinning it over a hairpiece to give it height. The kokoshnik settled into place as though the style had been made for it. A little nervously, as though afraid it might fall, Leon' stood straight-backed and motionless, as regal in bearing as her grandmother – her real grandmother – had looked when Laura caught her first glimpse of the kokoshnik fifty-seven years earlier outside the Kristov palace in St Petersburg. Kathy Walters clapped her hands.

'Perfect! I know it's an imposition, but may I, please?'

She produced a camera from her handbag, but Laura, using her unaccustomed stately voice again, intervened.

'No. My granddaughter is not a model.'

Leonie's stiff body relaxed into laughter.

'Oh, Grandmother, are you depriving me of fame and fortune? I hoped I was going to become a cover girl. Let me at least look at myself: Princess Leonie.'

There was no looking glass in the drawing room. As she picked up her skirts and swept out, the bodyguard followed.

Kathy Walters became businesslike again.

'Can you tell me anything about the history of the piece after it left your possession, Lady Knaresborough? I suppose my first question must be, was it stolen from you or did you pass it on to a legitimate owner?'

She must have thought it the simplest of questions, but Laura took her time about answering. She owed this young woman no favours, and what was most important was that there should be no indication of any link between the kokoshnik and Leonie Vereker. But although she tried to concentrate on that aspect of the conversation, her mind kept returning to one simple statement. 'He claimed to have been given the kokoshnik as a bribe. To save someone's life, apparently.'

Leon had made an equally matter-of-fact statement when he first returned to England. 'The British soldiers didn't like what they were being asked to do. One of them unbolted the door of the wagon I was in.' He had had no problems with that. It was only later that he learned about Anassa's presence in the area at the time. Discovering that she had been so close as he made his escape, and had died there, had been one of the things which seemed to knock him off balance.

That was not the unknown soldier's fault, of course. His intention must have been to do the prisoners a good turn. If he needed a bribe to make him take the risk to himself — and to open one particular wagon rather than another — well, it was for that reason, presumably, that Anassa had carried the kokoshnik across Europe. Yes, the answer to Miss Walters' question was indeed a simple one.

Nevertheless, Laura did not give it at once. Like the old woman that she had become, her thoughts wafted in different directions like a fluffy cloud blown by the erratic breezes of memory. She remembered Leon in his last months, drifting unhappily with no star to guide him. But that was a picture which she had long ago determined to banish from her mind.

Deliberately instead she conjured up the moment — the last of the moments — when they had all been happy: she and Fred, Leon and Anassa. It was the moment when Anassa had appeared in the drawing room of the Villa des Cascades wearing the kokoshnik with all the dignity of a true princess — just as Leonie had worn it a few moments ago. It had been Anassa's night of triumph; but none of their lives afterwards had ever been the same.

Nothing like that was going to spoil Leonie's future. Laura blinked once or twice, wondering whether she had almost fallen asleep, and gathered her wandering thoughts together.

3

The silence seemed to be enduring for ever. It was tempting to press, to rephrase the question, but Kathy kept quiet. She could tell that she had hit a target, although it was not yet clear whether it was the target at which she had aimed. By the length of the time she was taking to consider the straightforward questions, the old lady was revealing that there were answers she could give if she chose.

The quietness of the room was not greatly disturbed by the return of Leonie Vereker. She was still wearing the kokoshnik, and on her face now was an expression of awe. She had seen for herself how it could transform her from an English rose to a Russian princess.

Lady Knaresborough was quick to notice the effect, and came abruptly to life again, although she still did not answer Kathy's question.

337

'Give them back their kokoshnik, darling,' she said to her granddaughter. 'And then, when you've taken the wedding dress off and become your usual scruffy self again, will you do something for me? If you go into the box room at the top of the east wing you'll see on one of the shelves a wooden box just a little smaller than the case Miss Walters brought with her. It has some kind of a crest or monogram on it: I don't remember exactly. A Cartier box.'

Kathy's eyes sparkled with pleasure. Now they were getting somewhere. The old lady, who only a moment earlier had seemed to be falling asleep, had become alert and decisive.

'To answer your questions,' she said when Leonie had left the room, 'I was never the owner of this kokoshnik. I brought it out of Russia after the Revolution, at the request of the family I worked for there. From 1918 onwards it was the property of the Princess Tanya Pavlovna Kristova. But she was a child at the time and both her parents were dead, so the arrangement with Cartier was made with me. I presume that it's through the Cartier catologue that you discovered my association with the kokoshnik?'

'Yes. Is Princess Tanya still alive?'

'No. And I'm afraid I'm unable to help you any further in establishing the ownership of the kokoshnik. It must be almost forty years since I last saw it. She could have disposed of it at any time.'

'The story we were told. Do you consider it to be likely?'

'It's not for me to decide whether or not the present owner has a good title to the piece. All I can say is — in case you were worried — that there is nothing that I could do or would want to do to challenge it.'

'Thank you very much, Lady Knaresborough.' Fleetingly Kathy wondered whether to ask for a signed statement to that effect. But no; it was easy to tell that she was dealing with someone who would keep her word. Instead, she smiled gratefully. 'I'll send you the details of the auction in which it will be offered. It looked so exactly right when your granddaughter wore it. You might like — '

'No.' The interruption was definite enough to be almost brusque. 'I didn't expect to see the kokoshnik today and I don't wish to see it again.'

Kathy nodded. It was time to leave — but not before the Cartier box had appeared. 'May I ask you, Lady Knaresborough, how you came to be in Russia during the Revolution? Was your father a diplomat there, or something like that?'

'Nothing like that at all. My father was an Oxford don and I was brought up in Oxford. But I became a governess. Princess Tanya was my pupil.' There was a pause. 'I remember the first time I

338

saw the kokoshnik. It was only about an hour after my ship had docked in St Petersburg. We arrived outside the Kristov palace just as Princess Kristova — Princess Tanya's mother — was returning from a ball. I could hardly believe my eyes. Such jewels! There was a necklace to match the kokoshnik, you know. But I don't know where that is now. Ah, Leonie darling, you found it. Here you are, Miss Walters.'

The padded satin lining of the box still held the imprint of the kokoshnik. It was an odd thing, Kathy observed, that whereas the sight of the headdress itself had merely startled the old lady, the pattern of dents into which it could be fitted seemed to be moving her to tears. Kathy pretended not to notice.

'Thank you very much indeed for being so patient with me, Lady Knaresborough. And for the box.'

'It's not the original container, of course. Just a travelling box which was made when it went on exhibition in the 1920s. When I brought the kokoshnik out of Russia it was broken up into small pieces and sewn into my corsets!'

'I do wish ...' What Kathy wished was that she could stay and hear more about her hostess's adventures. But Lady Knaresborough was already signing to her granddaughter to help her up from her chair in sign of dismissal. The interview was over.

In the car going back to London, there was a lot to think about.

'She knows, doesn't she?'

'Knows what?' asked Mort.

'She may not have seen the kokoshnik for forty years, but she knows where it's been and what's happened to it. Why d'you think she wouldn't say?'

Mort, never chatty, had no answer to that question. But it continued to nag at Kathy's brain long after the kokoshnik had been returned to the strongroom and she, next morning, was once again seated in her office cubicle, trying to prepare the entry for the catalogue.

It was odd how her mind kept wandering, when as a rule she was so businesslike. It was one of the things which Mr Sampson had suggested: that she should see the piece in terms of its successive owners. At the time she had thought that to be a sentimental distraction, except in so far as it might help her to trace the erratic progress of a piece of jewellery from the design pad of M. Pierre Lamartine in Imperial St Petersburg to the dressing-up box of little Margaret Edwards in Coventry. The meeting with Lady Knaresborough had changed all that.

What an extraordinary life she must have led! Mr Sampson had empathised with the princess who had once been rich and had later perhaps starved. What Kathy longed to know was how the girl who had once been Laura Mainwaring, living quietly in Oxford, had become Lady Knaresborough, living quietly in a minor stately home, when the intermediate stages had included the smuggling of a kokoshnik out of Russia in her corsets.

Well, she was never likely to find out, any more than she could hope to discover who it was who had perhaps handed over the kokoshnik to a soldier in 1945 as the price of a life. Did he — or she — live happily ever after? Kathy sighed in frustration and then brought herself sharply back to the matter in hand.

Objects were what concerned her, not people. It was time to remember the second of Mr Sampson's two comments. 'An object has a life of its own.' The Russian tiara was an artifact, unaltered by its journey through six decades, through many pairs of hands, across many frontiers, through wars and revolution. If only the kokoshnik itself could speak of its adventures! But it couldn't, and so she must do the best she could without much help. She put a new sheet of paper into the typewriter and tapped out the heading.

THE KRISTOV KOKOSHNIK. *La Lachrymosa*. The tiara of tears.